# A Cat's Cradle

Carly Rheilan

Copyright © 2024 Carly Rheilan
All rights reserved.
ISBN: 9781797833668

## Dedication

This book is dedicated to
Mrs Nicky Model and Dr Kay Spicer,
two very wise women

# Contents

Dedication ..................................................................i
1. The Innocent ......................................................... 1
2. Taking Care ..........................................................10
3. Renewal ...............................................................19
4. Grave Matters .......................................................27
5. Secrets and Lies ....................................................36
6. Friendship ............................................................45
7. An Ill-Used Heroine ...............................................51
8. Flotsam and Jetsam ................................................65
9. The Visitation .......................................................70
10. Family Values .......................................................78
11. The Days of Magic and Glory..................................87
12. The Poacher .........................................................99
13. In Deeper Waters.................................................111
14. Bachanale............................................................124
15. The Creature in the Briar .....................................130
16. The Key to Happiness...........................................138
17. The Return of the Prodigal ...................................145
18. The Ties that Bind. ..............................................151
19. Church Going......................................................159
20. Metaphysics.........................................................167
21. The Invisible Man ................................................178
22. Cold Blood .........................................................190
23. Lost Time ...........................................................198
24. Rites of Passage ...................................................205
25. Parting Gifts........................................................213
26. As a Moth to the Candle Flame.............................222
27. On the Innocence of Adulthood............................237
About the author .......................................................244
Also by Carly Rheilan.................................................245

Carly Rheilan

# 1. The Innocent

Much later, white-coated figures would ask Ralph if he thought of the other child, the child he had killed all those years before, at the moment when Mary Crouch appeared at the window.

And he would think of how the story must be written in their file, and how everyone must have lied.

Then, because they prompted him and made him go back in his mind, he would remember the day and the warmth of the afternoon. He would think of the cats at the window and of Mary tapping and calling to him. He remembered how she trusted him: the terrible irony of that.

Of course he had thought of the other child. The other child was always with him.

The other child had a mark on her nose: a spider of thread-veins, stretching to her cheek. Yet she had been beautiful, which Mary wasn't. He did not say that though. He knew it would not help to mention that.

So in the end he would shake his head and form the lie again. *No. It was nothing like that. When I saw Mary, I never thought of the other child. There was no connection.*

On other days they asked him why he did it, as if, because of what he was, it was necessary to ask.

He knew what the newspapers called him and the word disgusted him. He knew what he was. He never claimed to be a hero.

He would try to think of nothing.

But in the pressure of the silence, he would remember the final moments – when Mary was struggling in his coat, and he covered her face, when he felt her life in his hands and the imperative engulfed him, when all his body was on fire and he knew what it would cost him but he did not care.

And even then, as they watched him and waited for his answer, he felt a kind of exultation. In all his pointless life: those few pure moments of glory. He had been, in those moments, a man.

*I didn't have a reason. I did it because she was there.*

They did not push him further. They were professional. They dealt with him, processed him, followed correct procedures. He would hear them writing on their boards, and then they would go.

There was only one, a woman, Irish, who would hang behind as the others left. Her words would hiss behind his head, and she would ask him, her voice contorted with loathing, *if he thought about burning in hell.*

"You had nothing to lose, did you?" she would say. "Did it make you feel big? Are you proud of yourself?" And she would tell him, as if it gave her the right to speak, that she had a little girl herself, and that nothing, nothing he ever did, would make up for what he had done.

Then he would hear her sucking on her tongue, and wait for the spit on his cheek.

He never spoke of it.

Only occasionally, waking in the night, he would sense without remembering that he had dreamt of them both together. Mary and the other child, point and counterpoint. A little stain on both their faces.

But really, the two events were separate and there was no connection. He was thirty-one that day with Mary, not a boy of seventeen. He knew what he was doing. Perhaps because of what he was, and what he had done before, he did not count the cost as he might have done. But it did not mean that he did not choose. He had free will.

And which of us sees the strings that tweak our legs and arms, making us dance?

\*\*\*

Mary was thinking about the white cat. She had followed it all the way from the war memorial, weaving after it, keeping it always in her sight.

She could see it was bleeding. It was her brothers' fault. They were horrible. Properly speaking it was Colin's fault, because he had thrown the stone. But Michael had started it.

Even when they were only throwing stones at the angel, she had protested, telling them to stop it because they'd get into trouble. But they'd ignored her, which wasn't anything unusual.

The angel was on top of the war memorial, to guard the names of the twenty-two lost sons of the village, from two world wars. Pavis and Sneddon and Fenner and Vardon. Mary knew all the names. She had sat on the steps a whole afternoon once, fingering out the letters and thinking about the war, while her brothers hatched plots and rode their bikes round the grass. The names on the memorial were the names of the village. The children at school had the same names, and some of the teachers even. Fenner and Sneddon and Vardon and Pavis. So many Sneddons. But there weren't any Crouches. If her family belonged, they would have their name on the memorial. Even at seven she understood that.

It was Michael who threw the first stone, taking aim at the angel's head. He missed, because he wasn't much good, but then Colin tried and the stone snapped sharply on the angel's breast.

"Smack on the bosoms!" he shouted and the two boys howled with laughter.

"Stop it!" Mary cried, all prim and disapproving. "I'll tell."

"No you won't," Colin said, but he looked unsettled.

"I will. I'll tell mum. And... and... And I'll tell the Vicar."

"Tell-tale tit" sneered Michael, in a sing-song voice. Then Colin joined in, with his thumb on his nose and his fingers waving. Mary knew it was very rude. "*Tell-tale tit, your tongue will be split, and all the little dicky birds will get a little bit.* Come on Col, see if you can get it on the gob!"

Colin took aim at the angel's face, but as he did so, the cat suddenly appeared under the fence. Michael glanced slyly at Colin.

"Bet you couldn't," he challenged with a grin.

Mary saw his thought. "No!"

But Colin was too quick and the stone clipped through the air, catching the startled animal on the side of its head. It yowled and turned. A sudden streak of blood ran through its fur, then it scuttled up the fence and over the back.

"You beast!" Mary shouted. "You're a beast and I'm telling! I'm telling on you. I'm telling mum. And... and... and I'm telling Miss Vardon."

"It was an accident," Michael said quickly. "Wasn't it Col? You didn't mean to hit it. You didn't, did you?"

Mary looked at them. "You hurt it," she said again. "It's bleeding. Come on... we'll have to catch it... We have to help it..." She looked from Colin to Michael, but they were losing interest. She swallowed hard. "It must have gone down the lane," she said. "You've got to go and see if it's OK. Else I'll tell Miss Vardon."

Michael pulled a face and shrugged. "OK Colin, let's go. We can catch the cat if that's what little diddums wants." He made a siren noise with his mouth, and they both jumped onto their bikes. But they didn't turn towards the lane at all. They skidded round the corner and back towards the shop and the village green.

They did that all the time. Mary had a scooter – a big, red, substantial sort of scooter, with two wheels at the back and one at the front, and a platform big enough for both her feet. It was scuffed now, because it had been Michael's before she had it, and before that, Colin's. But she could still see the picture of the pony on the platform and make out the word 'Mustang' on the handlebars. It was a good scooter, and she could ride it fast. But she couldn't keep up with the boys on their bikes. They were supposed to look after her, but they were always buzzing off. They didn't care.

Mary didn't care, either, really. She didn't much like their games, and they always came back in the end. If they went home without her, they'd be in for it, so she could have told on them anytime and sometimes she threatened to, which maintained the equilibrium. But most of the time they had an understanding.

Sometimes she went to the swings on the village green, and took her turn with the other little girls, watching out for her mum in case she walked up to the shops and saw her without her brothers. Sometimes she went to the field at the corner, to coax the ponies with handfuls of grass – her hand held flat, like the girl in *My Pony Annual*. But sometimes she stayed wherever the boys abandoned her, and walked round and round, making up stories till the boys came back.

In her stories she was always the heroine. Often, she was Lucy, from *The Lion the Witch and the Wardrobe*. She was clear in her mind that she was just like Lucy – although Lucy's brothers, even Edmund who was wicked, were nicer than hers.

And so she might have waited that day, if it hadn't been for the cat. The cat was a problem, but behind the problem there were possibilities. In stories, girls often rescued animals – from cruelty or mishap or injury – and this was clearly such a case. And it wasn't anything like teatime. The boys could take ages.

\*\*\*

The lane was little more than a path. The track was patched with flints and grit, and there were dips which filled with water in the winter. On one side there were fences – the back of the war memorial, then the ends of gardens – and on the other a copse with a pond where they weren't supposed to go, because it was dangerous.

"Puss-puss!" she called. "Here puss-puss." Then she spotted it, under the nettles on the verge: a yellow eye in a stained white face. There was more blood now. She squatted, holding out her hand. The cat stared for a second, but then skulked down the edge of the path, low against the ground. In seconds it was twenty feet from her, then fifty.

She dumped the scooter on the verge near the copse. An idea was forming in her mind now. She thought of the cat in her arms, soft fur yielding limply to her. She would need to bathe its wounds and bandage its head. She could carry it home and nurse it in the garage. Her mother never went there. The boys would find out, but they wouldn't dare tell. If they told on her, she could tell on them back, and they'd be in worse trouble then. Hurting a cat was much worse than the usual things she told of. Hurting a cat was wicked.

Encouraged by these thoughts, Mary trotted after the cat. Every few seconds it looked round, and she felt it was checking she was there. But it didn't stop. It wanted her to follow, she was sure of it.

Where the houses ended, the copse grew thin and there was a little wedge of field, bounded by the embankment and the railway. That was as far as they usually went, because there was only the road after that, where the bus went under the railway bridge. And of course, the witch's house.

The house was right at the end of the lane, set back from the road. The paint was peeling and there were broken panes upstairs. The garden was wild.

"Rita Vardon says a witch lives there," Michael had said, the first time they walked that way. "A witch and her cats. And Rita knows stuff about her that she's not supposed to tell."

"Only girls believe in witches," Colin had replied, and both of them laughed. Then Michael dared him to look through the window.

It was an old sash window, half covered in ivy, and rather too high for a child to peer through. But they could see the bottles and jars, lined up behind the glass. They might have been pills or they might have been sweets, it was hard to tell. The window was open, just a little, at the top.

"Dare you to get one," Michael had said. "Dare you sixpence. You could climb up the ivy. *Easy Peasy Lemon Squeezy*. If you got on the ledge you could reach through and get it. Dare you sixpence."

"You haven't got sixpence."

"I have, too. I've been keeping it."

"Liar."

"No, really. Got it off Gran. You're just chicken. *Chicken! Chicken!* I'm going to tell John Pavis that you're chicken."

"Well I'm not such a chicken as *he* is, anyway," Colin retorted. "John can't even go to school on his own. His mother has to…" Colin stopped. People said John was a sissy but he was Colin's best friend. "Anyway, I don't care. I don't want to get someone's stupid pills anyway. I expect they're poisonous."

Mary had been pleased when he didn't climb up. It wasn't that Mary believed in witches. Once, from the top of the bus, she had seen the district nurse go in. District nurses don't visit witches: that would be stupid. But all the same, she hadn't wanted him to risk it.

Nor did she plan to look through the window today, on her own, without the boys.

As she neared the house, she was catching up with the cat. Twice it stopped and shook its head violently. It might have been hurting. It was definitely moving more slowly. She wanted to catch it before it got to the road. She quickened her steps and crooned softly… "Puss-puss, here puss-puss…" The cat took no notice, but as it got to the house, it stopped abruptly and looked up at the window.

Then it jumped in a single bound to the windowsill and turned around, looking back at her. Its head was to one side as if asking a question. There was fresh blood now, a single drop glistening over the eye, and then falling.

Falling. A red splash on the windowsill.

Their faces were almost on a level then, just a few feet apart. Mary remembered what Rita Vardon had said. "A witch and her cats." But it wasn't a witch's cat. It was white.

For a second they eyed each other up, and Mary moved towards it, her hand outstretched. "Meow" said the cat.

It was perfectly clear. A pantomime meow, like someone reading a story and getting to the bit where the cat says *meow*. It was facing her, the wound giving it a rakish look, like a pirate. "Meow."

She took another step, willing it to stay. But will-power is nothing. The cat leapt up to the open window and disappeared into the darkness of the room beyond.

\*\*\*

The moment was always perfectly fixed in Ralph's mind. He had said goodbye to his mother upstairs and was standing by the sink with his water bottle. One of the cats had just come through the window and jumped across the draining board. He was worried about petrol, because his bike was almost empty and even if he found the garage open, he only had nine-pence. Some garages weren't interested for less than a shilling, and he didn't want an argument. It would be shortest to go through the village, but that was impossible because of *being seen*. He usually took the longest way, going under the bridge away from the village, then south towards Canningbridge and back by the main road. There was a third way, a kind of compromise, cutting down the lane and skimming the top of the village by Heckleford Hill. It wasn't quite so safe, but it would save a couple of miles. He'd have his helmet on and could keep his head down. Heckleford Hill was all new houses, fancy ones. No one would recognise him there. But still he hesitated.

And so he was standing, not quite ready for the world outside, a moment of indecision. Perhaps he had thought, just in that moment, of the other child – or perhaps that was only how it felt looking back, the way his memory played with him. Certainly he was thinking of the time, because it was half past four and he was late. It was June. The first Saturday in June, in 1962.

Then the hand appeared. It was just outside the window, reaching up through the ivy, tapping along the sill for something firm to hold on. Then the head came.

It peered over the sill just a few feet from him. A girl. She wasn't at all like the other child. She wasn't beautiful. Her face was round, owl eyed, with a large mouth. Her nose was pressed against the glass, grotesquely. The hand reached up to the top of the sash, and then, rather awkwardly, a knee arrived. As if in slow motion, he saw the little bare leg and the tartan skirt. He didn't move. There was a grunting sound as she heaved herself up to grab the top of the sash. Then her chin rested on it, and she peered into the kitchen.

It was only then that she seemed to notice him. He saw a cry forming on her face and then something else that stifled it. She screwed up her face as if to speak, then her eyes refocused, glancing behind him.

He swung round guiltily, but there was no one behind him. There was only the white cat, on the table.

"Your cat," the girl said. "Your cat's hurt."

Her voice wasn't local. She wasn't one of the village children. He looked at the cat and saw the stain down on its face. Blood. It must have been fighting. Suddenly there was a sense to the world again, a thread of connection. Something relaxed in him.

"Yes," he said. "It fights a lot. But it's not my cat."

The child stared at him dubiously. "Whose cat is it then?"

"My mum's. She lives here. The cats fight all the time."

"It wasn't fighting," the girl said. "It was..." She didn't finish her sentence. She suddenly looked anxious. He wondered if she knew something.

"I'm just leaving actually," he said quickly. "And I've got to shut the window. You shouldn't be climbing up there. You'd better scram."

Those were his words. Later, of course, he embellished them in his mind, so what he recalled was telling her off, and saying she should go home at once because she shouldn't be out on her own. But he did tell her, really, that she'd better scram.

Then she smiled. A small, apologetic, pleading sort of smile.

"I think I'm stuck."

He shrugged. "You got up there OK. You can get down. It's not far."

The child looked slightly indignant. She squatted a little, then stood again, shaking her head.

"It's too far."

It seemed to him, looking back, that even then it was she who forced him. He hadn't asked her to come. It was she who called for him, wanting his help. It wasn't something he looked for.

"OK, I'll come round. I'll help you down."

***

It was strange, she thought, the way he helped her. Anyone else would have done it better. Even Colin would have supported her bottom with one hand, and taken a foot with the other, to show her the footholds. And her Dad, in the old days, would have held up his arms and let her jump down to them.

But the man came out with an old kitchen chair and propped it on the verge behind her.

"Sit down on the sill," he said. "Then jump to the chair. Come on. Quickly now."

It was difficult to bend down without falling backwards. The frame of the window was crumbling, and she couldn't see behind her.

"I might fall," she said. "Can't you help me?"

"No."

"Stand close then. I might fall."

"You won't fall. The chair's here." There was something strange going on with his voice.

Awkwardly, she twisted to a squat, and clung to the frame as she tried to turn around. Then she lost her balance. She toppled a little, then jumped, for there was no choice now.

He didn't catch her, as he should have done, so she scraped her knee on the chair and tumbled to the ground. She had only been trying to help his cat, so she felt it was all a bit shabby.

"You're all right then?" It wasn't really a question – not as if he wanted to know. He was already turning away. He didn't even say sorry.

She stepped towards him and tapped his arm. His skin flickered as if a fly had landed on him. "I've got to go now," he said.

"But your cat... Your mum's cat. You need to wash the blood off." She grew bolder then, a note of bossiness in her voice. "It'll get infected. You need to bathe it with Dettol. Or that yellow stuff." She stared up at him, baffled. She didn't know anyone like this. He didn't seem to understand. "Or you could get your mother to do it. It could get poison you know..."

"I'm just leaving." He walked back into the yard. Through the gate she saw a motorbike, with a rucksack strapped to the back. She spoke quickly, afraid that he might shut the gate and all would be lost.

"But will you tell your mum? Will you tell her about the cat?"

"No. She's in bed. She doesn't get up. She's ill. Look, the cat's OK. You'd best go home."

"Oh." Mary pulled a face, but she didn't move. She thought of the cat, and the dark stain on its fur. The cat must be hiding in the house still, hurting. Then she said, almost pleading, "I could help you. If you just stayed a minute... It won't take long..."

It might only have been a second that they stood there, staring at each other. Ralph liked to think, afterwards, that it was a longer time. He wasn't entirely without will.

## 2. Taking Care

The kitchen was dark and airless, with a nasty smell. As her eyes adjusted, she sensed the movement, as if the room were furtively adjusting to her presence. She peered around.

For light there was only the filthy window, half obscured by ivy. It made no difference though. Even in the gloom, she could see the room was a mess. She'd been expecting a kitchen like the one at home – neat and cool with red Formica and everything in order. But the table was wooden and greasy and most of it was covered by a television with its back off and lots of dusty pieces spread out on old newspaper. Plates and cups were piled on the draining board and the sink had an ominous saucepan in it, blackened round the edges. There was a dresser, but it was piled with nondescript items, "all anyhow," as her mother would have said. Even the floor was all wrong. There wasn't any lino, just crumbling flags under layers of grime. There was nowhere clean at all.

The man didn't seem to mind. He pushed aside some television bits and put the cat down, holding it by the scruff of its neck. As he did so, there was movement round the room, and as Mary stepped back, she saw the eyes. They were everywhere. Behind the pots on the sink. Under the dresser. High on the shelves above the door. Cats.

The man gestured to the sink.

"Get me the cloth," he whispered. "Wet it a bit."

Mary looked dubiously at the sink. It was quite high and she couldn't reach the tap. The water in the saucepan was scummy and probably poisonous. The man was pointing to a tea towel, but when she picked it up, she felt the grease on it.

"You have to have cotton wool" she said firmly. There was always cotton wool. Even the dinner ladies, who said not to make a fuss, had bags of cotton wool and bottles of yellow ointment. It was the natural order of things.

"Haven't got any," the man whispered, and patted the air with his hands, the way the teacher did sometimes, when she wanted the class to hush. "Just let me have the cloth. Look... I'm in a hurry..." The cat was mewing now and trying to get down from the table.

"Is there some in the bathroom then?" Mary asked. At her gran's, the first aid box was in the bathroom, on a little shelf by the geyser. It had a special smell to it, because her Gran used TCP instead of Savlon, and her bathroom smelled of cold cream. Here, the staircase led straight up, opposite the door, so she stepped towards it.

"No!" The man shook his head vehemently and waved his hand in front of his mouth. "My mum," he whispered urgently, "she's upstairs in bed. Mustn't disturb her."

Mary saw the panic in his face, and fleetingly she remembered what her brother had said, about the witch. It couldn't be true though. The man was completely ordinary. And she didn't believe in witches, not as such. But there was something odd about it.

She also remembered, as if the thought were connected, that it was probably teatime and she really shouldn't be there. There were things her mother went on about. Like not going into other people's houses or talking to strangers, and this was both.

"Come on, just give me the cloth," the man hissed, sounding a bit cross.

Perhaps it was the irritation that reminded her, because she was always losing her hanky and her mother told her off for it. Whatever it was, Mary suddenly remembered and pushed her hand into her pocket. A moment of triumph. A little square of boiled and ironed cotton. Perfect. She pulled the kitchen chair to the sink, climbed up and twisted the heavy old tap till the water began to trickle. Then she took a bowl from the draining board and filled it with water. There should be Dettol really, but perhaps that didn't matter.

It was a strange thing, bathing the white cat's wound in the dark kitchen, while the man held it down. She'd never done it herself before, but she'd seen her mum do the boys quite often, and she knew what to do. It was important to get the dirt out, every last bit, even if it hurt. She moved a little, to get out of his shadow, but still they were close – close enough to smell the oil on his jacket and hear the coins in his pocket, close enough to see the dirt in his fingernails. Grownup people shouldn't have dirt in their fingernails. It was a bit of a puzzle.

Mary gently teased the blood from the white fur, moving in circles, dabbing away from the wound as she'd seen her mother do. She asked the cat's name and he said, after a pause, that it was Snowy, then she asked *his* name and he said it was Ralph. That was all he said, just "Ralph". It was a bit odd, because it should have been Mr something, as she obviously couldn't call him Ralph. And he should have asked her name back, to be polite. But he seemed a bit distracted, so she told him anyway.

"My name's Mary," she said. "Mary Crouch. But we're not Catholics. It's just Mary after my Gran. My Dad's mum. Mummy's mum is called Evelyn, but they didn't want to call me that, because it's old fashioned."

The man should have said something then — about her name or her two Grans or something like that. *Keeping the conversation going*, her Mum had called it, back before Dad left, when they had coffee mornings. Mary was good at conversation, much better than her brothers even. She particularly liked talking to grownups. In the old days, at coffee mornings, she could keep the whole room entertained, though sometimes she made things up and her mother scolded her afterwards. But Ralph wasn't even trying.

"Are you mending the telly?" she asked, thinking this might be more fruitful. He could talk about tellies for a while, and then she would tell him how theirs was broken and they were saving up to get it mended. If he knew how to mend them, he might even offer.

But all he said was "Are you finished now?"

"Almost," she said stiffly, feeling put out. Mr Ralph was really rather rude. She noticed how he glanced towards the stairs so he was probably worried about waking his mum. But he should at least have been polite.

The wound on the cat was more blood than injury. Once she got down to the skin, it was just a little nick, and it wasn't on the eye. She squeezed out the hanky, one last time, and rubbed it softly on the fur.

"That's better," she said, with a nod.

"OK then," the man said, letting go of the cat. At once it disappeared into the dark under the dresser. "Look, I've got to go." He touched her on the shoulder, pushing her to the door.

"When are you coming back?" Mary asked.

"I don't know. Maybe next week."

"But Snowy... Does your mum...?"

"There's a woman. She comes in for my mum. She feeds the cats. It's fine."

For a second, Mary thought again about taking the cat home, but somehow, in the real world with a grownup there, it no longer seemed possible. "Do you come every week?"

He didn't answer, but nudged her out of the door. It wasn't very nice, Mary thought. She had always got on with grownups, and usually they were friendly. She talked a bit too much sometimes – her teacher called her a chatterbox – but they usually seemed to like her. Mr Ralph was different.

Outside, the light had changed. Mary wondered, anxious suddenly, if her brothers were looking for her. She was a long way from home.

Ralph pushed the motor bike round and out into the lane. "Are you going home now?" he asked, but there was something odd about the way he said it.

"Yes... Well, my brothers. I've got to find them. They'll be looking for me."

"Look – Mary..."

He wasn't looking at her. He was glancing around, as if looking for someone else. Perhaps he was looking for her brothers.

"They're probably at the War-Morial," she said. "That's where they left me. I only came this way because of Snowy."

"Yes," he said. "OK. But Mary... Look..."

"What?"

"Please... You mustn't tell anyone. It's just a secret, OK? Snowy... and me... and you coming in. You mustn't tell anyone at all."

Mary thought about it. She hadn't been planning to tell anyone. "I won't," she said simply. "I'm not supposed to go into anyone's house – Mum gets cross."

"But not anyone, see? Not your brothers or anyone. You mustn't even say that you saw me. If you do..."

Mary smiled at him, kindly. It was funny having a grownup telling her to keep a secret. Perhaps his mum didn't let him have visitors. "OK," she said, sensing in some way that the balance had shifted. "I won't tell. But...." She shuffled a little, not sure how far she could go. If she kept a secret for her brothers, they had to give her something. She could have asked to come back, to see Snowy sometimes. She could even have asked to come to tea. But he wasn't very friendly, so perhaps she wouldn't want to. And there was the thing about his Mum. But there was something else. A delicious thought, forming in her mind.

"Will you give me a ride on your motorbike? A ride to the end of the lane?"

"No," he said. "You should go home." And he put his leg over the bike, kicked a pedal several times, and suddenly the beast thundered into life. There was a moment of roaring, then a scattering of dust, and he was gone, without even a goodbye.

Snowy was interesting, but all in all, Ralph wasn't a very nice man.

\*\*\*

The children were late again. Janet glanced at the clock and sighed.

She wiped the Formica and put on the tablecloth. It was important not to let standards slip. Anyone could knock the door, any time. Her situation, in the absence of Rick, left her open to gossip. She rather hoped that no one had noticed.

The departure of Richard Crouch, one Sunday morning some six months previously, was something Janet never referred to. She hadn't even got round to telling her mother, who would only have said *I told you so*. Rick had been to college and trained in engineering – *civil* engineering which was the cleanest kind – but his family were in *scrap* so although they had money it was dirty money and they were dirty sort of people. Janet had been foolish to fall for such a man.

He had taken his van and a suitcase of clothes. Nothing else. Janet supposed he must still be paying the mortgage, because the Building Society would have been round otherwise. And every Friday he sent an envelope with the housekeeping – no letter, no anything, but the same as he'd given her before. The postmark was Manchester, where Janet supposed there'd be lots of scrap, so she half suspected he'd gone back to his roots.

She had managed, she felt, rather well in his absence. Nonetheless, she felt the shame of it deeply, and the money was becoming a problem.

Mary's coat was mended and the boys needed shoes. The money Rick sent her was plenty for the groceries, but there was never any left for other things. When she first started worrying, she had determined to economise. She thought of her mother and growing up in the war. She bought marge instead of butter, made cakes without eggs, and padded out the stews till they were little more than gravy. When the boys complained, she told them firmly how lucky they were, and they should think of the starving in India. But then Mary had chipped in, trying to be helpful, about a girl at school who got potatoes for tea, just potatoes –

and the very next day Janet blew her week of savings on Sugar Puffs and sausages, because she didn't want them thinking they were like the village children. The Crouches were better than that. They lived on Heckleford Hill, not down in the village. They were nice sort of people, even if their shoes were rather tight. It was, undeniably, a difficult equation.

It was half past five. No doubt there would be all the usual excuses. "We didn't know," they would say. "We didn't think it was so late." And she would sigh and say they should have asked someone, and they would say they didn't see anyone to ask, and she would say there was always someone around and they should have thought of it. It was all a bit of a ritual. In truth, she didn't mind if they came a little late. It was more of a nuisance when they came home early, or insisted on playing at home: those days always ended with mud in the house, or toys left everywhere. Playing out was best.

It was safe in the country, because there were hardly any cars. That had been one of the attractions, when they moved from Croydon.

*\*\*\**

The boys had found the scooter early on. It was just by the copse, so they guessed she'd be down by the newt pond where they weren't supposed to play. They climbed the fence and spent a while searching the wood. Michael saw a ball that someone had thrown in the pond, and insisted on getting it out, and in the end he fell in and got muddy all up his legs. It wasn't even worth it, because the ball turned out to be burst, so it wasn't any good.

After that, they rode their bikes up the lane, calling her name. Colin was put out, because it would all be *his* fault if Mary made them late – it was always his fault.

As they passed the witch's house he stood up on the pedals and peered into the garden. There was a motorbike on the drive, which might have been interesting, but today there wasn't time. When they got to the road, they peered each way, and Michael shrugged.

"She won't have gone this way," he said, rather dubiously. "I don't think she'd go on the road."

But they checked the road anyway, riding as far as the railway bridge one way and the station the other. Michael said she might have gone to the ponies, so they rode up to the vicarage field, and checked the churchyard and the school as well, but she wasn't to be seen. Colin was getting worried.

"She might have gone to a friend," Michael said, but they knew she never did, and anyway, there was the scooter. She wouldn't just abandon it.

"Let's go back," Colin said. "She's bound to go back for the scooter."

They skidded to a halt by the scooter and peered all around. Colin called her name as loud as he could, and Michael added a Red Indian holler for good effect.

"Do you think she's hiding?"

"Better not be. I'll kill her if she is."

Michael shouted again. "Mary, Mary!" Then the sing-song chant, in case she was hiding. *Come out come out wherever you are! You win, I lose. Ha Ha Ha!* But the words disappeared in the still air.

Seconds passed. There was something neither of them wanted to think. "What d'you think the time is?"

"Must be gone five. Mum'll go barmy."

"Do you think... do you think we should check the pond again?"

The two boys looked at each other bleakly. The pond wasn't far away. Why else would the scooter be there, just there, abandoned? They scrambled the fence again and walked solemnly round the pond, not voicing their thoughts. They paused at the end, where the weeds grew thick, and poked about with a stick. But there was nothing.

"She must be flipping hiding," Michael said firmly. "We're ages late and it'll all be our fault."

"It's not fair. We shouldn't have to look after her."

"No. But what if she's gone home already?"

"She wouldn't have... Not without the scooter... "

"Let's go back to the scooter then. I'm going to kill her when she gets back."

So they were waiting in the lane when Mary walked back. She could see by their faces that she was in trouble. Colin ran up to her and whacked her on the ear. "Where have you been hiding?" he demanded. "You've made us late now – we'll be in trouble. Where've you been? Were you hiding?"

"No," Mary said. "I was... I was only in the lane."

"But we came up here!" Michael said. "Where were you hiding?"

"I wasn't," Mary said.

"You jolly well were!" Michael whacked the other ear. "Don't tell lies. We've been all round."

"And you left the scooter – anyone could have taken it. Where were you hiding?" Colin grabbed her wrist and twisted it round her back. "Come on – are you telling me or shall I make you?"

"Honest, I was just in the lane... You're hurting..."

"Truth now... Unless..."

He twisted harder, and it really hurt then, but Mary knew she mustn't tell. It would be worse if she told, because they might tell mum. That would mean bad trouble, for going in someone's house. Of course, if they told, they'd have to admit that they'd *left* her, so it wasn't very likely – but they might say she'd run off, which would make it different. Michael could lie with a straight face and look Mum in the eye, and then Colin might back him up. Mum always believed Colin.

"Stop it!" Mary shouted. "You're hurting."

"Own up then!" Michael hissed. "Where were you hiding?"

"Nowhere!" Mary replied, and tried to wrench her arm free, but Colin just twisted it more.

Then it came to her, in a moment of glory. The perfect story that would take care of everything. She kicked Colin's shin and twisted round to look at him. "Let me go and I'll tell you. Let me go. I'll tell. I promise."

Colin slackened his grip, but he didn't let go.

"No. Let go. Let go properly or I'll just tell mum." She paused, waiting for him to realise that the tables had turned. "Actually I might tell her anyway."

Colin dropped her arm then and stepped back. "What do you mean?"

She waited till they both were looking worried. She glanced from one to the other, and a tiny smile crossed her lips, but she crushed it into a frown.

"I was burying the cat," she said. "You killed it. It's all your fault. I had to make a hole and put it in. It was bleeding – loads of blood. I followed it all the way to the railway. Then it fell over." She made a gesture with her hand: the terrible flop of the cat as it fell, like one of the horses in a cowboy film. Seeing their awestruck faces, she warmed to the theme. "I had to bury it or a fox would have got it. It could have been all torn up like Mrs Fenner's chickens. All in pieces. So I had to bury it. But you killed it, Colin. You killed it. It probably belonged to someone. You'd be in trouble if they found it. Or *bits* of it. I could tell on you."

If he'd been a bit quicker, he could have asked how she made the hole, or checked for the mud on her shoes, because it was clay in the field near the railway and it always stuck. But he was quite undone by the horror of it.

"You didn't half whack it, Col," Michael offered, unhelpfully. "You got it on the bonce. Smack on the bonce. *Peeow!* It was bleeding. You shouldn't have done it."

It was then that Colin saw the blood. Two nasty smears of it, turning brown on the sleeve of Mary's blouse. And there were hairs, little white hairs, on her tartan pinafore. The skirt was dirty, and her knees all scuffed. So it was true.

Mary stared at him, savouring the moment. She saw how he coloured up, like he did when he was going to cry.

"You won't though," he said, in little more than a whisper. "Please Mary – you won't tell..."

"It depends," Mary answered, and she nodded at them softly, as if making up her mind. For once in her life she felt wholly in control. Things might never be the same again.

# 3. Renewal

A lot of things change in fourteen years. From 1948 to 1962 was a journey that others had made in hopeful steps, measuring out the path in years away from the war. For many the years had gone by at a gallop in a spirit of unlikely possibility – but at least there had been a progress to it, a moving from one time to another, a succession. Years were marked out in National Service and demob suits and jobs and marriages, new homes and new possessions – and most of all in children, whose determined race from one birthday to another forced the knowledge of time passing, in an orderly, inevitable way.

They were different people now, all of them – the gawking familiars who had passed from mouth to mouth the shocking news that was made that afternoon, so many years ago. And the facts had changed too: they had grown starker, simpler. On the day when it happened, the gossip had rattled through the village, half believed, not possible, constantly shifting, until it solidified, days later, into the monstrous verdict of the newspapers, and months after that into the terrible evidence from the trial. They had all known the details then, every moment of the story, the words like a necklace of razorblades. None of them had forgotten, but the story was simpler now. They were different people. They had moved on.

Even those closest to the child Ralph killed – even *they* had moved on through those years, after the first slow waltz of agonizing hours, through the days of holding close, helping each other to breathe, into the weeks when other things could be spoken of, at least apologetically, and to the months when finally other things mattered. In the end, through the passing years, they had moved to a kind of renewal, where the world took them back to itself, and they remembered Sonia's passing in only a ritual way, a wistful counting up of milestones never reached, an event in the dance of history across the story of their lives. They had moved on. They were somewhere else.

For Ralph, however, the time had passed with no sense of any journey. Not quickly, not quickly at all, but all in one piece, without change, without progress. After the terrible harsh daylight of the trial, the sun had disappeared in the spring of '49, and the twilight that followed had ground its way through his years in an endless circle, a purgatory of wretched discomforts, time without end. Looking back on it now, his years in prison seemed like a solid thing, almost half of his life, compressed into a single, seamless, paralysis of time.

Apart from the fact that it shattered – abruptly spitting him into the brave new world of 1962 – it seemed like eternity.

At the designated Labour Exchange they had a special desk, where a pasty young woman searched a cabinet until she found a thin file, with a flimsy carbon sheet and a letter on prison paper. He watched her read it and saw the look on her face turn sour. Then she disappeared into a room at the back, and a man came out instead. He asked what Ralph could do – which wasn't, it appeared, very much. There was nothing about Ralph – wiry and pale with hands like a girl – that marked him out as a labourer. Ralph listed his exams but the man just shook his head: fancy schooling was worthless, for a man who could never be trusted. In prison he'd stitched mailbags, but sewing was for women – unless it was tailoring, but he'd have needed an apprenticeship for that. He hadn't even done National Service. He was good for nothing.

They sent him to a factory, to a packing job which was really women's work and paid little more than a woman's rate. The middle-aged women who worked beside him had nicotine in their hair and vulgar voices, and all of them, by way of conversation, tried asking about his National Service. He didn't answer them. There was nothing he could say. After a while they ignored him.

Ralph had never lived in a town before. He had never lived anywhere but his parents' house and prison. But the signs on the boarding houses were reassuring: "No Blacks, No Irish, No Dogs". As he knocked the doors he felt his superiority without any irony. He settled on a house in a back street where he could share a room with a middle-aged man, in exchange for half his wages and compliance with a page of prohibitions, pinned to the back of the door. His roommate, Ted, was an amiable man who worked for a grocer and would regularly bring back pies – not fresh enough to sell but a welcome addition to the greasy stews that they ate each evening in the landlady's kitchen. Afterwards, Ted adjourned to a pub which he called "the local," while Ralph, keeping prison hours, would return to the room and settle himself in bed. He didn't sleep, but was comfortable with solitude, and liked to count his savings in his head and dream of a motorbike. And of seeing his mother.

He knew that his father was dead, because the prison Chaplain had told him so, one Friday morning, taking him aside after breakfast. The Vicar from the village had written, though he'd left it till after the funeral, thinking it best.

Ralph guessed, by that token, that his mother still lived, though she had never visited and his handful of letters had gone quite unanswered – even the latest with the news of his parole. He did not feel it was a matter for reproach. None the less, he thought of her often. There wasn't anyone else.

*\*\*\**

He had somehow expected her to be in the garden, weeding the flowers or hanging out the washing. As he juddered down the road on the second-hand motorbike, he was looking for a sight of her, as if that, on its own, would be enough. He hadn't thought ahead to any grand reunion. He had not even committed himself to knocking on the door. He had imagined, however, that he was bound to set eyes on her, and he felt that the two-hour ride – even the purchase of the bike and the privations it had cost him – might be justified by a fleeting vision over the little brick wall. It had been, after all, a very long time. Having waited so long, there was no great reason to hurry.

But as the house came into view, he realised with a lurch that things were not as he imagined.

It was two in the afternoon, four weeks before the day which he would call, when the time came, the Day of the Blooded Cat. The sun was shining on the house, and he saw at once the crisp black shadows where the roof tiles were missing, and ivy over the windows. Closer, he saw the thistles growing tall at the front, and the little front porch almost lost behind brambles.

He braked and slowed to walking pace, then the bike stuttered and stalled. He looked along the road without dismounting. Everything, even the arc of the railway bridge and the twist of the road by the oak tree, was poignantly familiar. But it no longer appeared that the house was inhabited.

He stared, not moving.

He wondered about the dresser in the kitchen where he kept his books and his cigarette cards. He wondered if his clothes were still there. There is always a fascination to an empty house, the possibility of something left behind. It was this, perhaps more than any thoughts of his mother, that took him to the back door, the one they had always used. Perhaps he should have noticed that the path was still well trodden.

The shouting started as he twisted the handle.

\*\*\*

Verity Sneddon sat up in bed. Even before the squeak of the handle, she had realised by the way the cats shot under the bed, that there was somebody there. Mrs Fenner, who did for her and brought her meals, had been already, so it wasn't her. In any case, the cats knew Mrs Fenner. Her step in the drive no longer disturbed them. Occasionally children came and rattled the door. So she shouted, knowing they would run.

But the door squeaked open and there were footsteps in the kitchen, and then closer, on the stairs. She should have been frightened, but behind her shouting, there was a terrible calm. She did not count her personal safety highly. She did not really have a lot to lose.

The thing she minded was how naked she felt. When Mrs Fenner came, the cats stayed on the bed, guarding her – which gave her the dignity of one not wholly unsupported. But now she was quite alone, facing her intruder with nothing but a winceyette nightie and a chicken-feather quilt for protection.

Then her door opened, and she saw him in the doorway.

She knew at once it was him. She had counted the years of his sentence and was not entirely surprised when she got the letter. She ought to have guessed that he might come home. But if she had, it was not something she admitted, even to herself.

So she ceased her shouting, looked him up and down as a dealer might look at a horse, and shook her head.

There followed a long silence. It occurred to her, without emotion, that he was probably shocked by her appearance. He could hardly have missed that she was not the woman she had been when he saw her last, in the court when the judge spoke the terrible words, and they took him away. She had been tall and strong then. Young almost. But it was clear in his face that he recognised her still.

"Do you want me to go away?" he said at last.

That voice. Her boy had turned into a man, but the voice was the same. It brought a pang that briefly threatened to crush her. It seemed necessary, after that, to say something back. Her face puckered into a frown. She made a gesture with her hand at the crumpled bedclothes, at her own broken body in the bed and then a larger gesture, taking in the room, the damp on the ceiling, the tiny square of railway embankment that was all she could see from the window, and she said the only thing that came to her, the thing she had said to him, in her mind, every day of her life for fourteen years.

"You ruined my life. You were never any good. I wish you had never been born."

\*\*\*

After that, Ralph visited every Saturday.

It added a component of purpose to his week and a focus to a day that otherwise seemed pointless. It was something he could say to Mrs Gregory, when she asked, as she usually did, if he was doing anything for the weekend. There was a subtext to the question, because she went to her sister's on a Saturday, and had made it clear from the start that the lodgers couldn't stay in. Ted explained, in the privacy of their room, that she thought they might have women in, and he poked Ralph in the stomach and said "She knows you're a bit of a lad." Ted seemed to find this funny – but he could afford to laugh, because he worked on Saturdays anyway.

"I'm going to my mum's."

From the very beginning, even before he bought the bike, Ralph told them he was going to his mum's. For months, every Saturday, he had walked with Ted to the shop, then on in the direction of the station, as if he were catching a train. When it rained, he would *really* go to the station, and spend the day on the concourse, with a newspaper and his thoughts. On other days he went to the park and watched the children.

"I'm going to my mum's."

Now that it was true, he felt a special satisfaction. He kept the bike on the square of concrete between the wall and the front door, and let Ted ride pillion as far as the shops. It wasn't any distance, but Ralph enjoyed the status and Ted seemed pleased. Afterwards, alone, as the smoke of Slough receded in the distance, he liked the feel of the wind against his face, the sense of power, the freedom. There wasn't any hurry. He mustn't arrive before eleven, because of Mrs Fenner; his mother was most emphatic.

The imperative of secrecy was a burden on the visits. If it weren't for that, there would have been things he could do, which would have leavened the hours for both of them. There was plenty he could have done in the house. There was the broken window in his father's room, and the tiles that had gone from the roof, which left patches of wet in his mother's bedroom. There were lights that didn't work, and everywhere needed painting. There was even the broken television, collecting dust on the table. It was a matter of frustration to his mother that his father had died in the middle of that. Ralph couldn't have done it, but if secrecy didn't matter, he could at least have taken it to a shop.

And of course there was the garden.

When Ralph was a boy, the garden had been beautiful. His dad was a signalman but the line was never busy and the duties weren't onerous. It was mostly potatoes, which was patriotic in the war, and a run at the end for some chickens, because of rationing. But there were leeks and onions and tomatoes too, all in rows without a weed in between, and flowers at the edges, for his mum, and a neat little apple tree. The dereliction of the garden must have pained his mother, before she took to her bed and saw it no longer. Ralph could have scythed the nettles and made a lawn. He could have cleared the paths, cut back the brambles and pruned the apple tree. All this he would willingly have done – indeed, he would have liked it – but Mrs Fenner would have seen, and then everyone would know.

So instead, he sat by his mother's bed, and they talked a little. There weren't so many things they could talk about. She never asked about his years in prison, and everything he could say about his life since then was exhausted in a couple of minutes. So Verity told him what had happened to the people he had known – jobs, and marriages, and births and deaths; some unexplained babies and the shame that followed. She even told him of the Pavis family, whose child he had killed, pointing out at the end that he had ruined all their lives. They'd had another child afterwards, a boy this time, but they never got over it, and the boy was a blighted thing. Ralph listened and bowed his head.

On his third visit, she told how his father had died. Ralph said he wished he'd known and that if only she'd written they might have let him out for the funeral. But his mother just snorted. "Oh yes? You'd have wanted to be there? Do you think I hadn't suffered enough?"

On his fourth visit, she spoke a little of the life she had led, not sparing his feelings. He had, after all, destroyed her life, destroyed her marriage, destroyed his father's life. Did he suppose that they had a life after? Did he think anyone forgot? Sonia Pavis was a bad girl – even after all these years, Verity could not entirely forgive the girl nor wholly believe that she had not, in some way, brought it on herself – but half the village was related to her. None of them forgot, and Verity Sneddon, who was related by marriage to the girl as well, had lied in court to protect the murderer.

*"It was a very hot evening and I wanted a walk. So I went to meet him and he had just come out of the house. Little Sonia was perfectly well then – I saw her waving at the window. I saw her clearly and waved back to her. It must have happened after that, after Ralph left."*

No one forgave her for that, not even her husband. Sonia's mother was his cousin and Sonia's father might have hung for it, if the lie had been believed. But she had done it for Ralph. She had damned herself for him.

Ralph needn't suppose that she didn't regret it. He had never been any good and hadn't been worth helping. *In fact it would have been better if he'd been a bit older, so they'd have hung him for it.*

Verity Sneddon had waited fourteen years to deliver him that verdict, and she delivered it without mercy.

Ralph bowed his head, and for a long while they didn't speak. Eventually, it was noon, so he brought out the pies he had bought at the bakery, and the two little cakes with sprinkles on the top. She didn't need them, of course. Mrs Fenner left a dinner every morning, and it was there under a bowl. There was pudding too. Verity paid for her meals and needed nothing from Ralph. But all the same, it was the pies and the cakes that she ate. Ralph was pleased about that. He put the plate of stew on the floor for the cats, and even they seemed uncertain about it.

After the cake, she had her nap. Ralph waited till she slept, then went downstairs and poked through the cupboards. Everything that was his had disappeared, and his bedroom stank of cats. But he found the photos. His father had an old box Brownie and the photos were a ritual. Unusual trains, oversized vegetables, faces of people in the family. Ralph never liked the photos as a child, but it was different now.

At four it was time to go, and he crept back up to whisper his goodbyes. His mother kept her eyes tight closed. Perhaps she slept. Fleetingly, he thought of kissing her cheek, but he didn't do it. Too many years had passed for that.

And that was the day when he saw Mary at the window.

***

It was not to Ralph's credit that after the Day of the Blooded Cat, he thought so much about the child called Mary Crouch. He knew perfectly well that it would be better to forget her, but still she kept occurring to him and he didn't do much to push the thoughts away. The recollection of their encounter wove through the dull days like a coloured thread among the grey.

He was renewed by it. There was something warming in the way that she did not shrink from him as others did. She had been, indeed, entirely the active partner. He had merely acquiesced and even then reluctantly.

The day had been sunny when she appeared at the window. He imagined them meeting again, by chance, in the lane. She would run towards him in happy recognition, and perhaps he would scoop her up and lift her in the air.

He thought of how her weight would feel in his hands.

The next week, when his mother took her nap, he went out into the garden and leant over the wall, looking each way. The lane was full of flowers. It was a nice place for a little girl. He wondered where she lived. Crouch wasn't a village name, so she might be one of the newcomers from the estate. But he couldn't be sure. She might have been anyone. Perhaps she was visiting relatives, and only there that day.

Or perhaps she lived close, and walked every Saturday down the lane, at just that time. He leant on the wall for a long time, looking each way.

But Mary did not come.

# 4. Grave Matters

Mary took only occasional advantage of the rope she now tweaked at Colin's throat. Indeed, she rarely mentioned it, but both of them knew that something had changed. Even their mother saw the difference – how Colin started humouring Mary's games and even got Michael to join in. It pleased her to see it. It was why she had had them so close together – not just the convenience of them keeping each other amused, but something more noble, about bonds of siblinghood, and blood being thicker than water. Janet herself was an only child, so perhaps she valued such bonds a little high.

It chanced, however, that a few weeks later, Mrs Fenner, the dinner-lady, lost her large ginger tom and put a notice in the Post Office with the promise of a reward. This was a matter for much discussion in the schoolyard since catching a cat seemed an easy matter, and compared to anyone's pocket money, the bounty seemed vast. Mary's friend Rita said it was probably shut in a garage, because her auntie lost a cat once and that's where it was found – in a neighbour's garage with six new kittens, almost dead from lack of water. Colin's friend John said it must have been stolen, because there were gangs of gypsies who stole cats, for their fur. His mum had told him there were gypsies everywhere: you always had to be careful.

"Is that why your mum still takes you to school? Is that why she holds your hand?" The Sneddon twins would sneer at anyone, but the others looked away. It was common knowledge that John Pavis was a dipper, and he never played out with the other boys. His mum and dad even came with him to the swings, and hung around, watching. But the older kids knew why, and they didn't speak of it.

At playtime all the talk about cats stirred up Colin's troubles and brought a tightness to his chest. But later, in arithmetic, he started to wonder why there hadn't been a notice about a *white* cat lost, if that was what people did. He rolled this thought in his mind for a bit, and it occurred to him that in all the recent talk – of cats lost years ago or miles away – no one had mentioned a cat with white fur, lost in the village just a couple of weeks ago. Between the lot of them, the village kids knew everything. But none of them had mentioned it.

He confided these thoughts to Michael in the dinner queue, but Michael just shrugged and said that the cat must have come from somewhere else, because cats walked miles, everyone knew that, and anyway, a cat was a cat, and if Mary told mum, he'd be in for it. Colin sighed. Michael was really very slow.

"But what if she *made it up*?"

Michael looked put out. "She couldn't have. There was blood on her jumper."

"So... it was bleeding. But maybe it didn't actually die – maybe she made that bit up."

Michael thought about this uneasily. "Well even if she's fibbing, she could go and tell Mum anyway."

"But if it's not true... Mum wouldn't believe her if it wasn't true. I mean she couldn't prove it."

"But if it *is* she could," Michael replied stoutly. "She could show mum the grave. Mum could dig it up even. There'd be bones."

They had got to the front of the queue by then, so the topic was over – though it was neck of mutton stew and Michael pretended he was Mum, digging about in the stew for bits of bone, and when he got to a lump of gristle, he waved it on the end of his fork, saying in a silly voice "Ooh dearie me, it's true. My darling boy has killed a little pussycat..."

Perhaps Mary heard some part of their chatter or watched from the lower table and saw how they played. Whatever it was, a sense of unease came over her, and her triumphant security seemed suddenly more precarious.

The next Saturday, Mary didn't insist on the boys staying close, as she had done before. When they got to the field, she said that the boys could go off if they wanted. She made it sound casual, but fixed Colin firmly with her eye. "I don't want to play today. I might go and put some flowers on the *grave*. I'll take my sandwich though. That one. With the pickle."

So Colin got out the sandwiches and reluctantly gave Mary the best one. Mary watched them go, then turned the other way, past the War Memorial into the lane.

\*\*\*

Ralph saw her from the motorbike as he came under the railway bridge. She was only a tiny figure, far on the other side of the field, but he was sure it was her. He recognised her sturdiness and the stubby cut of her hair. She was wearing a summer dress, white and yellow in the distance. He let his bike come juddering to a halt.

There were cows in the field, and she was picking her way round the far side, beyond the fence. He wondered where she was going. There was nothing up there except the plantation and the railway embankment.

She was heading towards the railway.

All through Ralph's childhood he'd been warned about the railway. His dad saw a man get killed once, splatted by the train as he took a short-cut over the rails. They picked up the pieces, his dad said, all the way from Canningbridge to Oatham Park. And one of his legs they didn't find for years, till some men were working on the line and found the bones, pecked clean by the birds. His father told the story often, to be sure Ralph understood.

So it was clear in Ralph's mind, these twenty-five years later, that a child like Mary could usefully be warned to keep clear of that place. He was suddenly very happy. It was a lovely, innocent thing, to walk along the field to meet her, to warn her of that. He felt that they would meet as friends and could talk for a while. He would tell her about Snowy – all recovered now – and ask about her brothers. It had been so awkward before, in the kitchen, with the risk that his mother might wake. He could make amends for that. Then he would explain about the dangers of the railway and walk with her back to the lane before going to his mum's. There wasn't much joy in those visits; he deserved a little brightness. It was a harmless thing, a responsible thing even.

He untied his bag from the back of the bike and climbed across the fence. The rain in the night had left a sweetness in the air. The fences were fringed with woundwort and bindweed, and there were larks in the sky. A smile, unbidden, played on his face. He was walking through the countryside of his childhood, on a mission of his own choosing. This was what it meant to be free. He had missed this, all those bleak dark years.

He kept his eyes on the child, waiting for her to see him, but she didn't look round. When she reached the embankment, she made no attempt to climb. Instead, she kicked the earth at the foot of it, then squatted as if doing up her shoes. Ralph was closer now. She would see him any minute. He felt nervous suddenly.

The embankment was built of compacted stones. He watched as she prised one up. She carried it back to the corner of the field and dropped it down. Then she returned to the embankment and picked up another. And again and again, stone upon stone.

Ralph smiled. It was obviously some kind of game; she was building something. But the place was ugly and unsuitable somehow. Though the day was sunny, this spot was shadowed by the railway on one side, the plantation on the other. He could show her better places.

"Mary!" he called. "Mary Crouch! Hello!"

She didn't respond but stood up and watched him approaching.

And then he was with her. Perhaps there was a shake in his voice as he spoke. "Hello Mary. What are you doing?"

She pointed, frowning, at the little pile of stones. "I'm making a grave."

\*\*\*

Mary had seen him, in fact, from the very beginning, when he leant across the fence, even before he started walking towards her. She knew it was him, from the motorbike, and the fact that he was there, just down the road from his mother's house. She recalled him saying he might return the next week. That was two weeks back, but perhaps there was a pattern, and today, like the last time, was Saturday.

She had considered waving but decided against it. She thought it was likely he would say hello but it was also possible that he wouldn't. She would wait and see. She was trying, these days – in a spirit of self-improvement – to be a little less *forward*.

It was something Miss Vardon, her teacher, had said to her. Mary had been having a cry in the toilets, because the other girls were doing skipping and they wouldn't let her play. She had previously offered some new skipping rhymes, because they kept on and on with the same old one, but one of the Sneddon girls had said something rude, and the others had joined in.

It made Mary miserable. At her first school, when they lived in Croydon, she had been quite popular. She'd never wanted to move to the country, where the children were mean and horrible.

"I'm sorry dear, it's just their way," Miss Vardon said. "They're not used to... It takes a while for them to accept... And they find you... They find you rather *forward*."

"What does *that* mean?" Mary asked at once, just a little indignantly. It took Miss Vardon quite a while to answer.

"I mean... you're a very clever girl, and that's very nice, but... well... sometimes you... sometimes you talk a bit much and put yourself *forward*. I know you're being friendly, but it... it's not what they're used to... The way you talk they...." She frowned, not liking to say it, though it had to be said. "Well, they think you're *showing off*. It's not their way, you see. They're quiet girls... They're... They're..."

And so she had petered out because despite her education Miss Vardon was still a village girl herself, a quiet girl, who didn't put herself forward. And clever Mary Crouch, though she was only seven, had come from Croydon and was really quite alarming.

So Mary had been trying to be less forward. As far as she could tell, this involved not saying much, and never speaking first. In a limited way she had found this helpful. She had established a marginal alliance with Rita – though Rita was related to Miss Vardon and it seemed quite likely that Miss Vardon had told her to be nice.

It had been clear to Mary, when she thought about it afterwards, that Mr Ralph was probably a village man, and that she had probably offended him too, by being too forward. She had certainly done most of the talking. He may have felt that she shouldn't have chattered on. He certainly might have felt she had been quite *forward*.

So when she saw him walking in her direction, she resolved to say nothing till he spoke to her, and if he spoke at all, to reply very simply. The strategy seemed to work, because at once he seemed more friendly.

"A grave, eh? I thought you might be building a house."

"No," Mary said, still careful of her words. "Just a grave."

He did a rather silly grin, Mary thought, but she didn't take it personally. In any case, he pulled himself together, and asked with a straightish face, "Who's the grave for then?"

"Your white cat. Snowy."

As soon as she said it, she knew how dreadful it sounded, and she felt herself blush. Mr Ralph looked quite peculiar for a second, and she realised he must have thought that she *meant* it. That was the problem with not being forward. Mary was a person who liked to explain, and if you didn't explain there was always the risk that people wouldn't understand. This seemed a case in point to her, and she found it quite frustrating.

"Not really though," she added, hoping that this would help without using too many words. "Only pretend."

"I see," said Mr Ralph, but it was clear that he didn't, and Mary suspected that he might be thinking that she *wasn't very nice*.

"I can explain if you want," Mary said tentatively. "Unless you're going somewhere." This wasn't being forward; it was leaving it up to him. If he didn't want her to speak, then he could just continue his walk. And if he did, then she'd only be doing what he wanted. It seemed simple enough.

He smiled. A nice ordinary sort of smile. "I'd like that," he said.

Mary was relieved. It had become a bit of a burden, the problem about the grave, and there was no one else she could tell. The lie had seemed so clever at the time, but lies had a habit of going wrong, and if Colin was going to be funny about it and tell the Sneddon boys, she could be in lots of trouble. And actually, it was all because of having to keep the secret, about going into the house... and she had been so terribly late and the boys had been so angry, so it had to be something special.

All this spilled out, in a rather messy sort of way. This time Mr Ralph didn't try to hush her and didn't seem to mind her chattering on. He even asked her to start at the beginning, so she did, and there was a certain comfort in it. She told him about playing out with her brothers, and them not being very nice and the incident with the angel. She explained about Snowy getting hurt, and the boys not caring, and how she had followed the poor hurt cat all the way up the lane to his house. The next bit Ralph was there for, so she missed all that, but she told him about teatime, and how they had to go home together or their mum would know they'd split up and they were supposed to stay together. She described – perhaps more luridly than she remembered – how angry the boys had been that day, because of her being so late, and how they had tortured her to make her say where she had been. She stressed that she had to give them some kind of story, or they'd have twisted her arm till it broke, and she was really pretty stuck because they'd searched all over the village, so there was almost nowhere she could pretend to have been.

All of this brought her, with a degree of embarrassment, to the horrible lie about the cat. She didn't say anything about the other aspect of it, about getting one over on Colin, but she stressed very earnestly that it was the only story she could think of that wouldn't betray their secret. She felt this was fitting, and it ought to exonerate her. After all, he had been so particular, so really she was covering for *him* as much as herself.

Such is the currency of secrets, and the alliances they forge.

He was very understanding. Halfway through the story, he suggested they sit down, and they went to the embankment where it wasn't so muddy. Even so, the stones were hard, so he took off his jacket and said he really didn't need it, and they sat together on that while she finished her account. He didn't say much, but at the end he nodded approvingly, and said he was glad she'd told him, and that he was really proud of her, for being so brave with their secret. Mary basked in this, though she felt, all in all, it was only right and proper.

Then he stood up abruptly, and said in a business-like way, "I suppose I'd better help you with this grave then. We can do a really good one if we do it together."

Mary beamed. It seemed to her suddenly that he was a really wonderful man.

And it was, when they finished, a pretty terrific grave. In his bag Ralph had the tools for his motorbike, which weren't ideal for digging but better than her hands, and with these he clawed a little pit in the clay. Then he pointed out that if it came to an exhumation, it would really be better if there were some *actual bones*. Mary looked dubious, but at once Ralph was over the fence, gesturing into the trees.

"There are foxholes in here. Could be bones anywhere."

So she let him help her over and they searched for a while. At first they found nothing except whitened sticks, which Mary thought would do very well, but then Ralph found something unspeakable in the undergrowth, full of worms and maggots. Mary refused to look, but she was rather pleased when Ralph said it was perfect, and he got it on the end of a stick and carried it to the hole.

"If your Colin digs *this* up, you won't have any trouble," Ralph said. "Run a mile he will." Mary laughed uneasily.

Then Ralph suggested gathering cow hairs from the fence and throwing them in amongst the earth near the top. The cows were Friesians so the white hairs had to be harvested one by one. Mary picked them out, and Ralph held onto them, and while they worked she told him about her brothers and how they always played boring games on their bikes, and how her scooter wasn't much good. Every now and then, she remembered she shouldn't be doing all the talking, and politely asked him a question, but he didn't have much to say. He wasn't, as she noticed before, very good at conversation. None the less, he seemed happy to listen, and so she relaxed. It was nice, having a grownup all to herself.

By the time they had scattered the hairs around the grave, it was time for lunch. Mary's sandwich had been in her pocket all morning and wasn't very nice, but Ralph, providentially, had two delicious pies and two fairy cakes, so apart from feeling thirsty they had a perfectly lovely lunch.

After lunch Ralph suggested some water from the stream, but Mary looked shocked. There was a drinking fountain at the playground but that was too far away. She pointed out, hopefully, that his house wasn't far, but Ralph wouldn't hear of it. So she swallowed her thirst and they finished the grave with a little circle of stones, and Ralph made a cross.

"I think I'd better go back now," Mary said. "But thank you very much."

Ralph looked disappointed. "Don't you think it needs some flowers?" he asked, and she remembered that this was what she'd planned from the beginning. "I know a place where the flowers are pretty," he said, and pointed away through the trees.

"There are cowslips in the field," Mary said, thinking about the time. "*They're* very pretty."

"But the cows might chase you. They don't like people going in their field."

Mary knew that was true. The cows were huge, and they scared her quite a lot. "There's an old barn the other side where there's lots of flowers." Ralph said.

So they set off through the plantation and Mary thought afterwards it was a jolly good thing, because just as they'd got to the cover of the trees, she glimpsed her brothers in the lane, two checked shirts, bobbing on their bikes.

She squatted quickly, taking Ralph's hand and pulling him down. He looked startled at first, and then a curious look came into his face as she pointed through the trees. "They know I'm here," she said. "They're probably coming to look for me."

He shushed her, though they were much too far to hear. Then he whispered, "I'd better be off."

But he didn't move, just squatted there, holding her hand. She felt his arm quivering, like a frightened animal. She saw how drawn and worried he looked. It was rather odd, she felt, since it wouldn't be *him* who got tortured if the boys found out. He probably needed geeing up, like the boys sometimes did. She patted his hand.

"Thank you Mr Ralph," she said. "The grave's smashing. And don't worry. I won't tell. Chin up."

She wasn't sure afterwards why she said that last thing. As soon as she said it, she knew it sounded odd – a bit forward even. "You wait in there," she said, pointing into the trees. "Be quick. And I'll go round the edge and meet them. They won't see you then." In the distance the boys were climbing into the field. "Quick. They're coming."

She stood there awkwardly, because he still didn't move. When he finally spoke, there was a strange tone to his voice. "Please Mary... please... Can we play again?"

Mary hadn't really thought they were playing, but she smiled at him anyway. "Yes," she said. "When?"

"Next week," he whispered. "But don't come to the house. I'll look out for you. If you come down the lane, I'll see you. Only on your own, mind. And secret."

"Yes," Mary said. "But quick, they're coming now."

"Absolute secret?"

"Cross my heart," Mary said. "Cross my heart and hope to die."

## 5. Secrets and Lies

Colin went white when he saw the stones, and worse when Michael pointed out the hairs in the clay.

"OK. OK. Let's go home."

"But we've got to dig it up, remember!" Michael crowed, sensing the advantage. "You said you needed to see the bones. You said that, Col – you did!" Then he picked up a stick and started poking at the earth. "Shall I dig up the bones, Col? Shall I? Do you want me to?"

But Colin had turned away. "It's all right. You don't need to. I believe her." There was, Mary saw, a horrible look in his face. She felt almost sorry for him.

But then Michael saw the footprints. "Hey, Colin, wait! Look, someone else has been here."

Mary stared where Michael was pointing. Her own little prints were clear enough – but not as clear as the bigger ones, all around the grave.

Colin turned and looked at Mary. "Did you see anyone? Did a grownup come?" He looked even sicker then.

"No," Mary said, a little awkwardly, then added as staunchly as she could "I only just got here. I was feeding the ponies before. I only just got here... I didn't even get the flowers yet."

She wanted to go then, but Michael was intrigued. "Who was it then? Whopping great feet, look! Must have been a grownup."

"They must have been there before," she said. "Someone looking at the grave. Maybe the person looking for their *cat*." She had meant it as a warning, but as soon as she said it, she knew it was silly. "Anyway, let's go home now. Colin... I want to go home."

Michael was looking at the footprints still. "They go off *there*," he said, pointing at the plantation. "Let's follow them. I'm gonna tell them Colin killed their cat, I'm gonna tell them it was you, Colin."

"No," said Mary, beginning to panic. "Let's go home."

Michael was beginning to climb the fence.

"No!" Mary shouted. "We're going home. Otherwise... *Otherwise I'll tell Rita about you wetting the bed. And I'll tell her you cried after Michael Fenner's party. And I'll tell John Pavis. I'll tell them at school."*

Colin just looked at her, gratefully, and squeezed her hand.

\*\*\*

Ralph Sneddon had always liked little girls. Even as a boy, he was never keen on football and amongst his cousins – which meant most of the children in the village in those days – he would always gravitate, furtively, to the company of the girls.

They did not reciprocate. There was something wrong about a boy who would ask about dolls and want to see the contents of tea-sets or needlework cases. If their brothers did that, they were usually sucking up because there was something they wanted, or they were pretending to be interested, only to poke fun later. They could see that Ralph meant it, so it simply seemed unnatural.

The boys had even less time for him, because he was manifestly a sissy, so all in all he was a marginal child. But there are margins to every world, and people to occupy them, so no one took much notice, except his parents who were sensitive to it. Once, in the pub, when the men were talking football, someone commented that he hadn't seen Ralph at the pitch, and someone else nudged him and said *no one* saw Ralph at the pitch, because he *wasn't quite one of the boys* that way. Reg came home mortified because it was tantamount to saying the boy was a *pansy*. It wasn't as bad as what they said about Bert Pavis – who had never got married and was generally agreed, with a certain amount of winking, to be 'artistic' – but as far as Reg could see the insult was still damning. Verity tried to calm him but she felt it just as much.

It was a relief to them all when he got into the County Grammar. Such achievement was almost unknown in the village, so it usefully removed him from the gaze of his cousins. It also gave an alibi in the face of other failings – he was the studious one, the clever one, who studied Latin and would take examinations. His mother even claimed – with no one to say otherwise – that he had found his feet at last and was having lots of fun with his County pals.

It wasn't true of course – there are bullies everywhere and the County was no different – but at home he was grateful to play up to the part. The adults were impressed. He cultivated the accent of the children at the

County – he sounded, people said, like someone on the radio. And everyone noticed how serious he'd become. He even became religious. He went twice a week to church, signed up to serve at the altar, and soon became a teacher in the Sunday School. He was in his element, the organist said, and the Vicar's wife agreed. He was made for it. Perhaps after National Service, he'd go into the Church.

And thus, when May Pavis wanted a babysitter, it seemed natural to ask him. She was a Sneddon before she married, so Ralph was *family*. And Sonia was in his class at Sunday school and he was so *responsible*. For a while, it was only Saturday afternoons – May did the cleaning at the church, and it all took so much longer if she had to take Sonia. But then, when her husband came back from the army, there were trips to the cinema and to dancing in Canningbridge. Minding Sonia was no trouble, Ralph said. He was such a nice boy.

Looking back, it wasn't true, what his mother said – that he was never any good. For a year or two everyone liked him, and he skimmed on the crest of a golden wave.

***

Riding back on his bike, after his day with Mary, Ralph thought of the injustice of his mother's words. He had done a terrible wrong, he didn't dispute it, but he'd done his time. That ought to have wiped the slate. He didn't deserve her bitter words, not now, all these long years later.

In Canningbridge, as he passed the grocer, he thought how she must have waited and watched the clock that day, getting anxious and peevish because he did not arrive. Something sharp flashed through his mind. She had not, after all, invited him to come nor ever made him welcome. It would do her no harm to miss him for a week. It might make her appreciate the next time.

There are moments in everyone's life where plans for the future split off into parallel tracks, each going off at their own due pace, wholly incompatible but each of them, separately, believed. Perhaps Ralph knew, even then, that he would not see his mother the next weekend either, but he still found satisfaction in the thought of it. She might perhaps chide him for her lonely day, but after that she would change her tone, and perhaps, at the end, ask softly if he would come again, and admit that she wanted to see him. He thought of her, reaching for his hand, and looking up, pleading.

At the same time, somewhere, he was thinking of Mary Crouch. He knew she would be there. He would wait at the fence by the railway bridge. She would appear on the other side of the field, and they would meet near the embankment.

He would show her the stream and the barn and the meadows of buttercups. They would all be hers. They could build a den together. They could make it a special place, a grand sort of den, a place they could go to if it rained. He wondered if Mary played out when it rained. Perhaps he would visit his mother then, and on fine days meet Mary. He mustn't, he told himself, take Mary for granted. There must be no demands, no demands on either side – he was wiser now.

Time stretched ahead now: the time of his youth that he had not had.

On another parallel line, he knew that this sudden blossoming was a dangerous thing, whose sweetness might open treacherously. He certainly knew that the world would not look kindly on this friendship, be it ever so innocent. But the world, he told himself, is not always right. A wrong path, taken once, does not mean that all paths afterwards will go awry.

And is not human friendship a precious thing, something meant, something ordained from the beginning of time, and somehow – exonerating all blame – a matter of secret chemistry, out of our hands?

It was perfectly clear that Mary Crouch liked him. She had made all the moves – he had only followed. She wanted him for her friend, and there was no harm in that. He would be careful, infinitely careful. He would be a good friend. He had always liked little girls.

After Canningbridge there were fields, and then a town, more fields, and another town. He knew the route without thinking now. He felt the bike bend into the corners, then surge again; it was a hard machine, effortlessly sensing his desire. He still carried L plates but he thought now of taking his test. That would be an achievement, something he could be proud of. A long time ago, at school, in a bleak place crowded with dangers, he had found satisfaction in tests and exams. Success was an endorsement that he wasn't so bad, whatever people thought.

The approach of home was marked by the smoke from the industrial estate. Slough wasn't a pretty town or a good place to live. He had no ties there – no ties anywhere, unless he counted Heckleford where he couldn't live again. But perhaps he would move closer. He could get another job. A decent job even, not labouring or factory work. He could still speak nicely, like someone on the radio. He'd lost a lot, but he'd never lost that.

***

Speaking nicely, however, is no guarantee of the respect that is due.

In the shop, that afternoon, Janet Crouch had asked politely for two ounces of ham, *very thinly sliced*. The lady at the counter must have heard what she said, but she left the slicer just as it was, and as two fat slices rolled from the blade, Janet saw at once that it was more than she'd asked for. Her heart sank. She had budgeted for two ounces, and each of the children would expect a whole slice, however thick it was.

"Excuse me," she had said, in her primmest voice, because it was all quite embarrassing, "but I did ask for *thin*."

"This *is* thin," said the woman flatly. "A ha'pence over – is that all right?"

"Well…." Janet paused. She did not like to make a fuss, but it really *wasn't* thin. "There ought to be four or five slices, you know, if you'd cut it thin."

The woman slapped the two slices on a sheet of greaseproof paper. "Will there be anything else?"

Janet hesitated. If she took the two slices, there'd be arguments at teatime. If she asked for more, she'd not have the money to pay. She gritted her teeth. "But I did ask for thin you know. Perhaps someone else would like those… *thick* slices. If you could just be so kind…"

The woman met Janet's eyes. "Luncheon meat's cheaper you know, *if you can't afford ham*."

Straight out, just like that, and loud enough for anyone to hear. Janet was mortified. She looked away, but as she turned, she saw the others – a couple of Sneddon women, smirking by the cheese counter, and the Vardon woman from the pub in her tarty makeup, looking on from the door. Janet gritted her teeth and pulled herself as tall as she could. "No, it's all right. I'll take those slices I suppose. They'll have to do."

Perhaps her hands were shaking as she fiddled with the clasp on her purse, for as it opened a shilling fell out and rolled under the meat cabinet. She knelt on the floor, trying to get it out. The assistant should have come and helped or offered to move the cabinet. Or the other women even. It was a lot of money to lose – everyone must have seen what had happened.

"Excuse me," she said, getting up. "I've dropped a shilling…"

The woman looked indifferent, sceptical even. "Oh yes? Well, if I find it later, I'll put it by."

Then one of the Sneddon women interrupted. "I think you'll find it was a *ha'penny* dear – I saw it go under. I did, Betty – it was only a ha'penny."

"But it wasn't!" Janet cried. "It was a shilling – honestly!" Without the shilling, she wouldn't have enough.

The woman shrugged. "So you don't want this then?" she asked, nodding at the ham.

Janet felt herself colouring up. She bent down again and squinted under the cabinet. But it was no good. "No, I'll leave it …" she said at last, feeling the wrench. "But if you find the shilling.…"

She turned, wanting to run. The tarty woman from the pub was still at the door, standing in her way. As Janet muttered "Excuse me," the woman stepped back, but then she took Janet's arm, and steered her firmly on the path towards the pub.

"Don't you worry," she said. "They're just a bitchy bunch, those Sneddons." Janet looked at her aghast. *Bitchy* was a rude word – almost swearing – and the woman was saying it, right in front of her. And she was actually touching Janet's arm! Janet tried to pull away, but the woman went on. "I was sorry about the… about the ham. Must be hard, dear, without your husband. You haven't got… you know… anyone *else*?"

Janet gasped at the impertinence, but the woman had not finished. "Look, if you come round the back, I can give you some. I mean… we changed the ham today and there's still a bit of meat on the old one. I could give you the bone, you know. You could do soup with it – or scrape it."

Janet tugged her arm away. This was disgusting. This woman, this *barmaid,* was actually referring to Rick's absence as if she had the right to, and asking if Janet had *somebody else!* And then, because she hadn't, she was *offering charity*. "Excuse me please!" Janet said, pulling away. "You've quite misunderstood. Now if you don't mind…"

She felt the woman's eyes as she stepped up the road. A horrible, vulgar, impertinent woman.

\*\*\*

By the time the children got home there was tea on the table. Pilchards were perfectly nutritious – though the tin was old because nobody liked them. The boys started whining at once, but Janet clapped her hands and refused to listen.

"Did you have a nice time, dears?" she asked, looking round with a fixed little smile. "Did you go anywhere nice?"

Michael seemed to find the question funny. "Oh yes, *really* nice. We went down the lane and we saw where..."

There was suddenly a movement under the tablecloth, and Michael yelped. Then he lunged at Colin across the table and said something rude. There followed an altercation and in the end the boys were sent to their room.

Janet's fixed little smile had quite worn away.

She scrubbed the plates as if she wanted the pattern off. Her position was intolerable. The injustice of it tightened her jaw. Everyone in the village sneering at her. The barmaid offering scraps of ham. It was so unfair. It wasn't as if *she'd* done anything wrong.

The future stretched ahead like a life sentence. Endless washing and squabbling and clearing up mess. Mary might learn to be helpful, but the boys... From what people said, boys got no better, even in Secondary School – just tearing around with enormous feet, spreading mud, and eating all the time. Three mouths to feed, and only Rick's pathetic little envelopes. Already there wasn't enough.

The thought of the ham, which she'd tried to suppress, came back to her bitterly. Everything seemed to be getting more expensive. And what if the envelopes stopped coming? What if the mortgage...? And what about the bills?

When Mary was a baby, Rick got pancreatitis and nearly died. Life was so unfair, Mary felt. Widowhood was respectable, honourable even. She'd probably have got a pension from his firm if he'd died, and anyway her mother would have helped her then, and so would his. And the people in the village would have shown her some respect. She banged the dishmop into the sink tidy and thought of Rick. It was so unjust. Death would have been infinitely preferable to Manchester.

\*\*\*

The boys had apparently made friends again and were playing noisily in the bedroom. But Mary didn't want to play with them.

She felt uncomfortable somehow. She thought about Mr Ralph, and the anxious look as he'd told her not to tell. She would have liked to tell her brothers. It was, after all, a bit of a coup to have a grownup friend. Back in Croydon, she had several grownup friends, and everyone was nice about it. There was the lady in the shop and the coalman and the almost grownup girl who babysat. They weren't *secret* friends though. The secrecy bothered her, even though she'd promised.

Her mum was on the sofa, staring at the television. It hadn't worked for ages, so Mary wasn't interrupting. She sat down close and snuggled in. For several minutes the two of them sat in silence. Mary thought any moment her mum would say "Bedtime," and that would be that. But she didn't. She stroked Mary's hair, in an absent sort of way, and Mary leant into her. She felt her mother relaxing, growing soft around the tummy. Such were the moments for broaching difficult things, for telling secrets even.

"Mum?"

"Yes?"

"Have you ever had a secret friend?"

Perhaps her mother tensed a little – perhaps it hadn't been so safe a thing to ask. But it was done now. "What do you mean, dear – a secret friend?"

Mary hesitated. "Someone you couldn't tell other people about, someone you really liked but weren't supposed to tell?"

"Mary, whatever do you mean?" Her mother's voice was sharp and she wasn't stroking any more. "Please! *What do you mean?*"

Mary was silent. She wished she hadn't said anything.

"Mary, what do you mean? What sort of friend?"

It wasn't any good. She would have to see it through. "Someone nice. A grownup friend. Like a nice man. Someone who's really nice and helps you with things, and you... you do things with... nice things... things other people don't know about... but he doesn't want you to tell anyone about him."

Her mother sat up, as hard as steel now. "Mary, I don't know what you mean! Who's been saying these things?"

Mary was startled by her mother's reaction. "Nobody... I was just... I mean... It was just something..."

"Mary, listen to me! I'd never have a secret man friend. Never. That's a *disgusting* thing. If anyone says anything like that to you, you mustn't listen to them. It's a wicked thing to say. A wicked wicked wicked thing. Now tell me – who's been saying these things to you? I want to know."

Mary was closing up into herself, fighting the tears. She wished she'd never spoken. "Nobody mum. Nobody. I didn't mean anything."

Her mother stood up. "I don't like that sort of talk Mary. It's your bedtime now. If anyone talks like that you mustn't listen and you're to let me know at once. It's a very naughty way to talk. Now, off to bed."

\*\*\*

There was so much in life that wasn't clear to Mary. Secrets and lies were difficult things, but so was the truth. She slunk upstairs quietly, tapping the steps with her hands. Downstairs, her mother – who had never had a secret man friend and never would – stood by the door, staring at the ceiling and breathing hard. The gossip in the village was clearly worse, much worse, than ever she'd imagined.

# 6. Friendship

The following Saturday, Ralph waited all day by the fence, looking out for Mary. The weather was cooler, and there was damp in the air. He screwed up his eyes and kept imagining he saw her. He had everything planned. She was bound to come.

At eleven he decided that she would come after lunch. Perhaps she couldn't get rid of her brothers and was waiting to shake them off.

At half past two, he ate a little of the feast, but left the best bits, in case she came.

At three, despairing, he thought of calling on his mother after all. He could say he'd got held up and could only stay a little. But on the first day, the Day of the Blooded Cat, Mary had come at four-thirty. It would be just his luck if Mary came then, and looked around and didn't see him. Or worse, she might see the bike by the house, and come knocking on the door. It would be best to leave it. He could always see his mother another week.

Minutes ticked by. The road was quiet, with just a handful of cars. If anyone noticed the young man by the fence, the motorbike under the tree, the rucksack on the verge, nobody found it interesting.

***

For Mary it had been a week of uncertain fortunes.

Rita Vardon had given her a little plastic pony, and in return she'd given Rita a fan. Mary guessed that this meant they were proper friends – maybe *best* friends even – but she didn't like to ask, because she was avoiding being forward. It seemed to be working.

The girls had let her join them at skipping in the playground – or at least, let her take an end for three playtimes in a row, which wasn't really fair, but was better than nothing. The girl with the calliper always took an end, but she couldn't skip so it wasn't the same. Even so, Mary saw it as progress and used the time for thinking.

She thought about the conversation with her mother. Having a secret friendship must be naughtier than she'd realised. Worse than naughty even. She thought of her mother's face, and the look of embarrassment and anger. She thought about Ralph and decided they wouldn't meet again, not at all. She would pretend she'd never met him.

She thought a lot about the grave and of Colin's face when he saw it, blank with shame and horror. He had been a bit quiet since then, and she knew that he suffered. She thought about telling him the truth, that it was all made up, and that he didn't need to worry. It would be difficult to do. He would get angry and probably hit her, but she could cope with that.

*\*\*\**

Perhaps she *would* have told him, if he hadn't tried to spoil the thing with Rita.

The girls in the village only knew one skipping rhyme. Mary knew lots from her other school but after what Miss Vardon said, she knew better than to mention this again. So she waited patiently while they did the only one they knew, over and over again.

*Ri – ta – Ri – ta – who – will you – ma – rry?*

Then they would call out the names of boys in the school, shouting in time till the skipping girl tripped, and she won the boy she tripped on. They always started with the infants first, then the unpopular boys from the juniors, and then last of all the best ones – like the Sneddon twins in the top class, who could already drive a tractor.

Once the partner was chosen, the counting part:

*Now – we – know – who – you – will – ma – rry*
*How – many – child – ren – will – you – ca – rry?*
*One – Two – Three – Four...*

There were girls who could go twice through all the boys and get over a hundred children – or so they said. But Rita was never in that league. She was a plump little girl – not actually fat like the girl with *glands* – but short with heavy ankles and clumsy feet. She skipped, with some relief, past the boy with the birthmark and a couple of other boys with runny noses and sweaty hands. Then someone called "Michael Crouch," and Rita slipped.

She untangled her feet and glared at the girl who said it.

Mary was puzzled when everyone laughed.

Michael wasn't the worst sort of boy. He was in the juniors, anyway.

Mary wasn't fond of him, but she felt – with a certain loyalty mixed with shame – that they shouldn't be jeering.

Rita looked round unhappily, and nodded at Mary to turn the rope again, so they could count her children. Mary did her best, but at the other end, the girl with the calliper was pulling the rope down, not ready to go on. The group tightened round, a little oval, staring at Rita.

"Lucky you, Rita Vardon!" a Pavis girl sneered. "*Missus* Michael Crouch! Poor little Rita's marrying Michael *Crouch*. Some of the other girls laughed again, uneasily.

Mary wondered what was going on. It was only a game. They weren't supposed to go on like this, as if it *meant* something.

"Mis-sus Crou-ouch. Mis-sus Crou-ouch..."

"You'll go and live in a fancy house up Heckleford Hill!" a Sneddon girl said. "You'll walk like this and talk like this!" She squashed her mouth into a tiny pout and spoke in the funny tone that they used when they pretended to be posh. Then she took a few mincing steps, wiggling her bottom.

"But it won't do you any *good*," another girl giggled. "He'll leave you for another woman and then you'll be sorry."

Rita was looking miserably from face to face – Sneddons and Pavises and even her own cousins. Then she stuck out her tongue at them all and turned to Mary.

"Come on, Mary," she said. "We're not playing with them. If I marry your brother you'll be my sister. So there." And she put her arm through Mary's and started pulling her away. If it weren't for the nastiness a few moments before, Mary would have been, at that moment, supremely happy.

***

She had not seen that Colin was looking on. She didn't notice him till she felt his hand on her shoulder, pulling her away.

"Come with me," he said. "Come on. Leave them alone."

"But I'm playing with Rita," Mary protested, gripping Rita's arm.

"No you're not. She's just making fun of you," Colin turned to Rita with a hostile look. "Buzz off, Rita Vardon. We don't want you." Then he waved his hands at the others. "You too! You're village idiots, all of you!"

Mary was appalled. "No Colin! I want to play with Rita! Let go!"

Colin was looking flushed, with little red blotches all around his neck. "You can't. Playtime's over almost. You shouldn't be playing with them. They're horrible girls."

"No Colin – not Rita!"

"They're all the same. You can play with me and Michael. You don't need Rita Vardon. She's a fat idiot."

He dragged Mary off, to the other side of the playground, and made her watch while he played a game with Michael. When the bell went for lessons, Rita was holding hands with her cousin again, and neither of them would look at her. Then later, after dancing, Mary's tunic was mysteriously missing, so she had to run round in her knickers, till she found it in the litter bin. She suspected treachery.

The next day she claimed a tummy ache, and to her surprise her mother didn't argue.

She sat up in bed all the morning, with her dolls and a colouring book, and her mother mashed a whole banana for her lunch. Then she went downstairs for *Listen with Mother,* as if she were still a baby, while her mother did the ironing. It was a lovely day. After school the boys were sulky and she heard them complaining that it wasn't fair – her getting the banana, when she was only bunking. So as a matter of honour she was ill the next day as well, even though it was Saturday.

It was all rather easier like that in fact. Being ill meant she didn't have to decide about going to see Ralph. She had her mother near and everything was comfortable. Her mother was never a simple book to read, but she seemed calmer now, a kind of blank serenity smoothing her features. Perhaps she had forgotten about the secret friend.

***

The next day Mary stopped being ill, and was glad, because at Sunday School she discovered that Rita had forgiven her. She even asked if Mary was better, and told her about a tummy ache that *she'd* had once. The Vicar's wife did a little story about how Jesus was a special friend to each of them, and could speak to them any time, in lots of ways that nobody else would know about, so they always had to be listening. Mary wondered if that counted as a *secret friend,* and felt a bit cross: adults were always saying one thing one day and the opposite the next, you never knew who to believe. Then they went into church and sang *What a friend we have in Jesus,* and afterwards they sat with their teacher and did colouring, and Mary and Rita swapped the little stickers that the Vicar gave them. Mary liked Sunday School. She was a good little girl.

On the next day, on the way to school, she told Colin that she was playing with Rita whether he liked it or not, and if he tried to interfere, she tell their teacher about *you know what,* because Rita was a proper friend, better than any of Colin's. And by the end of the week there was most satisfying proof, because Rita came to school with a note from her mother inviting Mary for Saturday tea. Mary's happiness, briefly, was complete.

After school, however, as her mother read the note, she didn't respond at all as she should. She just shook her head and tightened her lips.

"I'm sorry, Mary, I don't think its suitable. I'm not having you visiting a *pub.*"

"They don't live *in* the pub mum. They live in the house behind. Anyway, *Dad* used to go to the pub."

This didn't seem to help. "No, Mary, I really don't think so," Janet said very firmly. "I believe I've *met* Rita's mother. Not a nice sort of woman. A very rude *interfering* sort of woman. I really don't want you getting mixed up with those people. It's not suitable."

Mary stared, not able to believe. *Her mother was saying no.*

Mary was usually a good little girl, and rarely any trouble. That Friday evening, however, she was sent to bed early with the threat of a smacked bottom. Her mother didn't want a rude little girl who threw tantrums and ought to be ashamed of herself.

\*\*\*

After early rain, the sun dappled through the trees. Near the fence where he had waited the week before, Ralph made a secret clearing among the brambles. Into this he pulled his motorbike, out of sight of the road. It wouldn't do to have anyone wondering whose bike it was. Nobody knew he was there, nobody. Nobody knew he had ever been back, apart from his mother and she wouldn't tell.

This week he was more sober. He paced the verge less jauntily, less certain of pleasure ahead. He had felt, all week, a little cheated. But he told himself firmly that there must have been reasons. It would not do to let himself mind. In his rucksack he had another feast, and the two little toys he had bought the week before, and the little rug, folded up tight, and the knife and the string.

He stood by the fence again and stared across the field. The Friesians were already trotting towards him, but he had no eyes for them. What interested him was the little red dot, visible moment by moment through the trees across the field. It might not be her, he told himself. He did not want to be hurt again. But it *was* her, and after a moment he could see she was alone.

And all the larks in Heckleford seemed to be singing and soaring that morning.

# 7. An Ill-Used Heroine

Little girls' stories are thick with ill-used heroines. Uprooted from happiness, deprived of their protectors, despised and ill-treated by their familiars, they are generally an unfortunate bunch.

It was evident now to Mary that she was just such a creature. Her father had been snatched away, in circumstances not properly explained. Her brothers were cruel, her mother hated her and all of them were determined to deny her any friend.

She rehearsed these misfortunes as she sauntered down the lane with Rita's pony in one pocket and a sandwich in the other. She was not downhearted, for like the heroines in *Bunty* (which the newsboy delivered each Thursday with her brothers' *Eagle*) she was a stout-hearted girl.

She might not have admitted it, but her sufferings were made pleasant by a sense of her own virtue and the confidence that things must work out in the end. Her rescue of the cat, her befriending of the mysterious stranger, the magical gift from Rita – such complications in the story seemed entirely in order. It was always thus in *Bunty,* and it therefore seemed almost propitious. Sooner or later, such events would lead to a conclusion – involving, no doubt, the return of her father, the punishment of her brothers, her mother's remorse for treating her so ill, the affection of friends, and possibly even her happy restoration to Croydon. She was a patient child. She would play her part as fate required and wait for vindication.

Colin and Michael had gone off on their bikes, in a direction which suggested – though they never said it – that they were going to the farm to see the Sneddon boys. That was typical, Mary felt. Colin and Michael could have friends in the village and play where they liked. It was only poor Mary who was allowed no friends at all.

Such privations impel a girl towards secret adventures. She would, as she told herself, have gone to Rita's had it been allowed. Or if the boys were less horrid, she'd have made them play with her. But nothing was left now but to play on her own, and if she happened to meet a person in the lane, then it was hardly reprehensible if she said hello.

She knew she was a full week late for her rendezvous with Ralph. But she had come this way twice on a Saturday and twice she had met him, so she wasn't surprised when she saw him across the field. He did some complicated semaphore and then started round the edge. Neither of them ran or shouted, but when he came close, he did a little bow and held out his hand as if she were a grownup.

"Well met, Miss Mary. And a lovely morning. I was on my way to build a den."

Mary remembered her den by the newt-pond. "I wouldn't build it near here," she said.

Ralph shook his head. "I know a better place." He pointed through the plantation. "Through there. The old barn. You know where I mean?" Mary shook her head and he smiled. "Come on. I'll show you."

There wasn't a path through the plantation. Ralph took her hand on the rough bits, and twice, when they got to brambles, he picked her up to lift her over. When they came to a place where the nettles were tall, he lifted her over his head and perched her on his shoulders. Even past the nettles he didn't take her down.

"Have you and your brothers been round here?"

"No. Not ever."

"Hmm."

Mary felt the sway of his movement beneath him, like riding some wild creature through a jungle. She thought of the den and wondered how they would build it. "Have you built a den before?" she asked.

"Yes. Have you?"

"Only once. But the boys knocked it down."

"That's a shame."

So she told him about the first den, up by the newt-pond, and her brothers' wickedness.

"There was some of my tea-set, and a little bear. I don't know where they went. And the bear was a present from my dad."

Ralph was sympathetic. He understood everything and asked sensible questions. They had suffered, it appeared, quite similar privations.

He knew what it was like when she had to leave Croydon, because he'd grown up in the village but had to leave when he was only a boy, to go to somewhere else, which he didn't like at all. He knew about being new and getting picked on. And he knew what missing a Dad was like, because his own dad had died.

"I'm sorry," Mary said. "Why did he die?"

"I don't know," Ralph said, and was quiet for a while. "We'll build our new den somewhere safe," he said eventually. "Somewhere no one will find it."

Beyond the plantation there was a cornfield, still green but tall already. It sloped down into a little dip, with a row of trees at the bottom, and beyond that a stream. There weren't any houses in sight, just the skeleton of a barn, with its roof and most of its walls caved in. Ralph lifted Mary off his shoulders and laughed.

"You're a little ton weight you are."

"Yes," said Mary proudly.

"We'll build the den behind there," he said, pointing to the barn. "That's the best place."

They walked hand in hand down the side of the field. Mary tried to keep the conversation going, but she sensed a change in Ralph, and after a while he seemed not to be listening. She squeezed his hand kindly. Her mum was sometimes like that.

Only the back of the barn was intact. The other sides were crumbling. The space in the middle was piled with rubble, and a tree was growing inside it. There were flowers: poppies at the front and in the middle great clusters of furry leaves and a tall yellow spike, rising straight from the stones.

"You couldn't do a den in *here*," she said, staring at the rubble.

"Not inside," he said. "Too obvious. But at the back..." He helped her over the stones till they got to the corner where they could peer behind the wall. There was a dark place there, with the trees growing over, and patches of brambles and stinging nettles. Ralph's face clouded over.

"It's a bit overgrown," he said. "I had a den here before. Ages ago."

He seemed, Mary thought, upset.

'Wait here," he said. Then he buttoned up his jacket and pushed his way round through the nettles at the side. He seemed to be gone quite a time.

"Mr Ralph!" Mary called. "Mr Ralph!"

When he came back, she pointed to a place at the lower end of the field. It was under some trees with a bank of grass and the stream just beyond. The perfect place, Mary thought, for a den.

"No," said Ralph flatly. "It's too obvious. You can see it from anywhere. And there's a footpath just over the stream. People walk there. This is the place."

"But the nettles…"

"I'll cut them down. We'll make a path in." There was something urgent in his voice, but he must have seen Mary's dubious look. "No – the nettles are *good*. Nobody'll come poking. I'll make a secret path. It'll be good. Really." Then he smiled, a rather odd, awkward smile. "I had a den here before. It'll be good."

Then he went back behind the wall. Mary felt rather cross. If they made the den there, the nettles would always come back, however much he trampled them. After a while she decided to tell him this, so she made her way out of the rubble and gingerly down the side of the barn on the track left by his passing. One side of her legs got stung, which she felt rather proved her point.

It was a horrible place at the back. In between the nettles there were heaps of stones, but no sign at all of a previous den. A shadow of doubt began to grow in Mary's mind. Perhaps he'd made it up. In any case, it wasn't much fun, watching a cross-looking man kicking nettles about, in a dark little place behind a broken wall. The other side of the field, where she'd pointed before, had been bathed in sunshine and the grass looked soft and sweet.

"Mr Ralph… This isn't the best place," she said. "Really. It isn't."

He looked up, as if startled to see her. "*You don't understand,*" was all he said. Then he started kicking the nettles again, and when he got to a wooden beam, almost buried, he heaved at the end of it. It was a huge thing. He levered it round and dragged it backward, jolting it step by step, till one end could be wedged on the side of the barn.

"Like that, you see," he said, as if it were obvious. Then he pushed and tugged it, heaving it up on his shoulder, till the end rested high against the wall. Mary walked over. She could see, at last, what he meant. Inside the triangle between earth and beam and wall, was a space where even Ralph could stand. A den built like that would almost be a house.

"But it'll still be nettley," she said, feeling somehow put out at conceding his point.

"I'll see to that," he said. "I'll put something on the floor. It'll be good." Then he went back to his work.

It occurred to Mary that perhaps he was more like her brothers than she'd thought. He really just wanted to play by himself and she was in the way. She thought of going back, but she wasn't sure of the way, and anyway, it might seem rude. So she watched in silence as he heaved the great beams. There were lots of them under the nettles. Three... four... five... Half an hour passed, but he didn't stop. He was putting them a foot or so apart, one after the other. Nine... ten... eleven...

She saw the sweat all over his head, dripping down his neck, making his curly hair look like snakes round his brow. She saw the fierce, strained look in his face. She didn't like it at all. She tried to remember the way that they had come. She wasn't interested in the den anymore. She just wanted to go home.

A lot of the nettles were trampled now, and amongst them, near the wall, she could see some bits that might have come from an older den. They looked nasty now. There were scraps which must once have been material – decayed and crumbling. There were various pieces of rusted metal, and a book, all rotten and its pages swollen up. No one could read it now, even if they'd wanted to, and when she kicked it with her foot she found the back had been eaten away and there were creatures underneath

"Mr Ralph... I want to go home."

He looked up – that startled look again. For a second, there was some kind of battle in his face, but then he focused on her.

"No! No. Don't go home!" He let the beam he was pulling drop back on the earth. "Mary, Mary... I'm sorry. It's just the den. I'm building it for *us*. For you. I didn't mean to upset you... I just wanted to make it nice. A smashing den."

Mary felt this was more appropriate. "But I'm hungry now," she said, sensing her advantage.

He relaxed. "Of course you are! Mary, I'm sorry. I'm really sorry. But look... I've got everything."

He opened his rucksack and took out an inner bag with interesting bulges, and a flask, which was good because the last time they'd been thirsty. "I've got a good feast here," he said.

"Couldn't we eat it out there?" Mary asked, "It's too nettley here."

He looked disappointed but nodded. "If that's what you want. But I want to show you something."

From his bag he pulled the little roll of blanket, and carefully laid it inside the lean-to, like a rug. Then he pulled out two little parcels and put them on the blanket. And to finish he put the bag with the food on the corner.

"You don't have to eat it here if you don't want. But please... just come in for a moment. Just so you've been in."

"OK," she said, and took a step through the triangle at the end.

"No," he laughed. "You're walking through my wall. Only an invisible wall just now, but all the same – you mustn't walk through my wall. Our front door's the *other* way."

So she walked obediently to the other end, and Ralph pretended to open a door, making a slow squeaking noise. Mary laughed.

"Do come in," he said with a bow. "Welcome to Mary's Mansion. But please – allow me to show you round. In here, we will have the parlour." He gestured to the area where she was standing. "And over there" – gesturing to the eaves where it was too low to stand – "the babies' room." Then he gestured to the end, where she had tried to walk in. "What shall we have there? A bathroom? A garage? A bedroom maybe. Yes, a bedroom." He took off his leather jacket and laid it over the blanket. "Come and sit in our parlour. I've got these two little presents for you."

For a moment, the space before her seemed to shift and writhe, as it filled with meaning and possibility. The world is not a single place. It is full of secret doors and openings: wardrobes with magical backs that lead into other worlds, wormholes in time and space, rabbit-holes, looking glasses – infinite planes, each transecting the others, waiting for recognition.

The nettley place with its bits of nasty debris was only an illusion. Inside it, secretly, there was somewhere else.

Mary giggled. "Yes. I can see now. It's lovely." She looked around, enchanted. "It is. It's a smashing den. And I like the rooms just where you said." Then she sat on his coat where he pointed.

Ralph sat down next to her and passed her the presents. They weren't wrapped up like birthday presents, just paper bags with the ends folded over. The first was a little doll – with arms and legs that moved and little plastic furrows on its head, for hair. It was dressed in white knickers. The second was a little fluffy cat, with a red plastic collar and a bell.

"They reminded me of you," Ralph said. "Snowy and Mary. I expect Snowy would like to sleep in the baby's room, and when we've made a bed, you can put Mary in her bedroom."

Mary looked hesitant, not wanting to be forward. "Are they mine to keep?" she asked at last.

Ralph said yes, but then looked a little grave. "But you must leave them *here*. If you take them home and your mum sees them, she might be nosey."

Mary thought about it. It was true that her mother didn't like her getting things. She had even been suspicious of the little plastic pony, and when Mary had explained about Rita and the fan, her mother had got cross and said it was naughty to swap things.

"OK then," she said. "They can live here."

"Yes," Ralph said. "I'll make beds for them. Now madam, I believe you said you were hungry?"

And so, in the shadows of the new den, between the back of the barn and the pines beyond, they ate their second meal together. It was a feast. There were special biscuits with pink icing and a slice of gala pie, and a flask full of some special drink that Mary hadn't had before. It was just like a party.

Mary settled herself down beside Ralph and leant on him. She felt the warmth of him through his shirt. He must have been sweltering with his jacket on.

"We could bring flowers in," she said. "I could put leaves on the floor."

"Yes," he said. "That would be nice."

"I'll make it really pretty. Like a real house. But it should have a door. And a key. Mummy always locks the door when we go to bed. It's to keep out *bad* people."

"Hmmm," Ralph said. "But this house doesn't have a door yet."

"It's got a pretend door. It could have a pretend key."

"And we could keep out pretend bad people." Laughing, Ralph dug in his jacket pocket and pulled out the key to his motorbike. "Look, a real key. Let's lock the door now." He went as if to lock the space where the door might have been.

Mary giggled. "It would be better to have some walls first."

"You've got a point there," Ralph said sagely. "I was coming to that."

Mary held out her hand for the key, but he didn't give it to her. It was a little key, with a red enamel end. It was pretty. "Is it the key to your real house?"

"No. I haven't got that. My landlady lets me in."

"What's it for then?"

Ralph dangled it out to her, just out of reach. "Well, it's a magic key. If I didn't have this key, I couldn't come here. So I need it."

"Is it your mum's key?"

"No. It's my key."

"Is it the key to a cupboard?"

"No. It's a magic key. It makes the world change from grey and horrible to green and lovely."

Mary thought about it. She always liked riddles, and she was usually quite good at them – better than the boys. But this one puzzled her. "Is it the key to this house?"

"No." Ralph dangled it near her hand and Mary jumped up, trying to snatch it. But each time she jumped he raised it a fraction, keeping it out of reach.

"I give up," she said. She couldn't think of anywhere else he might have a key to.

Ralph grinned and put the key back in his pocket. "Like I said, it's a magic key. It's the Key to Happiness. Maybe it's the key to my heart. Would you like that?"

"Would you give it to me?" Mary looked up at him, expectantly. She suddenly felt that she'd like it very much.

"No," Ralph said. "But if you come next week, I'll make you some walls."

"Yes," Mary said at once, but then she wondered if she'd be able to. "Well, probably, anyway. Else I'll come the next week. It'll be summer holidays then. Do you only come on Saturdays?"

"It depends," Ralph said. "I could... I could come on a Sunday – if I knew you were coming. There's lots of nice things we could do. I know lots of good places. And good games."

"Shall I get some flowers now?"

"If you like. I'll just do a bit more work. Then maybe... maybe we could go for a walk."

Mary pulled herself up and went back to the front of the barn. It was the hottest part of the day, and after the heavy shade the sun was almost oppressive. It made the pale stones glow and the glare was in her eyes. It was better, after all, in the shade. The big yellow flowers were too tall and tough to pick, but she found plenty of others. She clambered over the stones to pick them and filled her skirt with them.

She was on her way back when she saw the little trinket, catching the sun.

It was a little gold cat on a chain, half buried in the grit, trapped between bits of rubble. The chain was a different metal, and flaked into pieces as she tried to get it out, but the metal of the cat was hard and shiny still. One eye was blind and full of dirt but the other was a little green gem. It was a pretty thing. Mary clutched it in her hand to show to Ralph.

Behind the barn he had been busy. As her eyes adjusted, she saw the sticks that he had tied across the beams. He'd only just started and there was much more to do, but she could see at once how they could fill the gaps with bracken, making walls like a proper house.

He had stopped though. He was sitting on the rug and rubbing his hands with dock-leaves. They were a mass of nettle bumps. She bent down to look, letting the flowers fall at his feet. "I'm sorry," she said. "Do they hurt?"

"Yes," he said. "You can kiss them better."

So she kissed them, solemnly, one hand and then the other.

"That's nice. That's better," he said. "But I've got stung on my head, too. Just there." He pointed at his forehead, just between his eyes. She couldn't see any bumps, but she kissed it anyway, and he laughed, and touched her lips with his finger.

"All gone now. You've got magic kisses."

Mary was pleased about that. "We can put the flowers in the wall to make it pretty," she said, gesturing to the pile of blooms. He smiled. "Yes," he said. "That'll be pretty."

She sat down beside him again. They seemed to be getting on better now. She wanted to keep him talking. "Was it as good as this when you built it before?"

"Yes."

"But it was a long time ago?"

"Yes. I was just a kid. I haven't been here for ages."

"How old were you?"

"Oh, I don't know. Just a kid."

"Did anyone help you?"

"No. Not really. I mostly did it on my own."

"How did you get the big wood up? If you were just a kid?"

He stared into the woods, frowning. "Slowly," he said at last. "I did it very slowly. It took me ages. Not all in one day, like today. I'm stronger now."

"That's good," Mary said.

"Yes. But it's not finished. I'm going to make it much better than this."

"Good."

Mary was feeling quite tired. She leant back against him, and he put an arm round her, making her comfortable.

"I found something out the front," she said.

"Mmm-hmm?"

She held out her hand and showed him the trinket. At first he didn't seem interested, but then suddenly he sat up, and she toppled a bit, scraping her arm against the wall.

"Give me that," he said sharply. "Let me have it."

She was affronted. "No!" she said. "Finders keepers." And she closed her hand into a fist.

"No. Mary that's not yours. You can't have that."

"It's not yours either!"

"Well – that doesn't matter. Give it to me."

"I'll swap it for the key."

"No." As he reached out for her hand, she pulled it back, but he grabbed her wrist. "No. I mean it Mary; you can't have that."

He tightened his hold and she saw something in his face that she had not seen before. She knew in that moment that he would have what he wanted. It suddenly occurred to her that he was going to hit her, like her brothers would do.

"OK," she said, and opened her hand. At once he snatched it from her. He turned it over and stared at the back. He had wanted it so much but he didn't seem to like it. He had a look that made Mary uncomfortable, somewhere between anger and grief, like the look on her mother's face, the day her father left.

Abruptly he stood up. "I need to pee," he said, and walked out of the den. He didn't turn down the path he had made. He simply continued into the nettles without even stamping them down, though he didn't have his jacket and his arms were bare. He walked straight through them, and into the darkness of the trees beyond.

*** 

It was half past three. At home, her mother was slumped on the sofa, staring at the envelope on the coffee table, and its contents, spread over the floor. The wrong envelope. Rick's envelope should have arrived that morning. It always arrived on Saturday. When it didn't come in the first post, she was sure it would come in the second. It was only a delay of course, but it disturbed her. It invited doubt – not for the present of course, because it was only a delay. But for the future. Would the envelopes keep coming, week after week – for years? Years and years? Forever?

So when the second post arrived, she had found herself, not quite able to explain it, crouched in the hall beneath the letterbox, her hands in anxious supplication as the envelope fluttered down. She caught it and for a moment she held it to her face.

She knew from the smell that it wasn't right.

It was a local postmark. And in the corner was a pompous little crest.

It was the letter from Colin's new school, with the list of all the things she'd have to buy. Tie and blazer and cap and jumper and special socks and a gabardine mack. An aertex shirt for games and special shorts. Football boots and plimsolls. A special bag for his homework and another for his kit. A special apron for technical subjects. A pencil case, a fountain pen, a set of geometry instruments. The list went on and on.

She gazed at it, disbelieving. She tried to put a figure on the cost of it all, but the prices weren't marked and she could only guess. Ten pounds? Fifteen? *Twenty*? However much she saved out of Rick's little envelopes, she'd never have *that* sort of money. What to do? She thought about her wedding ring. She thought about the children's Post Office books. It would only be borrowing. But all of what they had might not pay for all of that.

The awful truth of it was hovering behind her eyes. The thought that she wasn't ready to think, the desperate step she'd never taken, marking the threshold between the bright little world she was trying to preserve, and something shameful beyond.

*She would have to go to her mother.*

It was ghastly. She should have told her mother from the beginning –

not gone on writing as if nothing had happened – with endless excuses for the lack of an invitation. It made it worse that she'd waited till now, when she had to ask for money. And for a Secondary Modern, as well, which she'd also never confessed.

A *Secondary Modern.* Middle class children went to Grammar Schools or County Schools. The Secondary Moderns were not for them.

At first, when the results came, she'd been sure it was a mistake. Colin said John Pavis was going to the Grammar, which didn't make sense. John's dad was only a coalman. The envelope might have been wrongly labelled, or the list typed wrong. At the very least, she felt cause to be indignant. If the marks were right, then the teaching must have failed him – with all those farmers' children, they'd probably not attended to the brighter ones.

But when she went to the school, the Head Teacher shook his head. Colin was a good boy, a conscientious boy, a very nice boy. But there had never been any question of a Grammar School. He wasn't an academic child, no, not at all.

"Now you really mustn't worry," he had said at the end, as he ushered her out of the door. "Your Colin will do nicely at the Secondary Modern. He'll miss John Pavis of course, but his other chums will be there. I'm sure he'll get on fine."

It seemed inexplicable to Janet. The school had never warned her that anything was wrong.

Tie and blazer and cap and jumper – all that expense, and all with that shameful crest. It was Rick's fault of course. If Colin was stupid then it came from his side, because Janet's family were *professional.* She had gone to the grammar school, which was only to be expected. Rick had got in as well, of course, but that was just him, and it didn't wipe out his family. "Glorified rag and bone men," her father always called them, and things like that could come back in the blood.

She wiped down the kitchen table and got out the Basildon Bond. The horrible time had come and she could put it off no longer. She would write to her mother.

*\*\*\**

Mary sat on Ralph's jacket in the den.

At first, she had expected he would come back any minute. He had only gone for a wee. There were loads of trees, so it shouldn't take long.

But the minutes ticked by and he didn't come.

After a while the thought came into her head that *he might have gone for good*. Something turned over inside her. He had been cross about the trinket, and perhaps he had just *gone*.

It didn't seem fair. The little trinket wasn't his thing either. And it was she who found it – he shouldn't have got cross about a thing like that. She hadn't been naughty. He had said she had magic kisses.

On her own, the shadows round the den seemed darker somehow. She wanted to go home. Uneasily, she went to the front of the barn, where it was sunny still, and walked along the field. She peered through the plantation, but there weren't any paths. It hadn't seemed far when they came but she couldn't be sure which direction it was. She thought of going back to the den and calling him.

But going back behind the barn seemed scary now. There could be something there. Something might have gone into the den and still be there, waiting. She felt it, deep inside herself, the presence of something nasty behind the barn. She started to cry.

***

Perhaps Ralph had also been crying. He seemed different, somehow, when he finally appeared from the back of the barn. When she saw it was him, her relief was absolute. She ran and put her arms round his waist.

But he pushed her away, rather stiffly. "I'm sorry," he said. "I didn't mean to be so long. I didn't mean anything."

"I'm... sorry too," Mary said, with a terrible hiccup in her voice. "I didn't mean to upset you – about the little cat. I'm really sorry."

"No, it's all right," Ralph said. "It's all right. It isn't anything." Mary wondered if he was going to give it back to her then, but he didn't. "It's late," he said. "You'd better go home. I'll take you to the embankment."

They walked back almost in silence. When they got to the bit with the nettles, he stamped them down for her, and where the branches swung low, he held them back. He did not pick her up this time, nor even hold her hand. She felt the change and knew she had done wrong.

When they reached the field with the cows, she knew where she was.

"I'll be all right now," she said, because it seemed to be what he wanted, and they stood there, both of them, suddenly awkward. Ralph started rubbing his hands again. They were a mass of white wheals. She thought of his arms. He had his jacket on again, but they were probably the same.

"Would you like me to get you some dock-leaves?"

"No. You must go home."

She wanted to ask if he still would come next week, but she feared it might be forward, now that they didn't seem such friends.

She wanted to make up. She wanted to retrieve the happy mood, when he'd shown her the rooms of his den, and given her the toys. She looked at him, and smiled, hoping he would speak, but he didn't.

Reluctantly, she turned away. "I suppose I'd better go," she said. "Maybe..."

"You mustn't tell anyone," he said, just as she turned. "Nobody. Nobody at all." She heard the urgency in his voice and turned around. At least it was conversation.

"I won't. Not ever. I promise." Mary willed him to say something else, but he neither spoke nor moved away. She saw how his face was drawn and strained. He wasn't looking at her, only at his hands. In a moment of inspiration, she took his hands in her own. And she kissed them again. Magic kisses.

"I'm sorry about your hands," she said. "Please come next week."

Then she turned and walked briskly down the side of the field, not daring to look back.

# 8. Flotsam and Jetsam

Ralph had not thrown away the trinket. It was still in his pocket, its one green eye trapped in the dark. On the way back to the bike he had thought of tossing it into the field for the cows to walk on, or pushing it into the grave with the unspeakable thing, or hurling it up on the railway where the trains would crush it. But nothing had seemed safe.

It wasn't really anything. It would have no meaning to anyone. Justice had been done, long ago, and it would make no difference now. What was it, anyway? A stolen trinket that had never been missed? A clue to a crime that was long since solved? No one would be interested. It hadn't come up at the trial.

At the trial they talked only of the evening when it happened, up in Sonia's bedroom while her parents went to the pictures – that and the Sunday School, which made copy for the papers. They didn't ask about the rest, and he didn't volunteer it. They made it seem like a sudden, random act, a moment of singular, unspeakable, evil.

Nobody knew that they had really been friends, that there was history between them. Nobody knew what he had done for her, and that it had meant something, the first time, deep in their den, with the birds singing and the flowers all round. It was different afterwards, but he knew she had wanted it, that first time. It was a kind of worship.

She was beautiful. Nobody else saw it because of the mark on her face, but he saw she was beautiful. He had loved her. And she had wanted it.

It was different afterwards. Nobody knew how he had gone on trying to please her, how she had teased and promised to do it again, only to say *no* when it came to it. And the presents she demanded – the ever more impossible presents – and how she had threatened, each time, to tell her father. It was a kind of torture. Nobody knew how he had worshipped her.

All this he had tried to explain to his solicitor, stammering out the truth of it, not as an excuse but so someone else would know. Yet the man turned away from him and shook his head.

"Look son," he had said. "You want to be crucified? I'm your lawyer and I don't want to know what you just told me. You got it? *I don't want to know.*" Perhaps it was unprofessional, but he probably meant well. Who could say if it was good advice? It probably made no difference. Neither jury nor newspapers had spared Ralph anyway. If he hadn't been so young he would certainly have hung.

Several times on the way home, Ralph decided he wouldn't see Mary again. The little gold cat, scratching its way into *now* from another time, had been a warning to him. It had all been a mistake. It would be better to forget the child called Mary Crouch, forget Heckleford, not even visit his mother. His mother didn't want him. He didn't have to go back, not ever.

The thing to do would be to start again. A different, lesser, life, but one without danger. Pain was a cleansing thing. The nettles, still burning, had brought him to his senses.

He could take up evening classes, work for promotion. Find better digs. Pass his test on the bike. He could even join a church again. He could help the elderly. He could make a little, good enough life. That ought to be plenty.

But several times he also changed his mind.

Mary had come of her own volition. Of all the strangers in the world, she had chosen *him.* It was meant. Mary wasn't Sonia, and he was older now. He knew what he was doing. He wouldn't touch her. He didn't have to touch her.

He thought of the feeling of her hand in his. Her kisses. Her legs around his shoulders when he carried her. Her knickers against the back of his neck. The warmth.

*Please come back next week... Promise you'll come back.* That's what she'd said. He knew what people thought but they weren't always right. There was a truth inside him, a truth that called to him. The world was a big place. There was room for more ways than one.

He thought about the den and the simple pleasure of rebuilding it. It was good to be working outside again; there was something pure in it, like the old days, before. And Mary was a simple child, a sweet child. It wasn't the same at all.

Sonia had forced him into it, what happened in the end. She had made him do it.

His solicitor hadn't wanted to hear that, either.

***

There are always more ways than one to construct the world. It was certainly true, at just that moment, that Mary wanted Ralph. As she walked back down the lane she was thinking of him, and worrying that she had upset him. She was afraid that he might not come back again, and it was all her fault. There had been moments in the day when she felt that things weren't as they should be, but looking back she wasn't sure which moments they were. He was really her best friend. He was a smashing friend.

Time stretched ahead rather bleakly if he didn't want her anymore. She thought about Rita and wondered what she'd say at Sunday school in the morning and whether she'd forgive her for not coming to tea. She thought about her Dad, and whether he'd ever come back. It was in her mind that she had done something wrong with her Dad as well. With him, too, there had been times when she felt that things weren't as they should be, but she didn't know why. Perhaps it was something about *her*.

When her brothers found her by the memorial, Colin thought she might have been crying. Perhaps he felt guilty for leaving her all day and having a brilliant time without her. They'd gone to the farm with some other boys, and made fun of the pigs, and then someone's big brother had made a ramp in the yard and they'd done wheelies on their bikes. Acceptance is a fragile thing. If they'd taken Mary, she'd have been a liability. But still he felt ashamed, when he saw her sitting there. She was only little and must have been lonely, doing whatever she did.

"We went to the Farm," he told her on the way home. "It was pretty boring. Didn't do much though. Did you do anything?"

"No," Mary said. "Not really."

"You can come with us if you like, next week. They've got piglets. You'd like them."

Michael glared at him. "Hey Colin... They won't..."

Colin glared back. There were plenty of things that Michael didn't know. "Or we could go for a picnic. You'd like that, yes? We could save up some stuff... Mary – you won't tell mum about today, will you? I meant to come back for you at lunchtime, honest, but I thought..."

"No," Mary said. "I won't tell. I was OK actually. I made a sort of den."

"That sounds fun," said Colin, relieved. "Maybe you could show us, next week I mean..."

"But we're going to the farm," Michael interrupted. "You wouldn't like it anyway. The piglets – they're only fattening them up so they can kill them for bacon." He made a gesture of a knife across the throat, and gruesome face, which he meant as a baby pig, dying. "They'll probably have killed them by next week in fact. There'll be blood and stuff."

"Shut up," Colin said. "You're a pig yourself."

"Anyway, my den's secret," Mary said. "It's private."

"Well, we won't go there then," Michael said with a note of satisfaction.

"No," said Colin, relaxing a little. Perhaps Mary liked it on her own. She was a girl, after all. She had girlish things to do. He resolved, without saying anything, to be particularly nice to her, providing she kept quiet and didn't make trouble.

"And anyway," he added after a pause. "It's the holidays after that. We can do loads of stuff. All of us. We'll have fun."

"Maybe Dad'll come back," Michael said, and they were all rather quiet for the rest of the walk home.

*** 

It was past seven when Ralph hit the outskirts of Slough. He had ridden more slowly than usual, and in a kind of daze, not thinking of the route or feeling the excitement of the bike. Distracted, he had taken a wrong turn and not realised it for miles, until he passed a pub that he hadn't seen before. If he'd had any money he'd have stopped for a pint, though he wasn't a pub man, really. It would have been a relief, to sit in the bar, with people all around. It would have calmed him.

But he had spent all his money on the feast and the presents for Mary. There wasn't even anything for petrol, and the extra miles were a bit of a risk.

He thought of cutting across country, down little roads, and finding his way back by some other route. On other days that might have pleased him. The evening was warm, and he could see a bit of the world. But today he didn't want it. He wanted the road that was familiar, regular, safe. So he turned the bike around, regretting the wasted miles. It had all gone wrong.

He told himself firmly that it wouldn't matter being late. The worst that would happen was that Ted would have snaffled his share of the sandwiches. But he felt uneasy. He wanted to get back at the usual time, the proper time. He wanted the day to have an orderly quality, and to finish as it should, as if nothing were different. He didn't want Ted to ask about his day, or enquire why he was late, or comment on the mud on his boots.

He wanted to go to bed.

Almost home, by the canal bridge, the motorbike juddered to a stop. He kicked at the pedal a few times, but there was nothing, and he knew that the petrol was gone. He was late already, and the last few roads, which would only have been seconds on the bike, would take twenty minutes, pushing it.

He leant the bike against the bridge and stared into the water. It was muddy and sullied with litter. Flotsam and jetsam, he thought, and there was comfort in the words. Flotsam and jetsam. Flotsam and jetsam. He watched as a lollipop wrapper floated across the water. It got caught for a moment in some scum near the bank, but then an eddy released it and it moved on its way. He felt compelled to wait till it reached the bridge and disappeared beneath.

The water flowed on without ever stopping or turning or coming back on itself. However long he stared, the wrapper would never come back. Things decay. Things disappear. And behind them, pressing into the present, there is always something new. Time passes and never comes back.

He remembered the little gold cat with its lost jewel eye. That was flotsam and jetsam, too. It was a scrap of the past, snagging randomly on the present. It was worth something. He should sell it. But he knew he never could.

He pulled off a glove and felt in his pocket. He glanced all around. There was nobody nearby. He put his hand on the parapet, casually, and when he put his glove back on, the tiny cat was on the ledge, an inch from edge. Then he turned around again, as if checking the road, and let his elbow brush along the bricks. When he looked again, the little cat, with its cruel green eye, had disappeared forever. It was not of this time. The past is nothing.

# 9. The Visitation

Evelyn Parker, as everyone acknowledged, was a resourceful woman. In response to Janet's letter, she arrived the next Thursday in her little Austin car, with a nicely packed suitcase and a box of apples for the children. It was time, she felt, to take things in hand. She was not a woman who was given to self-reproach, but she said to her hairdresser on the day of her departure, that she blamed herself.

"She's such a dreamer, you see," she confided, as the woman plucked out the curlers. "She always has been. I blame myself really. I should never have let it get to that point. It was a foolish marriage, and I told her so, and now she's gone and let him fly the coop and done nothing at all to get him back. I should have taken her in hand."

"But Mrs Parker, you mustn't blame yourself," the woman said, rather absently.

"Well, no dear, it's hardly *my* fault," Evelyn replied, forgetting for the moment that she had offered to blame herself. "I told her from the start that she was making a mistake. And now it seems he's been gone six months and she's not lifted a finger. Just sat there feeling sorry for herself and didn't even tell me. I *knew* there was something up, but I wouldn't interfere."

"No," said the woman, "Of course not."

"Well, at least she's told me now, so I can sort it out. Daughters! Where would they be without us?"

And then she did a cheerful little nod of her head and inspected the curls in the mirror. They always looked stiff at first but would look more natural in the morning. She thanked the hairdresser and gave her sixpence for a tip, which was more than generous. It might have been better, she thought, to have left the next morning when the perm had settled. But it didn't really matter. Out in the country such subtleties would be wasted.

She felt at that moment a most agreeable sense of challenge. If only Janet could be more like *her*, then none of this would have happened. But she was on the job now. She would set things right.

\*\*\*

"It's not fair Mum!" Michael protested. "There isn't any room!"

"Michael, please. *Gran's* having Mary's room. So Mary's in here with you boys for the moment. That's all there is to it."

"But I hate Mary."

Mary stood in the doorway, listening and watching. It was always like that, she thought – Mum and the two boys, completely ignoring her. She didn't want to sleep in the boys' room either.

And then an inspiration. "Why can't I sleep in *your* room mummy? There's room in your bed now Daddy's gone."

Michael looked put out and shook his head. "No – that's not fair. She could sleep downstairs though. Dad slept on the sofa before he left. Mary could sleep there."

Colin knew that wouldn't work, but his mother's room seemed reasonable. "She *could* mum – sleep in your bed. There isn't space here. And I'm eleven now. You shouldn't make me share a room with a girl. She'd be better with you."

Janet felt the pleading of their faces, and the cackle of their voices – and the whole of the holidays ahead of her, and never any let-up. The pressure of time running out was pulsing in her temples: her mother arriving and nothing quite ready, the certainty of criticism. *I told you so, I told you so.* She felt the urgency of the absent envelope – though it would have to come on Saturday with the two weeks' money, because he couldn't forget *twice*. She felt the emptiness of the larder, the possibility that there might not be enough when her mother arrived, even for a meal. *Not good enough, not good enough.* She felt the cumulated pressure of the last six months, and the weight of all the years stretching out ahead. She wanted to run away, lock herself in her bedroom and hide in the blankets. *Her room.* And they wanted to take even *that* from her. She looked from one face to the other, and saw three vultures, eyeing up her liver.

None of them could really make out the words, but they had certainly never heard her shout so loud.

Evelyn heard the sound as she opened the door. It had been clear from Janet's letter that things had been getting on top of her, but she hadn't expected *hysteria*.

She waited, listening, till everything went quiet, then she made a big rattle with the door, as if she'd only just come in.

"Cooee dear!" she called, in a bright little voice. "Only me!"

***

After the ceremony of *"my how you've grown"* and all the formal kisses, the children were dismissed and allowed to play outside. It was quite a relief. The beginning of the holidays, so long awaited, had not gone as pleasantly as any of them had planned – what with having to tidy up because Gran was coming, and moving the bedrooms and their mother being funny, and nothing but toast for lunch.

Their gran spoke briefly to Colin, because he was the eldest.

"Now run along dear," she said. "Your mummy and I have things to discuss, and I think she's very tired. Now, why don't you go to the swings and play with your little friends?" And she presented them each with an apple and waved as they walked down the hill.

Mary suggested that the boys should go ahead and she'd meet them later. The truth was she didn't want to walk past the pub. The last week of term had been difficult and if Rita's relatives saw her, she might get a telling off.

It was the awkward matter of the invitation to tea. Rita's mother had baked a cake and got everything ready and at three o'clock the whole family was waiting. At the very least, there should have been a phone call from her mum with some suitable excuse. But instead there was nothing: just a terrible, insulting, absence. The offence, it appeared, was unforgivable.

*"She just didn't come."* Hiding in the toilet at break time, because everyone had been horrid, Mary faced the further trial of hearing all about it. "Little Miss Toffee Nose," a Pavis girl sneered. "And poor little Rita was only being nice because she felt *sorry* for her. But she's learnt her lesson now. Stuck up little madam." Then another girl did a horrid impression of Mary's accent, and the first one said something rude about their Dad.

Mary had sat back on the toilet seat and pressed her feet on the wall, so nobody would see her if they peered beneath the door. It was a great relief that the term was almost over, because the posture was uncomfortable and she saw no alternative.

So as they headed down the hill, Mary felt it would be better if they didn't go by the swings, which were just across the road from the pub, and not a safe place at all. In any case, she had other things to do. "You could go to the farm," she suggested to the boys.

"Yeah," said Michael at once.

"Well...", said Colin, torn between duty and pleasure. "Last week we..."

"Don't be stupid!"

"No..." Colin glanced across at Mary. "We could go to the horses – we could give them the apples."

Neither Colin nor Michael was fond of apples, and these were the sharp ones that grew in Gran's garden, all spotty and full of core. And they were old as well, rather wrinkly and smelling of newspaper. No one could be expected to eat them.

"I suppose," Michael said. "But couldn't she..."

Mary suddenly interrupted.

"If you give me your apples I'll go up to the horses. I'd like that. You don't need to come. You can go to the farm. I don't want to, anyway."

Colin and Michael grinned. The day had improved at last.

*\*\**

Mary wasn't sure, but she thought she could find the way. To the grave took twenty minutes and that bit was familiar. It was only the last bit that worried her, the bit where there wasn't a path. It hadn't seemed long, the first time, sitting up high on Mr Ralph's shoulders, though it was longer coming back, when he was cross with her.

As the term had creaked to an end, this mission had assumed an increasing importance. She had to have a friend for the holidays. At least one friend. And Ralph – if he *was* her friend – was her best friend ever.

Sitting alone in the toilets at break time, with her feet on the wall again and her bottom getting sore from the toilet seat, she had reflected on the events of that Saturday – each turn of their conversation, each kindly word and act. She thought of Ralph lifting her over the nettles, the gifts, the feast, the den. But these comforting remembrances always led to the part when something, somehow, had gone quite wrong. She had perhaps, been forward without realising. Perhaps he would never come back again.

In any case, even if he did, there was something of a problem. If he came at all, it would be on Saturday. But her Gran being there made everything uncertain. Gran liked to take them shopping in her car and buy them horrible clothes, and Saturday might easily be tied up like that. What if he arrived, all ready to be friends, and she wasn't there? What would he think? Would he ever come back after that?

She needed to leave him a sign. She had presents in her pockets.

The ground was wet from the previous day's rain, and her feet were soon heavy with clay. When she got to the grave, she rested a moment and scraped her shoes against the fence. The circle of stones was still perfectly clear, though his footprints all around it had turned into puddles. Her own had disappeared.

She stared at the shape of his boots in the mud and felt a curious wave of affection. His footsteps, there in the earth beside her – the visible, tangible, relic of his presence. She felt a magic in it. If she only shut her eyes, he might be there beside her, and pick her up again. For a second, a longing overwhelmed her, and she did shut her eyes, but when she opened them the world was just the same, except the magic had gone.

She turned to the plantation. The trees stood in ranks like soldiers, row upon row in sinister regularity. Between them were spaces where the brambles grew, but the route she needed cut across at an angle. Within moments the cow field was completely out of sight, and it would be several minutes before she emerged in the cornfield. Without Ralph it seemed a frightening place – a liminal, dangerous boundary between worlds.

At last, through the trees, she saw the watery sunshine of the cornfield. And there, just a little further, was the barn.

When she reached it, she was deeply perplexed. Mr Ralph had certainly made a path to the back, and stamped down the nettles. But where the path should have been, a huge branch had fallen, blocking the way. It seemed most unlucky. It was a great big thing, with its limbs reaching higher than her head, clothed with twigs and withering leaves – the barrier seemed insurmountable.

She thought of the presents in her pockets. It seemed so cruel a chance that the path should be blocked like this. It wasn't even clear where the wretched thing had come from. There was a row of beeches near the back of the barn, but none that should have dropped a branch just there.

She pulled at the biggest fork but it moved not at all. She tried to break one of the smaller sticks, but the wood was fresh and it bent without breaking. She peered behind it, and saw a clearer space, in heart of the branch, between its three great limbs. She pulled the sticks back and pushed herself in. From the outside the leaves made a solid wall, but it was hollow inside, like a little house. Carefully, because her legs were bare, she climbed over one limb and under the other, and then she stood, at last, on the path to the den.

It wasn't as she remembered it.

The path of trampled nettles was neatly carpeted with pine needles, soft beneath her feet. The air was sweet like Christmas. Bewitched, she ran to the back where they had sat on Ralph's coat in the skeleton of the den.

But it was skeletal no longer. The walls were solid and thatched with pine. There were crisp gaps for windows, and at the end an opening, curtained with ivy. She pulled it aside and peered in.

As her eyes adjusted, she saw the neat divisions, marked as he had said. In the body of the den, which he called the parlour, there was a space quite tall enough to stand and underfoot there were reeds, laid criss-cross on the floor. Opposite, under the eaves, with a little log to mark it, was the babies' bedroom, and there, in a nest of bracken were the little doll and the cat, just as she might have put them. She pushed through the trailing leaves and spun herself round with her arms outstretched. There was so much space! At the further end, in the darkest part where there wasn't a window, was the place he had called the bedroom. The bed was a mattress of bracken, and his blanket was there, the one he had laid for the feast, with tassels at the edge.

She jumped on it and lay, looking up at the vaulted roof. All around, was the heady sweetness of the bracken and the pine. But there was another smell in the blanket beneath her, deeper and more mysterious. She turned over and rubbed her face against the softness. There was a fragrance caught in the wool, a lingering sense of leather and motorbike, labour and desire. She lay on her tummy and breathed it in, and a slow quiet smile passed softly on her face.

After a few minutes she rolled herself onto the reeds. She would have liked to stay, but it must, she felt, be halfway to teatime and she had to get back. Her mission – which had seemed so bold when she first conceived it – seemed almost redundant now. If the whole situation had been other than delightful, she would have been disappointed.

He couldn't have been cross; she must have been mistaken. She didn't need to wheedle or cajole: he must have come back – the very next day perhaps — to build this palace for her. There could be no doubt that he was still her friend.

She pulled the presents from her pocket. First there was a handkerchief, with an M embroidered on the corner and a little spray of flowers in green and pink. She placed it carefully over the doll and the little cat, like a bedspread.

She pulled out the apples and laid them in a row by the log. No one could eat them but they would be fine for playing.

Then she got out the card. It was a little bit crumpled from being stuffed in her pocket, so she straightened it carefully. She had taken a lot of trouble with it. It had a picture of a cat, in a basket which was quite a lot like Snowy. Inside there had originally been a rhyme, about "my precious little dear" and "a very happy year," which was certainly not right, so she had cut that bit out, along with "Happy birthday darling, all my love, Gran." On the back, to cover the hole, she had pasted a piece of her mother's Basildon Bond, so the hole looked from the inside like a big blue cloud. In her best writing, she had written on the cloud "Ime sorry please still be my frend". In view of everything, this no longer seemed quite apt, so she sat on the reeds and carefully added, just above the cloud, "Thank you Mr Raf. Lots of love from Mary." Her writing was quite big and there wasn't space for more, but all along the bottom, underneath the cloud, she made a row of little kisses.

She hoped he would realise they were magic kisses — all of them magic.

\*\*\*

It was only when the children were asleep, and Janet crept in to fold up their clothes, that she noticed the fragrance of Mary's cardigan. She held it up to her face and wondered where she had been, to come back smelling of Christmas trees.

She glanced at Colin, who was snoring slightly, just like his father, and Michael, who had thrown off his blankets, exposing the shameful teddy-bear that no one was supposed to see. They weren't bad children. She thought of them, trotting down the road together, happy in the sunshine.

Her mother had said that they played out too much — they ought to be useful in the house and have little jobs to do, not running round unsupervised, like savages. So Janet insisted that they *did* help in the house and that they only played out every now and then, and that she was always around if they needed anything.

Then her mother had complained that the village was dreary. At least in Croydon there was a library and a proper park, and the Civic Centre, and Cubs and Brownies. Children, she said, needed stimulation, and the boys needed discipline. Without it, their brains didn't grow so she wasn't surprised that Colin was getting nowhere. A Secondary Modern indeed! He might even end up delinquent. It was a cruel way to talk, Janet felt. Her mother was beastly.

Janet felt the pressure to go back downstairs. Her mother had suggested they might have a little chat when the children were in bed, which was ominous enough in itself, and then added, absent-mindedly, "just a nice little chat over tea and biscuits", which made it even worse. The absence of biscuits might be glossed over of course, since at least there was milk – but in the morning, when the milkman came, he would want to be paid, so at breakfast even milk might become a problem.

Wearily, she gazed at the sweet, calm face of her daughter, and envied her tranquillity. Then she folded the knickers and the vest, and put the muddy socks in her apron pocket. It was nonsense what her mother said. They were good children, happy children, wanting for nothing.

Mothers are not always right, no matter what they think.

## 10. Family Values

The diminishment of their mother, which invariably accompanied their grandmother's visits, was something the children could never have named, yet they felt it intensely, all of them. It was a challenge to the flimsy rocks their life was built on, a turning over of unquiet truths.

The boys, being boys, felt it mainly in their arms and legs and voices, and after the initial repression of "being polite to Gran," it made them shout and run around and break into fights. Sensing their grandmother's contempt for their mother, they hated the old woman for the echoing contempt that she sowed in their own entrails – the wounding, unnameable suspicion that their mother was no good. This injury made them rude, but because their grandmother was alien and frightening, they turned their rudeness on their mother instead, for being inadequate and allowing this to happen. Their impudent giggling and running about and the language not usually permitted were an armour to them. It turned the situation around; it gave it a reason. From time to time it forced their mother to explode at them, which was a temporary reversion to the proper order of things, so they did it all the more, in search of reassurance.

But behind their mother, even as she shouted, they saw the figure of their gran, looking on, shaking her head, unnaturally calm. They did not understand, but they saw in her eyes the triumph of being right, a silent, self-satisfied assertion that everything proved her point.

Mary felt it differently. Little though she was, she was embarrassed by the boys, and angry because they made it all much worse. It seemed unforgivable, at this time more than any, that they should *let the family down*. They were pigs, both of them. But she still felt the shame of it: their mother looking smaller, pleading with them, dithering and flustering as her own mother looked on.

*\*\*\**

Mary held her mother's hand tightly on the way to the village. She was worried about Rita's relatives, though she didn't want to mention it. She felt the tenseness in her mother's fingers and saw how drawn her face was.

"I love you mummy," she said. "You're the best mummy, ever."

And her mother smiled at her, not the best sort of smile, but a smile at least. So Mary said it again, and then her mother, who was not on the whole a demonstrative person, bent down right there in the street and kissed the top of her head. When her mother spoke, there was something odd in her voice, a funny clipped sound, like someone on television.

"I'm so sorry darling." she said. "I'm just all in a lather with Gran here. It's really quite hard being grownup." Then she laughed – a brittle, embarrassed sort of laugh. "When you're grown up, you'll understand."

Such confidences made Mary uncomfortable, so she was glad when they reached the Post Office. Her mother had the little book with Mary's savings, and her card with some Savings Stamps stuck on, which her other Gran had sent her for her birthday – the least desirable of all possible presents. There was a little form, her mother said, a little form Mary had to sign. So Mary signed the form where her mother said, and afterwards her mother bought her a little ring from the stationery counter, a ring made of yellow metal like the little cat, with a little green stone, like its eye.

"Don't tell the boys," her mother said. "This is just for you, for being a good girl." Mary hadn't been expecting a present, and the ring seemed lucky. It was a sign.

Then they went to the shop and bought all sorts of shopping, and after that her mother seemed happy.

Her mother, Mary noticed, was particularly pretty when she was happy. Today, with her spotty green dress and her big wicker basket packed with treats, she looked like a mummy in a book, only lovelier. It was sad that being grown up was hard and made people cross. Perhaps that was all that was the matter with Mr Ralph, the kind of crossness that grownups got, that could be soothed by a word and a hug.

The lucky ring was on her middle finger, and she stroked it fondly. She was glad she was a child.

\*\*\*

Back at the house, Evelyn Parker had checked all the cupboards. All were creditably tidy, and everything seemed in order, though there was hardly anything in the larder. That was, however, the least of her problems.

Even when they had their *little talk,* Janet hadn't admitted to the problem about the money – but Evelyn had her suspicions. When Janet told her about the envelopes she had asked at once what Janet meant by "the housekeeping" and whether it was regular. The sum Janet mentioned was clearly not enough – not in the long term, anyway – and in Janet's voice there had been something, just *something*, that made her suspect that things were worse than she was admitting.

It was beyond any question that Janet had brought it on herself. The poor girl was mercifully blameless, of course – but she hadn't played her cards right, not at all.

Whatever Janet said, there *must* be another woman. It simply wasn't plausible that Richard would have walked out, just like that, with nowhere particular to go, for no other reason than he was tired of the rows. After all, whatever the difficulties, he had a regular job, and the home was nice, and there were all the usual comforts of bed and table. Evelyn had it in mind to ask her daughter, as tactfully as may be, about whether the former had been everything it should be, because poor Janet was just the sort of girl who might not realise that she had to play her cards there, too. There was probably some secretary – or worse, some fancy little madam from behind a bar. Evelyn Parker had seen it a dozen times; it was tawdry of course, but nothing irredeemable. Such a man could certainly be brought back.

It was the staggering lack of initiative that made Evelyn roll her eyes. It had taken her almost an hour to worm out of Janet the story of Richard's departure. It was perfectly clear that her daughter had done absolutely nothing about any of it.

She hadn't even phoned Richard's office, let alone dropped by – as Evelyn would have done – to sniff out the news from colleagues who would know him. And no, she hadn't contacted his parents or his sister, though when her mother mentioned it, she had to admit that they would probably have an address or at least some news, and that they could hardly have refused to pass it on.

Rick had a box of papers at the top of his wardrobe, which related, Janet felt, to matters like the mortgage, but she hadn't seen fit to go through the contents. They weren't, she felt, the kind of thing that would make much sense to her. There were also, she eventually admitted, a number of letters that had arrived since he left. They were addressed to *him*, so she had added them to the box and hadn't opened them.

With some hesitation, and under more pressure than she felt was quite nice, Janet pulled out the box and allowed her mother to go through it. There was nothing that led, as her mother had hoped, to her son-in-law's current address or his bank account, but there were rather a lot of unpaid bills and worst of all a threat to cut off the electricity. It was ten days old already. There wasn't even much time.

There was nothing about the mortgage, and after the first few weeks there had been nothing from his bank – which must have meant, Evelyn said, that he must have given them his new address. But Janet was vague about which bank he was with, and then started dusting the furniture.

It was just as if (as Evelyn would confide much later to her hairdresser) the girl wasn't *bothered*. Which would have been all very well, of course, if she had a private income. Or was a modern sort of woman with a job and some hope of independence. If that were the case, then divorce, however shameful, would have been the logical option. There was obviously some other woman, so adultery would probably have been easy to prove, and really, Richard Crouch was a mucky man, and never much of an asset.

But in the absence of any income, divorce was unthinkable. Alimony was never reliable and it wouldn't be long before the house became untenable. So *then* where would Janet go? Evelyn knew the answer, and the very thought put steel in her heart. It was clearly essential that Richard be taken in hand. He had married her, and she was *his responsibility*. Evelyn had no doubt that with a little intelligence and a dose of determination, the man and his income could still be retrieved.

She stood by the window and watched Janet toiling up the hill with Mary. Janet was slouching a bit, which was always a vice with her. And she looked such a mess. That dress! Quite apart from the polka dots and the ghastly green, it was terribly dated, and even in the country – where nobody had any taste – it was really quite *ageing* to wear a thing like that. Anyone could take her for forty in that dress. It was certainly not a look that a man would come home for.

There was nothing for it, they would have to go shopping.

Evelyn would regard it, she told herself, as an *investment*. She would fork out for some presentable cthes and a decent hairdo. She would also – rather against her inclination – settle the most urgent of the bills. She would draw the line at Colin's uniform, however. It wouldn't be needed till September and she'd get Richard back by then. Evelyn was never a woman who doubted her abilities.

Janet paused at the drive, not sensing herself watched, and patted her hair with an anxious gesture. Evelyn sat quickly back on the sofa, as if she hadn't moved from the spot. She shook her head as the key turned in the lock. That hair! Well might the girl look embarrassed, she thought. She could really do with a *perm*.

\*\*\*

Lunch was sliced ham – nice thick slices with lots of pickle and new potatoes and carrots – and pudding was a new sort of mousse made from a sachet of powder that her mother had brought in her suitcase. Colin and Michael said it was scrumptious, but Mary said pointedly that she liked mummy's puddings best. Her mother smiled at her gratefully.

"Now dear," Evelyn said, once everything was eaten. "What are the arrangements for *tomorrow*?"

"Tomorrow?"

"Shopping dear. For some clothes. Arrangements for the *children*."

Janet saw the boys' heads turn, and her heart sank. She had told her mother that she never let the children play outside except when she was home. It wasn't strictly true, but it had seemed the right thing to say. She regretted it now.

"Oh... well I haven't actually thought. I mean... I thought they'd be coming with us."

"Oh Mu-um!" Michael moaned. "I'm not going *shopping*."

"Yes you are. You know I can't leave you on your own."

"But we'll be out," Colin said, in a matter-of-fact tone. "We always go out on Saturday."

Janet shot him a warning glance. "Only when I'm *here* Colin. You can't go running round the village with nobody to turn to. Now, no arguing." Janet wanted it to sound rather final, but Michael wasn't sensitive to things like that.

"But it's the holidays. I'm not going. You can't make me. Not *shopping*."

"But it'll be fun," Janet said, that pleading note coming back to her voice. "We'll be going in Gran's car. Now that will be nice, won't it?"

"I expect I'll be sick," Michael said. "You remember how I got sick in Dad's van?" Then he made a pantomime of being sick, with a disgusting noise in the back of his throat. "And then I'll have to go round with sick down my front. It might even go on you. Or Gran."

Their grandmother, who had never experienced going shopping with boys, looked on with dismay. She had been picturing a pleasant little stroll around the dress shops, picking things out for Janet to try on. She would buy her an outfit as an early birthday present – something nice, that would make the right impression. Then they would go to Lyons and have a coffee and a cake, and at some point in the conversation she would broach the delicate matter of *foundation garment*s. Evelyn had checked her daughter's cupboards and had found, as she suspected, a lamentable neglect of proper underwear. With that midriff bulge she could do with a long-line brassiere, or even a well-fitted all-in-one. A little support might help her posture too. But these were hardly things that could be broached with *boys* in tow. Let alone with a boy who might have sick down his front.

"Now Janet, there must be some neighbour you could *leave* them with. Or some little friend they could go and play with...? I do think that would be best you know. Now, who can you think of? I could drive them round and have a word perhaps."

A momentary panic flashed across Janet's face. Since Rick had gone, she had quite neglected the neighbours, and there was nobody in the estate she could ask for a favour. And she could hardly ask any of the *village* women.

"No, I don't... not really..."

"Oh, for heaven's sake Janet! It wouldn't be much to ask."

Janet hung her head, ashamed, and her mother rolled her eyes. Then she turned to the boys.

Suddenly Colin got it. "Well, we could go to the *twins*." He smiled at his grandmother winningly. "They're our friends. Their mum said we could come round anytime... We could probably stay to lunch."

Michael, not understanding, looked a little worried. "Well, maybe... If mum talked to her... Gran could drive round..."

Colin glared at him. "No Gran doesn't need to do that. Honestly Gran. Their drive is very mucky. It's a farm you see. You know – cows... We'll just walk – it isn't far."

Janet looked gratefully at him. Colin wasn't a bad boy. Once in a while he showed a bit of maturity, a bit of family feeling.

"That's a very good idea," she said firmly, trying to sound in charge again. "So it'll just be Mary with us, and she's no trouble."

"Well, I think she could go with the boys, don't you?" her mother said. "I could drive them up and have a word... There'd surely be room for one extra *on a farm.*" And she laughed, as if she'd made a joke.

"No she couldn't!" Michael said at once. "The twins don't like girls."

Colin nudged him. "No Gran, I'm sure it will be all right. She can come with us."

"No she can't! She never comes..." Colin nudged him harder, because he wasn't supposed to say that, and then suddenly, from nowhere, came a moment of inspiration.

"She could always go to Rita Vardon's."

The words dripped into the waiting air, like oil into water, shifting their shape for just a moment before settling into globes of perfect plausibility.

For a moment, Janet looked perplexed, then her face went blank. Her eyes slid gently to a point to the left of Colin's eyebrows, and Colin pressed the matter home. "Rita was asking her to go round you know. She said it would be fine any day. We could drop her off on the way to the farm. I'm sure Mrs Vardon won't mind."

It was done now. Janet smiled. A grateful, puzzled, only slightly wary smile.

"Well, we've sorted *that* out then," their grandmother said, with satisfaction. "Do you think we could set off about half past ten?" She looked round the three of them, all standing there like idiotic dolls, with stupid expressions on their faces. The boys must have got it from their father, which was rather unfortunate, but there wasn't any excuse for Janet. It was well past time that she pulled herself together.

***

Oddly enough it was Colin who minded – though he was the one who had started it off.

That night he lay awake, staring at the ceiling. His mother must have *known* that he was fibbing. Especially the thing about going to lunch. And going along with the thing about Rita – when she'd said all those things just the week before, and hadn't let Mary go round to tea, even with a proper invitation.

It wasn't that Colin held truth in great regard. He was perfectly happy to fib to his mother, and he regularly did. But his mother's collusion made it feel uncomfortable. It made her smaller somehow and he felt unsafe.

He saw, of course, that it was all about his Gran. In the horrible gaze of his grandmother, his mother had somehow shrunk. She was almost *one of them.*

'Do you think it's all right?" he asked the air, not knowing if Mary or Michael were asleep. "About tomorrow?"

There was a pause, but he sensed from the breathing that Michael was awake and Mary wasn't.

"Yeh," Michael said at last. "It's fine. Gran won't see us."

"Mum knows, doesn't she?"

"I dunno. I suppose so."

After a little while, Michael's breathing came slower and he started to snore. But still Colin couldn't sleep. Something unpleasant was going round and round, a fish in a dark pond. He thought of his grandmother, bossing his mother and telling her off. He thought of his mother, knowing that Mary wasn't really invited to the Vardons. Where did his mother suppose she would go?

And where *did* she go?

Once he drifted off into a dream about Mary and his mother, but then they were chasing a little white cat and he jerked back into wakefulness.

"Are you asleep?" he whispered, but this time only silence came.

He felt cold and unsettled. He thought about creeping into the bottom bunk with Michael. It was usually Michael getting in with *him,* so he shouldn't complain. He thought of his mother's bed, which had never been allowed. But he didn't want Michael or his mother really. He wanted his dad.

*\*\*\**

A mile away, in the den, in a deeper darkness unbroken by the moon, Ralph was also sleepless. He too had been thinking of Mary, but his thoughts were happier. There was an excitement in them, an urgent, insistent beating of a drum.

The bracken was soft beneath him and the night was sultry. He lay on the blanket, gazing into the dark. Only a tiny starlight crept through the thatch. He had built the den well.

Arriving at twilight, he had found Mary's message and the little handkerchief. For a while he had been drunk with the unexpected pleasure of it. Afterwards, however, he had thought of the risks, and made a mental note to speak to her. Then as night fell, he set a little fire of twigs and carefully burned the card with its childish writing and the little handkerchief with the tell-tale M. They were threads that could snare him if anything happened. He had to be careful.

Not that anything would happen.

He did not doubt for a moment that Mary would come in the morning. It was Saturday. He wouldn't have to wait by the field, because she knew her way now and waiting in the open was dangerous. And she would come without calling, because she wanted to be with him.

There could be no harm in that.

# 11. The Days of Magic and Glory

In every childhood, however brief or unsatisfactory, there must be a moment of glory, an epoch when the pleasures of childhood are perfectly defined, to be sealed in the memory and delivered to the future as a keepsake. A Christmas, perhaps, when everything was perfect, a birthday, a holiday by the sea... For less fortunate children – such as those for whom Mary prayed in Sunday School – it might be no more than a day of sufficient food, or an afternoon's respite from brutality, recalled with nostalgia. Even for the fortunate, the perfection, whatever its form, might be greater in the memory than the momentary reality. The sea in the world may have been less blue than the sea recalled, the day less golden. But who is to say that the present is truer or more precious than remembered history? Who would deny the taut, remembered glory of the perfect tense?

If Mary were one day to reflect on these things – though perhaps she would not – then the next few weeks might have served such a purpose. Certainly, her childhood had been broadly satisfactory from the start, and she had known no signal disappointments let alone real suffering. She had always been well-fed and warm, and for the most part, despite the recent vexing absence of her father, she had felt secure in her family's affections. She was clever at school and the current crisis in her friendship with Rita did not cause her more anxiety than its substance deserved. She was, in short, a generally fortunate child.

But there were days that summer that held a gasping, ineffable magic, like dawn dew on a spider web.

\*\*\*

She took the scooter as far as the lane and left it in the bushes behind the war memorial. The day was hot and she had in her pocket the little bag of sandwiches, handed to each of them awkwardly in the moment of goodbye. *Just a snack, dears, in case you feel peckish* – their mother said awkwardly glancing at their grandmother. It seemed a bit odd to Mary, since they always got sandwiches on Saturday, for lunch.

The sandwiches felt sticky already, and she did not doubt that Mr Ralph would bring a feast, so she fed them to the horses, and skipped on down the lane. On the way, she met Snowy, on the fence at the end of someone's garden, which must have been a sign because she hadn't seen him since the day in Ralph's kitchen. She stretched up and crooned "puss-puss," and he bent down his head with an engaging look, quite as if he remembered and was grateful. Then he leapt down the other side of the fence and was gone.

From the grave, she peered across the field, to the point near the road where Ralph might be waving, but she wasn't too dismayed when he wasn't there. She skipped through the plantation, finding the way without trouble now, and found herself again in the cornfield, with the barn ahead of her.

The heavy branch was pulled aside. Where it had been, there were two little bunches of flowers, and the pine needle path looked freshly laid. Mary slowed her steps, and walked, with careful, reverent steps like they used in church. In the shadows behind the barn, left neatly near the door of the den, was Mr Ralph's rucksack.

Satisfaction flooded over her. She pulled back the ivy curtain from the door and looked into the dark. She saw his shirt first, light against the shadows, and then, as her eyes adjusted, his face, smiling back at her from the bed.

She ran to him and flung her arms round his neck and kissed his cheek with her special magic kisses.

His cheek was spiky, like her father's sometimes, but the smell was different. She kissed him again, despite the spikiness, and breathed the lingering scent of him. He held her, just a moment longer than she really wanted, then sat up and released her.

"You like it, then?" he said, with a grand gesture at the contours of the den.

She nodded. "Did you find my card?"

"Yes, I did. I really liked it." Then a pause. "Yes. Yes. I did." There was a sobriety to his voice then, and Mary felt for a second that there might be something wrong. She hesitated but then spoke.

"And... and the little sheet? Did you see how I put them to bed? Snowy and Mary...I wanted to say..."

"Yes." He held out his hand to her and then patted his lap. "Come here."

Obediently, she went back and sat on his lap. He put one arm around her and rubbed her tummy through her dress.

"I really liked the little card, Mary. I promise I'll keep it always. And the little sheet with your special M. I'm going to keep that in a special place at home to remind me of you when I'm not here." He paused, and she relaxed, relieved that everything was all right after all. She was about to get up again when she felt his hand grow tense on her skin. "But Mary, you mustn't put anything of yours here, not ever. Do you understand? Nothing at all. The little card and the hanky were lovely, but you mustn't do it again... OK?"

"I didn't... I'm sorry..." Mary remembered the week before when he had suddenly grown unhappy about the little gold cat. She didn't want that to happen again. "I'm sorry... I didn't mean..."

"No, it's all right. They were lovely. It's just... It's just really important that we keep it secret. Just our secret. Nobody must know... even if somebody finds the den, they mustn't know that it's yours and mine. It's got to be a secret. Our special secret. Do you promise? Promise you won't leave anything that's yours here anymore?"

Mary looked into his face. There was something tortured there, disfiguring him, and she thought of her mother. It was very hard, her mother said, being a grownup. It was obviously true. "All right," she said, and smiled kindly, wanting to reassure. "I won't bring anything. Nothing at all." She stood up and laughed, pulling out the pockets of her little cotton dress. "Look, nothing. I had some sandwiches but I fed them to the horses. Nothing left."

"Just you," he said. He was relaxing, Mary saw, but it still wasn't right. "And you won't tell anyone? You'll keep it secret?" That look again, and his voice insistent: that probing, anxious command.

"I promise," she said. *"Cross my heart, hope to die, stick a needle in my eye.* I won't tell anybody. I wasn't going to, anyway. I already promised."

He smiled. "Can you stay all day?" he asked and stood up as if ready to go out. Mary knew then that everything was all right.

"Yes," she said. "What will we play?"

\*\*\*

In the morning they picked armfuls of flowers from the edges of the field, and brought them back to the den to make it pretty. Rosebay willowherb and campion and woundwort. Speedwell and butterbur and Venus-looking-glass. Ralph hacked down a spike of great mullein which he fixed on the roof of the den, like a spire.

"It's a church, now," Mary said. "You can be the Vicar and I'll be... I'll be..."

"You can just be Mary," Ralph said. "The Virgin Mary."

So they played a game where Ralph was the Vicar and Mary was a statue of the Virgin. Ralph kept going out to visit his parishioners or find flowers for weddings and was always most perfectly astonished when he found that the statue had moved when he got back. Because of course it was a magic statue, and in the end he declared it a miracle. Then he said it was time to take the statue outside, and just as he put it down on the threshold, it ran away laughing into the sunshine.

"And suddenly the Painted Lady statue turned into a Painted Lady butterfly and flew into the sunshine. And try as he might, the Vicar couldn't catch it," Ralph declared – and sure enough, though he chased her all through the corn, he simply couldn't catch her.

Ralph knew the names for all the flowers and for the butterflies that danced among them. Tortoiseshell, Fritillary, Painted Lady. When he was younger, he said, there were others as well: Emperors, Graylings, Skippers, Hairstreaks... They had gone now, all gone; he didn't know where. He made her look, very carefully, at an ordinary Marbled White as it rested on a leaf. Then he named all its parts – proboscis, antennae, abdomen, thorax... Before it flew off, he made her look at the fine-haired limbs with their tiny joints and the magical pearly scales on its wings.

She wanted to catch it but he wouldn't let her. She must, he said, be very careful with it. It was very precious. Touching it at all might make it die.

So they waited till it flew and then they chased it, following it through the corn, stepping between the rows so they wouldn't leave a mark.

In the very middle of the field, where no one would see till harvest time, Ralph lay on the ground and flattened the corn with his legs. A secret circle of flattened stems, just enough to lie down.

"This is our magic circle," he said. "Come and tell me a story."

So Mary sat down beside him, leaning against his chest, and told him a made-up story about a girl who went through a cupboard, a bit like Lucy in *The Lion the Witch and the Wardrobe*, and found herself somewhere else.

Then Mary was tired as well and she lay in the sun and shut her eyes and he told a story back, about a prince and a little girl. *And the girl had beautiful skin* – he stroked her cheeks – *and beautiful hair as soft as Mary's but terribly terribly long* – the lightest of touches from the crown of her head, all down her back, down to her waist, to her bottom, to her feet – *and the little girl was trapped in a tower by a very bad witch, and only the prince could rescue her.*

Mary knew the story already, but she lay in the corn with the touch of the sun and the gentle caress of his fingers, and listened to the end as if it were new. She felt an excitement in the moment, something that she could not name. There was something in his voice, a tremble perhaps… a delicious urgency of wanting to please her. When he got to the bit about the tallness of the tower, he held the Key to Happiness high above Mary's head, and locked the invisible door so she could never escape. When the witch cut off the princess's hair, Mary felt Ralph's nails on the back of her neck, a long sharp stroke as if a knife ran on her skin. And when the prince fell in the briars Ralph took Mary's hands in his, and ran her fingers over his tight closed eyes, and she knew she must kiss them to make him see again.

As her lips touched his eyelids, his eyes opened abruptly. Blue eyes, speckled with a darker grey. And his tawny hair all curly like a halo round his face. It was somehow disconcerting. He stared at her, intensely, as if asking a question. Then he laughed and the moment was gone.

"And they lived happily ever after," he said quickly. He jumped up and stretched. "But first they ate an absolutely *enormous* dinner in their palace."

So they went back to the den and made a special feast for the Snowy cat and the Mary doll, and ate it themselves, sitting in the shadows under the window of the den.

"Do you like this?" Ralph said.

Mary wasn't quite sure if he meant the gala pie or the feast with the dolls, or the den where they sat. But she spoke for all the glory of the day when she answered.

"Yes," she said. "I like it all. You're my best friend ever."

And perhaps he was. Certainly, no other friend, adult or child, had ever played so attentively, had ever offered such invention, had ever shared so freely.

"You're my best friend too," Ralph said, and her happiness was complete.

***

At four they were sitting in the sun, perched high above the field, sitting on top of the broken back wall of the barn. Mary had been frightened to climb so high, but Ralph pulled her up in his arms and placed her carefully in a crook of the wall where the golden stone was secure.

"From here you can see forever," Ralph said, gesturing to the horizon.

"Yes," Mary said, gazing at the receding ranks of fields and hills. "Do you think that's a different country over there?"

"Oh definitely. It's probably.... Arabia." Ralph picked stones from the crumbling mortar and tossed them gently into the tumbled rocks below them. "This is a magic place, up here," he said. "You can see everything that's far away but nothing that's close. Look – Heckleford is over there but you can't see it at all."

Mary stared where he pointed. There were trees and a little fold of land, but it was true, you couldn't see anything of the village. "It's all behind the hill," she said sensibly. "The hill where we live."

"You live up on the hill, do you? In one of the new houses?"

"Yes." The thought of home tugged a tiny thread of unease in Mary's mind but then it snapped and troubled her no more. She looked around, trying to get her bearings. "Can you see your mum's house from here?"

"No. Not in summer, anyway. In the winter you can see the smoke from the chimney." Ralph twisted round and pointed, but then he saw how the trees in the plantation had grown since his childhood. "No, maybe not even in winter anymore. I told you, it's magic."

Mary traced the outline of the horizon, blue hills against blue sky. She thought of the most distant places she knew.

"Can you see Croydon?"

Ralph made a show of looking around, then pointed to an area in the distance where pale square shapes like cliffs were shimmering in the mist. "Yes, over there."

Mary peered. It was far, far away, but not the furthest thing they could see on the horizon. "What about Manchester?" It had never occurred to her that the places that mattered might really be so close.

Ralph shuffled round, wedged his knee against a stone, and carefully manoeuvred himself to a standing position, balancing precariously with a hand on Mary's head. Then he pointed to a patch of something darker, far on the horizon. "Ah yes. I think that must be Manchester," he said, solemnly. "Look... just a little to the left of... of Palestine."

"My daddy's in Manchester," Mary said.

There was a silence then, as Mary peered into the distance and thought of her father. Perhaps Ralph thought of his own father, too, both of them lost.

"Can you see where *you* live?" Mary asked at last. "Where you live when you go off?"

"Oh, definitely." Ralph pointed vaguely towards the west, past the place where the railway twisted round behind a hill, where the afternoon sun made the sky too bright to look. "Over that way. I'll show you another time, but it's not very nice."

"Why don't you just stay? You could stay at your mum's house. Or here even. It's the holidays now... I could come..."

"I've got to go to work," Ralph said. "And anyway..."

Mary watched his face. His lips were moving as if he was speaking, but no words came. She wondered if he might be praying. There was a catholic girl at school who moved her lips like that, every day before dinner, with her eyes closed. But there was something else in Ralph's face, like the look he had that first day, in the witch's house.

She wished she could think of something to say, to keep up the conversation. She thought of his mother's house and guessed that he didn't like staying there much. It certainly wasn't nice. She thought about his mum. Maybe he didn't like staying with his mum, either. "My friend Rita says your mum's a..." She stopped herself abruptly, realising how rude it was.

"A what?"

"Oh... nothing really." Mary felt herself blushing. "I saw the nurse going in there once," she said, trying to cover up. "With her bicycle. Is your mum very old?"

Ralph pulled a face. "Not very," he said. "She's just not very well."

"Did you live there before? When she was better?"

"A long time ago. When I was a kid."

"Do you *belong* in the village?"

Mary caught the flash of something strange in Ralph's face, and saw that the question disconcerted him. She knew she shouldn't have asked.

It was a vice in her. She asked too many questions.

Ralph poked at the mortar again and threw some more stones into the rubble below. "What do you mean?" he asked at last.

Mary screwed up her face. "Well, *we* don't belong in the village," she said. "Mum and me and the boys. Because we come from Croydon really. And Dad. We don't... you know... we don't really belong. Not like – you know – Sneddons and people. And Mum thinks that's why they don't like us."

She looked up at Ralph, hoping that he understood. Perhaps it was a change in the light but she noticed that his face seemed different now – less golden than before.

"No," he said firmly. "I don't belong in the village. Not at all. Actually, I *am* a Sneddon but they don't like me either. Any of them." There was a vehemence in his voice, and it was Mary's turn to feel disconcerted.

"I didn't mean... I mean... I'm sorry..." Mary was afraid she'd upset him again. She didn't want to spoil a lovely day.

"No, it's OK," Ralph said. "But it's time you were going home."

He lowered himself down from the wall then reached up towards Mary in her tight little perch.

"Come on," he said, smiling. "Jump. I'll catch you."

It seemed a long way down. Mary remembered another time, when he had not caught her. And anyway, she didn't want to go home, not yet. "Do I have to go now? What time do you think it is?"

Ralph pulled up his sleeve. "Five and twenty past four. I don't want to go either but..."

"I'd better come down," Mary said at once. It was later than she'd meant. The boys would probably be waiting. "Are you sure you'll catch?"

"Promise," Ralph said. "One two three..."

And she closed her eyes and jumped, feeling the momentary air all around her, then the firm grip of Ralph's hands under her arms. Instantly she closed her legs around his waist and put her arms round his neck. She didn't let go. It was the way her father used to carry her, long ago, when she was little. She put her cheek against his, feeling the stubble, breathing his breath, and let him carry her down over the stones to the edge of the corn, like a baby. She could have let go then, but she didn't move.

"When will you come again?" she asked, half whispering the words into his ear. She let her lips stay there, gently nuzzled against the delicate curls of his hair.

"When do you want me to come?" he said.

"Every day," Mary whispered. Then she lifted her head, knowing it was time to be sensible. "Except I can't come every day, either. My Gran's staying. But will you come next week?"

"What are you doing tomorrow?"

Mary leant back a bit to look in his face, and with the shifting of her weight he almost stumbled. She clung tight as he recovered himself. She wondered what he meant. "Why? Will you still be here tomorrow?"

"Would you come?"

"I've got Sunday school," she said, apologetically. "And there's Sunday lunch. It takes ages. I don't think..." She felt appalled at the thought that he might be here and she wouldn't be able to come. "And Gran makes us do jobs. We're not really allowed... not on Sunday."

"No. No of course not. Sunday school is important... *Suffer the little children to come unto me.*" Mary saw the strange look in his face as he said that and wondered what it meant. But then he shrugged. "Anyway, it's time to go. Come on!" He bounced her to get her more comfortable in his arms, and laced his fingers under her bottom to take her weight. Then he strode along the edge of the field, towards their secret route through the plantation. "But Mary... you won't forget what I said, will you? About not bringing anything?  If you come... Even if you don't come... you mustn't tell anyone about the den. Or about us. Not even your brothers."

Mary put her cheek on his neck again. "I promise I promise I promise I promise," she crooned into his ear. "I don't want anyone else to know, anyway. They'd only spoil it."

"Yes," Ralph said. "That's just what they'd do."

*\*\*\**

Their mother grew different that summer.

The Saturday after their gran came, their mother's body changed. It lost all its softness, it almost stopped feeling like a body at all. Colin noticed at once, that first time, when she got out of Gran's car. She was moving differently. She manoeuvred herself from the front seat without bending in the middle. And the bosoms.  He noticed the new pointed bosoms and whispered to Michael, who giggled uneasily. Both of them stared a bit at teatime, and perhaps they pulled a few faces. Whatever it was, Gran suddenly turned to Michael, and told him to mind his manners and concentrate on his tea – though he hadn't done anything and it obviously wasn't fair.

At bedtime, when Mum came to kiss them goodnight, there was no longer any question. They all felt the thrusting cones as she bent down over them. And as they hugged her, they felt the hardness round her middle, tight as a new football.

"It's like she's wearing armour," Colin whispered afterwards, once the footsteps had died at the bottom of the stairs. "Or as if she's made of plastic. Did you feel it? She feels like Gran does. Like a robot in a dress."

"Yes," Michael said, his lips turning down. The idea made him uncomfortable. She didn't feel quite like a *person* anymore. "What do you think she's done? Do you think Gran's…" He tailed off. It seemed possible that Gran had done something unspeakable to her. For a second he remembered how the Sneddon twins had pulled the head off one of their sister's dolls and stuck it on a pig's trotter. Then they'd chased him with it, and he'd fallen over and cried. The memory was shameful but beneath it was a terror. "Do you think Mum's…?"

"It's only one of those *Playtex* things like they've got on telly," Colin said knowingly. "In the adverts. It's like a really tight swimming costume. It squeezes you in to make you thinner. And so your bosoms stick out."

Michael giggled, relieved by the banality. "Do you think Gran made her wear it?"

"Yeah," Colin said. "I think Gran wears one, anyway. She always feels like that."

There was a long pause. It was stuffy in the bedroom, with the three of them crowded in and the heavy curtains drawn to make it dark.

"I really hate Gran," Michael said, and Colin grunted his assent.

Mary thought of saying something, to tell them off for being rude, because it wasn't nice to say they hated Gran, let alone to talk about ladies' underwear. But she didn't really care, and there were other thoughts dancing in her head and spinning her towards sleep.

\*\*\*

For a while, each day brought a new change in their mother – the acrid aroma of a perm in her hair, the addition of lipstick, a different dress, a different look in her face. The boys were generally hostile, detecting in each transformation the sinister input of their grandmother. Mary was ambivalent. There was, she dimly felt, a kind of disloyalty in it, but she sometimes looked at the ladies in *Woman's Realm,* and she could not help noticing that her mother now looked more like them. She had always regarded her mother as pretty, but now she was transformed. She had become, Mary felt, quite glamorous. Despite herself, Mary felt a certain approval.

It seemed to Mary that the transformation of her mother was just the kind of thing she could have talked to Rita about, if only they still were friends. Rita was always interested in clothes, and Rita's mother wore makeup every day. It seemed somehow a wasted chance, that Rita had turned away just now, when at last there was something that Mary could have told her.

But she did not let it trouble her unduly. It was the summer holidays, so she only saw Rita at Sunday School, and in any case, there were plenty of diversions. On rainy days the children played upstairs. The boys took sheets from the linen box and made a secret place between the bottom bunk and the top, where they told rude stories and drew silly pictures. They had to let her join them, because otherwise she might have told. Sometimes on sunny days they took their bikes and the scooter up the hill to the very top, and then raced down, feeling the tightness of the wind in their faces and the thrilling closeness of death. Each Tuesday that summer they went to the library in Canningbridge and had to pretend to their gran that they always went, because that was what Mummy had said, hoping to impress. Behind the library was a playground with a slide and beyond the playground a stream where they dropped bits of litter and watched them floating away down the eddies to the Cann. Colin and Michael played war-games there, and once, when they met some bigger boys, Michael somehow lost a shoe in the stream, and had cried because he was going to be in trouble. Mary got it out for him and after that he owed her one, because she could have told Mum. It was a wonderful summer.

But all of that, though it was magical enough, was no more than a backdrop, a pleasing intermission to the summer's real drama.

Mary counted the days from Saturday to Saturday. Even on the other days, the lesser days with their cheerful diversions, Ralph was always with her. The secret wove through her days like a magical, distant music. But it was Saturdays that mattered.

In earlier times it might have troubled Mary that the path to the den, trodden with such eagerness each Saturday morning, was paved with so many small dishonesties. Fibbing was part of the normal weave of life, but such systematic deception slightly scared her. She felt uneasy as her grandmother tied the bow on her summer dress and told her to be sure to say *thank-you-for-having-me* to Rita's mummy. She felt, as the boys clearly felt, that there was something misbegotten in their mother's collusion. There was something unspeakably *not right* in the blank little stare to the left of their eyes, and the furtive packs of sandwiches. She even felt awkward with Colin, as he looked back at her from his bike, when they parted at the war memorial. He obviously felt guilty, leaving her alone. It was the same look in her mother's eyes, in the teatime conversations when their grandmother asked if they'd had a nice time, and suggested, in a mercifully vague sort of way, that one of these days they must invite their friends back.

Mary wasn't a naughty girl and she knew when things weren't right.

But her friendship with Ralph, in all its magic and glory, had a truth all its own, that snaked through her mind and wiped the lies aside. She wasn't a naughty girl, not really.

## 12. The Poacher

Ralph peeled off one sock and then the other. Then he lay back on the grassy bank, stretched, and let his feet dip gently into the water. The stream had a sharp, clean chill to it. Ralph let it flow across his toes, and he focused on the moment. The cold was almost painful. Purifying.

In prison, Ralph had learnt to live in the moment. It was a trick of survival: a scrupulous avoidance of past and future. By focusing his mind, just there, in the momentary pain of his present heartbeat, by looking neither forward nor back, not joining one thought to another, not allowing any sequence of consciousness that would awaken memory or hope, he could get through the day without sensing – or at least without wholly sensing – the terrible chasm of time.

It was always there. Keeping it at bay was like holding his breath.

But it was easy now. He focused on his skin and felt the early sunshine: an almost imperceptible warmth after the morning's long ride. He felt the happy emptiness of a skipped breakfast and the dampness from the grass. He heard the stream and the breeze and the song of a blackbird. Above that, higher pitched, there was the rise and fall of the larks. Far in the distance he could hear a train. The sound grew, moment by moment to a roar, and opening his eyes, he saw the flash of its passing on the distant rails, and it was gone. An express train. For the blink of a second, Ralph thought of the speed of it, the racing movement from past to future, from London to the sea, and in that blink, losing the instant of presence, he found himself caught on its wave, veering back to the past. His father worked on the railway. His father knew the times of every train and the sounds that they made. He could tell a mile away if the train was running empty or full, how many carriages it had, whether it would stop at Heckleford or speed on without stopping. A mile away, an ordinary person would hardly notice the sound. An ordinary person might think there was nothing there, just the whisper of the wind round the bend of the line. An ordinary person might think there was time to cross. *They picked up the pieces, son, all the way from Canningbridge to Oatham Park.*

Ralph shook his head, as if shaking off a fly.

He sat up and looked at his pale feet in the water. The boots for the bike were second-hand and they rubbed one of his ankles. He pulled up his foot and peered at it. There was a tiny blister. He would show it to Mary. She would give it a magic kiss.

Mary.

Mary determined everything. She gave meaning to his days in the factory, the tedious evenings at Mrs Gregory's, the otherwise pointless traverse from one week to the next. He planned things for her. He thought of contingencies for rain or sun. When he walked round the town in the evening, he gazed in the toyshop window, wondering what she would like.

He didn't have the money of course; he couldn't do everything at once. But it was good to have an idea, to think of things. When it rained, he went to the library. There was a corner at the back, where the children's books were. He hadn't read much since school, but he read for Mary. He read the whole of *The Lion the Witch and the Wardrobe*, because Mary had said that her teacher had read it to them and she liked it a lot. It made him feel, though he couldn't say why, uncomfortable. But he also read books she wouldn't know, to have stories to tell her. Distant adventures of dragons and fairies; princes and princesses, ill-used heroines and rescued ponies and happily ever after. They were nice books. He had always liked girlish things.

The woman at the desk looked somewhat disapproving, but she didn't make a fuss. A lot of odd-balls used the library, and Ralph wasn't the worst. He didn't slip books under his coat or bring sandwiches. He didn't fall asleep or fiddle with himself and he didn't make a noise. And he was nicely spoken. There wasn't any harm in it.

On other days he gave thought to the feast. Mary liked her food, and when they were together he watched her carefully to see what she chose first. Gala pie was a favourite and little fairy cakes with silver balls or coloured sprinkles. To save a little money he dispensed with the Mars bar that had previously been the focus of his tea-breaks. Mary liked Fruit Salad chews, and Sherbet Fountains and Flying Saucers.

There hadn't been anything like that in the old days, with Sonia, because of rationing and the war. But anyway, Sonia wasn't interested in sweets.

She wanted bracelets and rings and necklaces – not plastic things that were meant for babies, but proper ones, of metal with little stones. Most of all she wanted gold. When he gave her a ring once, a cheap one that he'd bought from a jumble sale, she had fiddled about with the metal till it bent and showed the grey pig-metal under the paint. She had been contemptuous and thrown it in the stream. And he was only a kid himself then. He only had pocket money – two bob a month if his father felt generous. He thought of the little gold cat, what he'd had to do to steal it for her, and how carelessly she'd lost it. Even now, an adult with a job, he couldn't buy things like that. And still she had wanted more.

But Mary never asked for anything at all.

He saw her as she emerged from the plantation. The corn was high now, and from where he sat, by the stream, he could only see the top of her head. When he stood, she spotted him and started to wave. She skipped round the field, past the barn, to join him by the stream.

"Hello Missy", he said. "It's going to be hot today. Really hot."

"Yes. It's nice."

"It's cool in the den. We can go in if it gets too hot."

She smiled, still catching her breath. "Yes." Then she looked down at his feet. "You've been paddling."

Mary sat down on the grass and started taking off her shoes. Little red sandals, rather scuffed, with crepe soles and a flower cut out from the front. Ralph picked one of them up and put it in his pocket.

"I like this shoe. I'm going to keep it."

Mary laughed. "I'll have to hop all the way home."

"Bet you couldn't."

"Bet I could. I'm good at hopping."

"OK then. So I can have the shoe?"

"No."

"What are you going to give me then? Can I have your socks?"

Mary had taken off her socks now, and rolled them into a ball in the other sandal. She laughed again. "No, you can't. Mum'll tell me off. Anyway, there's a hole in one of them."

"I like holes. I'll have the one with the hole."

"Why do you want my socks anyway? They won't fit you." Mary giggled at the idea of it.

"I want to keep a bit of you."

Mary was standing by the stream now, with one foot stretched towards the water. Ralph took her hand so she wouldn't over-balance. Gingerly, she put in a foot then quickly withdrew it. "Ooh! Freezing!"

"Yes. It'll be nicer later. When it's really hot."

"But you went paddling already."

"Not really. My feet were sore. I was washing them. He sat down abruptly and picked up his foot to show her. "Look, I've got a blister."

Mary knelt down beside him and looked carefully.

"You need a plaster," she announced solemnly. "You should put a plaster on for when it pops. Stuff'll come out of it. Watery stuff. If you haven't got a plaster it'll get infected."

Ralph remembered the conversation about Snowy and her demand for disinfectant. "I forgot you were a nurse," he said. "But it's only a little blister. I thought you could give it a magic kiss."

"OK," she said, and kissed it.

Her lips on his ankle were soft as a butterfly, a tiny tickle and then gone.

"Better already," he said.

***

Till lunch time they played along the bank of the stream, following it along the edge of the meadow and into the next. There was an open footpath the other side, but Ralph said they had to stay on their own side, making their own path. *Just ours,* he said. *Private.* At the corner of the field there was a patch of brambles, with blackberries not yet ripe. Beyond it was a little copse of birch-trees, and a barbed wire fence that blocked their way. Ralph got several scratches, but he held Mary over his head, and planted her safely on the other side so she didn't get hurt. Mary looked dubious. It was a bit dark under the trees, and the bracken at the edges grew very tall.

"It's cooler in here," Ralph said. "I used to come here, a long time ago. Look. I'll carry you." And he lifted her onto his shoulders, to push through the bracken.

At the centre of the copse there was a gap where the branches parted and bracken gave way to a circle of delicate grass, translucent where the dappled sunshine caught it. Ralph put her down in the middle of it.

Mary looked round, smiling.

"It's pretty here," she said at last.

"I thought you'd like it." Ralph watched her reaction, somehow wanting something more, as if she should have known, as if she should have felt it – the aching, yearning imperfection of the past. But she was distracted already. There was a squirrel in a tree, and she was watching its dizzy race through the branches. She wasn't to know. Of course, she wasn't to know. It was better like that.

"There are loads of squirrels here," he said, forcing himself to speak. "And pheasants too. Lots of them."

"That's nice," said Mary, distracted, still watching the squirrel. "What are pheasants?"

Ralph laughed. "Birds. Big birds. Coloured birds. You must have seen them."

Mary shook her head.

"Do you want to see them?"

"I don't know," Mary said, looking round. "Why?"

"They're pretty."

"OK."

"Look." Ralph picked up a stick from the ground and ran to a patch of brambles, banging the stick on the arching growth. There was nothing. From the corner of his eye, he saw Mary watching, but he knew he wouldn't disappoint her. He ran to another great mound and then another. Then at last, abruptly, there came from inside the unmistakeable sound, and a large cock pheasant emerged, followed by two hens. For a second the three birds stood there, heads nodding this way and that, then all three of them batted their wings and flew up through the branches into the air beyond. Glory.

Mary clapped.

"Magic, see?" Ralph looked at her, seeing her wide eyes, feeling his power at last.

"Yes," Mary conceded. "They're really big. And one of them was pretty. Can you do it again?"

"Yes, watch." Ralph ran around again, beating the brambles, waiting again for that moment of delivery. But nothing happened. He kicked at the undergrowth. There had to be more. There were always more. He ran from one mound to another, beating and beating. Frustrated, he ran right into the brambles determined to find them. The thorns clawed at his arms and scratched his hands. He hit at the branches with his stick, then it fell from his hands into the deep of the thicket, and he was impotent. There was nothing there.

As he pulled himself free from the brambles, he thought of the butterflies. Long ago there had been butterflies everywhere, and they were gone, almost all of them. Perhaps it was the same with the pheasants. He was older now.

Mary was watching him, her head on one side, a hand on her hip, like a grownup woman. She was shaking her head, as if she found his behaviour absurd. He felt, for a moment, humiliated.

"Mr Ralph, I really don't think there's any more," she said, stating the obvious in a tone that seemed somehow smug.

He turned away and walked back towards the stream. There was something in her voice that echoed from the past, and he didn't want it now. He stared at the stream, forcing himself back to the moment. If he stayed in the moment, he felt nothing, nothing. He looked at the water and the steep banks either side, dropping down, several feet to the water. His arms were sore from the brambles and he thought of jumping down to dip them in the stream. But that might, he thought, have looked foolish. Perhaps he'd get stuck climbing up again. They were only scratches; they didn't need a fuss. He sat down on a fallen log and stared at the dappled water, pretending not to care.

Mary sat down beside him. Perhaps she sensed his disappointment, because her voice was different now, cajoling. "They were nice birds Mr Ralph. I really liked them. You were clever to know they were there. How did you know?"

Ralph made himself speak, but his voice was flatter now. "They live here. That's why the farmers leave bits like this." He gestured round at the copse, with its mounds of brambles. He saw her face, looking up at him, anxious. There was comfort in that; there was a little power. So he went on. "They keep it specially for them. Otherwise they'd just cut the trees down and plough it up. This whole place. It's to give the pheasants somewhere to live."

Mary looked sceptical. "But I thought farmers didn't *like* birds. I thought that's why they had scarecrows."

"They like pheasants," Ralph said, and he laughed. "They really like pheasants."

"Why?" Mary asked. "Is it because they're pretty?"

"No," he said. He hesitated, but then spoke firmly. "They shoot them.

They like shooting them." He pointed a finger at Mary and mimed the shooting of a gun. He saw the look on her face and felt a frisson of something bitter in his spine. But perhaps Mary did not feel it.

"So why do they give them special places? Places to live... if they're going to shoot them?"

In the green light of the trees her face was pale, prim. The old trees were vast above her. She was very small.

He looked intently into her face, probing her eyes. He suddenly wanted her to know. He wanted her to be frightened, to feel the power and danger of it, to understand. The words came fiercely, deliberately. "They like them because they hunt them, Mary. They leave this place all nice for them because then they come here. Sometimes they even look after them a bit. They feed them up. But it's all because they want to hunt them in the end. They want to make them feel safe so that in the end they can chase them out, and shoot them down, and kill them and eat them."

There was a long silence. Mary stared at him and their eyes locked. It seemed as if they would sit there forever, fighting out the future with their eyes.

But then Mary stood up. "Let's have lunch," she said. "I'm hungry."

***

For lunch he had brought a different sort of gala pie and some cupcakes and red apples and a packet of jelly babies. There was a bottle of drink but he had left it at the den, so they scrambled down the bank and scooped the clear cold water from the stream and drank it from their hands.

Purifying. The moment had gone.

Afterwards they sat on the log again and threw pebbles into the stream. The sun was past its highest now, and the stream made a corridor in the trees, plunged in light. Mary was leaning against his arm and telling him a long story about her mother getting new clothes and looking prettier than before, which seemed – though the connections seemed unclear – to be something to do with her grandmother's visit, and an argument with someone at Sunday school. Her words were like birdsong in the heavy air.

She had a strange way of moving her hands as she spoke, like a deaf mute or a foreigner. In prison, there had been men who did that: foreign men. He wondered where she'd got it from. Crouch was an English name; there was nothing foreign in her. Ralph looked down at the flickering hands: little, dirty hands with plump fingers, dirty fingernails, and dimples on the knuckles and wrists.

Something had changed since he met her, all those weeks back. He traced the shape of her, from head to feet, proprietorially. There was something different, but he wasn't sure what it was. She was a little plumper, perhaps. Her arms and legs were growing brown from the summer, and there were new freckles on her nose.

He looked at the freckles and thought uneasily of Sonia. Sonia had a mark on her nose, a little spider of veins that stretched towards her cheek. But Sonia had been beautiful. Mary was not even pretty, not really. Her face was too square, her owl eyes muddy coloured, her hair unattractive. At the beginning he had thought about that, but now, he told himself, he no longer felt it. It didn't matter that she wasn't beautiful. Why should it matter that she was not beautiful? She was not his.

Why should it matter that she was not beautiful?

She was his.

She was not his.

Ralph felt himself falling into a black place he had determined not to go.

He shuffled a little so she could not lean on him. She looked up at him, reproachfully, and he pretended to be shifting about to look for something in his pocket. He pulled out a threepenny bit and the key to his bike. The Key to Happiness. He put it back quickly because he did not want to think of that. It was true, he had been happy that summer, waiting each day for his Saturday pilgrimage. He was happy.

But there were things he should not think of. He made himself focus on the threepenny bit, turning it over and over. Mary asked if he was going to throw it in the stream and make a wish, and then she giggled. He put it quickly back in his pocket with the key. He needed his few coins for petrol. He couldn't afford the fancy of wishes.

It was the heat. Even under the trees it was much too hot. Mary adjusted her balance, and chattered on, lost in her own story.

He only had to say "yes" or "really?" or "dearie me". She did not ask for much. But there was something oppressive about it. He wanted to move on. It was much too hot.

From time to time, he bent and picked up pebbles near her feet. He noticed the little red sandals again, and her bare ankles. Her dress was blue and white: rows of little blue cats on a white ground, stepping in ordered ranks across the gathered skirt. It was tied with a bow, and there were buttons, little white buttons all down the back. The spaces between buttons gaped a bit, because the dress was a bit too small. Mary sat with her legs together and she had a funny way of smoothing out her dress as if trying to hide her knees. But it was too short for that.

"We could go paddling now," he said abruptly, interrupting her prattle. "It's hot enough now."

"Here?" she asked.

"No," he said. "Somewhere sunnier. I know a place."

She followed him, obediently, along the side of the stream, out of the copse, over a wooden fence and into the stark sunshine of the field. For a moment they both stood there, blinking in the glare of the sky and the yellow corn.

"It's hot enough here," Mary said.

"Too close to the path," Ralph said. "I know a better place. Secret."

Over a stile, the stream twisted down into a little valley, with scrubby trees. Then the place became steeper, so the stream was tumbling over boulders. Mary had never been this far. They were walking downhill, and it felt like a long way from home.

"I'm tired," she said. "We could paddle here."

"Almost there," he said. "Next bend. Just past that big oak. You'll see."

As they turned the next corner, Mary saw what he meant. Ahead, the water cascaded down a bank of boulders, and at the bottom the stream was suddenly wide: a shallow pool in a hollow of green. Broad flat stones lay under limpid water. Tall plants grew all around, but on the sandy ground near the water, the grass was short and soft.

Ralph surveyed the hollow of land. It was smaller than he remembered, and even more enclosed. Perhaps the young alders on the further bank had not been there before. The oak had not changed though. He looked up through the branches to the blue beyond, then back to Mary.

The sun on the shallow water twinkled in her eyes, and she smiled at him in wordless acknowledgement. It was the perfect place to paddle.

They raced to pull off their shoes. Ralph took his shirt off and rolled his trousers above his knees. Mary tucked her dress into her knickers, like she did at the seaside, then stepped into the water. Underneath, the ground was soft, like sand, with a few flat stones, carpeted with algae.

"Look Ralph!" She kicked the water into the air making a spray of silver and diamond. Little drops of water rained over Ralph, leaving polka dots on the pale twill of his trousers. She laughed and did it again and he pretended to chastise her, which made her laugh more. Again and again she splashed him, and he chased her round as she tottered through the water. Laughing and laughing – both of them laughing and laughing.

The water was crisp and cool on their skin and the stones below were slippery. The afternoon sun was blinding in their eyes. Of course, he knew what would happen.

He could easily have caught her when she fell. Paddling towards him, she tripped on something and lost her balance. He was only an arm's reach away but he did not catch her. He watched as she fell, and her laughter shattered to a frightened cry.

The water was never completely over her. It was shallow; there was never any risk. For a couple of seconds he watched her thrash, spluttering and kicking, then he bent and lifted her in his arms, raising her onto his shoulder.

He carried her dripping from the water and crooned the words of pity and comfort. He took her up the bank to the place where he had left his rucksack, and sat down, still holding her. She was drenched all over, and soon he was too, clothes and hair and skin. Even in the sunshine, she shivered in his arms. She started to cry. Her little dress clung to her: bedraggled blue cats on a white that was now transparent, taut across the pink of her skin and the deeper white of her vest and knickers.

"I'm all wet!" she cried, as if it weren't obvious. "And I'm cold. Dry me Mr Ralph, I'm all wet." Then she sobbed some more, and he held her tight. Without letting her go, he slipped a hand into his rucksack and, like a magician, pulled out one of Mrs Gregory's bath towels.

He put the towel loosely over her, like a tent. Then moving his hands beneath it, feeling his way, he peeled her wet clothes from her body. Dress. Knickers. Vest. Tenderly. Lovingly. It was only for a moment that he saw her naked: naked all over like a little doll. Her legs and arms were brown but her chest was white, with little blue veins stretching down across her belly, down to the place where her legs crossed. He glanced, only for a moment: that little, naked, slotted place. Then he wrapped the towel tighter around her and pulled it up a little to rub her wet hair. Through the towel, tracing the contours of her body with his hands, he patted her dry all over – legs and body and arms, and between her legs and under her arms, and her face and her neck.

Comforted by his touch, warmed by the big towel, she softened and her sobbing subsided. He pulled the towel neatly round her body, swaddling her arms and legs, and held the little bundle close to his naked chest.

"Poor little Mary," he crooned. "Poor little wet Mary." And he rocked her in his arms, rocking and rocking. And carefully, without putting her down, he wriggled out of his own drenched trousers, and held her, swaddled, in his lap.

They were high on the bank overlooking the water, in a place where the short grass yielded to taller plants: willowherb and ragwort and cow parsley. Carefully, Ralph lay back into the greenness, letting the flowery stems rise back above them, arching over, hiding them from view. No one else knew this place, anyway. Only the hot, high sun could see them now, just a little through the leaves.

The child was quiet now, warming, recovering. Still he held and rocked her. She was a bundle of white towel, her bare legs poking out on his, her wet hair on his chest. And as he rocked her, she became a little limp and her eyelids flickered and then closed against the glare of the sun. Gradually, as the minutes passed, he rocked her faster and more rhythmically. And he stroked her through the towel, her legs, her back, her legs, between her legs... rocking and rocking, faster and faster, and his breaths came hot and urgent and sighing, and then he was still.

***

When Mary woke, she was wrapped in a towel and he was sitting a little away from her, watching. He looked anxious, and as she sat up, pulling the towel tighter round her nakedness, he handed her his shirt.

"Put this on," he said. "I'm drying your clothes, but you can wear this for now." And he looked away while she slipped the shirt over her shoulders. It was hugely big, like a nightgown, but she was used to that from the dressing up box, so she knew what to do.

Her clothes were draped in the sun. They were drying, but crumpled and misshapen from the water and in need of ironing. She wanted to play some more but he told her to stay where she was, hidden in the plants.

"You're not dressed," he said. "You can't run round like that."

There was something stern in his voice, as if she had done something wrong. She knew that she *could* have run round like that: the shirt went well below her knees – she was perfectly decent. But he looked a little cross.

"I'm sorry," she said. "It was an accident."

"Yes," he replied. "It was just an accident. I know." But still he sounded stern. After a few minutes he pulled out a comb from his rucksack – a hard, brown one, like her father used. "Your hair's a mess," he said. "You'd better comb it." Mary wasn't used to combing her own hair. Sometimes she played with the ornate ivory comb in her mother's bedroom, but that was only playing. Whenever her hair was tangled, it was her mother who combed it.

Ralph watched her and after a few moments he took the comb from her.

"I'll do it" he said. He held her head and pulled the comb firmly through the tangles. Several times she told him to stop, because it was hurting, but still he tugged. She knew, by the roughness, that she had done something wrong, so when he was finished she sat silently, not daring to speak.

He got up and paced around the top of the hollow, scanning the fields. Every few minutes he felt her clothes, to see if they were dry enough. After half an hour they were damp still, but he brought them to her anyway and told her to put them on. Then he turned abruptly away. When he saw her dressed, his face cleared a little.

"We'd best go back," he said. "It's getting on."

Somehow it seemed a long way back. It was all uphill and the heat of the afternoon lay like a blanket in the still air. On a different day, she would have held his hand, or even asked him to carry her, but now she didn't. She felt somehow ashamed. She had spoilt the day by falling in the water. She should have been more careful. And she would be in trouble at home now, too. It was perfectly obvious that her dress had been wet. There was nothing she could do to hide it.

"I'm really sorry, Mr Ralph," she said. "I didn't mean to fall in. I was just playing."

"Yes," he said. "We were just playing." But it was funny the way he said it.

\*\*\*

Did you fall in the pond?" Michael demanded. "Did you go to the newt pond and fall in?"

Mary didn't say anything. Her dress was almost dry, but it was crumpled and her hair was all bedraggled.

"Mary, you mustn't go to the pond by yourself," Colin said earnestly. "You know you mustn't. It's dangerous. You could have drowned."

"Mum'll go barmy," said Michael, with perceptible satisfaction. "And Gran's bound to see. You're in for it now, Mary Crouch."

"Shut up, dimwit," Colin said. "We're supposed to have taken her to Rita's. We'll all be for it."

So Michael whacked her as usual for getting them into trouble, and she cried, but still she didn't speak. The whack was somehow comforting and ordinary. She was thinking of other things.

## 13. In Deeper Waters

"He's got himself in deep water," announced Evelyn. "I don't doubt he's regretting it. If you play your cards right, he'll come back with his tail between his legs. You mustn't mind. It's just been a little *episode*. It happens to men sometimes – like the *seven-year itch*. They go out of their senses for a while."

Janet looked sceptical. She didn't think Rick was the kind of man who would have an *episode*, though her mother assured her it was scientific and there were articles about it in magazines. It sounded, Janet felt, a bit like a mental breakdown and he certainly wasn't *that* sort of man.

But her mother insisted.

"Lots of men get it at that age, dear. It's because they don't talk about their feelings like women do."

Janet, who never talked about her feelings, found the whole thing improbable. It seemed much more likely that Rick was a bit of a cad.

\*\*\*

The arrival of Rick's envelope – just the next morning after several weeks with nothing – was a matter of much triumph to Evelyn. It didn't contain everything for the weeks he'd missed, but it did contain more than a normal week, which indicated contrition.

In the short term, if she counted what it cost her, she would have to conclude that she had paid a lot more than her son-in-law for this triumph. And she had certainly worked harder for it than Janet had done, though it was all for Janet's benefit. The girl had no idea.

It had taken her several days – with Janet trailing after like a wounded puppy – to track down the mortgage on the house and the precise location of her son-in-law's bank account. Once they got to the bank, the tellers were unhelpful, but Evelyn stood her ground rather forcefully – with *bravura* as she put it later – and the Manager was called and was trying to claim that he couldn't tell her anything, because the customer's business was confidential, even if he *did* have a wife and children.

Janet by this point was trying to leave: she never did, Evelyn felt, have much staying power. So it was just at this moment (a moment so ghastly that Janet couldn't refer to it afterwards, even to reproach her mother, whom she would never forgive for it) that Evelyn declared, right in front of the tellers and the customers, that 'customer confidentiality' didn't really apply, because as far as she knew Richard Crouch (and here she adopted a stage whisper that might have been audible in the street) *was in prison* – so he was hardly a customer in any case, and unless the bank was just *laundering the money*, his account should probably be closed. The Manager was so startled by this that he dispatched a teller to bring him the statements, and ushered them into his office. In what followed he let slip quite a bit of information, and when Evelyn suggested that it was all a deception and she was thinking of contacting head office, he had actually shown her the bank statements.

"It's simply a matter of playing your cards right," she explained to Janet in the kitchen. Janet (who had never played her own cards right so should have been full of admiration) was being very dense and not in the least appreciative. "You just have to get the upper hand, dear. And it always helps to be dressed the part. I'm so glad you were wearing your corset."

Janet was doing the potatoes. She stabbed at their eyes with the peeler and gritted her teeth. She couldn't have been more embarrassed wearing nothing *but* the corset. Her mortification had been absolute. She would never be able to go to Canningbridge again, not ever, not for anything.

The following day her mother had dragged her to the office at the edge of town, where Rick had worked. At the entrance there was a pleasant reception room, with a girl in a cheap twinset, sitting at a desk, with a phone and a typewriter. The girl looked flustered when Evelyn asked about Richard.

"I don't know," she said, blushing. "Mr Crouch left before I joined. I'll have to get the manager...." And then she got up and went round a screen, and behind it there was whispering. Then a door opened somewhere, and there were other voices, and after a few moments the girl came back.

"The manager's in a meeting," she said, apologetically. "If you'd like to make an appointment..."

"We'll wait," said Evelyn firmly. "If you could be so kind as to tell the manager."

There was a corner with little chairs and a bookcase with copies of Civil Engineering Monthly. On the walls there were nicely framed diagrams of bridges and roundabouts, all delicately labelled. Evelyn looked round, approvingly. It was an engineering firm, which could never be *professional*, but there was really no evidence of *muck*. She had quite expected to find greasy rags and unsuitable calendars, like in the garage where her car was serviced. She'd even advised Janet that they shouldn't sit down when they got there, not in their good clothes. But this was apparently some *superior* sort of engineering. Richard really had been silly to leave it.

"So you're new," Evelyn said pleasantly when the girl came back.

"Not new – not really... six months I've been here. Almost."

"But that nice girl you took over from.... I can't recall – what was her name?" Evelyn frowned and put one finger on her mouth, in a pantomime of thinking. "Was it Lindsay?" Lindsay was the receptionist at her hairdresser, but she said it with conviction.

"Oh no," said the girl. "It was Valerie."

"Oh yes, that was it," said Evelyn, and busied herself with her compact. Then she looked up, casually and asked, as if the answer were just on the tip of her tongue. "Valerie what was it? Valerie..."

"Smithson. Valerie Smithson."

"Oh yes of course," Evelyn said. "I believe she left just when my son-in-law did. But anyway, you seem to have picked it all up very well. And you're so young as well – is this your first job?"

"Well, sort of... I was at Woolworths for a while. But I did typing at school. I was only waiting for an office job."

"Well you're doing very well, I must say. I bet they're very pleased with you – someone so young taking over from a woman of thirty-something...."

The girl looked puzzled. "No... no she wasn't... She was more my age..."

Evelyn put her hand to her mouth. "Oh dear! So I've got that wrong too. I'm a silly old thing. Of course, you *all* look young to me, but I thought someone told me that Valerie was thirty-one. We do mean the same girl, don't we?"

"Well... I suppose so... Otherwise there's only Mrs Murphy, but she's old. I mean, she's mature. I don't mean..." The girl giggled nervously, but Evelyn hushed her.

"No really, I understand. I do apologise. Don't take any notice of me, I get quite muddled."

As the girl went back to her typing, Evelyn smiled at her own cleverness. She glanced at Janet, who should, of course, have been looking on, impressed, but she was slumped in a chair and staring at her shoes. She hadn't taken any of it in.

Even on the way back, in the car, Janet hadn't seemed to grasp it. She seemed more concerned about whether the remains of the joint would be enough for a shepherd's pie, and about the washing on the line, because it had rained while they were out, and it would all have got wet.

"It makes it rather hard, you see," she said, with a pleading note in her voice. "All this gadding about. I mean, I don't have time to get my work done."

*Gadding about.* Evelyn raised her eyes to heaven. There she was, salvaging the poor girl's marriage and she called it *gadding about*. But at least the end was in sight. The discoveries of that day had brought them nicely to the point where they could phone Richard's mother.

*\*\*\**

"Can't help you, I'm afraid. Haven't seen him." The voice was rather stiff. Old Mrs Crouch did not seem at all pleased to be phoned by Richard's mother-in-law.

At the other end of the line, Evelyn raised one eyebrow. "Oh, I *am* surprised," she said sweetly. "You see he drew some money out last week – and it was from the branch in Basingstoke just round the corner from you. It never occurred to me that he'd come all the way from Manchester and not call on *you*. I'm so sorry. He must have been visiting someone else."

There was a pause then, a very gratifying pause, and in the end Mrs Crouch remembered that he *had* made a visit, but she really couldn't talk about it.

Evelyn made a tutting noise. "Oh dear," she said. "It's so embarrassing, isn't it. His *mid-life crisis* I mean… Did he bring little Valerie? Miss Smithson, I should say – that little girl from his firm. Just a teenager I believe… just out of school. It must be hard for you. He's made himself look rather silly."

The silence then was more gratifying than the last. Recovering, Mrs

Crouch insisted that she couldn't get involved, then she moved to criticising Janet: if things had been right at home, then it never would have happened. "And anyway... he's not a child you know. Honestly, I don't know why you're phoning *me* about it. I can't get involved. It's really nothing to do with *me* if they split up."

"But the *mortgage* of course," Evelyn retorted, her tone a honeyed arsenic. "He's been falling rather behind you see – I thought the building society might have contacted you. It was kind of you to stand as guarantor" – a pause, to let it sink in, while Evelyn silently applauded the thoroughness of her research. "So very kind. I know how they both appreciated it – because it's hard these days for young people, isn't it, getting started up...? But then you see, if they were to separate, my Janet would still be entitled... to the house, I mean... with her having the children, you see. So of course, with you as the guarantor, it seemed... I mean you'd be liable.... I mean if he... So you see, I feel that really you *are* involved, it can't be helped."

At the end, when her cards had all been played and the silences had finished, Evelyn made sympathetic noises. "You never stop worrying about them, do you?" she crooned. "If only they knew! It's a life sentence, being a mother, I swear it's a life sentence. Well, I must let you get back to your family, but when you do speak to Richard, do let him know that the children send their love. And to you of course... It's Michael's birthday next month. They'd so love to come over..."

So, all in all, she wasn't surprised when an envelope arrived. She was virtually home and dry, she felt. He'd had plenty of time to get tired of little Valerie. She was doubtless a fast young thing, and it was probably going sour by now.

"So don't you worry, dear," she said to Janet. "He's had his little fling, but we'll just have to overlook it. It's just *men*. You have to feel sorry for them really – any bit of fluff and off they run after it! But they're never so keen once they've had their way. By now he's probably feeling quite ashamed. It's just a question of reeling him in."

***

In Ralph's case, certainly, a degree of shame soon followed his satisfaction.

For a little while, it overwhelmed him. On the Day of the Fall in the Pool, he had driven his bike home fiercely, grinding his teeth, vowing he wouldn't come back.

He felt the closeness of the towel in his rucksack. Of course, he had only brought it because he thought they might go paddling. That was all.

That was all.

He knew he had let himself down. He had betrayed himself.

And afterwards it was meaningless. Dirt on a wet towel.

Halfway home he stopped the bike and pushed the towel behind a bin in a layby. If Mrs Gregory missed it, he could always replace it. He could afford it. He'd have more money now, if he wasn't coming back.

Seeing him that evening, Ted didn't ask him, as he often did, if he'd had a nice time with his mum. He saw the scowl on Ralph's face, the twisted look. When Ralph looked like that, it was best to say nothing.

But the next day Ralph was better. At work, filling up the boxes, he saw a scrap of packing that was just the shade of Mary's dress, the blue of the little cats. He placed it in on his palm and he felt, just for a second, the stirring of desire.

He tore it into tiny bits. He thought of her body, naked, just for that moment, in his arms. And he made a little tear in the last scrap of blue. The little slit that he had not touched.

But perhaps she had wanted him to. She had not protested. She had pressed herself against him. She had led him on all day, sitting on his lap, kissing him. Afterwards she had seemed so keen to please. Perhaps she wanted it.

Then the supervisor arrived, a woman in her fifties with nicotine hair, and asked if he was all right, and he said yes, he was all right, and he threw himself back into the task with a vehemence that almost alarmed her.

That night in bed, once Ted was snoring and everything was safe, he thought of Mary – of the little slit, of her flat little chest, of the plumpness of her thighs. He made the pictures in his mind but he did not touch himself to seek satisfaction as he might have done. He just thought of her, waiting.

*\*\**

It was, Mary felt, a bit of an odd week. Their mother, although definitely very pretty, had a distracted air, and the boys were whispering in corners. There was something going on, but nobody was telling her.

She had begun to think that perhaps the boys were suspicious and were planning something sneaky. Colin had gone on about her being all wet, and twice he'd asked her where it happened, and who she was with.

"I know it wasn't the newt-pond. You'd have been muddy. Where was it? "

She had told her mother that Rita had the paddling pool out and that somehow she'd slipped in. It was a silly story, because Rita didn't have a garden, except for the place where the men drank beer behind the pub, and they'd hardly have a paddling pool *there*. But their mother and gran had seemed busy with each other, and had let it go at that.

It was Colin who worried about it. A nagging thought about her drowning. Mary hadn't been round at Rita's and she hadn't got muddy so it couldn't have been the newt-pond. Someone's paddling pool seemed almost more plausible.

"Were you with someone, Mary? Did you go round somebody's house?"

But she didn't answer.

"Where did you go? Were you with someone?"

Still she did not answer.

He had heard, all his life, of children who got drowned. Never anyone they knew, but he didn't doubt it happened. Little children and playing near water: it was one of those vetoes, like taking sweets from strangers, or getting into cars. He felt resentful that she wasn't being sensible. If she was going to be stupid they'd have to keep her with them. So he thought it was pretty mean, all in all. She was spoiling everything. The gang at the farm was a boys' affair. Colin and Michael were peripheral in any case, because they weren't anyone's cousins, and some of the boys made fun of their clothes and voices. If they had to drag Mary along, then they wouldn't stand a chance.

So he twisted her arm till she squealed a little. "You've got to tell me, Mary. Where were you paddling? Where was it?"

"I can't remember."

"How deep was it?"

"It wasn't deep." He pulled her arm round again, twisting her elbow upwards. "Only up to my ankles. I just fell over."

"And who was with you? Who were you playing with?"

"No one," said Mary firmly. "I was on my own." But she had a funny feeling that he didn't quite believe her.

***

The week seemed long to Mary. Colin kept insisting that they all kept together, although Michael was horrid and neither of them wanted her, not really. By Thursday she was desperate. She had to be free on Saturday. She had to make things right again.

She had felt it all week – Ralph's turning away from her after the accident in the pool. He hadn't got cross but she knew he had minded. She had disappointed him. She'd let herself get silly and let him down. She mustn't do so again. If she didn't go on Saturday – if he waited for her and she didn't even come – then he'd probably stop being her friend, and never come again. The thought was unbearable.

On Friday, walking home from a dreary afternoon behind the station, playing football, she finally asked the boys "Are you going to the farm tomorrow?"

"Yes," said Michael quickly, looking at Colin. "We are, aren't we Colin?"

"No," said Colin, though Mary saw he was torn.

Mary walked a few steps, and then said, as casually as she could, "You might as well go to the farm. I'm not coming with you."

"It's not up to you," Colin snapped. "We've got to look after you. We can go… we can go up the coal-yard or something. We can't go to the farm." His resentment was palpable.

Michael glared at Mary then back to Colin. "It's not flipping fair! She spoils everything. If she's too stupid to look after herself she should stay with Mum."

"Oh just shut up!" Colin said, but after a moment he looked at Mary, something sly coming into his face – a look that wasn't quite at home there. "You *could* though, Mary. They're going to get the telly back tomorrow. You could go with them. In Gran's car. Then you could watch it. You'd be the first then. If you stayed home."

"Yes!" Michael cried. "Colin'll tell Gran you want to go with them, and she'll have to then! Then we can go to the farm! Nyaaaaarrr… Nnnnnyyyyyyaaaaaarrrrrrrr!" He whooped and ran round them in a circle, pretending to be an aeroplane.

Mary put her foot out and the plane crashed to the ground. She ignored his howling as if nothing had happened and turned to Colin.

"I'm *not* staying with Mum," she said, very firmly. "I'm going to play out on my own and I don't care if you go to the farm or what you do. And if you say anything to Gran, or Mum, I'll tell them about *all* the times you've left me. And about you hitting me. And I'll tell John Pavis what you said about him being a sissy. And I'll tell everyone that Michael cried at the dentist and wet his pants. And I'll tell the Vicar about you killing the cat. And about the grave."

It was done now..

\*\*\*

On Friday night it poured with rain. It had stopped by breakfast, but even so there was talk of staying home, and the boys looked like they were going to comply. It was only the mention of *tidying their room* that rescued the day from disaster. They were going play in a barn, Michael said abruptly. The boys at the farm had invited them. They'd be out of any rain. Of course it was all right. "And Mary can come too," Colin added, catching her warning look. "We'll look after her."

Once their ways had parted, Mary tracked up the side of the cow field. The ground was waterlogged. When she got to the grave, she saw the top had washed away. She didn't look too closely, but she thought she could see part of the unspeakable thing, half unearthed at the top.

As she pushed through the trees in the plantation, they shed their water on her hair and clothes. She shivered a little. Where the trees gave way to the field, she stared at the corn. It was flattened by the rain. It would never be harvested now.

She felt despondent. The rain would probably deter Ralph from coming. Or if he did, he might be angry because her clothes were wet again. She had wanted the day to be perfect.

He had said last week that the blackberries might be ready, so she had planned to gather baskets of them, and take him to their secret place in the standing corn, and feed them to him, one at a time, so they didn't leave a mark. She had wanted *sunshine*, so she could lie with her head in his lap, and he could stroke her and tell her stories. It was all spoilt now.

When she reached the barn, however, her heart lifted. The branch had been pulled back. The nettles were freshly stamped. And as she pulled back the ivy, she saw his rucksack propped inside the door.

"Hello Mary."

He was lying on the bracken bed, sprawled on the blanket. His wet clothes were hanging from the roof, dangling down like ghosts. He had nothing on but his underpants. Mary was really quite astonished. She stood there, blinking, letting her eyes adjust.

"I got drenched," he said. "On the motorbike. You get really wet on a bike."

"Oh dear," Mary said, not sure how to take it. There was something not ordinary in his voice. She wished she could make things dry for him again.

"You're wet too," he said. His voice seemed kind enough, but the last time he'd got all cross when she got wet, and she wished she was dry this time.

"Only a bit," she lied. "It's only my hair, really. It'll soon dry."

"I see. And I thought you'd be just as wet as me! I even brought a towel for you. Look."

He lifted his head and pulled out the towel he'd been using as a pillow.

"Come here. Take the mack off. I'll dry your wet hair."

Mary smiled, and pulled off her mack, obediently. She looked at him shyly, trying to read his expression. "I'm really sorry about last week. About getting all wet."

He laughed then. "Don't be silly. I liked you all wet. Come here."

She went over and sat on the bracken beside him. He pulled himself up and patted her hair. "Oh dear," he said. "It's *very* wet, isn't it." And he rubbed it with the towel, and then smoothed it out. She was afraid he was going to get the comb out again, but instead he just teased out the strands with his fingers, and arranged them either side of her head, restoring the parting.

"Are you cold?" Mary asked. His fingers seemed warm as it brushed against her face, but his hands were shaking.

"Just a little," he said. "If it weren't for your wet clothes, you could warm me up." And he laughed, a funny laugh, not his normal laugh at all.

He pulled himself up and knelt on the reeds beside her. "Your boots, Madam. You can't come in here with muddy boots. Give me your boots." He picked up her foot and she toppled back onto the blanket, laughing. He gently pulled one boot off, then the other. Then he held her feet in his hands. Still his hands were shaking.

"Your socks are wet as well," he said. And he pulled off her socks. "This time I *am* going to keep one," he said. "My special souvenir. So are there holes this week? You know I like holes."

He pushed one hand in the sock and found a little hole. "Yes!" he said, "Here it is." And he pushed a finger through the hole and wiggled it. "Look, there's a snake in your sock. You never told me you kept snakes in your socks. What a very cheeky little snake." Then he laughed again, pulled off the sock and tucked it in his pocket. Gently, he picked up the towel again, and dried her damp feet.

"That tickles!" she said, and he did it some more. It was a nice towel. Pink. It was fluffy and soft and felt very new. He tickled her feet with it, and the back of her knees, and under her wet skirt, and the bit above. She laughed and laughed, feeling that things were improving.

"Well then, Madam, is that the last of the wet bits? Is the rest of you all dry?"

"Pretty much," she said, giggling, not wanting to say otherwise in case he got cross. His hands were shaking terribly now, and there was a shake in his voice as well. She was almost frightened for him. "You must have got horribly cold on the bike," she said.

"So are you going to warm me up then?" He held out his shaking hands, and she took one in her own. Despite the shake, it didn't feel very cold.

"You might be getting ill," she said. "You should get under the blanket till your clothes are dry."

"Only if you come with me," he said.

He pulled back the blanket so they both could get under. To her surprise, beneath the blanket there was another towel, blue this time but just as fluffy, waiting for them to lie on.

"I thought the bracken would be tickly," he said. "I thought this would be nicer."

It did not occur to her to question his foresight. He always had everything perfect. There was always everything they needed, packed in his big brown rucksack. Ralph wriggled under the blanket, pulling her with him.

"I'm really cold Mary. I need you to warm me up."

Perhaps in the dark of that place, Mary felt a moment's anxiety, wriggling down into a bed of bracken, with this man whom she loved, almost naked. She felt his hands on her dress, stroking.

"Oh Mary," he said, in mock reproach, "there's a wet bit here." His hands were touching the neck of her dress. "And all down here," he said, running his hand down her back, where the rain had got in. "And here." It was the back of her skirt, on the hem, from climbing the fence.

He made a show of shivering. "You're making me even colder," he said. "Let's get your wet things off, heh?"

And she sat up obediently and he pulled off her dress and her vest and patted her all over with the fluffy pink towel. Then he lay down again and pulled her back under the blanket. And this time, it seemed as he held her – both of them naked save the fig-leaf of underpants – that he found her warm and to his satisfaction.

"That's better," he said. "That's nice and warm. Put your hands on top of my hands Mary. I'm all shaking."

And she put her hands on his hands, as he told her, and her hands followed his as he stroked her tummy and her legs and her face and her neck.

"Do you like it, Mary?" he said. "Do you like it here, like this?"

"Yes," she said. "It's really nice." But as she said it, she knew there was something not right about the game. As each step played out, it had seemed quite all right, but in total there was something, she knew, that was not to be approved of.

His hands under her hands, his belly by hers. She liked the feel of skin on skin and she couldn't deny that her hands were nice and warm now. It was nicer than being wet. Then he reached down, under the blanket, right down to her cold little feet. Her hands couldn't follow and he lost them and laughed.

"Your arms aren't long enough" he said. "Put them here, instead." And he tucked her hands under the waistband of his underpants. "That's nice," he said. "Down a bit."

Unprotesting, she moved her hands, though she knew it was naughty now. He was hairy just there, like a monkey, and it made her giggle. She had never known anyone who was hairy on their tummy. And as he pressed against her, he was all a funny shape, as if there were a pocket in his underpants with something solid in it. Perhaps he'd brought another present for her, another dolly or a cat and she was supposed to find it. She fingered the coarse fur on his belly, a gentle, delicate exploration. And his hands stretched out along the length of her legs, on her calves, around the backs of her knees, the inside of her thighs.

"Do you still like it?" he asked, and his voice was just a whisper, with something catching in it, like the voice of a runner at the end of a race.

"I think so," she said, because she knew it was very naughty, though the truth was that she liked it quite a lot. She liked the feel of his hands on her skin, and she liked the closeness of it, the secrecy and specialness. That urgency again, the delicious imperative of it. And most of all she liked the fact that he loved her again and hadn't gone away.

His fingers traced the outline of her knickers, at the tops of her legs. After a moment or two, one finger, poked through, under the elastic.

"It's that snake again," he whispered. "It's a very cheeky snake."

And she caught her breath, and held it, not knowing what to say.

The finger was sure, tracking its route to the place it wanted to go, gently, gently. She felt his breath exhale on her neck as he found the place. A place that was secret and wet.

"Mary," whispered Ralph. "Mary..."

She couldn't speak. She was holding her breath.

There was something about his hands that was fiercer now, and although he was warm, he was shaking again, shaking all over, so he could hardly speak. But he spoke all the same.

"Mary... Do you know about sex?"

## 14. Bachanale

In truth, Mary wasn't wholly ignorant of sex. The bald facts of reproduction had been recounted by her brothers, though they often invented disgusting things just to see if she would blush, so she still wasn't sure how much of it was true.

The bit she knew as 'sex' was the unlikely claim about the father starting the baby by weeing in the mother's bottom. Mary knew that the baby came out of the mother's tummy, because she'd met a pregnant lady at the clinic once, who had let her feel the bump and told her all about it. But the weeing thing was something else completely. Mary would have dismissed it, were it not for an occasion when she had seen her father weeing on a flower bed. He had looked rather sheepish, but then he had winked and said it was to make the flowers grow – "Good stuff, wee. Makes things grow. Don't tell mummy, but it's a shame to waste it." This had seemed, Mary felt, to corroborate the argument.

It was perfectly clear, however, that there must be alternative methods. For one thing, it was obvious that her mother would never have permitted such behaviour, and even her father – who was sometimes rude and might wee on the garden – could never have been so disgusting. For another, one of Rita's cousins had a baby by accident, when she didn't really want one. This clearly precluded the wee-wee theory, because that wasn't the sort of thing that could happen 'by accident', and anyway, that baby didn't *have* a father – Rita was adamant on that point – so it must have been made by some other method, unknown to her brothers.

There was also the Virgin Mary, who had Jesus with an angel, and there couldn't, Mary felt, have been any wee-wee involved in *that*.

Her brothers had also pretended that the baby came out *there,* which wasn't at all convincing. That hole was obviously not big enough, and anyway, it was related to toilet matters, and babies, she knew, must be kept very clean. It was much more likely, she felt, to involve the tummy button. It probably came undone, like a drawstring bag.

She didn't even have a word for *there*. 'Bottom' was the best she could do, but the term was problematic. Boys had bottoms and a willy, and she had a bottom and another place, which manifestly should have had a name. Her mother would tell her, on the days when she didn't have a bath, to wash her hands and face and *between her legs*. She always said it in a certain way, that made it somehow embarrassing.

In bed she would touch the special place and trace the mysterious wetness of it. It seemed clear to her that it was a kind of second mouth, with lips, and a tongue, and a place inside, not wholly reachable.

She wondered in fact, if the bit in the middle might be the other end of her tongue. Clearly there was some kind of passage from her mouth to that part, since she drank with her mouth, and her wee came out there, so it seemed quite possible that her tongue, as well, went all the way through her. A careful investigation brought other support for the theory. That part had the same pleasing quality as her mouth, the same redness and wetness. There were also, to her scientific mind, the structural parallels. Sticking out her tongue and peering in the mirror, she noticed the tiny papillae that covered it, just like the tiny pearls in that other tongue, palpable under the skin. And when she pushed her real tongue backward, she could see in the mirror that it was joined to her mouth by a tiny bridge, with a little bobble at the root. Something similar, she had noted, went on with the other tongue, with the root of it joined by a little bridge, and at the base that same little bobble, very pleasing to the touch.

Finally, adding sociology to science, there was the issue of touching. As a little child, she had liked to suck her thumb, particularly in bed. She liked to rub her thumb on the roof of her mouth and feel round it with her tongue. It had been a matter for battles with her mother, who insisted it was naughty and dirty and would lead to unclarified ills. The same prohibitions applied to that other place, which was also a secret place for touching in bed. Mary could not recall how she had been discovered, but she remembered the shameful repercussions. Her mother had pulled all the bedclothes off and sent her to the bathroom. Then she called out after her – quite loud enough for the boys to hear, and they had teased her horribly afterwards – "Now wash your smelly hands, Mary Crouch! Properly I mean – and under the fingernails. They'll be full of germs now." She remembered the look of disgust on her mother's face, and even now, years later, the shame burnt in her mind.

Mary also knew, in a childish way, the indescribable excitement of sexual submission. She had long passed the age when she would share her brothers' bath, and she was a modest little girl who could even get changed on the beach without *letting herself down*. Occasionally, however, they still played a secret game called 'Strip and Poke Her', where the boys took turns asking difficult questions, like sums or spelling, and for every error she had to take something off, until she was completely naked, and then for the next mistake they could pull her legs apart and have a look, and for the next they could lift her legs up and poke a crayon in her anus. She had to pretend that this was all a hateful penance – but in truth she was cleverer than her brothers and the game would scarcely have progressed without deliberate wrong answers. All three of them knew it was a terrible, wicked game, which if discovered would have led to mortifying punishments. But they played it none the less, as children do.

There seemed little to be said about the boys' role in these mysteries. Their chief involvement, clearly, was as envious observers. Mary had seen them naked and it was painfully clear that where there should have been a mouth, with all its secret and pleasurable organs, there was nothing but a floppy thing for weeing with, made of ordinary skin, no more engaging than an earlobe. Particularly appalling was the blankness of that lumpy region between the anus and the penis. She had inspected it in the bath with Michael, and its bland topology, devoid of any specialness, had filled her with awkward pity. She knew they couldn't help it and had been born like that, and that it must be same for her father. She knew that she wasn't to remark on it, and that somehow this deficiency was at the heart of everything and was probably the reason why her mother scorned their father, and why her brothers liked to hit her.

So, all in all, she was quite a knowledgeable girl, and what is more, had opinions on these matters. What she lacked, perhaps, was any grasp of their connections – or even, for the most part, that there *were* connections. Reproduction, anatomy, sociology, diplomacy. Pleasure, desire, shame. Difference, envy, violence. Desire. Submission. At seven, after all, the world is full of mysteries and it is far from obvious where the jigsaw pieces fit.

So perhaps, when Ralph asked her if she knew about sex, she should have answered "No".

But none of us wholly knows what we do not know, and she wanted him to see that she was a well-informed little girl. And it wasn't, in any case, an uncompromised moment - with one of his fingers resting in that naughtiest of places that even *she* was not supposed to touch. So she answered – her voice a little shaky because of the nasty matter of weeing in bottoms – "Yes, of course," and in the half-light she tried to look insouciant, though she knew for a certainty that his question was rude.

There was that look again, disfiguring Ralph's face. Sometimes, when he was worried, particularly when he was worried that she would give away their secrets, his face took on that strange, taut look: his nostrils a little wide and his eyes a little narrow. It wasn't a look that she liked, though it usually passed quickly, with a little reassurance.

So she put her hand under her knickers, and placed it on top of his, and she gently stroked his finger.

"Don't worry," she said. "I promise not to tell."

\*\*\*

Looking back, she knew there was a point when she stopped liking it. Certainly, there was a time, at the beginning, when she liked it rather a lot, and afterwards a time in between, where she still quite liked it, but would rather have stopped. He was quite hot now and his hands had stopped shaking, so it really wasn't necessary to continue the game. She thought of suggesting that his clothes might be dry now.

But there was an excitement in his breath that caught her by surprise. She felt his skin on her body, and the smell of him. His hands, coming firmer, playing a game that wasn't quite what she thought. He was poking the special place with a finger now, too hard, and it was starting to hurt. She wriggled awkwardly to get away from the finger, but it followed her, and his breath came harder. He was lying on her as her brothers sometimes did, but he was heavier than them, and he was rocking. She didn't like it at all then.

She tried to call out, but he hushed her. He was pulling at that last small garment and she was holding it to herself, somehow wanting its comfort. She felt the cloth ripping, and under the blanket she felt against her body that thing he'd been hiding in underpants. It was sticking out now, hot against her legs.

And she realised that it was *him*. Some impossible excrescence of himself, like an extra limb. It was something unnatural, some dreadful deformity.

"No!" she said, trying to get away from it. "Stop it! No! Let's..." Her eyes were accustomed to the shadows now. She saw his face, inches from hers, curiously distorted.

"Mary, Mary," he was saying. "I love you, Mary. Please! Please Mary, let me! I won't hurt you. Just let me..." The hard thing was pushing at her, and he was prising her legs apart, guiding the hard thing into the space between.

Sometimes she wrestled with her brothers, and they struggled with her, wrenching and pulling and rolling on the floor. Long ago, when she was little, she had a game with her father where she fought him and he picked her up and threw her in the air, over and over, or held her up by her feet, as she kicked and giggled and struggled in his hands, her skirt over her face, her knickers showing, helpless.

It might have been a game like that. There was something of that game in it, but Mary knew it was really something else.

She wriggled backwards and bent her knees upwards as she would do with her brothers, to lever them away with her feet. But as she did so, she saw the desire in the rictus of his smile, and smelt the poisonous sweetness of it. "Yes!" he said, with a snort that was not laughter. "Good girl. That's it. Good girl." He pushed her knees apart and forced his body between them. The solid thing was closer now, high by his belly. It was purple.

Then, as if a light switched on, she realised what it was. It was his willy. It wasn't like her brothers' in the bath, or even her father's when he weed in the garden. It was monstrous, absurd, like a cartoon thing. But it was still just a willy.

"Mary, Mary," he was moaning. "I love you Mary... please, please... Just let me... just a moment... just once... please... Mary you can't... I've got to..."

And in a momentary chill of understanding, she knew what he was doing. He was going to wee in her bottom, to make a baby.

\*\*\*

She had resisted, on and off, up till then, but now it was different. Where before she had struggled without needing to win, she now jerked away violently. Fiercely, she kicked at his stomach, his hideous willy. "Stop it! Ralph, stop it!" She was angry now. It wasn't just alarm about being hurt. It was shame and loathing. She didn't want anyone's wee in her bottom, not anyone's, ever. And she was much too young to have a baby.

"Stop it! I don't want to! Go away!"

It hadn't occurred to her, till then, that he wouldn't stop if she really told him, if she really meant it. He had always done what she wanted before. He had always been attentive. He had played her games and never ignored her as her brothers did. But this time was different. He was pushing her down, wrenching at her legs, taking no notice.

There was still the final weapon that worked with her brothers. She spat out the words, knowing the terrible power of them, feeling all the promises of her summer tearing open, *"Stop it or I'll tell of you!"*

The words echoed in the air.

She saw the look in his face, the look of distaste and resentment. But he did not stop.

"You won't," was all he said, and there was something in his eyes that she had not seen before. "You won't tell *anyone*." She tried to hit out at him, but his hand caught hers, and pushed it down behind her head.

"I'm telling of you," she cried again, trying to free her legs. "I will. I'll tell my mum!" She was urgent now. She no longer cared about promises or all that had gone before. "I mean it, I'll tell my mum. I'll tell my teacher." She fished in her mind for something yet more potent, but could not find it. "I'll tell my mum." There had to be more. There had to be something worse. "I'll tell her everything. And I'll TELL MY GRAN!"

His hand clamped round her face.

"No! Stop it! Nnnnnnn..." His palm was blocking her mouth, and all that came out was an inchoate spluttering. But Ralph was not listening anyway. His eyes were somewhere else, in some other plane: great ugly eyes like a startled bull.

"Mary... just a bit, I've got to..." and his voice trailed into a groan. And she realised, in that moment, that he wasn't going to stop. She had been quite wrong. He didn't care. He was going to do it regardless. Desperation clutched at her, because he was strong and she was little, and what he wanted was horrible. His hands were like a vice, and the weight of him was like a falling horse, crushing her.

And then the little pain that had been troubling her – the sharp little pain, like the soap that stung her tender places in the bath – turned to something else. At first it was a bit of a wrenching like the Indian burns that her brother's did on her wrists, then something ripping, tearing, searing. Then the darkness started coming on her eyes, a blindness without form or shadow. And a burning, terrible wetness.

# 15. The Creature in the Briar

It was then that the dog barked.

At first it seemed nothing. In the urgency and panic of the moment, the dogs might bark, the world might end, but it hardly needed to matter. The darkness had consumed her, and a different feeling was coming, a feeling that tore in her chest and crashed across her face.

But then the sound again, and closer. Three sharp yaps and a pattering on the path.

Ralph froze. He pulled himself up till he was kneeling and looked all around. Mary felt the weight lift from her, the pressure subside, and the pain, which had threatened to engulf her, pulled sharply back into some inner place. She opened her eyes and the world rolled back to her. The man who had terrified her moments ago, was kneeling in the bracken, almost naked, his white skin scattered with bits of leaf, his face like a cornered fox.

He looked smaller now, just a man as he had been before. Just Ralph. And all at once she was embarrassed by his nakedness. She saw his willy poking out from his underpants, and looked away. It was, after all, an ordinary willy. She reached over and pulled the towel over her tummy. The game had been nasty and much too rough, and he had really hurt her. She touched herself gingerly and felt the tearing soreness in her special place. It had been a horrible game. He had injured her. Even her brothers stopped short of that.

Another bark. It was only a dog, and from the tone not even big, but she saw the cornered terror in Ralph's face. It was just outside, behind the den, snuffling under the thatch. Then a silence and a pattering, and its face appeared at the door.

It was a tiny thing, a Jack Russell, all white except for a patch on one eye. It was hardly more than a puppy.

Ralph stamped and rushed towards it, shooing it away. "Go away. Away boy. Go away."

But it stood its ground and yapped some more.

Mary was grateful. Ralph clearly didn't like it, but at least it had distracted him. She focused on it, making herself think of it, blotting out the moments before. It looked like a nice little dog. She wondered if anyone owned it, and whether perhaps she might keep it. She looked for her clothes and saw with relief that Ralph was doing likewise. He was frantically pulling on his trousers and wrenching the shirt from its hanging in the rafters. He looked much more normal with his trousers on, though still there was something different in his face, something nasty.

"It's all right," she said. "I don't think it'll bite." She was conciliatory now, wanting things to be normal, so at least she could get dressed and take herself home.

Ralph span round to her. "Shut up," he said. "Get under there. Quickly." To her surprise, he pushed her back onto the bed, and shoved her into the shadows of the eaves. "Back, right back," he hissed, "Get under the bracken."

"No!" she said, "No! I don't want..."

She squeaked a little and struggled to sit up, but he pushed her back roughly. Then he scooped up the bracken and threw it on her face. Then the towel and the blanket. The darkness under the blanket seemed dank and unpleasant, and suddenly she thought of spiders. She felt the scratchiness of the bracken, the earth just beneath her and the prickly branches behind. But above all, she felt the indignity of it, and the betrayal. He was being horrid today, completely horrid. And she hadn't done anything wrong, not really, certainly no more than him. And he had really hurt her.

She pushed herself up from the bracken. There was a horrible pain in her bottom and it was all his fault. She felt the tears coming. "I don't like you!" she said, "I don't want to be your friend now, not anymore." The terrible words came out with a sob. "I'm going home now. I'm telling my mum."

He turned round and stared at her. Then he hit her round the face.

She toppled backwards and his hand came down on her mouth. It was strong and hard, and it made her bite her tongue. Then his voice came hissing, close to her ears.

"Shut up Mary. If you make a sound, I'll kill you."

\*\*\*

Ralph had seen, almost at once, the problem about the dog. He pulled on his shirt, not bothering with the buttons, and looked around for his boots.

"Keep still," he hissed, sensing a stirring in the bracken behind him. "Don't move at all. I mean it." The bracken was still again.

The dog was clean and had a collar on. It wasn't the sort of dog that arrived on its own. Whoever its owners were, they couldn't be far away, and the yapping would call them. Whoever it was, it could only be moments before the noise would bring them to the den.

He had to get rid of the dog. He had to make it go.

The bracken moved again, and Mary's head appeared. "Please... I want to go..."

He looked at her tousled head. A bitter grief washed over him. But she had to be quiet. He had to stop her prattle. He bent down close to her and snarled into the darkness. "Don't move, Mary Crouch. I've got a knife. Don't move or I'll cut your throat,"

He heard a quick inhalation of breath, and then she was quiet.

He stepped quickly to the door, and aimed a kick at the dog, but it was quicker than him and ran just out of reach, barking all the louder. Then it ran in a circle round him, expecting a game.

From the corner of the barn Ralph stared down the field, towards the stream and the footpath. There was nobody that way. Then, looking back, he saw the figure. The man was barely past the stile, perhaps a hundred yards back, walking towards him. He had a walking stick and a heavy jacket – the farmer perhaps, coming out to see the damage to his crops.

Ralph cursed his own stupidity. The path to the den lay open from the field. It was marked with little stones. The carpet of needles. It was too late now to pull back the branch.

And still the dog was barking. Ralph thought of Mary, in the den behind him. Under the bracken, under the blanket and the warm fluffy towel. Under it all, she was lying there, quite naked. And the man was getting closer, striding purposefully down the field.

Ralph felt in his pocket, where his penknife was, and worked the blade open. It was self-defence. He had no choice.

He pushed his way through the bank of wet nettles and into the trees beyond. The rows of pine were dense to the ground and made perfect cover. As he pushed his way from one to the next, the little dog followed him, yapping a bit, just beyond his feet.

He kept himself out of sight, but he could see the man clearly now – grey haired, thickset, walking a little stiffly. Ralph's chest tightened as the man drew closer. He knew that any moment he must let himself be seen. He clutched the knife harder. He wondered if it was big enough. But he didn't have a choice. The man mustn't walk any further. The man mustn't see what the dog would show him.

"Bramble! Bramble! Here boy!" The old man was looking around now, scanning the trees, wiping the rain from his glasses. And for a moment, just for a moment through the dripping branches, Ralph saw his face.

It was old Max Pavis. It was Sonia's grandfather.

It was possibly to Ralph's credit that the knife stayed in his pocket. Perhaps in the snapping of a moment Ralph weighed up his chances and found them wanting. Perhaps he had no stomach for it, not today, not here, with the smell of Mary still fresh on his hands. Or perhaps the past rose up in his throat, and his hands shook, and he couldn't hold the blade. Fight or flight or freeze.

A terrible coldness closed around his chest.

And because, for whatever reason, he could not fight, and if he froze the dog would give him away, he did the only thing that was left to him. He turned his back on the field and on the den where Mary lay naked. He turned his back on the dog and the once-familiar man. He thrashed through the nettles, through the brambles, through the trees, into the plantation and back towards the embankment. He ran away.

It was that, in a sense, which saved them all.

His careless thrashing excited the dog and alerted the man. The man peered round, and saw the curious gypsy figure in sodden shirtsleeves, disappearing into the trees. The dog, delighted by this new activity, barked all the louder and followed him.

"Bramble! Bramble! Here boy! Come Bramble!"

The man called urgently, then whistled and called again. But the dog – who was young and a terrier – ignored him as before.

"Bramble! Bramble!"

Ralph no longer thought, no longer planned, no longer nurtured any purpose – except to get away. The dog yapped joyfully at his feet and when he stumbled, the dog bounced onto him, licking his face. Ralph pushed it away, but still it followed him, yapping and wagging its tail.

At last: the edge of the plantation. He headed past the grave towards the road. But after the rain, the clay was sticky, and within moments his boots were caked, and he was running as one runs in dreams, leaden footed, without progress. It was no use. He turned from the field and clambered to the welcome firmness of the embankment.

It was rocky and the wet stones slipped a little, but as he scrambled upwards there were patches of ragwort which gave him some purchase, and after desperate minutes he was at the top. He caught his breath and threw himself down beside the track. His ankle had been wrenched in some awkward moment, but it didn't matter. He was out of sight now. He was almost safe.

"Bramble! Bramble!" The old man's voice was coming from below, getting closer. Raising his head to glance backwards Ralph saw the patch of tweed near the edge of the plantation, moving through the trees. He flattened himself again, feeling the wetness of the stones on his face. He would lie still, let the man pass.

But at just that moment, the dog scampered onto the track beside him and crouched just out of reach, wagging its tail and barking. Ralph cursed. He made a hissing noise, which would have sent the cats running, but the dog only bounced towards him, imagining some game. It came right up to him and licked his face. Then it ran in circles round him, barking. Ralph closed his eyes, willing it to lose interest and return to its master.

But then, as his face grew cool on the black stones, his mind grew clearer. The man's pursuit of the dog meant the den had not been found. They were not damned, not yet. But if the dog went back, Old Max would resume his walk. Back along the field by the barn.

There was another way. Into the blindness of inevitable damnation, there came a tiny crack of hope.

Ralph reached out his arm and tried to grab the dog, but it darted from him. He held out his hand as if offering it a titbit. "Here Bramble," he hissed. "Good boy. Here Bramble." But there was nothing in Ralph's hand, and perhaps the dog had been tricked before.

For a moment it turned its back on Ralph and cocked its head to the sound of its master's voice. Max was climbing the fence now, looking around and calling.

## A Cat's Cradle

\*\*\*

The dog never saw the boot. There was metal in the toe and Ralph's aim was true. There was a sharp thud, and a single yelp as the tiny creature twisted upwards, then fell, catching the side of its head on a rail. It did not get up.

The rain dampened the dog's cry. In the field below, the man had not turned. He was sitting astride the fence, scanning the field.

Ralph shuffled to the place where the tiny dog had fallen. He could see that its back was broken. For a moment he felt the cleansing rush of relief.

But then the dog moved and he saw he had not killed it.

Like a dog that dreams of running with rabbits, its front legs were twitching in a tiny spasm. Its eyes were open and one of them seemed to look at him, a little tip-tilted stare, the more painful for its absence of reproach. The tongue was lolling out and the mouth was stretched as if frozen in mid-bark. And there was a silence catching in its chest, a bark obstructed in the moment of eruption. Again and again, a juddering, unearthly gasp, trapping the awful present in a moment of silent pain. It was not finished.

Ralph looked away. *Finished* was unnecessary. Only silence mattered and the dog was silent now. He knew he must flatten himself back on the stones, keep still, wait. Without the barking, the old man would have no reason to look up, let alone to climb. He would go on through the field, calling and searching, further and further from the terrible danger of the barn. And then, in the end, he would go home, disappointed.

A crack of hope.

Ralph stared across the stones at the horrible, unfinished death. He told himself it wasn't his problem. It would finish in its own time. Any action now would be dangerous. He knew he must either stay lying or else run.

But he did neither. He pushed himself up till he was kneeling by the track, though he knew he would be perfectly silhouetted on the skyline. He reached in his pocket, opened his knife, and with a careful, grating stroke, he sliced the dog's throat. The blood poured across his hands. Ralph retched, but he did not let go. For all the moments that it took, he held the dog's head, and whispered soothingly to it, crouched where anyone could see him, taking his time, risking everything.

There was no mercy in the gesture, but there was no cruelty in it either. Perhaps there was even courage, since even the bleakest of sinners may be capable of that. Above all, there was relief. A flood of something completed, something that would disappear into the past and be gone. The past is nothing.

Only then, slowly, he looked back to check if the man had seen. He was fifty feet behind and twenty feet below, standing by the empty grave, wiping his glasses on his sleeve, looking this way and that, perplexed.

"Bramble! Here boy!"

Ralph lowered himself back beside the rails. High on the dark stones, pressing his face into their sharpness, he lay and waited for the man to pass.

And after a while, he knew that the closest danger was gone. Max's voice – calling his dead dog's name to the empty air – was moving away. But as the danger subsided, and the crack of hope gaped wider, the knowledge came to Ralph that it was not over, and other thoughts buffeted him, in waves of horror and nausea.

He thought of Max Pavis trudging into the distance, along towards the road and the railway bridge. He had not changed so much in the years that had passed, since he had stared at Ralph from the gallery of the court. He thought, inevitably, of Sonia and then of the days they had shared and of the years he had lost: the terrible price he had paid. He thought of Mary, naked under the bracken. The cost of staying alive, the cost of a moment's happiness. And the cost, it seemed then, was infinitely too high and he had lived too long already. Then he let himself think, for a moment and just for comfort, that it would probably be better if they caught him again, and it was all over for him.

But even then, if the old man had turned and seen him, Ralph would have run, and if he had been caught, he would have pulled the knife.

*** 

Ralph was shivering all over as he pulled himself up from the stones.

He looked at the broken dog, and thought ruefully of the grave down below, of the white hairs lovingly collected, of the stones and the unspeakable thing. There would have been a poetry in it, the closing of a circle. But there was no need for poetry. Gently, he draped the lifeless creature on the rails.

# A Cat's Cradle

*They picked up the pieces, son, all the way from Canningbridge to Oatham Park.*

It was nothing now. An unspeakable thing. Everything is unspeakable at the end. The little dog, the little girl. It made no difference. He thought of Mary. She would be there still, lying under the bracken. He thought of her face in the dim light of the den, her hands on his hands, urging him onwards. It was her fault really. Whatever had happened afterwards, she couldn't deny that look. She made him do it.

The thought relieved him though he knew it was irrelevant. It was too late. *Stop it or I'll tell of you.* Nobody would be interested if she wanted it or not. *I'll tell my mum. I'll tell my gran.* What had happened had happened. He had no choice anymore.

He stumbled to the edge of the slope and slid awkwardly down the embankment. He was soaking wet, even inside his boots, and muddy from his knees to his chest. Without thinking, he had rubbed his hands on his shirt so it was streaked with the dog's blood. His trousers were torn at the knees. As he got to his feet, he felt again the wrench in his ankle. He thought of taking off his boot and binding the ankle with a strip from his shirt, but it would take too long. It was only a little pain.

Awkwardly, he climbed the fence.

Rain dripped silently from his curly hair down the back of his neck. Ralph felt no joy in what he had to do. At that moment, he would have wished the path through the plantation, the secret path they had made together, between the bracken and the pine trees, to wind onwards forever. But already the field was opening ahead of him. In the chink between the trees, he could see all the way from the muddy path to the far side of the field. And between, he could see the devastated corn, the place where they had hidden and played in the sun, all flattened by the rain, all lost.

# 16. The Key to Happiness

Mary felt acutely that things weren't as they ought to be.

For a while she had been terrified by Ralph's threats and she lay in the bracken with her heart pounding and her breath catching in her throat.

But once the immediate fear grew still, she pushed the bracken from her face and took stock of the matter. The game had gone horribly wrong, and Ralph had been perfectly awful. But he couldn't have meant what he said. It was just the kind of thing her brothers said. Never a day passed without terrible threats from Colin or blows from Michael. It didn't mean anything particular. It was just what her mother called 'boys being boys'.

The thought grieved her, because Ralph had been, all summer, her very best friend. She wondered if his beastliness had been somehow her fault. She wanted to forgive him. Even now, despite the distracting pain inside her, she felt the lure of his friendship, and it didn't seem impossible – not wholly impossible – that he might come back and apologise. She could hardly ignore how nasty he had been. Whatever he had meant, he had actually injured her. He would have, at the least, to say a very big sorry and give her something, because he'd hurt her such a lot.

She thought of how it happened and she felt a bit awkward. It had been, undeniably, a naughty sort of game. But she wasn't the one who started it. She thought of the moments before the hurt. It had been a kind of a cuddle at first, because he'd been cold. And afterwards, a bit of a fight. She tried the words out in her mind, and they seemed quite plausible, though she knew all the same that they weren't quite true. Sometimes when she fought with her brothers it got, as her mother would say, 'a bit out of hand'. Once, when Michael was pinning her to the ground and Colin was tickling her, she had bitten Michael's arm and left quite a mark. She'd expected a lot of trouble for that, but when Michael went crying to their mother she just looked exasperated and asked him what he expected if he horsed around like that. 'Horsing around' was probably what it was. Just horsing around. She thought of the horses in the field and the danger and thrill of feeding them. They were great big things with enormous teeth, and if you didn't keep your hand flat they might bite it off. But Mary fed them every week, and didn't come to harm, because she was a sensible girl and knew what to do.

The thought reassured her.

So she dug herself out of the bed, feeling the injury with each movement, and she wiped the bracken from her skin. Her clothes were trampled in the reeds and her knickers terribly torn. It was Ralph's fault for that, and she felt aggrieved. He wouldn't have liked it if she'd spoilt *his* clothes. The knickers weren't even wearable, so she hid them in the bracken and pulled down her vest. With her dress on she'd be decent. Nobody would see.

She looked around for her socks but could find only one of them. Then she remembered what Ralph had said. *This time I'm going to keep one. My special souvenir.*

And he'd actually meant it. He had stolen one of her socks.

Quite suddenly, she was overwhelmed: a grief and indignation that she couldn't quite explain. The knickers might have been an accident, but the sock had been *stolen*. She remembered him laughing about it, making fun of the hole, and poking his finger through. It was horrible. He had no right. It was her sock. It was hers and she wanted it back. It was a mean thing to do. *She hadn't said he could have it.*

She looked round the den, and suddenly it seemed a hollow, dirty place. It was dingy and damp. It smelled of decay. The branches which had been fresh and green at first were brown now, and their needles were sharp and falling. She hadn't ever wanted the den there, anyway. It was much too shady even on sunny days and horribly dark when it rained. It would have been better where she'd said in the first place, down across the field, by the stream, where it was nice.

She had made a mistake about Ralph. It began to seem possible that he wasn't, in fact, a nice person at all.

She pulled on her boots and buttoned up her mack. Then it occurred to her that she might take something of *his*, to pay him back for the sock.

By the door there was his rucksack. She pulled it open and poked around. There was funny stuff in it. There was rope and a box of matches. There was a little book with pictures of ponies, but it was a baby thing. There were spanners. A bottle of cream soda. And of course there was the feast: a bag with fairy cakes, and slices of pie. She wondered what the time was. Nothing looked quite as nice as it might have done, but she ate a fairy cake anyway, and dropped the paper on the floor, which she knew was naughty. Then she stuffed the other in her mouth as well, so he couldn't have it, even though she didn't really want it.

His jacket was still hanging from a beam. It was odd, she thought, that he'd gone without it. In the rain he should have needed it. In one pocket was a wallet, like her dad had, but there was nothing in it except a sixpenny bit and three ha'pence in coppers. But she wasn't very interested in money. In the flap there was a crumpled old photo of a woman and a man, standing hand in hand and smiling awkwardly. She thought about taking it because he owed her something, but it wasn't at all pretty. She thought of the little gold cat and wondered where he'd put it. She tried the other pocket, then the one inside. It was hers by rights already, because of *finders keepers*. He was a thief. He had stolen that from her too. At the bottom of the pocket, half into the lining, she felt the metallic cool of something small and angular and thought for a moment that she had found it. But when she pulled it out, it was only a key. The Key to Happiness.

She put it in her pocket.

\*\*\*

She was already by the plantation when she heard him coming. At first it was only the crackling of twigs, which might have been the rain and the wind in the branches. But then she saw a flash of white, far off through the trees, and she knew it must be him. He was returning.

Despite her resolve, she was pleased by that. There had been something rather shocking in his sudden departure – at such a moment, just after their little fight.

*Their little fight.* She felt it was easier if she thought of it like that.

He had done it before – the abrupt departure, striding into the woods and leaving her all frightened. But just like that other time, he was coming back. She felt quite mollified and thought of calling him, but then she remembered the stolen sock and how carelessly he'd hurt her and the beastly things he'd said. She wouldn't, she decided, be the first to speak. She'd see what he said. If he wanted to be friends again, she'd need a proper 'sorry', and her sock back. And she'd ask for the cat as well. He certainly owed her something, for hurting her like that. It still hurt badly, even now. He would have to give her the cat.

Closer now, she saw the patch of white again.

She was glad she'd left the den. He would see she was going home and that she was cross with him and that he needn't suppose that she wanted to see him. If he wanted to make up, he would have to be extra nice. She'd let him see that she was really upset.

She crouched down low, though it hurt her bottom when she squatted. She focused on the pain of it and tried a tentative sob. It would be quite right if he saw her crying. But the excitements of the day had exhausted all her passions. There was an emptiness in her head where the tears might have been.

As he turned the final twist of the path, she saw him clearly. She saw his face, contorted by a terrible emotion. She saw the strange way he was walking – jerking as if invisible strings were plucking at his limbs. She saw the front of his shirt, not white as she remembered it, as it had seemed as she glimpsed it through the trees. It was smeared with red. His clothes were covered in blood.

Something dipped and flickered in her mind, like the television set before it died. Sense and nonsense clattered together, and then, in an instant there came an urgent certainty. This wasn't Ralph at all. It wasn't the person she was waiting for. It was someone else. Instinctively, she pulled back into the shadow of the tree, and pressed herself, gasping, behind its slender trunk. Then she did not breathe again until the man who was not Ralph had passed.

***

Sometimes terror comes quickly, snapping at the throat in an instant, bringing its own strength. But sometimes it comes like night, a little at a time, a remorseless, nibbling away of hope. Ralph stood in the empty den, and slowly took in the import of its silence.

It simply had not occurred to him that Mary might have gone. So unwelcome had been the task ahead that he had not thought of the possible complications. And at first, in that bewildered moment of discovery, her absence seemed almost welcome: a sweet thing, a redemption, a lifting of a terrible burden. Though of course, it was nothing of the sort.

It took him several moments to take it in. He tossed the bracken from the bed. Nothing. The dangers moved around each other, in a slow, mawkish, hideous dance.

He wondered, then, how much time he had. She must have left at once or he would have seen her on the way. She might be home already.

*I'll tell my mum. I'll tell her everything.*

He wondered what she would tell. Perhaps, at the first, she would be disbelieved. Surely there would be no evidence to speak of. He paused for a moment, nauseous, remembering. But he had not, surely, done very much. Nothing that should damn him, nothing so very bad. He had not, he told himself, actually *hurt* her. He had only done what she wanted, surely... He had only followed where she led him. But he was not sure. Looking back, he was not sure if there might be some mark on her.

A word flashed through his mind. The word they would call it. Sonia, in the end, had been silent, but Mary would speak.

He was older now, so many years older, but scarcely wiser.

He had never taken care, as he should have done. Mary knew his name, where his mother lived, he had made no secret. It would not take long for connections to be made. They would find out where he worked, where he lived.

Last time the knock had come in the night: two policemen at the door, ash-faced themselves, waking his parents, stamping up the stairs. And they had found him, lying in the dark, lost in what had passed, no thought of escape. In those days he was young and life seemed infinite. He did not know, as he now did, the sound of the closing doors, the keys in the lock, the endless grinding of years.

He would not let that happen a second time. He would move on, disappear. He had a full tank of petrol. He could ride through the night and be anywhere by morning. He could sleep out, make a little shelter, take vegetables from the fields. He had a blanket and the towels to sleep on. He could wash in a stream and steal clothes from washing lines. He could chum up with travellers, get work picking hops or potatoes. In prison he had heard men talk of such things.

He would choose a new name. Ralph Sneddon would die and a new man rise from the ashes. There were more ways than one to build a life. He could start again.

He pulled on his jacket. The rain had chilled him like a little death. He thought of winter.

Before he left, he paced once more round the den. He scattered the bracken from the bed and picked up the little cat and the doll. Crushed in the mud he found Mary's knickers and here and there on the floor a handful of relics – a bunch of dead flowers, the paper case from a fairy cake, a button.

Relics. He thought of the little cat with its emerald eye, lying in the stones for fifteen years. He stuffed the relics in his rucksack.

On the way out, he scuffed at the path and he kicked the stones from the edge of it. Then he pulled back the branch and walked the other way. He would take, he decided, the long way back to his bike. He did not think she would lead them to the place, not now, not today, and every extra yard was a pain on his twisted foot. But it would be wise to take another route, just in case.

He was tired when he got to the road and his ankle had swollen in his boot. The thought of a long ride gave him no pleasure, but there would be comfort in taking the weight off his foot, and relief in the miles growing long between himself and danger.

He dragged the bike out from its hiding place and he pulled on his helmet. He was ready to go.

Then he felt in his pocket for the key.

***

Michael and Colin bounced down the lane on their bikes. It was full of puddles and it was a matter of pride to splash through each of them, getting each other if they could.

Michael whooped and hooted, too excited to find words. He stood on one pedal and waved a leg in the air. He held one hand over his head and hollered at the sky. He rang the bell over and over. His front tyre was flat and the wheels slammed each stone, but he didn't mind. Nor did he care about the rain or even, really, the delay in finding Mary. He was so happy he felt he might burst. It was the best day ever.

Colin felt it too, though he remembered Mary's terrible imprecations and had asked if perhaps – despite everything – they should wait till the usual time. But even as he said it, he knew that it was nonsense. The nature of the news was far too pressing. It was the kind of thing that even Mary, who was often pig-headed, would immediately understand.

They had trundled round the field with the horses, calling out her name, but she wasn't there, so they cycled down the lane and set off for the newt-pond, but all of it was boggy, because of the rain. "The station then!" Michael shouted. "She'll be at the station. We can go to the witch's house and down the road from there."

"But the road... we're not supposed to go on the road."

"Sissy! Nobody'll see. Come on. Beat you there, sissy." So saying, Michael clambered back on his bike and clattered down the lane.

Colin, who wasn't a sissy and had a better bike anyway, overtook him in a puddle, and splashed him down the trousers. "Gotcha that time!" he laughed, but Michael just rang his bell again, and hollered and hooted, and screeched his happiness to the passing air.

Halfway down the lane they met John Pavis's granddad, who had lost his little dog and asked if they'd seen it. Colin, who liked to be helpful said they'd keep an eye out, and Michael did a dumb show behind the old man's back, of taking an eye out and waving it round.

Colin looked away to stop himself from laughing, but Michael was enjoying himself. "There was a dog on the village green," he said. "A black and white dog. You should check there."

The man looked happier then and smiled at them. "Thanks sonny, I'll do that," he said.

When the old man was gone, Colin kicked Michael in the shins for being so cheeky. "That was the dog from the pub, stupid. You know that."

Michael shrugged. "I only said it was a dog," he said. "Just trying to help." And he laughed, and swerved off on his bike again, with Colin following after.

They saw her from the lane. She was far off, near the railway land, struggling through the clay between the field and the plantation. She was holding on to the fence, walking awkwardly and stopping now and then to look behind. She must have been playing by the grave. She must have been taking flowers.

Perhaps in the rain she didn't hear what they were shouting. Michael was standing on the fence by the lane, waving his arms and yelling out the news, but she didn't react or wave, or even seem to see them. As she got closer, Colin saw the look on her face. He wondered if she'd eaten something she shouldn't. Michael had eaten a crab-apple once when the twins had dared him to, and his face had gone just that way because he realised, too late, that it must be poisonous. Colin put his hand on Michael's elbow and shook it a little.

"I think something's up," he said. "I think she's not very well."

"Nah," Michael said, without turning round. "She's just dippy. Come on. I'll hurry her up." He swung his leg over the fence and started off down the side of the field, yelling and waving his arms.

"Mary! Mary!" he was shouting, and Colin joined in now. "It's Dad! He's come back, Mary! Dad's here. We saw him! Gran's gone and Dad's come back!"

## 17. The Return of the Prodigal

Evelyn was pleased, ever after, that she had insisted on collecting the television. If she'd let Janet have her way, they'd have given in to the rain, and all stayed home. Then when Richard arrived, he'd have found things all *anyhow*, with the children making a mess, and teacups in the sink and Janet with her hair not done and probably wearing a housecoat.

Even so, Evelyn felt, Janet did herself no favours. Arriving back at the house, and seeing her husband's van, she had burst into tears and then refused, for all too many moments, to get out of the car and greet him. He was sitting in the van and must have seen her.

Evelyn did her best to rescue the situation. She waved breezily, then switched off the wipers so he wouldn't see Janet crying. "Now stop blubbing," she said firmly. "You're not a baby anymore." She dug around in her handbag for a handkerchief. "Come on. Dry your eyes. Now go in and be *nice* to him dear. And tell him I'm just *leaving*. I'll just get my case – no really, dear, I've kept it all packed up, it won't take me a moment. Now Janet: out you get. Go and give him a kiss. And *be pleased to see him*."

Evelyn did not see, and did not want to see, how the lovers greeted each other after their six-month separation. It was all rather touch-and-go, she felt, but there was nothing more she could do. It was up to Janet now.

By the time her son-in-law was in the hall, Evelyn had stripped her sheets from Mary's bed, straightened all the bedclothes on Janet's, picked up Janet's washing from the floor and retrieved Richard's pillows from the top of the wardrobe.

"Lovely to see you Richard dear," she declared as she deposited her suitcase at the bottom of the stairs. "What excellent timing. We've got the TV in the car and I had no *idea* how we'd get it in. We've just got it fixed at the shop. But now you're here... if you could just be so sweet... Mind the rain on it though: if it gets at all wet you'll have to let it dry before you switch it on. Even a spot mind – you can't be too careful."

While Rick was at the car, Evelyn tweaked Janet's hair and whispered to her firmly.

"You've got him all to yourself till the children get in. You must make the most of it. Get him a nice lunch because he won't have eaten. I suggest you cook the chops. Do all of them – I'm sure he'll like two. The children can have pilchards. Now remember, dear. You have to think of your *future*." She fixed her daughter's gaze till Janet nodded in meek acknowledgment of this truth. "So, when the children come in, give them half an hour with him while you make their tea. Then put them to bed. They'll get over-excited otherwise, and Richard won't want that. He'll want a nice quiet evening with *you*. There might be something nice on the television. Just a bit of relaxation *and an early night*. And make sure you make him welcome. You know what I mean, dear. In the bedroom. It's very important that you make him *welcome*."

Then a kiss on Janet's cheek and she was out on the drive, stepping onto the grass to let Richard pass with the television.

"Thank you so much, Richard, that's lovely." She smiled approvingly but noticed how he needed a haircut and his shirt needed ironing. It was blatantly clear that he hadn't been looked after. "I'd be really grateful if you could put my suitcase in the boot. And I'm terribly sorry I can't stay. If I'd known you'd be here this evening I'd have arranged things differently, but I've absolutely *promised* to get back. But I'm so pleased I didn't miss you completely. Janet dear, do say goodbye to the children for me."

It was satisfying, she felt, to have managed things so well.

\*\*\*

The boys, who had spotted their father's van as he drove through the village, then seen their grandmother leave and endured almost an hour of exquisite delay for the sake of retrieving Mary, greeted him with a veritable explosion of exuberance.

They flung themselves at him, they hung round his shoulders, they both talked at once, at a pace and volume that made comprehension pointless. Like puppies whose master has returned from long absence, they greeted him with no memory of betrayal and no burden of recrimination. In the passionate delight of his restoration, all the grief of their long abandonment was a dream forgotten.

But Mary, hovering in the doorway, still in her mack and boots, did not echo their exuberance. She was worried about the missing sock, and worse, her knickers. She wondered if she could get upstairs without anyone noticing. There would be dry things in the airing cupboard, but in the meantime she didn't want to take anything off.

And her father was there. Her father.

She knew she should feel something, but deep in her belly she was hurting, and higher up, where feelings should have been, she felt only numbness. She saw him as if from a terrible distance. He was sat in his chair, just where he used to sit, with the boys clambering over him. Somehow, none of it seemed anything to do with her.

It was her mother who noticed her, creeping towards the stairs with her head right down and her mack still on.

"Mary!"

Her mother would normally have been cross, because outdoor clothes weren't allowed upstairs. But today she came over and put an arm round her, and whispered in her ear as if she understood, and forgave. Mary suddenly wanted to cry.

"I know, poppet. I know. But it's all right. Now don't you worry."

Mary wondered, distantly, what it was that her mother knew. But it was obvious from her next words that she understood nothing.

"I know dear, but he's back now, and that's all that matters. Now he's just as pleased to see you as the boys, little one. Really he is. In you go. The boys just got there first, that's all."

And she started unbuttoning the coat as if Mary were a baby. Mary shook her away, but then her father turned and held out his arms.

"And my little girl!" he said, "Come and say hello to your naughty daddy. Come and give me a kiss." He pushed Michael sideways to make a space on one knee and patted it for her to come and sit.

Perhaps it was only because she had no knickers on that Mary could not do so. Or perhaps there were other reasons. Whatever it was, the very thought of such intimacy brought a tightness in her chest and suddenly she was crying out "No no no!" and pushing past her mother to the stairs. She ran up on all fours, threw herself into the bathroom and turned the key in the lock. It was quite forbidden to lock the door, and she had never done it before. Indeed, the key was only there because her gran was particular about privacy. But at that moment, the key was a comfort, and even when they all came upstairs and wheedled through the key hole, even when her mother got cross with her, even when her Dad said jovially that he'd have to call the fire brigade, even when Michael suggested they should knock the door down like they did in *Dixon of Dock Green,* Mary sat with her back to it, and would not let them in.

***

Verity Sneddon watched the last of the rain on the window as the light changed imperceptibly from teatime towards dark. In the corner was a place where the roof had lost a tile, and on days like this the patch of damp would swell pregnantly and eventually drip. There was a bucket underneath it and the dripping of the water made her think of going to the toilet, but she had done that when Mrs Fenner came, and would try not to go again till dark. It was hard to do it on her own, and she marshalled her strength carefully.

When it was sunny, the shadows moved round the room and she could tell the time by them. But when it was rainy there was nothing to look at, only the drips. She watched without interest, but intently, since there was nothing else.

Even the cats were meagre company. Two tabby cats slept on the end of her bed, and Snowy was draped on the dressing table. One of the tabbies was unreliable so the room stank of cat-pee. But the old woman never smelt it; it was only the visitors who complained.

The nurse came once a week to change the dressings on her legs. She was a nice enough girl and in an absent way, Verity quite looked forward to her visits.

But she would not miss her, if she did not come. Not the way she missed her son.

The departure of Ralph from her life, as unheralded as his return, was something that pained her. She had been rather peeved at the first of his absences, because the week before, just as he left, he had said "I'll see you next week then. I'll bring a nice pie." But then he had not come. Over the weeks that followed she had come to feel this betrayal – though she would never have said so, not even to herself – rather more intensely than the other one, all those years ago. What is closest hurts the most. There was a kind of backwards forgiveness in it.

She did not blame herself. She did not link his absence to the poverty of her welcome or the bitterness of her words. She did not feel that she owed him platitudes. *"I speak as I find,"* she had often said years ago – and with a certain smugness, as if cruel words were virtuous, provided they were true. Her ruthless honesty had not won her any friends – though to be fair, it never cost so many friends as that one desperate lie had done, standing in the courtroom. So perhaps truth really was the better strategy, all in all.

Truthfully, she thought he was pretty shoddy. It might have been shame that stopped him coming, which was a proper response but no excuse. And he might have been grieved that his father was not there, but that wasn't her fault and her widowhood only added to her claim on him. He had never been any good. He wasn't worth thinking of. Yet still she still wondered, every Saturday morning, if perhaps this day he would come again, and as the sun turned back in the afternoon, she felt regret. He had been such a good boy once.

So if it had been earlier in the day, she might have registered the footsteps. But her head was full of whispers and it was evening, when the house was cooling down and the staircase always creaked on its old timbers. And it was rainy that day, with a dripping bucket, and noisy pattering on the skylights. Even so, if she hadn't been drifting towards sleep, she might have put more store on the sudden friskiness of the cats. They never moved for the ghosts in the woodwork, nor for the rain, nor even for Mrs Fenner. She would have wondered, when they suddenly jumped from the bed and retired beneath the wardrobe, if perhaps he had come.

On that evening, however, she had long stopped listening for him. The sounds of the house were like a blanket over her, and she was drifting through thoughts about ham and fairy-cakes, and the rather grey stew that Mrs Fenner had brought, in a modern plastic bowl with a tight-fitting lid. Mrs Fenner was a dinner-lady at the school, and Verity occasionally wondered, uneasily, if there might be some connection. Certainly, the stews weren't the *best* cuts of meat. And they were always cold by the time she ate them. Perhaps she would ask for a pie instead, or a nice piece of tongue from the butcher. And in place of the dreary slab of suet pudding, a little shop-bought cake or a freshly mashed banana for a treat. In the evenings, when she was safe in her bed and Mrs Fenner had gone, Verity often made such resolves. It wasn't, after all, as if she were asking for charity – she paid Mrs Fenner the bulk of her pension, so she was entitled to some standards. But in the morning, when she was cold and vulnerable and invariably wet, she never got round to mentioning it. Mrs Fenner was all she had, and if it weren't for Mrs Fenner, the district nurse would put her in a home.

At some time that evening she certainly slept, and her thoughts gave way to broken dreams in which Ralph was home, and took her into the garden, and her husband was there, leaning on his spade and calling out to them, something about some pie and Ralph's bicycle and burying something. It may have been that in her dream she was riding the bike herself, because there was a moment when she suddenly jolted, as one does in dreams, and it seemed that she was awake again and her eyes were open.

It was, in its own way, a most pleasing dream. She dreamt that her husband was standing over her, in her bedroom. It was almost dark, but she could see his pale fawn trousers and the light checked shirt that was new when he died. He was looking down in a tender sort of way, not at all the hateful face that he had shown her, all the years from the trial until he died. And when she opened her mouth to speak, he put his finger on her lips and stroked her eyes shut again and whispered, "It's all alright... I'm sorry... I'm really sorry... Please... please go back to sleep". He spoke as a parent might speak to a child, and there was something infinitely tender about it, and she knew herself forgiven.

Except it wasn't her husband's voice that whispered, and it wasn't – at least, not quite – her husband's face. It was more like Ralph.

# 18. The Ties that Bind.

Ralph stood motionless. He watched the old woman in the bed and saw her face begin to settle again, then finally grow still. The lines that had tensed around her eyes relaxed, and her skin resumed the amorphous texture of old porridge. At last, her breaths grew slower and she started to snore again. She had not really woken. In the morning she would have forgotten.

The clock downstairs ticked quietly, and somewhere outside he could hear cats fighting.

He waited till at last she turned over. Then till her breaths grew quiet and slow, and with infinite care he bent again, and felt once more beneath her pillow. He tested the dark interior like a surgeon. But there was nothing. Nothing anywhere. There had been no envelope behind the clock, no bundle of notes in the tea caddy. He had carefully opened the great wardrobe in the corner and felt through its bundles of rubbish till he was sure that nothing was there. He had even lain on the floor, and blindly run his fingers down each slat of the bed base, feeling for anything under the mattress. There was nothing except a few protruding wires, and an unpleasant dampness. And now there was no money under the pillow, either.

There was always supposed to be money in houses, especially with old people. Old people didn't use banks. They kept it hidden in teapots or under the bed. The glib prison certainties had failed him, the only time he needed them.

He looked at her face. She was barely in her sixties but looked twenty years older. His mother. She had been a handsome woman, once.

Gently he pulled his hand from the pillow. There was a greasy coldness to it, even where her head was resting. The room smelt of piss, but this was a deeper, older dampness, that hung in the air and seeped into the rug. He thought of the slates on the roof, the peeling paint by the window, the mildewed stain on the ceiling. Her bedroom was the dampest place in the house. If things had turned out differently, he could have helped with that. But it was too late now.

*You ruined my life. You were never any good. I wish you had never been born.*

He had never considered the question of forgiveness, but he had imagined, arriving that morning in June, seeing her so broken, that perhaps he could be a use or a comfort to her. He had thought he could be dutiful and she might come, if not to forgive him, at least to remember him as he once had been, in the days when she loved him, before the fall.

He was so close now he could feel her breathing. He could see in the darkness her silvery hairs across the pillowcase and the tiny jewel of spit at the edge of her mouth. Gently he touched the worn stitches on her pillow: little flowers that he had traced with his fingers, decades past, beside her. Daisies. *She loves me, she loves me not, she loves me.*

She must have loved him, whatever the daisies said. The past flooded over him like a wave, snatching his balance. He suddenly longed to touch her cheeks, her earlobes, to climb into the bed and lose himself as he had long ago. He was tumbling through time, all the mess of all the years and all their darkness. He was just a boy, and it all had been a dream.

Without knowing why or what he did, his hand reached out to her face. For a second he felt her skin: the gossamer touch of his boyhood fingers on her throat, a little boy in the first exquisite stirrings of the heart. Then he looked from her face and saw his own arm.

Time ground on its axis, like a stone on broken glass.

The smooth skin of childhood had rotted away and where it should have been there was a dark, sickening thing, hairy and taloned. A hideous, predatory arm, protruding from an unfamiliar shirt and reaching for his mother's neck. On his wrist there was a smear of blood. The past is nothing.

He stood up, stifling his breath. He straightened himself and stepped carefully to the door. Whatever he was looking for, it was not here. There was nothing here to help him. The past is nothing. The knowledge that poisoned everything was nagging behind his eyes. He had to move on.

He thought of his bike, lying pointlessly in the brambles with its tank full of petrol. There were ways, he knew, to start a motor without a key. For that matter, there were ways to ride the trains without a ticket, to get money from strangers in the street. Dimly he searched his mind for the secrets of these things but he did not find them. The boy who had served at the altar and had left the world before he even found it, had learnt nothing in prison. His poverty was abject.

\*\*\*

Mary, at that moment, was not quite asleep. She was in her own bed, back in her own room, and she was feeling rather frightened.

Perhaps it was no more than the absence of her brothers' breathing, which she had grown accustomed to in the weeks of her grandmother's visit. Or perhaps it was the recollection of the day, oozing back through the cracks where she had tried to hide them.

Her room still had a little of her grandmother's smell and her grandmother's dressing gown, forgotten in the hurry, was still hanging on the door. Mary had seen it as her mother undressed her – but now she began to wonder if there was something inside it. Something not nice.

Bad things happen to girls who have been naughty, and she knew she had been naughty. It was naughty not to speak to her father, and to lock herself in the bathroom. It was naughty to put on clothes that weren't hers, so they'd have to be washed and ironed again. In the end, her father had climbed to the bathroom with a ladder and got in through the window. Everyone, by then, was very cross with her, because she was stubborn and selfish and was spoiling everyone's day.

For a little while her mother had crooned from outside the door. She had sent the others down and said she would deal with it, because Mary was just little and over-excited. At first, she whispered through the lock, then spoke in a little sing-song way. "Please little one, I know it's all a bit of a big surprise, but it'll be all right. Daddy really loves you. Please Mary… Be a good girl. Come downstairs and give him a kiss. For me, Mary, please Mary dear. I've got you some nice tea, and then it'll be bedtime. He really wants to see you. He says he'll read you a story when you're tucked up in bed."

But Mary wouldn't answer so her mother went downstairs again, and when she came back, she spoke rather more loudly and crossly.

"Mary, you've got to come out now… We've all had enough of this… Michael's waiting to use the toilet. Come on Mary, I'm ashamed of you… You must stop showing off… I don't know what's come over you…"

Mary sat behind the door, and it all seemed a long way away.

She had taken off her mack and all her wet clothes, and washed herself all over. It had stung a lot *down there* but she knew that Ralph had weed in her bottom and it was horrible. So she took the soap and scrubbed with it, not heeding the pain.

Then she had rifled through the airing cupboard, looking for something to wear. Above all she wanted knickers, but there were only some bloomers of her granny's and a pair of Michael's pyjamas. She put the pyjamas on first, then the bloomers over the top.

After that she found a vest of Colin's and two old socks that weren't really a pair. She put them all on, and then two petticoats of her mother's and one of her own cardigans. Each garment was an armour for her. She opened the towel box and took out all the towels. Sitting against the door, with the all the towels on her lap, she felt a little safer.

Her mother's voice seemed a long way away – her mother and her brothers, but none of them seemed to matter. Then there were voices outside in the garden, her father's voice, and the boys. She hoped they were going out. She wasn't at all ready for her father. She wanted to be left alone.

Then she heard the ladder on the wall outside.

Looking up, she saw the shape of hands on the window, then a horrible face distorted by the frosting. She stifled a cry though she knew who it was. He was calling to her, a horrible urgency in his voice.

"Let me in Mary. Please, just pull up the catch. Or the door Mary, just do the key. Be a good girl Mary. Do it for Daddy. Please Mary, just open up." Her throat constricted. She felt her body closing like a lock, her arms tight round her knees, her lungs gasping. She saw his face press against the frosted glass, and then his voice came crosser, more urgent. "For heaven's sake, Mary, just open up. I'll have to break in, otherwise, and you don't want that. You could get hurt."

A long, ugly, silence, then a banging on the window frame. Through the glass she saw his hands and some horrible implement in them. He was prodding the frame of the window with it, getting in where he wasn't wanted. Then a heaving and a groaning and a pushing and the whole of the frame fell forward, landing in the bath so the glass smashed to pieces.

She had screamed then, and had gone on screaming as her father pushed his body through the window and as he clambered from the bath and as he picked her up from the floor. She screamed as her mother dragged her to her bedroom, stripped off the clothes and put her into bed.

She did not doubt that her mother was right. She was certainly a very wicked girl.

All the same, she wished that they had given her a teddy. She had never gone to bed without a teddy before.

***

Ralph should, of course, have gone the other way. If he had really wanted, with the virtue of the angels, to spare Mary or his mother or even himself, he would have turned the other way – out past the front of his mother's house, along the road, under the railway bridge and on through open country towards Canningbridge. There were barns where he might have slept till morning. And a few miles further he would have reached the road to Guildford, where lorries passed and he could have hitched a lift. But he did not turn that way.

The way of the angels is cold and lonely, and even danger, snapping at the feet, cannot quite sever the ties that bind. The tongue is always drawn to the broken tooth. None of us is free.

When he was a boy, there had been fields on Heckleford Hill, just cows with their backs to the wind, and a few little trees. But now the new estate stood out like a beacon, glaring with horrible streetlights. The houses were modern, built of brick, with wide casements and garages at the side. Most of them had lights on, and in some he could see the cold unworldly glow of television sets. The people here had money. They were not like him.

One long road swept through the whole estate, till it met the backroad to Canningbridge, coming out of the village. Off this there were four or five little cul-de-sacs, all identical. Beside each house there was a little passage to a garden at the back. A few of the passages were gated but most gaped open into dark beyond.

Ralph's fingers played on his wallet, feeling the outline of coins beneath the leather. Seven-pence ha'penny. It would buy a meal if he wasn't ambitious, but not much more. Cautiously, he let himself think – only in the abstract, as if he had plenty of money and it were nothing to him – about how easy these houses might be. The smart modern doors would be locked of course. The cottages of the village would be easier and probably not locked, but he couldn't go there. Here, however, was anonymous. A door could be forced. A careless window might be left ajar. There was even a house with a ladder in the passage, propped on an upstairs window with the glass all out. The window was unlit, a rectangle of black against the lighter blackness of the wall. It would be easy. It was almost an invitation.

The men he had known in prison would have mocked his hesitation.

All the houses here were wealthy. The little pickings that were all he wanted would barely ruffle their complacency. Ten shillings would get him to some distant town and a dry bed and safety. For less than that he could probably find someone to start his bike. Who could begrudge his escape at so small a price?

But it wasn't money that he wanted. It was Mary.

She was there, on the estate, somewhere. He felt her closeness and scanned the gardens for a sign. Her scooter, perhaps, propped against a garage. Some familiar toy on the lawn or an envelope with a name dropped on the driveway. One of the houses had a name on a plaque: 'The Dawsons'. But there was nothing that said 'Crouch'. He had felt, at the least, that he would somehow know the house, that it would call to him. But there was nothing like that.

As a child he had dreamed that angels came to him. They had bright, eager faces like little girls, and they would dance out of doorways as he passed or fly through windows. They would circle around him, like little girls playing, or take him by the hand and carry him into the air. It was a shameful dream. Perhaps he had thought that Mary would come to him like that. Perhaps he had thought that they could fly away together, never to return. He had always been prone to girlish thoughts.

In the deep pockets of his father's coat, he clenched his fists and dug his fingernails into his palm. The rain dripped down the back of his neck. His rucksack, stuffed with his father's clothes, chafed on his shoulders. His twisted ankle was strangled in his boot. It was much too late, and there was nothing to be done. He had been stupid to come here.

He turned, limping back down the hill.

\*\*\*

Mary had been watching him from her bedroom.

Earlier, she had certainly been sleeping. Waking from a dream of unbearable desolation, her eyes had opened in the street-lit darkness to a huge yellow lion in the bed beside her. Its broad head occupied the pillow, and its feet were under the bedspread. This was undoubtedly a miracle, for she surely would have heard if someone had come in with it. She wriggled away from it and looked at it from the corner of her eye. It certainly wasn't hers. It was meant to be a proper lion like Aslan, but in its blind-eyed gaze there was something she didn't like. An Aslan that leered in her bed, in the night. She wondered if she was dreaming, so she shut her eyes and hoped it would go away.

The images of the day splashed round like shattered water. Perhaps they lured her to another sleep, for when she opened her eyes, there was another wonder. The lion had turned into the little white cat that Ralph had given her. It was lying on the pillow but was quite alive now, and big as a real cat. It was speaking to her. She felt she ought to listen, but she was quite distracted by its tail, which was purple and perfectly bald, protruding from its fur like a giant finger. As its words wove through her, she realised that it was not, as she had thought, a nice kind of cat, because the things it was saying were really very rude. She reached to push it from her bed, but it took her hand in a paw with human fingers and pulled her up the bed. It wanted her to do something, but she wasn't sure what.

Mary woke abruptly. She was sitting up, with the unfamiliar lion back beside her. Her elbow was jammed against the windowsill and one hand was clutching the curtain.

Then came the third miracle. She knew before she lifted the curtain that he would be there.

Perhaps there was something in him that called to her in her sleep. Perhaps she sensed the weight of his footsteps, the particular way that his presence disturbed the air. The sight of him standing outside was not quite welcome, but it had a quality of inevitability. Ralph's comings and goings had never belonged to the ordinary world, not entirely, but he had a way of being there, whenever she looked for him.

She stared through the window. She was wide awake now. The streetlight was just above his head and it caught him in its radiance. The blooded shirt was gone and instead he was dressed as he had never been before – strange clothes, with an old-fashioned grandeur. His coat was long and his trousers were pale. He looked like a bishop or a magician or the master of a circus. Only the rucksack was familiar.

He was staring at her house, scanning the windows. For a second, it seemed that he caught her eyes. His lips were moving but she could not hear the words. She thought of waving, or calling, but no movement came, no voice. As he scanned the windows, the streetlamp captured him. For a second, his face was transfixed by light and his wet hair glistened like a halo of sparks. There was something in the moment like the magic of communion, when the bell rang on the altar and God crept in through the bread and the wine. He had come for her.

The world shifted round on its axis, its meanings moving across each other, like boulders under the sea. And she knew in that moment that she had been entirely wrong. What had happened, had not, as she thought, been a horrible game. It was something else: a mystery, a secret, a magical test. It was something that no one else knew about, only her, only him. She was a secret book and he was the eyes that read it; she was the locked door and he was the key that opened it. She didn't belong to this house or to the stupid balding man who had climbed through the window and picked her up like a plaything. She belonged to Ralph. He had come to say that he would never really leave her. He'd weed inside her so she'd have a baby. Whatever she did, they would always be bound together.

She waited, because something was certain to happen, but then he bowed his head, and the light was gone. He turned and started walking up the road.

For a long time, after he had gone, she watched the space in the air where he had stood and formed the shape of him in the dark of his absence. And then, after a while, her head nodded and she lay back on the bed, and did not wake until the light came, cold on the counterpane, her hand on the yellow fur of an unfamiliar toy.

# 19. Church Going

There was, as always, a tiny red light over the altar, but it was not enough to see. Ralph let the door swing shut behind him and waited while his eyes adjusted to the dark. The smell of the church flooded back to him. The faint perfume of lilies and incense, the fusty aroma of old hymn books, then duller and deeper, the smell of stone, old hassocks and bat droppings.

There had been a time once when he knew every corner and cupboard of the village church. It had been his sanctuary and had lent him a certain importance. Ralph was first amongst the altar boys. It was always Ralph who stayed back after choir to put the hymnbooks away. It was Ralph who picked up the surplices and arranged them in the cupboard – shortest to longest, each on its own hanger. He was careful, and quiet and orderly. His hands would stroke the dust from the altar and rub the untidy trails of wax from the holy candlesticks. But he also swept the porch and cleared up droppings from the belfry. He wasn't proud.

The vestry key was still in its niche. There were matches there too, for the altar candles, but Ralph didn't need a light. He opened the cupboard where the vases were kept, and found the key to the organ loft, on its hook behind them.

The organ staircase led up from the choirstalls, in narrow, twisting steps not much more than a ladder. At the top was a tiny space, where the floor was just a board across a scaffold and even a child could not stand. It was there for the ecclesiastical engineer and his mysterious rites of maintenance. It wasn't a place where anyone else went, though Ralph had often gone there when the organist practised, to lie on the boards with his eyes shut, and to feel the music running all through his body and the walls singing.

And once he had been there after Sunday school, with Sonia.

In the old days he had swept this little eyrie every week. And just that once he had put flowers there. But clearly nobody had been there for years. As he knelt, thick dust fluffed into the air, tickling his throat. He took off his wet coat and laid it on the board. The coat would be filthy by the morning, but it didn't matter. If he'd wanted comfort he could have brought hassocks for a mattress, and armfuls of surplices for warmth. But he wasn't particularly bothered. He groped through the contents of his rucksack: Mary's blanket; the towels; a little bottle of water. He stretched himself, put the towels under his head and pulled the blanket over. And at last perhaps he slept.

\*\*\*

It was well past dawn before the first dim light, but Ralph had been awake for hours, lying in the dark.

He rummaged through his rucksack. He had eaten the pie for supper and would have welcomed a fairy cake, but Mary must have taken them. For a moment he pictured her: a square little girl, crouching by his rucksack, helping herself. The thought was reassuring. She would hardly have stopped for the fairy cakes if she'd really been upset. Perhaps she'd been quite happy about it really.

The urgent certainties seemed less obvious now. It was not clear, after all, that she meant it when she said she would tell. She had spent all summer with him, and she had not told. Something had happened that should not have happened and something had changed that should not have changed. He regretted it in a sense, or at least, some part of him felt that he wouldn't, if he lived the day again, have let it go that way. But it need not happen again, and anyway, had she not been, in a way, a willing partner? She had wanted it too; he was sure of it. She had led him on. Later, she'd pushed him away and shouted a bit, but girls did that. They didn't necessarily mean it.

He pulled the blanket back over, and let the scene play out in his mind, though certain moments of it he did not play. She had taken off her clothes and climbed into the bracken beside him. And she had let him touch her – indeed, she had held his hand, just so, keeping it there, where the wetness and the warmness told their own secrets. He played those moments over and over, and thinking of it he felt a glow of remembered excitement.

He did not let himself think of the moments afterwards. He had his passions but he was not, by nature, a violent man. Such moments had no pleasure in them.

It was the little dog's fault. If it had not been for the little dog, then it all would have been quite different. There would have been a gentler, tender time, afterwards. He had left her, not of his own wanting. And being left alone, and the day being cold, she had eaten the cakes then decided to go home. That was all. For a while, half asleep in the dark, he felt that perhaps it had been no more than an unfortunate disturbance, a little falling out, that in the passing of days would all go back to normal. It was only the problem of the motorbike that remained. In the morning he could find the key and then ride back to Mrs Gregory's. Then, in a week, Mary would be there again and he would tell her stories and they would play. He would have liked it thus. He wished her no ill.

But later, in the bleakness of daylight, he knew it was folly. As long as she lived, she could always tell.

Pulling on his boots, he felt the soreness of his swollen ankle. But perhaps it was no worse than the day before. Downstairs, he saw how small the church was, how much smaller than his memory. The low sunlight cut through the altar window and sparkled on the dust. Such dust! It would never have been like that, in the bright fresh days before the fall, when Sonia's mother cleaned the church. She had taken Sonia with her for a while, and sometimes, because Ralph was always hanging round the church, they'd done it all together. He thought of the blocks of beeswax and the sweetness of them on a yellow duster, and being helpful, and rubbing the altar till the wood glowed. But that was long ago. His tasks were quite without sweetness now.

He let himself into the vestry. Nothing there had changed. He lit the little burner and put the kettle on. In the cupboard under the hymnbooks there was still a box of tea, but all portioned out in tiny, netted bags which he had not seen before. He tore a bag open and made the tea as usual. There was no milk, but there was sugar and a tin of biscuits – unprecedented previously because of rationing. The world had more luxury now. After this fine breakfast, he carefully put everything away and left by the door at the side, going round the back so nobody would see.

It was half past seven and the morning already beautiful. On another day he would have felt the promise of it, the crispness of the air, the brightness of sunlight on wet leaves. But today, as he walked back grimly, he saw none of these. Each step still hurt his ankle, and as he walked through the plantation, he scanned the ground for the key. Then along the field and back to the empty den. After half an hour of fruitless picking through the reeds, he trudged back to the embankment. Painfully, he climbed up to the railway and scoured the stones for a glint of metal.

He found the place where he had lain among the ragwort. He even made himself search where the dog had fallen, which wasn't, in the end, as bad as he had imagined. The body had disappeared – taken no doubt by a passing train – and even the place where the blood had poured was almost clean now, washed by the rain.

He knew, before he left the place, that the mission was hopeless. The key was tiny and the stones were large. It could have fallen anywhere. He thought of the little cat with its emerald eyes, lying unseen for fifteen years. He thought of the mud that hid it now. He thought of the train, taking everything away. Everything.

In the end he was back at the road. He pushed himself through the tall weeds, into the little space where his bike was hidden. He looked reproachfully at the ignition. Other men could have done it without a key. Half the youngsters in the village probably knew how. It was a question of finding the right wires, twisting them together. He stared at the metal creature and tested the dull covers that hid its entrails. The metal plates were firm to his touch and it was not even clear how they might be removed. It was no good. He was no more a mechanic than a vet; he had no knowledge, no tools, no sense of direction. The bike was as useless as a dead horse.

It was worse, in fact. If anything happened, they would search the area and find it, an enormous calling card. It was registered in his name, a liability. He couldn't even get rid of it. If his foot were better he could push it down the road into Canningbridge, but it was several miles and a hundred people would see him – people from the village even. If he waited till nightfall there would be fewer passing, but anyone seeing might stop and offer help, and afterwards they would remember. And, anyway, even in Canningbridge, it wouldn't be safe. Perhaps in the night he could drag it to Whitewall Lake and push it in.

Angrily, he kicked a wheel of it, then took hold of the saddle and rocked it till it toppled. Then he pulled at the brambles and tugged them partly over. It wasn't any use. The metal gleamed through the tangle of thorns. Anyone could find it.

It wasn't yet nine in the morning when he got back to the church. He skirted the graveyard and found a place to wait, deep in the shrubbery near the lych-gate. The bellringers would be there by ten. At eleven there was Sunday School and the morning service. He had to be ready.

*\*\*\**

Janet spread a tablecloth on the kitchen table and laid the plates for breakfast. The children would have cereal but there was an egg for Rick. Bacon would have been nice with it, but it was no bad thing, she told herself, that there wasn't any. He needn't suppose they'd been living in luxury.

Teatime, unfortunately, had been somewhat spoilt – what with Mary playing up and Rick's finger getting cut on the window and bleeding on the towels. But from now on, she told herself, things could get back to normal. *Normal.* Whatever her feelings about Rick (and she certainly would not speak of them) the idea of 'normal' had a charm to Janet's mind. *How nice to be back to normal.* It was also particularly nice – though there was no one she could say it to – that her mother had gone.

She had, as instructed, made her husband welcome, and in the awkward intimacy that followed, he had apologised after a fashion. After that, he had lit up a cigarette and spilt ash on the carpet. Janet pulled a face, rather ruefully, remembering. She had chided only a little, because she remembered what her mother said and she was thinking of the future. But her mother was right, of course: he was a deep-down mucky man and she would have to live with it. She pulled the napkins from the drawer and thought about the extra washing, and then put an ashtray on the table in case he lit up after breakfast.

Halfway through breakfast, Rick asked about Sunday School. Colin immediately protested, because it was the last weekend of the summer holidays. Michael joined in and said it wasn't fair and nobody *else* would have to go to Sunday School when their dad had just come back. Rick laughed at this, and said it was a *particularly* good idea for children to go to Sunday school when their dad had just come back, and then he winked at Janet, which made her heart sink. She'd already made him welcome once and she never liked doing it in daylight.

She looked at Mary who had made a mess with her cereal and was staring across the kitchen with a blank little look. "I don't think Mary looks very well, dear," she said hopefully. "I wonder if she's really up to Sunday School."

Rick laughed again. "Not sickening are you, little cabbage?" He leant over and chucked her under the chin. "Come on – chin up for your Daddy."

Mary turned her head to escape his hand.

"It'll be good for you," Rick laughed. "Think of how naughty you were last night. It'll make up for that."

Janet glanced at him sharply, because they'd agreed, after Mary was asleep, that she was only over-excited and they shouldn't get cross in the morning. But it didn't make much difference. Mary's eyes were fixed on a spot just over the cooker, and her hands lay limply on the table.

"She *is* ill, too," Michael said quickly. "I think we'd better stay home and look after her. She's probably got 'flu. John's granny died of 'flu."

"And we might get it too," Colin added cheerfully. "We're probably infectious already."

Janet looked slyly at the two boys. "Well, it might be best..." she said. "A quiet morning at home for all of us. The boys could clear up their bedroom..."

Rick looked a little put out by that, and the boys decidedly dubious.

"Nonsense," Rick said. "And it's a lovely day. Go and get dressed all of you. Sunday best! You too Mary. Upstairs with you!"

\*\*

Mary clutched her attendance card as they walked down the hill. They were all supposed to have attendance cards, with their name and class on the front and a space inside for the Vicar's little stickers. The boys had lost their cards long ago, and anyway, they didn't care about pictures of lambs and palm trees and men wearing dresses. Michael had cut up a sticker of Jesus once and stuck the head and arms on the cereal box, so it looked as if he had fallen in a bowl of cornflakes. Even their mother had laughed, though she told them off afterwards.

Mary never did such things. She was a good little girl. She liked the pictures and the colouring and the songs and the bit when they all trooped into the church. On an ordinary day, she found it rather fun.

Today however, was different. She felt herself burdened by a new responsibility. She wasn't the same creature she had been before. And there was something about church that made her uneasy. She thought about Ralph, the night before, in his halo of streetlight. And of the morning in the den, and everything that had happened. She wondered what God thought about it.

She looked at the picture on the front of her card. It was Jesus, holding out his hands, and underneath it said *Suffer the little children to come unto me.*

Ralph had said that once. Ralph and Jesus.

The picture was the same as the one in the school hall. Jesus, like

Ralph, had golden brown curls. The good little children who had come to him were sitting round his feet and smiling. One of them was holding a little white lamb in her lap, like a cat. They did not look like they had suffered very much.

But there did, after all, have to be suffering.

Something strange was happening, Mary noticed, to the air around her head. The boys were right beside her, squabbling as usual, but if she looked at them in a certain way, they appeared to recede into the distance. She could hear what they were saying, but it seemed to be coming from the other side of glass.

She looked again at the card in her hand, and it seemed that Jesus smiled at her, a slow sad smile. It was becoming increasingly clear to her now, though the details were uncertain, that she was really very *special*.

They were passing the school now. A little way ahead, by the church, Mary saw Rita holding hands with a cousin, and just in front of them a family of Pavises, all with hats on.

"Do you think," she said slowly, forming the words carefully, "Do you think…" She wanted to ask if they thought God was watching, all the time, whatever they did, like the Vicar said. She wanted to ask if they thought Jesus really was everywhere, even here. She wanted to know what it meant when the Vicar said Jesus loved them, really loved them: Ralph had said he loved her, really loved her, and it occurred to her that it might be all the same. But even as she pondered the questions, she knew there was no point asking. Her family weren't special. They wouldn't know.

***

Ralph, at this moment, was squatting uncomfortably in a gap between rhododendrons and yew trees, deep in the bushes, with two ranks of gravestones between himself and the path. From his fragile hide, he had seen the Vicar trotting up in his cassock, and the bellringers following after. Then there was a pause before the bells started tolling, hesitantly at first, then growing stronger.

And, at last, the villagers came.

They came in twos and threes at first, with minutes between, then more of them, family groups and couples, stepping quickly down the mossy path of the churchyard, chattering past their dead.

Ralph knew them. Their faces called to him across the years and plucked at his eyes as if he still owed them tears.

Sneddons and Pavises and Fenners and Vardons, relatives by marriage, and relatives of relatives. There were aunties and uncles and cousins and second cousins; old men and women who in their prime had bought him birthday presents and attended his confirmation; children he had taught in Sunday school now wearing adult bodies, and children he had never seen but with faces still familiar – little ghosts from the future.

In the midst of them came a middle-aged woman with badly permed hair and too much makeup, who laughed as she rounded the corner, then dropped a cigarette on the gravel and ground it with her foot. He knew her at once, though he had not seen her since the night of Sonia's death, when she thanked him lightly for babysitting and gave him a threepenny bit.

As the woman neared the church, she turned and called behind. "John! John! Keep up can't you!" And a boy hurried up to her – a serious, wide-eyed boy, perhaps eleven or twelve, as beautiful as a girl. Ralph's heart missed a beat. The boy was marked with every angle of Sonia's features: the shape of her eyes, the turn of her neck, the pale, high forehead and straight dark hair. All that was missing was the little purple stain that flickered in his memory. Time tumbled into confusion, and he stared through the leaves, disoriented. The child was older than Sonia but Sonia had no brother. It was impossible.

But then the years made sense again and Ralph understood. Another child. A child out of time, a replacement. Sonia, had she lived, would have been a woman now. He wondered what life must have been for the boy, cursed with his sister's face – a substitute, second-best child, an empty consolation. Ralph glanced at the boy once more, then closed his eyes, unable to look.

Perhaps that was the moment when Mary turned the corner. He had not seen her walking behind the Pavises, but then when he opened his eyes, she was already past him. Two boys, no doubt her brothers, walked a step behind, blocking her from sight, and all around her were the stragglers, hurrying into church. He had waited there for nothing.

But it did not escape him that she arrived as she did, chaperoned only by a pair of little boys. If she had spoken, her mother would have kept her home, or walked beside her, looking around, guarding.

So in that moment he knew that Mary had not spoken – not yet – and the possibilities of escape twisted in his heart, like vipers.

# 20. Metaphysics

Mary had always gone to Sunday School, even in Croydon where the church was largely empty. In Heckleford all of the children went. The school in the village belonged to the church – built on church land, with the graveyard pressing on the playground fence. There was Religious Knowledge every Wednesday and Friday, and once a month the Vicar came and talked to them. But despite this pedagogic rigour, Mary had not, until this time, been quite confident in God. She had even suspected that He might be just pretend – like witches and germs and Father Christmas.

She hadn't ever believed in witches, not completely, or at least not for ages, and she had found out the previous year about Father Christmas, from Michael. There were various parallels between God and Father Christmas – not least their omniscience – so the discovery that one of them was pretend somewhat compromised the other. She would have liked to be sure, but when she tried to raise the matter one evening after school, her mother just told her to *stop talking like Michael*, which didn't seem to answer the question.

Grownups had whimsical rules, Mary noticed, about talking of such things. It was quite approved, for example, to deny the existence of witches, but it wasn't polite to do the same with Father Christmas, because grownups liked children to pretend about that. And if any child admitted that they didn't believe in *germs* – although germs were manifestly invented – then the grownups got cross and told horrible stories about germs coming up invisibly out of toilets and killing people.

Such prevarication on what was real and what was pretend forced Mary to draw her own conclusions. She rather resented this, since grownups must know and could easily have told her. What was more, their lack of candour exposed her to errors. She had been wrong, for example, about Germans, who appeared with regularity in Colin's *Dan Dare* comic, invariably malevolent and prone to killing people. Mary deduced, through rational comparisons, that Germans were really just germs drawn as men, so Germans, like germs, must also be pretend.

Later, at school, she had propounded this view and it had led to some trouble, and her teacher had said that *of course they were real*, and not to be so naughty. Men from the village – uncles and grandads of her classmates even – had been *killed* by the Germans. That was, she now knew, the meaning of the War Memorial.

She realised with discomfort how close she had been to the same mistake with God. Up until now He had never exactly spoken to her nor answered her occasional prayers. His interest in her life seemed slightly implausible and His invisibility – although not an insuperable obstacle – was hardly a recommendation. She hoped, in the light of recent events, that God had not looked to closely in her mind, because if He had done so, He might have spotted that she had been inclined to disbelief.

But that was past now. Mary's morning had passed in a metaphysical blur. The pain in places that she could not talk of was matched by unspeakable thoughts that swirled through her head and left her staring, not even hearing when her mother grew cross with her.

Everything that had happened from the moment when Colin threw the stone at the Angel until that morning in the den, was clear in her mind. But as she traced the course of it, she came to a fork in the path. Something important had happened whose direction was not clear. She could take one path and it meant that she had been terribly naughty all summer and, worse than that, she had been terribly wrong about Ralph. He was a bad man. He was not her friend. He had hurt her. She should never even have spoken to him. She ought to tell her mum and let him get into trouble. But on the other side, there were different possibilities: vaguer, stranger, calling her on with terrible siren voices. And as she stared at the pictures in the Sunday school hall, and groped in the air for meaning, things began to seem clearer. Everything was meant.

Most of all, there was the possibility of being special. She must have been chosen, just as her namesake had been. Mary and Mary: it wasn't a co-incidence. The thought promised vindication. Somewhere at the back of her mind, she had always suspected that she was special, though nobody else saw it. Now, letting herself think in certain way, she could see it must be so. For a moment she even thought, with a certain resentment, of times when other people ought to have seen it, but hadn't. It seemed possible now that God would show them, and punish them for it. She could feel the bitter, numinous magic of God's presence in her body, as palpable as the nagging discomfort between her legs.

It also, reassuringly, meant Ralph was special too. He had always been special. She had always known it. Everything that had happened was meant. The thought relieved her, cancelling amorphous fears, like a sweet rush of air after holding her breath.

She wondered what people would say when she had the baby.

*** 

Rita sat next to her in Sunday school and wanted to show her a little French-knitting doll that her granddad had made for her.

It wasn't just a cotton reel, like most of the girls had, but a proper wooden dolly, drilled all the way through with a little painted face. At the top, the tiny nails for the wool were lacquered gold, like a little crown. It was, of course, an offer of rapprochement, because any of the girls would have liked to hold it, but it was Mary whom she chose. In the ordinary run of things, Mary would have been enchanted.

Rita demonstrated, under the table, how the wool looped over the nails and how the thick woollen rope went all the way through and came out the other end. There was something about it, Mary thought, that wasn't very nice. A little girl with a hole all through. A rope of wool coming out from the painted skirts, like poo from a bottom. A crown of nails. A crown like Jesus. Everything suddenly seemed suffused with worrying meanings. She stared at the little dolly, chasing the thoughts in her mind.

There must have been something odd about her face, because the Sunday School teacher, who was cousin to the twins, suddenly leant right forward and spoke to her. "Are you all right, Mary?" she asked. "Was there something you didn't understand?"

The girl had a little Fuzzy-Felt board, with some cut-out pictures on it, of grownup Bible people and a bush and a lamb and a little child. She must have been saying something, but Mary couldn't think what it was.

"No... I..." She looked around the little class, trying to focus. But there was, of course, so much she didn't understand. "I mean, no, I didn't really understand," she said lamely. "The bit about... the bit about... the bit about Jesus."

There was a little titter around the class, and the teacher, Shirley Sneddon – who was only a teenager herself and not the brightest – looked decidedly put out.

"We weren't even *doing* Jesus," she said, and she tapped on the little board. "Look. This man is Abraham, and this is his little boy called Isaac and Abraham was going to kill Isaac to please God but God let him kill this little sheep instead." She tapped them each in turn, as if that might make it clearer. "So that shows you how kind God is and how he loves us and how he wants us to love him." She said it with a kind of finality, and then looked at Mary expectantly. "You understand now?"

"Yes," said Mary meekly, and she looked down at the table, though she didn't understand at all. The air was full of possibilities, and Mary clutched at them, desperate for an anchor. She wondered why Abraham was going to kill Isaac, and what the sheep had to do with it. It was, she felt, a funny kind of loving, that would be shown in such a way. She also noticed, as if it were connected, that the teacher's hair was just like Ralph's, but longer, and that it fell in waves, like Jesus's did.

"How did Isaac kill the sheep then, miss?" It was the girl with the calliper who wanted to know, and she always asked stupid questions. She was almost as bad as the boys, Mary thought – though everyone made allowances.

"With a knife," the teacher said, rather crossly, "How do you think?"

"You have to cut the throat," one of the other girls said firmly. She was a Sneddon, too, so she knew about things like that. "Then hang it up in a shed so the blood comes out. Otherwise, it's no good. After that you can skin it."

"But why did God want him to kill it?" The girl with the calliper never knew when to stop.

The little Sneddon girl glanced across the table and whispered, between her teeth, "For his yummy lunch," and then she giggled. Rita giggled as well then, and for a moment it looked as if the class might fall apart. Mary thought of Abraham afterwards, with the sheep's blood on his shirt.

"It was a sacrifice," the young teacher interrupted. "To please God." She looked around the hall as if seeking inspiration, then glanced again at her notes. "Now, anyway... let's get on. I've got some nice pictures here. You can all have one and colour it in. No more talking now. While you're colouring in, you can all think of the different ways God shows He loves you, and the things you can do to show Him you love Him back. Then it'll be time to go into church."

Mary took her colouring sheet and stared at it, long and hard. It was a picture of Abraham bending over Isaac, with the sheep hiding in the corner, behind a bush. The child was just lying there, on a rock, dressed in nothing but a little cloth round the middle, and the man was bending over with a wild sort of look, as if he might, any moment, rip the little garment off and do whatever he wanted. She thought about the moment before the knife fell, and of the little sheep that took the blow. She was also thinking about the little dog and the man who wasn't Ralph, or might have been Ralph, with blood on his shirt. *Don't move or I'll cut your throat.* Things were beginning to come clear to her.

Again she felt a churning in her belly and the sense that everything had secret meanings that nobody else, nobody ordinary, would be able to see. She was, after all, quite different from the rest of them. She sat in her chair, not picking up a crayon, not even trying to colour in. Distantly she was aware of Rita and the Sneddon girl and further away, on the other side of the hall, her brothers in their own class, and their teacher talking. But she couldn't look at them. She was locked in the picture, with Abraham and Isaac and the lamb, and Jesus who wasn't even in the picture, and the dangerous mysteries of love and suffering, of substitution and sacrifice. She tried, as instructed, to think of God and all the ways He loved her and all the things she could do to show Him that she loved Him back.

But whenever she tried to picture it, it seemed that God wore a leather jacket, and a blooded shirt, and that he showed his love with hungry hands and a terrible, urgent passion.

\*\*\*

"Now any more of this and I'll get your father to spank you," Janet said to Michael. "I mean it now. I've had enough of this. I'm at the *end of my tether.*" They were on their way home on the train, two days later, on the final day of the summer holidays. It had rained all day, and they had spent the afternoon in Canningbridge, buying sensible shoes and the manifold items of Colin's new uniform. Janet hadn't been happy in Canningbridge, not for a moment.

The boys were always difficult on the train. This time they were trying acrobatics, hanging from the luggage rack, and they'd almost kicked a gentleman who was getting off.

In fact, the children had *all* been dreadful. None of them was grateful for the money being spent on them. Colin got quite insolent about trousers from the Home & Colonial – which were half the price of the school supplier – and when they got to the uniform shop, Michael swung on the clothes rail and made the blazers fall down, right in front of the manageress. Then just after that, Mary insisted, for the third time that trip, that she had to go to the toilet. She was obviously *playing up,* so Janet told her crisply that she'd just have to wait, but then the manageress sent her to the toilet meant for staff, and said reproachfully to Janet that she was *just a little girl.* Janet felt aggrieved. Mary had been to the toilet twice already, in the public toilet and in Woolworths. All of it held them up, and she wasn't a baby.

\*\*\*

Mary knew it was shameful, the way she kept on weeing. It confirmed in her mind that Ralph must have weed quite a lot in her bottom, to account for all the extra wees she'd been having to do since then. And it stung as well, which her own wee never did, and made everything hurt even more. Mary had found blood on her knickers, twice, and had hidden them under the mattress. She knew she shouldn't mind, because it meant she was special, and it might be the same as the Blood of the Lamb which came up in prayers sometimes. But still she felt ashamed.

She wondered if her namesake had felt shame about Gabriel. They'd never said at Sunday School about him weeing in her bottom – but they did say she was frightened, and she protested at what happened, because she was only a young girl and not even married. Before, it hadn't been clear to Mary, but it was clear to her now. Perhaps everyone else had understood all along.

The events of Saturday played constantly on her mind. She wished she had understood then, as she understood now. She would have done better then. Things wouldn't have gone wrong. She thought of the angels, standing invisibly outside of the den, and of God being everywhere and seeing what she did. *Suffer the little children to come unto me.* She had not suffered it as well as she might have done. She had not looked heavenwards with sainted eyes and endured. She had not let him wee freely into her, as perhaps she should, as the other Mary must have done with Gabriel – so God might be disappointed, or even angry. A terrible regret flooded through her. She wanted to be good like the other Mary.

She was better than her brothers, anyway. They had wandered down to the other end of the carriage, and Mary could see them, from the corner of her eye, trying to peel the 'no smoking' labels off the furthest windows. She snuggled next to her mother and softly touched her hand. Even the Virgin Mary had been allowed to tell a cousin. She looked up at her mother's face. Perhaps her mother knew everything already but didn't want to say.

*** 

Janet, quite exhausted from the shopping, felt the tender touch of Mary's hand and was pleased she was saying sorry. She had, after all, been naughty all afternoon, which wasn't really like her.

"I do love you, Mummy," Mary said.

"That's all right, little one. We'll be home soon."

Outside, the fields rushed by, and the loops of the telegraph cables swished across rainy windows like interference on the television. Janet's eyes began to shut.

"Mummy?"

"Mmmm hmm?"

"About Saturday..." Janet's head was beginning to nod, and Mary stroked her arm. "But mummy... I wanted to... About Saturday... There's something I want to..."

Janet pulled herself up and tried to attend. Of course, it was all about Saturday really, all this naughtiness. It was Rick coming home that had quite upset her. She hadn't been herself since then.

She patted Mary's hand. "Don't you worry. I understand. But it's all going to be fine." Mary's look of relief confirmed her suspicions. Poor little Mary. She had been very naughty, and the tantrum she'd thrown had made things rather difficult. But Janet wasn't inclined to blame her. Rick wasn't *entitled* to a hero's welcome – if there had been any justice, they might *all* have thrown tantrums.

"But there's something.... I wasn't very... On Saturday... "

"I know, dear," she said. "But it's all forgotten. Nobody's cross with you. Everyone understands."

"But mummy... on Saturday... Something..."

Janet sighed. Perhaps they really did have to discuss it. Mary had been quite dreadful to Rick ever since he got back. She wouldn't go near him. She refused to sit on his lap and would barely sit next to him at table. She wouldn't even kiss him goodnight. Janet was clear in her mind that they had all been ill-used, but that didn't mean Mary could misbehave. Like her own mother said, they all had to think of the future.

"Now Mary, I know all about it. I know you're upset, but you shouldn't have pushed him away you know. I know it's not nice with him going off, and coming back like that, but he loves you very much, dear... Even when he wasn't here, he never stopped loving you. You must make an effort. I mean, it doesn't hurt – being nice... a little kiss..." Janet felt, as she said it, a certain twisting inside herself. She hadn't wanted to do little kisses, either. But it was what they both had to do; it was the female condition. So she squeezed Mary's hand and spoke more softly. "Sometimes we all have to do things we don't like. I know it's difficult now, but one day you'll understand... when you're a mummy yourself..."

Mary started at that and shuffled in the seat. So her mother *knew*. "But mummy... about Saturday... If I'm going to have a..."

"Now, not another word!" Janet held up a hand. "There's nothing to be sorry about. We're not going to say anything else about Saturday. You're going to be a good girl now, and it's all going to be fine. We're going to be a nice, happy family."

Walking back from the station, Janet thought of the article her mother had shown her, about how important it was to *talk* in families. She felt a little smug. Her mother was very clever of course, but it was all theoretical. Janet had never confided in her mother, the way Mary confided in *her*. That was because her mother never really *listened*. She was never really *understanding*.

"Come along sweetheart," she said, as Mary dragged her feet up Heckleford Hill. "Almost home."

"But Mummy...you know about *Jesus*...? You know about when he comes back?"

Janet wondered what nonsense they'd been telling her at Sunday School. She'd always approved of them going before: it gave her some peace to get the Sunday lunch prepared, and possibly taught them some manners. But suddenly Sunday School seemed rather unnecessary. And Rick had certainly been unreasonable about it. They weren't babies anymore. Michael already knew, clearly, and Colin probably. If all the children knew, then perhaps she could put an end to it. She wondered about saying something now, whispering to Mary not to worry about Jesus, because it was all just stories really. But with these thoughts, they got back to the house, and the boys were scrapping, and there was no more time for *girlish confidences*.

***

For three hours, in the rain, Ralph worked away at the den. Every branch, every beam, every piece of thatch. He carried the branches far into the woodland, to drop them here and there so they wouldn't stand out. Again and again he filled his arms and between each trip, he checked the path along the field. But there was no one.

He thought, though he tried to avoid it, of the beginning. The branches were fragrant then and the morning had been warm. Living branches and dead. The tying and untying of a knot.

Each time he stopped he felt slightly faint. He was hungry. He thought of the sugar in the vestry cupboard and wished he had brought it with him. Sugar would be something. He had eaten the last of the biscuits a day ago, and since then nothing except apples, not yet ripe, and blackberries from the hedgerow. For an hour, in the rain, he had fished in the river with a makeshift net, but he caught nothing. Once the den was gone, he told himself, he would try for a pheasant: at dusk they were stupid and it wouldn't be so difficult. He had trapped a pheasant once, as a boy.

When the thatch of branches was off, there were the cross struts, woven and tied. And then the heavy beams. Twelve great beams, from the original barn roof. Twelve times he squatted and then heaved himself upward, pushing the wood from the wall till it stood almost upright, then letting the huge thing topple back into the nettles and against old trees. By the end his shoulders were bleeding.

But it was done. The beams lay now like a criss-cross of bones, as if some great beast had died there. A dinosaur skeleton: a creature whose time had gone.

He looked round one last time. A tell-tale rectangle of battered earth. Nothing else. In a week the nettles would grow back and in a month they would be tall again.

It would all be clean then, and the page on which the den was written would have disappeared from history. It would never have been there.

***

It was not that he did not care about Mary Crouch. To be sure, he did care, though confronted with the certainty that she would talk, sooner or later, he cared more for his own life, for freedom. When he was younger he had thrown away freedom without even running. He did not know then what he knew now. He had sleep-walked into the solid darkness, open-eyed, unknowing. For a moment, remembering, he felt the dog-breath of prison grow close again; the infinitesimal slowness of flesh growing older; the years settling onto his eyes like dirt. But even that was life. A chill knowledge twisted in his head. *He was older now and they could hang him.* Even for this, which was nothing really. He had not hurt her and she had asked for it. Yet because she was a child, and because of what happened before, they could easily hang him this time. His life.

He would not throw away his life, not for Mary.

He sat under the wall and looked up into the trees. Then he shut his eyes, and thought himself backwards, finding the moment to which time must return.

History is not truth; history is memory and belief. Nothing had happened that could not be erased.

There was an afternoon in early June, when he had been at his mother's and a child had come chasing a cat down the lane, banging at the window. His mother had been upstairs and he told the child to go away. The sun was shining. His mother would remember the day, though she had not seen the child. That afternoon in June was good enough: it would not be so difficult to go back to there.

Nothing had happened after that. Nothing. He had never been to Heckleford after that.

Even as he thought it, he felt time turning backwards, shedding its load. He had from the start been a rather careful traveller. He had left few footprints. There was only the den – and that was gone now, waiting only for the nettles. Beyond that there was a little cat and a little doll, a sock with a hole, some torn knickers, and a little book with ponies. They were nothing but ashes now, ground into the earth. There had been, further back, a little card from Mary and a handkerchief, and intruding from another time, a golden cat with an emerald eye. But those were also gone, like ripples on water. They were nothing now.

Only his memories then, for a little while. Then nothing. He would forget. He would make an art of it. He would stifle all memory into a tightening space until all of that summer – as a million years can be compressed into a line in a rock – would be less than a hairline fault in the depth of his mind. He would forget that he ever met her. A secret memory, buried in one mind only, crushed infinitely small, is almost nothing. He would forget this summer. It would never have happened.

For a second, the infinite sadness of oblivion opened up before him.

The summer had been a beautiful thing, the happiest time of his life. To unmake that summer, out of all the summers in his bankrupt life – that was a sacrifice, and he felt it, exquisitely.

The consciousness of sacrifice is treacherous, corrupting. The sense of how much he was giving up, how much he would lose, was a curious strength to Ralph. Perhaps even Abraham, walking up the mountain with his son, had allowed himself to feel a little smug. Perhaps, as he lifted the knife, and thought of the child he would lose, he let himself believe that the sacrifice was his.

***

That evening, Ralph scratched up potatoes from the edge of a field, made a smoky fire and cooked them as well as he could. He would have pheasant the next day, he told himself. As night fell, he sheltered where a footpath went through a little tunnel under the cutting, wrapped in the blanket from his rucksack. The circle of sky, framed in the fronds where the footpath opened, was clear and full of stars. Long he lay awake and gazed at their brightness. Once or twice, incongruously, he thought of showing these stars to Mary, telling her their stories and seeing the wonder in her face. But then he remembered, sickened, and pushed the thought away. That was not what stars were for.

The comfort of stars was their infinite coldness and distance. Stars had a time of their own, in which the moments of human life were nothing. None of it mattered, none of it. Life, any life, was just a blink – a tiny movement that passed and was gone. All the battles ever fought, all the struggles of good and evil, all the human disasters and triumphs – they were nothing in star-time. And how much less was Mary Crouch than that? That was what stars were for. Beside the stars, what he planned was nothing, nothing at all.

## 21. The Invisible Man

The bread was buttered, the sausages in the oven. It was a special tea, because of Colin's first day at Secondary – but if the boys weren't back soon, it would all be spoilt. Janet was irritated. It was so *irresponsible* of Rick, taking them out after school, without regard for tea or homework. And they'd left Mary behind, not even inviting her. Of course, it was Mary's fault too, because she was still being dreadful – but Rick ought to make an effort.

Mary was sitting at the table, making something. She'd started as soon as she got back from school, cutting out felt from a kit she'd got at Christmas. When Colin came in, all full of his new school, she had hardly looked up, and when Rick suggested an outing, she'd stood up quickly and gone to the toilet.

There was a funny look in her face: teeth clenched and eyes intent. Janet had asked her twice what she was making, but she'd been quite unforthcoming. "Do you need some help, dear? Do tell me what you're making…"

Mary put her hands over her project, as if she didn't want to show it. "Nothing really. I'm just playing."

"Well, it's a shame to waste the felt, then."

Mary looked put out. "Well, I *am* making *something*. It's a sort of present for someone. It's just…"

Janet saw how Mary was biting her lip, and suddenly wondered if she was going to cry. She sat down beside the little girl. She wanted to say something helpful. "Men are difficult," she said at last. "You mustn't mind. And boys too. They're all the same you know." She waited for Mary to answer, but the girl just stared at the table, that funny look on her face. "But anyway, you really shouldn't think about it." Janet felt on safer ground now. *Not thinking about it* had always worked for her. "Just let it all wash over you. Don't take any notice. You're a very *special* girl, Mary. You're a very good little girl. And really he does love you. I know he does. And I know you love him too. But you need to show him, dear. You need to show him how you love him."

Mary looked up abruptly and almost smiled. Janet realised, with satisfaction, that she'd said the right thing. "You see? It'll all be alright. Now let's see what you're making. Is it a tiny dolly dress?" Janet couldn't think of any dolly quite so tiny so perhaps that wasn't right. "Or... or...". She dredged through the possibilities, wishing it were more obvious. Mary was easily offended at such moments. "I know," Janet said, getting desperate and wishing she hadn't started. "Is it a pin cushion?" She looked at Mary's face but saw no reassuring acknowledgement. "Well... It's very pretty, *whatever* it is."

It was, so far, a tiny little pocket the size of a finger. Mary's stitches were uneven and there were points where the thread had got knotted. But the two bits of felt had clearly been cut to a shape and stitched together in a purposeful way. And there were stitches in the middle which looked – though Janet couldn't be sure – deliberate. "And you've... you've embroidered on the front... Is that .... a flower?"

"It's an R," Mary said, with a note of irritation. "An R and some kisses. It's a little bag. It's a present."

"Well, that's lovely dear," her mother said. "It's very pretty. A present with an R on it. Now who could *that* be for?" Janet smiled, indulgently. Things were obviously improving. Her voice took on a teasing tone. "So, who do we know whose name begins with R? I think there's a very lucky man somewhere…"

Mary frowned, crossly, then caught Janet's eye rather slyly. "It's R for *Rita,* actually."

"Oh... Oh I see. Yes." Janet looked at Mary, trying to read her face. "Well I'm sure she'll like it. She could use it to keep... to keep... She could use it to keep really *little* things in. *Anyone* would like a little bag like that."

Janet turned back to check the sausages again. It was obvious from Mary's funny look that the sewing was really for Rick. She must have meant to surprise him with it. She made a mental note to mention it once Mary was in bed, and to tell Rick to be nice when she gave it to him.

*\*\*\**

Tea was rather spoilt by the time the boys got back, all three of them wet and dirty. Janet started to complain, but it did no good.

"We went down the newt-pond," Michael said, excited. Then he bent toward Mary and whispered "We were looking for your den. I was going to *smash it up*."

"But we didn't find anything," Colin added quickly. "Then we went down the lane and got blackberries."

"So I *see*," said Janet, reprovingly. "Look at the state of your..."

But Michael interrupted. "And we found a motorbike in the brambles – a good one. Someone's dumped it there!"

"It was all in the mud," Colin added. "In the middle of the bushy bit."

"But Dad and me got it up and I had a go on it... Vrrrrm." Michael made a gesture with his hands as if gearing up a bike and ran round Janet, pretending to ride it.

"Don't be stupid," Colin said. "He didn't really ride it, Mum. He just sat on it."

"Well that was naughty," Janet said. "It must belong to somebody. Honestly Rick, I'd have thought you'd have more..."

"No mum, it didn't belong to *anybody*," Michael insisted. "It was just in the verge where the blackberries are, in the long bit. Somebody must have thrown it away. I think we should bring it home..."

"Hang on, boy," Rick laughed.

"I hope that's not *oil* on your shirt," Janet said, pointing at his sleeve. "I just don't know what... Oh, and you too Colin! I'd have thought you'd know better! Your new uniform!"

"Anyway," Colin said, ready to change the subject. "After that we walked back down the other side of the railway. And I went in the woods and there was a fire..."

"A fire dear?" Janet looked sceptical. It had rained that week and was hardly the weather for campfires.

"No... it's true mum. A cooking fire. It was smoking."

"Dad said it must have been a tramp."

Janet looked outraged. "Well I hope you didn't touch anything! Honestly Rick, I think you could have tried..."

"No mum, no... we didn't even see him. Must've legged it when he heard us ...But he'd been cooking something, we saw it."

"...a little chicken on a stick. A stick up its bum!" Michael made a rude gesture to illustrate his point, then did it again and laughed so much then that he fell over and rolled around the floor. Colin kicked him.

"I think I've heard quite enough," Janet said firmly, taking charge at last. "I can see it's very amusing going round the countryside interfering with other people's property but I'd be pleased if you'd just go and wash your hands so that we can get on with our tea. You too, Mary."

Upstairs, the boys ran the tap as usual, to make it sound like they were washing their hands, though they never did. Mary *really* got her hands wet, just to show them, and she quizzed them about their tramp. But they didn't seem able to focus on her questions. The boys were stupid and didn't understand *anything*.

*\*\*\**

The next day, her second day in the Juniors, Mary got in trouble for not listening to the teacher. It was a bit of a shock, because Miss Vardon, who had taught her before, had never told her off. At the most she had tutted because Mary was 'a bit of a dreamer', but Miss Vardon knew she was a clever girl really. Sometimes, when the others were being slow, she had even given Mary a reading book, to keep her occupied while the others caught up.

But her teacher in the juniors, a man who wanted everyone to know that he had been in the war and commanded *men*, was different from Miss Vardon.

Mary had finished her sums, and was staring out of the window, looking towards the church. She thought she had seen someone, darting behind the row of trees between churchyard and playground. It had only been a second, but her heart had fluttered, a mixture of pleasure and fear. It could have been him. It was brown like him: brown clothes and a certain way of moving. But then it was gone. It might, she thought, have been something magical, like when Jesus appeared to the disciples after Easter, magically there and then magically disappearing.

When the teacher spoke her name, she heard it, in a way, but only as she might hear birdsong, or traffic in the distance, or grownups talking about things that didn't matter.

Then he threw a piece of chalk and it hit her on her face, and she suddenly turned, and said, without thinking "Hey – stoppit!"

This added the crime of *bolshiness* to her initial inattention, so he made her stay in at playtime and write lines.

> *I must attend in class. I must not be rude to the teacher.*
> *I must attend in class. I must not be rude to the teacher.*

Mary was both mortified and aggrieved. It wasn't that she minded missing playtime in the rain but she had been thinking about important things and she was a special child, a chosen child. The teacher had started it by throwing the chalk, which he shouldn't have done, so it certainly couldn't have been rude to ask him to stop it. No doubt God would punish him for it sooner or later. Mary was a good girl. She had never been kept in to write lines before, not ever.

By lunchtime, Michael had heard about it and said something mean in the dinner queue – which was useful in a way because it gave her an excuse to say she wasn't going home with him.

Michael hissed back that he didn't want to, anyway. He didn't care if she got run over. In fact, he hoped she *did*. He was going back with the Fenner boys. They were going down to the station to wait for Colin, and they didn't want girls there, anyway.

Mary smiled to herself, satisfied. If Michael dawdled a bit and played by the station, she might get back in time to meet him, and then they could arrive back home together as if she'd been obedient. Or maybe she wouldn't, but she could say was his fault.

After the bell rang, she waited in the toilets till the chattering had finished then went to the gate and looked along the road. True to his word, Michael had gone without her: she could see him in the distance, mucking about in puddles with the Fenner boys. So she turned and went out through the churchyard, past the vicarage, down the road towards the War Memorial and into the lane.

The sky had cleared now, and the puddles were shiny. In her satchel, inside her pencil box, in the special compartment reserved for rubbers, Mary had the Key to Happiness in its little felt case. Several times that day she had taken it out, and magic had almost vibrated from it. She could sense it now in the satchel, jogging about on her back as she walked. The Key to Happiness. She hadn't, she told herself, *stolen* it. She had only borrowed it to make a cover for it, because it was precious. She would return it to him now, with the cover as a gift. The tiny felt bag was a perfect fit. When she'd started the embroidery, she had been thinking of the hassocks in church, with their beautiful crosses and roses. It hadn't, she felt, worked out quite as nicely as she'd imagined, but it was still embroidered and anyone sensible would be able to read the R.

She did not doubt that Ralph would be grateful and she thought of him bending down to take it with a solemn smile, taking it from her hand, perhaps picking her up to give her a kiss.

She could not help wondering what would happen next, but she tried to think of other things. *You really shouldn't think about it. Just let it all wash over you.* Her mother was probably right about that.

Or perhaps not.

Without meaning to, she thought of his hands, and felt again a curious burning low in her belly, in secret places. The discomfort that had troubled her for several days had largely subsided and though she still felt something like fear, it was mixed with other things. It had, after all, been part of something larger and important. She had been frightened at first, but that was a mistake. Ralph was her best friend ever. He loved her. Even her mother, who wouldn't talk about it, clearly knew and understood. Whatever happened would happen because it had to. He loved her. He wanted her for his own, whatever that meant.

She thought of him touching her skin, teasing at the elastic of her knickers. She thought of everything she had felt at first as his fingers slipped down to secret, special places. Remembering disturbed her a little but she set her teeth firm. She would let him touch her if he wanted to. She would let it flow over her, like her mother said. She wouldn't cry out. It would be what God wanted. *Suffer the little children to come unto me.*

Then she thought of the other thing, the thing that had hurt.

*"I come not to bring you peace but a sword."* It was written on one of the posters in the porch of the church. She thought of him poking her with his willy, between her legs, getting it in so he could wee in her. He had done that now, so he wouldn't, surely, need to do it *again*. Remembering was horrible, but there was a kind of fascination in it. She had found, several times in the last few days, that if she started to think of it she couldn't stop and somehow she had to go on thinking it, and then someone would look at her strangely and she would worry that they had guessed what she was thinking about. She had that feeling right now though there was nobody looking at her. She looked round quickly, just to check, but there was nobody. Nobody.

She did not doubt that he would be there at the den, though it was strange to think of him there on a Thursday. It was clear from what the boys said that he hadn't gone back to Slough. His motorbike was hidden up the road by the railway bridge. He must still be living at the den, making campfires and waiting for her. This also explained, she thought, why she'd kept on feeling that he was somehow close by her, that he was there, just behind her, almost touching her. He probably had been. Perhaps invisibly even, like Jesus.

She climbed the fence and walked along the side of the field. When she got to the grave, it looked as if someone had tidied it. The stones round the side had been straightened up, and there was a feather in the top. It must, of course, have been Ralph. She smiled at his whimsy.

There was something else different though. She climbed the fence in the usual place, but the little path they'd worn there was completely blocked. Brambles had somehow arched across the way. Nettles had tumbled over the path. A few feet down, a branch had fallen, just like the one that had fallen by the barn. It was all very odd.

Determined, she pushed onwards, though she lost the path and came out further down than she intended. After that, she wasn't surprised when the branch had reappeared across the path beside the barn. It had obviously been windy. She climbed through the branches, getting a little scratched as she went. Then she saw.

The carpet of pine needles was all kicked away. The stones that marked the path weren't there anymore. And even before she turned the corner, she knew from the light that something had happened to the den. She walked to the corner, and then stopped. That other Mary, coming through the garden to an empty grave, could hardly have been more appalled.

Whatever enemy had done this had been utterly remorseless. The destroyer had left nothing. Everything was gone.

Suddenly she was running, pushing back through the branch, panting down the side of the barn. She could not go back through the plantation. So she ran into the field where the corn lay flattened. She did not want to be near the trees.

At the end of the field near the stream was the place she had always wanted for the den. Perhaps even then Ralph had known there might be enemies. He had always wanted to be hidden and perhaps that was why. Whoever had done this would clearly stop at nothing.

A sentience of deep magic stirred inside her. Manifestly, what had happened had been part of a terrible struggle, a conflict of forces both visible and invisible. She thought of *The Lion, the Witch and the Wardrobe*.

Perhaps it had killed Ralph too.

This thought, which might have instilled a new terror, was curiously reassuring. Mary was virtually a stranger to death. One of Rita's aunties had died and much was made of it, but after a little while Rita seemed quite cheerful. Michael, back in Croydon, had a fish from a fairground, which had festered for years in a bowl till it finally expired. Beyond those limited contacts, death was a storybook thing. Wicked people in stories were regularly killed and sometimes most gruesomely – which wasn't a matter to worry about. When good people died – though it was usually quite affecting – it was invariably temporary and generally presaged a *happily ever after*. Aslan had been killed by the Witch, Jesus by the Jews; the Beast had died of love. Ralph in Mary's mind was all of these, so it naturally implied that if he were dead then it wouldn't be for long and a *happily ever after* would be just around the corner.

At another level it also meant (though she wouldn't for anything have spoken the thought) that it was all just a game.

So as she hopped from stone to stone across the stream and clambered the fence to the footpath, the terror that had gripped her was becoming more manageable. To be sure, she still felt the thrill of its hold – she could not at that moment have gone back to the barn. She still felt the excitement of nearby evil and the tragic frisson of a friend who might be dead. But behind it now at some other level there was a grounding sense of safety. What would happen next, what she would find or do, was all to be discovered – but the ordinary world was still there waiting and there would still be tea and bedtime in the usual way.

The path was a long way round compared to the plantation but she knew the little tunnel where it went under the embankment, and from there it went back to the road beyond the bridge. She guessed this was where the boys had walked just a day before. She scanned the territory for a sign of Ralph, not omitting the places where he might be dead in the grass. If she found him thus, she would certainly kiss him, like Beauty with her Beast. Her mother had been very clear about kisses and perhaps that was why. But she wasn't surprised when she did not find him.

Back at the road it was all familiar. Ahead was the bridge and beyond it the cow-field. The verge was wide and the weeds and brambles were tall. It was natural, she felt, that he had left his bike there. It didn't take long to find it.

In the secret clearing she squatted down and gazed. It seemed a vast machine, infinitely male. She did not try to lift it but she stroked the raindrops from the saddle and touched the black handlebars. She thought of the first time, at the witch's house, when he had kicked it into life and there had been dust and roaring and then he was gone. The wet bike smelt of grease and leather. It smelled like Ralph. Suddenly a yearning overwhelmed her. He could not be far away. He had been there yesterday, when the boys had found his fire. Whatever had happened he was close by somewhere. He needed her. She felt his presence everywhere. An invisible man.

It clearly meant something, all of it. She struggled in her mind for the meaning.

She wasn't supposed to walk along the road. She ought to have climbed the fence and walked round the far side of the field to the lane. But that would mean walking in the direction of the barn. She walked by the road past the witch's house.

When she got to the house she stood for a while at its gate. There was a little brick path to the door at the front but it didn't look used. She walked round to the lane where the back door was. Under the window where she had climbed that first day, there was a big green bicycle that looked slightly familiar. A lady's bicycle. She looked at it, puzzled, then peeped through a crack in the back gate. She saw the path to the door, and a stripy cat with two black kittens. Encouraged, she was about to push it open, when there was a rattling from the house and a shadow behind the door. Then, to Mary's astonishment, there was Mrs Fenner the dinner-lady, coming out with a bowl in her hand and a laundry bag under her arm.

Mary bent behind a bush and squeezed herself under. It was damp and prickly but she didn't want Mrs Fenner to see her. Mrs Fenner would know who she was and would ask what she was doing. She might even mention it to her mum.

She watched as the woman tied the laundry to the carrier, climbed onto the bike and rattled back to the road.

Mary hesitated for a moment in her hiding place. Up until then she'd sensed magic in her path. Near the road she had let herself feel that Ralph was calling from the house, wanting her to come. But the unexpected appearance of Mrs Fenner, with a grubby bowl from the school canteen, had quite undermined the moment. It seemed suddenly unlikely that Ralph could be there. He could hardly be in a house with Mrs Fenner there: they didn't belong to the same world at all.

And anyway, she might be late and she should be getting back. She crept out carefully from her hiding place, but as she did so, two things happened.

Her satchel, almost forgotten on her back, snagged on a little branch, disgorging its contents. Pencil case, pencils, the last of gran's inedible apples. And all on its own, like a spot of blood in the afternoon sunshine, the Key to Happiness in its little felt pouch. She reached and held it in her hand.

As the very same moment, there came a sound from high on the fence across the lane: the sound of Snowy's meow. He was there, watching her, looking at the key to happiness, calling her to the house as he had done before.

***

It must, Verity thought, be Mrs Fenner, come back to apologise.

The question of the dinners had come to a head. Verity Sneddon had found that day, in the sludgy gravy at the bottom of her stew, a repulsive chimera that turned out to be a little girl's hair-slide and a number of hairs. Since Mrs Fenner only had boys at home, the conclusion was inescapable. Verity fumed all afternoon. She knew Mrs Fenner was a dinner-lady. She had never much liked Mrs Fenner's dinners and now she knew why. She had paid for quality but got nothing but slops, either stolen from the children or perhaps even worse – maybe scooped from the pig-bin. Either way, the woman was a fraud and a trickster and a violator of trust. She should be reported to the police, to the council, to the headmaster. Even to the district nurse and to Public Health at the council. Slops from the children. It was a wonder that Verity had avoided dysentery. It was scandalous. The woman was a criminal.

By the time Mrs Fenner arrived to take the dinner things, the old woman had worked herself to a state of outrage. All the resentments of her abandoned old age found form at last in this disgusting betrayal. When she heard Mrs Fenner at the door, she pulled herself onto the side of the bed and was ready with a barrage of complaint that would, in any proper world, have reduced her betrayer to ashes.

But Mrs Fenner gave as good as she got. She had never, she said, been so insulted in her life. The hair-slide must have come off Verity's own head. In fact, she recognised it. She had seen it in Verity's hair, just the day before. The district nurse must have put it in. And her cooking had always been good enough for her family but since it wasn't good enough for Verity then of course she wouldn't bother any more. She didn't care if Verity starved, if good home cooking wasn't good enough. In any case the job was more trouble than it was worth – it was almost a charity and if Verity thought she could do better without her she was welcome to try. Then she pointed out that the bed was wet again and it was the second time that day. Even the sheets were a kindness since they'd come from Mrs Fenner's linen drawer out of the goodness of her heart, because Mrs Sneddon made so much washing that she couldn't keep up with it. But since nothing was appreciated, she'd have the sheets back, and in future Mrs Sneddon could make her own bed or lie in her stinking wee – it was all the same to Mrs Fenner.

So without any ceremony she swung the old lady onto the commode and stuffed the wet sheets into the bag. She didn't remake the bed. "You needn't think," she said as she stood in the doorway, "that I'm going to come back. I've had a bellyful this time. I've done my best for you and it's more than you deserve. And I've taken some stick for doing for you, I can tell you. There's not many in this village that would help you out, believe you me. But I've had enough now. You can go into a Home for all I care."

At that moment, as Verity heard the footsteps on the stairs, the awfulness of her predicament seemed no more than a rhetorical flourish. The woman couldn't seriously be walking out on her, leaving her there on the commode and not planning to come back. The district nurse wouldn't come again till Monday and no one else would visit. She didn't have a phone or any means to summon help. She could swing from the commode to the bed, but the bed wasn't made and the blankets were on the floor where she wouldn't be able to reach them. She could get, with some difficulty, to the doorway, but she could never get downstairs. There was a cup of water on the chest beside her bed and after that *nothing*. It was a death sentence. Mrs Fenner couldn't have meant it.

So, when she heard the tentative turning of the door handle and the squeak as the door came open, she assumed it was Mrs Fenner coming back to say sorry. It had been a nasty trick to scare her but she couldn't have meant it. She must be coming back, shame-faced, because she had been so unreasonable.

The cats had already disappeared with all the shouting so they weren't on the bed to tell her any different.

Halfway up the stairs the footsteps stopped. Verity wondered what Mrs Fenner was playing at. Her rage had evaporated now. It was only a storm in a teacup. Perhaps Mrs Fenner had been right, after all, and the hair-slide *had* been hers. In any case she'd probably been unwise to make accusations. It might be better to be a little conciliatory.

"Oh, come on," she called out, impatient now. "Just come up here. I know you didn't mean it."

She heard one more step and then silence again.

"For heaven's sake!" she said. "Just come *up*." But there wasn't a sound.

She was irritated now. The woman was playing hide and seek, sneaking up the stairs and pretending not to be there. She was trying to frighten her. *I can't be doing with it,* she said to herself. *I'll show her.*

She pulled herself to standing. Every step was painful, but she had to do it. It was two steps to the doorway and as she took the second she heard a sharp intake of breath from the person on the stairs. And she knew in that moment that it wasn't Mrs Fenner.

Verity Sneddon stumbled the last step to the doorway and stood, clutching the doorframe and peering into the shadows. It really wasn't Mrs Fenner.

It was a muddy child, a little girl, no more than seven or eight, standing on a step near the bottom of the stairs with a curious look on her face.

Verity stared. The child didn't look malevolent. She didn't even look hostile. Children sometimes came to the house but only to torment her with stones at the windows or bangs on the door before they ran off laughing. They never came in. None of them would have dared to. Perhaps the girl's arrival was lucky. Perhaps she could send the child to the surgery to get someone to help her.

From top and bottom of the darkened stairway the woman and the girl stared long and hard at each other, sizing each other up. At last, the child spoke.

"Is Ralph here?" she asked, dropping the words into the silence like stones into a well.

Perhaps she saw the horror in the old woman's face because she went on quickly, in her best polite voice, as if to reassure her. "It's all right, I'm Ralph's friend. He plays with me. I've got to give something back to him. But I'm sorry if he's not here. I can come to see him some other time. I didn't mean to bother you."

In that moment all the years collapsed in Verity's eyes, into a single point of darkness. She looked at the child, the little vixen, standing in her house, on her stairs, breathing her air. A little girl, just that age, *a little friend of her son.*

And the last of Verity's courage and the last of her breath coalesced into a single cry.

"Get out! Get out! You filthy little... filthy little *whore!* Get out of my house!"

The child was down the stairs and out of the door before the cry was over. She did not hear the woman fall.

## 22. Cold Blood

History is not truth; history is memory and belief.

It was a matter of local history that Mrs Fenner had been something of a saint, in her care of Verity Sneddon.

Mrs Fenner didn't come from the village, so perhaps she felt the evil less intently than the others, whose memory flowed in the blood. But even so, her husband was half Pavis so her sons were cousins to the murdered girl. It must have cost her something, day after day, year after year, tending the witch who had spawned the monster, and had lied to protect him.

As if proof were needed, her sanctity was confirmed by the fact that *on the very day* when the old woman died, Mrs Fenner had a vision, or at least a premonition. She had left the old lady in bed as usual – as she explained several times to anyone who would listen – sitting up nicely with a sandwich for her tea. But then in the evening, halfway through the news, she got this funny feeling and felt the need to check her.

She never went after teatime in the usual way. That she felt such a call, on that night of all nights – albeit too late to help the old witch – was manifestly proof of an exceptional compassion.

Such was the local history.

And certainly, in her own eyes, she had always been faithful. Verity was an ungrateful woman, but Mrs Fenner had stood by her. She had never complained about the sheets, though she only had a mangle and had to wash them all by hand. And whatever the provenance of the dinners, she could vouch they were nutritious and hygienically prepared. Verity's words had been deliberately insulting – and a little girl's hair-slide, after all, was not something *dirty*. Such a thing could have happened in a restaurant even. It was hardly the end of the world.

The body was twisted at the bottom of the stairs, cold in a puddle of blood from the wound on her head. Perhaps in those first shocked seconds Mrs Fenner blamed herself.

But quickly she put such feelings from her mind. The woman, she told herself, had always been perverse. A desperate venture down the stairs had been quite unnecessary – she'd only been left for an hour or two, and there was everything she needed in her room. And anyway, she must have known that she wouldn't *really* be abandoned.

Thus thinking, the woman made peace with her conscience. Nobody knew what had passed between them, and nobody needed to. A secret memory, buried in one mind only, crushed infinitely small, is almost nothing.

She pulled a rug over the body so she wouldn't see the eyes, then stepped carefully round the blood, and went upstairs to the bedroom. She made up the bed, but ruffled it as if someone had lain there, and put Verity's glasses and an old Woman's Own by the pillow, as if she had been reading. She emptied the commode and opened a window to let out the smells.

Then she went to the chest by Verity's bed and felt for the old camisole where Verity hid the change from her pension. She carefully scooped up the notes and the coins and put them in her handbag. She had, after all, done more for the old lady than she'd ever been paid for and it was really no more than wages in lieu of notice. Her husband was, for that matter, related to the Pavises, so she owed them compensation. And no one would want her *heir* to benefit.

After that she washed the dishes and cleared up the kitchen. She wouldn't like the doctor to think she'd been remiss. There was still a nasty smell but the house was always damp and the lady was incontinent, so a bit of a smell was hardly her fault. At the end she chased out the cats. It wasn't nice, she felt, to leave them with the body: they might walk in the blood – or worse. They might, it occurred to her, be something of a problem. Nobody would want a cat from that house. She might have to get her husband to drown them.

Outside, the rain had stopped and the air was fresh. She cycled round to the doctor's house and told the story to his wife. It had been, all in all, a rather emotional day, and she cried a little as she told her tale. She was fond of Mrs Sneddon, despite everything, she said, and she'd been *so well* when she left her earlier.

***

To be properly understood as accidental, and to arouse no suspicions, a tragic event must evoke an obvious story. Those who come to it afterwards must see in the dust a clear road that has led there, spoilt only by mistakes that anyone might have made, or a bolt from the blue, where the blue is nothing unusual and the bolt bears no fingerprints.

It was around the time when Mrs Fenner was talking to the doctor's wife that Ralph finally settled on a spot.

He had assumed that he would take Mary up the embankment, from down by the grave. If he took her that way, even if she came unwillingly, its very familiarity would calm her; she would be less likely to protest. It was also a place that was known to her brothers – they had been to the grave, so they knew that she played there. Yet each time he rehearsed it, he found more things wrong. It was much too close to his mother's house, to the den, to the place where old man Pavis might remember something. There was also the question of the motorbike – he had to get rid of it, but in the meantime, it might have been seen. It was all too close. Even the curious grave – it had satisfied her brothers but might, in the searching gaze of adults, provoke too many questions.

So in the end his thoughts turned down the track, to the other end of the village, towards Oatham Park.

He walked in a careful detour, keeping amongst trees, behind hedges, off the road. He checked at each turn for lines of sight, because that was the way he would walk with Mary, their last walk together.

He thought of her, walking beside him – trustful and chattering perhaps, or possibly reluctant. Then an image came to him, a composite of all the walks they had taken together, through all the Saturdays of summer. The memory twisted inside him. He felt the pain of what was coming like a cold hand on his throat. He felt pity biting at his eyes, though as much for himself as for Mary. The task was vile and he would not have chosen it.

It was inevitable now. There was no other way.

He passed the fork where the track led to the Farm. As a little boy, he had walked that way often – reluctantly, for endless parties with the cousins. But as a teenager he had taken the other fork – over the bridge, across the railway to the open country beyond.

When people found it, the story would need to seem obvious. Mary's brothers were regular visitors at the Farm: she could easily be looking for them. And once before she had followed a cat down another lane – her brothers knew that, and might mention it. A little girl, following a cat or looking for her brothers, might end up here as naturally as anywhere.

He stopped on the bridge and looked down to the railway. Very little had changed. There was still the slight gap at the edge of the bridge, and the faint path beyond, leading down the cutting. Near the line there was the little brick hut with its corrugated roof. It was something to do with the railway, and the space behind it was dark and secluded. It would do well enough. He pushed through the gap and walked down.

When he reached the little hut, the metal door that had been locked all the years of his childhood, was half off its hinges and gaping open. That would be even better. Ralph peered inside. It was empty and smelt of mould and piss. Mary wouldn't like it, but she would run in cheerfully enough, to see what was there. Ralph thought of the moment, and for a second the revulsion tightened round his chest. But it wouldn't take long. It was necessary.From the hut, he stared along the railway. A hundred yards further, just as he remembered, there was a bend. That would be the place. It wouldn't be far to carry her.

He thought of the weight of her body in his arms. He remembered picking her up in the meadow, and how light she had seemed as she touched his face and whispered to him. But the thought hurt him and he pushed it away.

He left the path and clambered down to the track. From there he looked down the line and was satisfied. The bend wasn't much, but enough to make a blind spot just beyond it, where the driver would see nothing until he rounded it. If he saw at all – and perhaps he might not – it would be only for a second, a glimpse and then gone. There would be no time to slow, let alone to stop.

Folded in a certain way, propped up a little, it could look in that split second as if she were crouching there, squatting on the track with her back to the train. There would be nothing anyone could do.

Ralph walked up and down, checking the view from different spots till he was sure of the place.

Then all he needed was something for the cat. He was thinking of fishing line. Once, as a boy, he had found a moorhen almost dead in the river, its legs tangled up in discarded line. But fishing line on a railway track would seem a bit unusual – people might question it. Then, as he walked down the track, he saw something better. Here and there along the line, there was rusted barbed-wire from a long-forgotten fence, hanging loose between rotten posts. Ralph dragged a length of it from the brambles and heaped it near the edge of the line.

A cat out mousing could easily get caught. A cat might chew through fishing line, but not through wire. A cat entangled in it, bleeding perhaps, trapped at the edge of a railway line: anyone would understand that it would tug a little girl's heart. Mary was a kind girl, resourceful, fond of animals. It would be natural for her to help, however unwise. And in the end they would find it all: her satchel, on the ground where the accident happened; her pencil case open, and a pencil stuck in the wire as if as if she had been trying to bend it; the cat, still trapped, just inches from the line.

For a moment, Ralph thought of it, and felt sick. *They picked up the pieces, son, all the way from Canningbridge to Oatham Park.*

But after that they would understand and time would be smooth. It would be history then; a story that parents told their children ever after, to keep them safe. Snowy had brought her to him, and Snowy could take her away. Ralph felt the justice of it.

*\*\*\**

Walking back, he felt a dull relief. The answer to a question. He had tracked her all week, not sure what to do. But now it was settled. It was not, he told himself, so great a thing. Children's lives were flimsy and they were careless with them. His parents had told him of children in the war – in the cities, where the bombing was. And children, everywhere, dying of famine, illnesses, on the roads even... One more death – tragically explicable – would add little to the burden. "At least it must have been quick," people would say. "She would have known nothing."

And though it wouldn't, perhaps, be quite as quick as people thought, by the time they spoke it would at least all be over; she would know nothing. The days they had spent together, the days they should not have spent, were a ripple in the fabric of time. And soon it would be smooth.

Slowly, he retraced his steps up the cutting, slipping a little where the ground was muddy. When he got near the bridge, there was a woman on a bicycle, heading back towards the village or the Farm. He crouched down low and waited as it passed. It would be better, really, to wait until dark. So he made himself a little comfortable beneath the bridge and thought about the future.

With everything settled, the future seemed more possible. He would live quietly, save some money, lie low, forget. A secret memory, buried in one mind only, is almost nothing.

Walking back at last, in the dark, he even felt he could make amends. He would start again. Once he'd got a bit of money he could find new digs in some distant town, get a proper job, join a church...He would write to his mother. He would send her money. He would go to evening classes and make something of his life. Then, once he was somebody, he would visit her again. He could get another motorbike. Or even a car. She would be grateful to see him. He could mend the roof and deal with the damp. He would redeem himself.

\*\*\*

The large black vehicle was a puzzle at first. It was in the road by his mother's house, parked with the lights on. He saw it from the field, and it didn't seem right. There was nothing to stop a vehicle just there. The house stood alone and nobody visited.

After a few moments the vehicle pulled away, followed by a bicycle. Ralph hurried across the field, but before he reached the gate, another car pulled up.

The house he grew up in had always been dark. In daylight it looked like a box of darkness, with blackness looking out from its tiny windows. And at night there had never been more than one light. His parents had always been thrifty. At the most there should have been one lamp, glimmering faintly from his mother's bedroom. Yet suddenly all the lights came on, upstairs and down, flooding the field. And there were people behind the windows, dark silhouettes, moving from one room to another. For the first time ever, the house looked full of life.

But he had seen what vehicle it was that pulled away, and he knew otherwise.

\*\*\*

Once the doctor had been and the body was removed, Mrs Fenner must have spent a busy evening. Half the children in the school claimed she'd talked to their mums, or they'd met her in the street and heard the terrible tale.

"Mrs Fenner's my Auntie," a little girl boasted to a group of younger children who had gathered by the climbing frame. "My actual Auntie," she added, since others had claimed as much who were really only cousins. "So she came right round to my mum, straight after – I heard them talking. Mrs Fenner had a *premission*. So she rushed round on her bike, and there was the witch, all dead. She'd fallen down the stairs and broke her neck. Mrs Fenner gave her the kiss of life but it didn't work, because of all the blood being gone. It had all come out on the floor."

One of the twins said he'd heard the same from the barman, who had heard it from one of Mrs Fenner's sons. "There was blood all over the house as well. But it wasn't proper blood, like people have, it was black, because she was a witch."

"It's true," another boy agreed. "That's what Mrs Fenner told my mum. And the whole house was full of cats and they were drinking it. Mr Fenner's going to drown them. That's what Mrs Fenner said."

Rita had also been talking to the barman, though it seemed her conversation had been rather more prosaic. "The funeral's on Thursday. They're going to do it quick. Mum's even cancelled the quiz night on Wednesday."

"But not to be nice to the witch," her brother added quickly. "It's because of John Pavis's mum and dad. Mum thinks they'll get upset if there's a quiz."

"My Dad said she couldn't be buried in the churchyard, especially the Sneddon bit. He said she should be fed to the pigs." The oldest of the Sneddon girls looked round defiantly, enjoying the shocked expressions.

"They don't *do* that," the girl with the callipers objected. "She'll have to be buried with her husband, because they were *married*. In the Sneddon bit. It's the law." Her father was the sexton, so she knew about things like that.

"Well she's a witch so it doesn't count."

"Don't be stupid. And anyway, my dad says there are lots of bad people in the churchyard already. In the *Sneddon* bit too. My dad said she'd *have good company*." She said this rather pointedly, because several of the Sneddons were horrid about the calliper.

"Anyway," said another girl, "my Uncle's going to mow up a place in the *nettles* for her. Where they throw the dead flowers. And afterwards he'll throw the rubbish back and let the nettles grow and that'll be the end of it."

"There'll have to be a cross," insisted the sexton's daughter sulkily. "She'll still need a cross."

"Not necessarily," said the older girl, with a sneering look. "Someone has to *pay* for the cross, you know. It's not just free. And there's nobody to pay for it."

"Well then," Rita said, because she wanted to kind, "they'll probably just put a *little* cross there, a cheap one, so they know where it is. Everyone at the funeral can pay a bit, for a little cross."

"Don't be stupid. Nobody's going to the funeral."

"That's right. Nobody's going. My Uncle said that."

Michael had been listening in the corner. The talk about the witch had been making him uncomfortable. He'd known for a long time that witches weren't real, but the children were talking as if all of it were fact. He didn't know the story, but he knew there *was* a story. None of the children was supposed to know, and though they *did* know, none of them would tell him.

"Didn't she have any children?" he asked, interrupting at last. "Won't her children go to the funeral?"

There was a long silence, till the girl in the calliper giggled. Then one by one the backs turned, leaving Michael in the corner, on his own.

# 23. Lost Time

It was lucky for Mary that she wasn't at school that day. She had run back crying from the witch's house and when she got home, just a little before Colin, she was so upset that she escaped a telling off. So Michael got told off instead, for not having waited for her – though he said it wasn't fair, and he'd waited ages anyway. Mary didn't say anything and hardly touched her tea, so Janet sent her to bed because she was probably brewing a chill.

She stayed off school the next morning but was better in the afternoon and played with her dolls. It wasn't a very nice game, Janet thought, since it seemed to consist of just dressing and undressing them. It had a curiously repetitive, mechanical quality, like someone in a factory, doing it for money.

Michael got back earlier than usual and brought the news about the woman in the witch's house. Then he told them the story of Mrs Fenner's premonition, and how she had gone there and found the woman dead.

"It was just a co-incidence, dear," said Janet firmly. "She must have just called because the lady was poorly. What a nasty shock for her."

"No," said Michael, "It wasn't that. Rita told me, and Mrs Fenner told her mum. And anyway..." He hesitated, trying to remember the details. "Anyway, Mrs Fenner heard a voice in her head, saying *Come – to – me... Come – to – me*, and it was like a spell so she couldn't stop herself, she had to go. And there she was, all dead. All her blood had come out."

"Oh, Michael!" Janet looked exasperated, because she could see it was frightening Mary. "You shouldn't listen to the village children, dear. It's a lot of nonsense."

Mary was staring curiously at Michael, trying to work it out. She had seen Mrs Fenner come out of the house, and then she had gone in herself, straight after, and had spoken to the lady at the top of the stairs. But Michael was saying she'd had been dead when Mrs Fenner arrived: dead already and cold on the floor, so she must have been dead before Mary went in.

She remembered how cold the house had been, how unnaturally cold. And perhaps there had been a voice in her own head, pulling her to the house. In fact, she could remember it now: a horrible voice saying *come – to – me*. Mary shuddered and her face began to crumple. Witches weren't real, or at least she didn't think so, but she knew that ghosts were real because of the Holy Ghost, which they said about in Sunday School. The jigsaw fell horribly into place. The screeching, pallid figure in the long white gown had evidently been *a ghost*.

Janet put an arm round her and shot a warning glance at Michael. "Now upstairs at once please, and get out of your school clothes. And when you get down, I don't want any more of this nonsense. You've really upset poor Mary, and she's not well anyway."

Colin had heard the news on his way to school. On the train, with all the village children, he found it quite exciting. But then when he heard it again, in the lunch queue with children from the town, it seemed a little silly. It was only an old woman who had died, after all, which was what old people did. His new friend, a boy from Canningbridge, poked fun at one of the Vardons, because witches were kids' stuff, and nobody had black blood – unless they were black in the first place, of course, like a black G.I. And anyway, if she'd fallen down the stairs and hurt her head, she'd have called an ambulance and had stitches in the hospital: she wouldn't just lie on the floor while she bled to death. Colin was impressed by the solidity of the argument. The boys from the town had a certain authority, and he was happy to find that they were open to his friendship. There was even a boy from Purley who supported Croydon at football. Compared to such alliances, all the village rivalries seemed petty. It suddenly didn't matter what the Sneddon twins thought. Colin felt his world growing bigger again.

Rather the opposite was happening to Mary. It seemed to her that the world was imploding – right there in Heckleford, as if it were Bethlehem, or Narnia – a momentous vortex of meaning. After tea she sat at the table and stared at the milk jug. She was certainly at the centre of *something*, sucked in perhaps like Mrs Fenner, and called to play a part that she didn't understand. It was something about Ralph and his terrible ghostly mother, and about herself and being his secret friend, and having a baby. It might be something about Jesus coming back. She remembered how the den had been demolished and the grave renewed. There were things going on.

"I need to go to the funeral," she said suddenly.

This remark brought a curious silence, and then, after a moment, they all spoke at once. Janet said not to be silly, because funerals were for grownups and anyway, you didn't go to funerals if you didn't know the person. Michael said there wasn't going to *be* a funeral, and Colin said it was on Thursday. Then the two of them traded hearsays and Janet tried to shush them.

At that point their father arrived, and it started again from the beginning. Halfway through the story, Evelyn suddenly looked to Janet and said "You mean that woman from the house by the railway? The one that was the mother of that...?" Janet raised an eyebrow and nodded pointedly towards Michael and Mary. There was no point protecting Collin, since it was he who had told them. But Michael and Mary were not supposed to know. It was a horrible story and certainly not suitable.

"I need to go to the funeral."

"No, no, little one." Rick tried to pat her hair but she pulled her head away. "I don't think a little girl needs to worry about that. So are you better today then?"

"I'll be better on Thursday. I can go to the funeral."

"Now stop being silly, dear. I've told you. Funerals are for family. They're not for strangers to go gawping."

"Anyway, nobody's going," Michael said. "They don't need to have a funeral. She hasn't got a family."

Mary looked up at him puzzled. "But she does have a family. She's got a son. He's called Ralph."

***

If Ralph had still been preoccupied with Mary, then her absence from school on Friday and her continuing disappearance on Saturday might have raised his anxiety to fever pitch. Saturday was the day when he had planned to meet her. He needed to get it over. Everything was ready.

But Ralph was not thinking of Mary anymore. The aching enormity of his mother's death had expelled all thoughts of the future, even of safety. It wasn't about love: perhaps he had not loved his mother very much. But she was all there was, the only audience for his pitiful groping through life, the only one. He had, after all, always planned to make amends. If he thought of Mary now, it was only with vague resentment, because she had lured him from the path of reconciliation. She was a pitfall, a snare. She had stolen the last few months that he might have had, just as Sonia had stolen fourteen years. There was no one now. He was a ship with no anchor, adrift.

And this time it was impossible, utterly impossible, to undo time.

He had watched from the dark of the field for several hours. People kept arriving at the house. Several cars came and left, and then a van. He watched – too dismayed to care, too dismayed to think. But in the end it was dark again.

The back door, that had never been locked in thirty years, resisted his hand. Someone had put a padlock on it.

There was a passage at the back, between the outside toilet and the back of the hall, where the dustbin was kept and the tools for the garden. Even in the dark it wasn't difficult. He had done it often as a child, just for fun. He clambered from the dustbin to the roof of the bathroom, and from there through the skylight onto the tallboy on the landing.

The door to his mother's room was slightly blocked. Inside was desecration. Clothes and bags and boxes were scattered on the floor, on the bed, like rubbish. The dressing table had gone, and even the old commode. Someone had tried to get the wardrobe out. That was oak though, solid, and it wouldn't go past the bed. Only the little chest was left and even that was broken. Without putting on the light, not wanting to see, he piled the things back into the wardrobe, and heaved it back against the wall.

He sat in the dark on his mother's bed. It was stripped and smelt of urine. But the pillow still smelt of her and he knelt beside it and wept. Hours later he woke on the floor, and the terrible truth of it came back to him. So he wept again. His life had been for nothing. Fourteen years and one summer, gone forever, and now it was too late. Time was not as malleable as he had wanted to believe.

When light dawned, he walked around the house. He saw at once the spaces where things had gone. There had never been anything worth stealing, but still things had gone. The most obvious was the great old dresser from the kitchen with the dusty plates that had sat there all his life. The old green carpet from the back room had gone, the two art deco vases from the mantelpiece and the clock his father got when he retired. The cutlery from the drawers. The wooden rocking chair, where she had sat all those years ago, to nurse him as a baby. Even the broken television – gone with all the pieces, leaving only the ghosts of them outlined in the dust.

The things that were left only made matters worse. There were piles on the floor, where drawers and cupboards had been emptied. The unwanted detritus had a terrible, painful intimacy. Its worthlessness crushed his heart. Old Christmas cards, and books of accounts. A pencil case he had used at school. His mother's apron. A glass jar he had painted as a vase for her, twenty birthdays ago, broken on the floor. These were intimate things. It was a violation.

A fire had been lit in the grate, but not, it appeared, for the warmth. It was choked with charred remains of something black and papery: his dad's photographs. Ralph had not loved his father and he had not shared his father's passions. But each of the pictures had been a moment: a fragment of time that had been framed, achieved, made solid across the years. Perhaps his father, too, thought that time could be tamed. He too was wrong.

Ralph could not think of the future now. The imperative of action, of changing history, which had seemed so urgent just a day before, seemed utterly distant. The wall of his grief was so absolute that nothing could pass it. He went back to the gloomy bedroom and ran his fingers round the imprint of his mother's body on the mattress. That was all there was of her: an empty, damp, hollow place. He sat there, silent, till the sun grew high and at last its rays came through the window. As it fell on the chest by her bed, he saw the dust on the flaking varnish, and without thinking he wiped it with his fingers. They left a mark, and so he rubbed it with the sleeve of his shirt till the dust was gone. Perhaps it was that which freed him.

He went downstairs and walked from room to room, taking in what they had done to her, looking very carefully, one final time, so he wouldn't forget. Then, starting slowly at first, he put things back in the places they belonged. He swept the floor and cleared the grate. He carefully built what was left from the dresser into a shape against the wall: the shape of a dresser, in silent accusation.

He boiled up water and sliced up soap. Then he washed the paintwork in the kitchen and cleaned the filthy glass. He scrubbed the draining board and brushed out all the cobwebs from the corners. In his mother's room, he swept the floor and scrubbed the mould from the walls till only the pinkness of the plaster remained.

Incongruously, the bathroom rug was at the bottom of the stairs. When he pulled it back, he found the terrible stain where she had bled.

He burnt the rug at the end of the garden, then scrubbed the flags till they were grey again.

And then, when it was evening, he lay on her bed and slept.

The next day he woke with an aching hunger. He had eaten nothing for thirty-six hours. Downstairs, the new-scrubbed sink and the iron hob had a homely feel. In the cupboard beneath the stairs, there were rusted tins that had been there since the war, and boxes of porridge with weevils in them. There were peas and mandarins, corned beef from the Argentine, spam and ancient pilchards. The contents were grey and they smelt of tin, but some of them were edible.

When he had eaten, he went out to the shed. There he found cans of paint and brushes covered with cobwebs. By nightfall he had done the first coat. The damp still showed where the roof had leaked, but the room looked brighter already. It seemed like a bedroom again, a place where his mother might have sat up in bed and worn a bedjacket and read a magazine.

The next day, he told himself, he would patch up the roof. There was a ladder in the garden. After, that he would have time, either that day or the next, for another coat in the bedroom, and perhaps the kitchen as well, and the landing. He would leave it as bright as a diamond. The weather was set fair and there was plenty of time.

Time laughs at all of us. He knew he was much too late and there wasn't any point. But sometimes, when time mocks us, there is strength in laughing back.

\*\*\*

Thursday the 13th of September, the day of Verity Sneddon's funeral, brought the last real sun of the year. There was to be no Indian summer in 1962. There would be sleet and frost before October, prefiguring the snow that would begin in November, get worse after Christmas, and end up lingering till March: the coldest winter of the century.

So perhaps the roses and the dahlias of the village would not have lasted much longer, anyway.

When the villagers first saw it, they each made sense in some personal way. At the farm the only flowers were a pot of busy-lizzies and a rosebush at the gate. The twins got the blame for the pot because they'd had been playing football in the farmyard: they must have broken it and hidden the evidence. Nobody noticed that the roses had gone.

At the pub, they blamed vandals from Oatham for the hanging baskets, because their team had turned up anyway and been more than put out about the cancelled quiz-night. Up the street, Mrs Fenner's husband, staring at his ravaged border, suspected his rivals from the horticultural society: his dahlias were always the biggest and he generally scooped the prizes. The stationmaster, seeing the neat stubble where his zinnias had been, thought it must have been gypsies, stealing them for the market.

It was the sexton who found the answer. He had checked the new grave the previous day, to be sure that it was deep enough and straight. They had dug it against the churchyard wall, behind several yards of nettles. It was an ugly spot, near the compost heap, which seemed to the sexton quite unnecessary. But he wasn't of the village and had no part in their feuding. It was all hallowed ground, he told himself, and the Lord wouldn't care.

He only came early for the ringing of the bell. But the scent called him back to the grave, as he told people later – the beautiful fragrance in the air, like the smell from a florist.

There were branches of fir arching over it, woven together like an arbour or a den that a child might build. And for six feet either side, the ground was no longer nettled. It was a carpet of flowers.

## 24. Rites of Passage

The death of the witch was a relief to everyone: the final falling off of a scab. May Pavis, waking at dawn and remembering the day, rolled over and whispered to her husband. "Not long now. It'll soon be over." Her husband had declared the day a holiday, because no one that day could be interested in coal. For the hour before their son woke, they lay in each other's arms, not speaking any more, remembering the years. The death of the witch marked an epoch, a time for moving on.

At the school there was a curious sense of occasion. No carnival, certainly, but there was something in the air, an excitement, a sense of things happening. Mary felt it when the register was read, and then at playtime it was stronger. The girls stood whispering, huddled by the churchyard fence, but as Mary approached, they grew silent, and their huddle dissolved. She knew perfectly well that they were speaking of the funeral, though only the girl with the calliper admitted it.

"It's Mrs Sneddon from the witches house," she said. "But nobody's going because of what her son..." But a Sneddon girl dug her in the ribs and told her to shut up. These things were private. Everyone knew what the son had done, and whose family he came from, but it didn't do to speak of it. And it was over now.

*\*\*\**

Verity Sneddon had played out her part. Perhaps she had even proved useful.

When the news of the murder erupted, the families drew apart in their grief, and in the aching gap between them all manner of bitterness festered. The Pavises muttered about the Sneddon blood. Ralph had never been normal, everyone knew that – but all of the Sneddons were inbred. They married each other's land, to keep it in the family. Ralph's grandparents were cousins, and everyone knew what *that* could lead to.

The Sneddons fought back with whispered slurs. The girl had always been sly and wayward, she must have led Ralph on. Even as an angel in the nativity play, she'd been wearing lipstick! And her father was at fault

– taking his wife out gallivanting, leaving a boy to look after the girl, and at bedtime too. And if everyone knew that the boy wasn't right, what were they doing even asking him?

Most of the village had blood from both sides. Sonia's mother had been a Sneddon before she'd married, and even Ralph's father, who was Sneddon through and through, had Pavis blood in him, further back. The pressure to take sides was tearing the village apart – husband from wife, mother from daughter.

But Verity Sneddon was not from the village. By her treacherous perjuries at the trial – reckless, transparent, scandalous – she drew the poison to herself. By the time the witnesses got home, the families were united by their loathing. The pathetic Ralph Sneddon, in the dock with eyes like a bullock in the slaughterhouse, weeping like a girl and carted away like a sack of rubbish – he was almost a side-line. It was Verity who had betrayed them all.

And with her death it was finished.

***

They came in twos and threes along the lanes and footpaths leading to the church. None of them wore black, lest anyone imagine that they had come to pay respects. A few came in garish rags with elaborate contempt, and the farmhands, let off for the afternoon, came just as they were. But most of the others came carefully dressed in summer colours, because they were coming for Sonia. And they came together, Sneddons and Pavises and Vardons and Fenners. At the front came May Pavis, with her husband on one arm and her Sneddon sister on the other.

They saw the hearse turn down the track to the church, and a sigh passed amongst them. By the time they reached the gate, the hearse was empty, and they gathered by the lych-gate, leaning on the fence.

With nobody attending, the service couldn't be long. Perhaps the undertakers would stand to attention, as the Vicar said a prayer and sprinkled holy water. Or perhaps even that would seem pointless, with no one to watch but the professionals.

It seemed a long wait, none the less. The villagers started to grumble.

"Get a move on!" someone shouted from the back of the crowd. "Bring 'er out!" An old lady shushed him, but he had voiced what everyone had been thinking. Someone started humming and others joined in. Then the tune gave way to its words: *Why are we waiting? Why-y are we waiting...?* Then one of the farmhands got out a bottle of cider. There was some scuffling at the back and some whispering that wasn't very pleasant.

At last, there was movement from the church. As the door juddered open, there was the sexton in his frock, fussing all round as the bearers shuffled out. The man who had shouted did a cheer. Another joined in, and a third one whistled. One of the Fenners protested – *it was a funeral, not a bloody football match* – but that only drew laughter: a hard, brittle laughter tainted by trouble.

The four men round the coffin must have heard the commotion, but they made no acknowledgement – unless perhaps to walk a little slower. The Vicar walked before them, treading the ground in solemn, careful steps, and the sexton took the rear.

The little procession rounded the back of the church and disappeared from sight. Again, a sigh, rippling through the crowd, and then silence.

"That's it then," Max Pavis said firmly, addressing the crowd. "That's the last we'll see of her. It's finished now. Let's get home." He put out his arms in an expansive gesture and indicated for the crowd to part.

Most of them would have complied, but some farmhands took exception.

"Hey shut it Granddad. You're not on the council *now*, you know."

"An' I want to see her going in the ground! I want to throw some earth on!"

"Hey, sonny, no!" Old Max Pavis was looking alarmed. "We agreed. We agreed remember... It's best to..."

"I never agreed nuffing!" said the lad defiantly. "An' I went to school with that murd'rer. I wanna throw some muck on for 'im. Some muck on 'is mum." And he started pushing towards the gate.

"An' I want to piss on her!" His friend sounded somewhat slurred, but there were those in the crowd who sniggered at his wit. "I wanna piss on the witch. Come on Davie..."

The two of them trotted into the churchyard, a little unsteadily. For a moment the crowd hesitated. Discipline was discipline and they knew what they'd agreed. "We have to be dignified," Max Pavis had said. "We have to think of Sonia. We'll be there for Sonia, that's all." Max Pavis had been chairman of the Parish once. He was the voice of reason.

But it didn't seem right, in that moment, that they had waited so long and seen so little. They'd done what they agreed about the Church. Honour was satisfied. It was only the bit by the graveside that was left.

As the crowd hesitated, on the edge of a decision, the school bell went, and within seconds the children were flooding from their classrooms. Some of them recognised parents by the lych-gate. A couple of Vardon boys saw their Uncle Davie jogging off towards the grave, and they clambered over the fence to join him. Others followed, and even the ones who'd been heading round the path started climbing the fence instead. It was all too much for the crowd by the lych-gate. They surged into the graveyard and headed towards the grave. All of them, even May Pavis who was weeping, and her Sneddon sister who was pulling her back. Even Max went in the end.

Everyone knew where to find the grave, because they'd gossiped all weekend about the nettles and the compost heap. It was round the back, in the overgrown bit where the shrubs weren't cut. It was...

As the first ones rounded the corner they stopped abruptly. The others, rushing behind them, jolted into their backs, and then stopped in turn.

"Bloody hell!" Davie said, his jaw dropping open. "Cop a load at that!"

And they all looked, pushing between the laurels into the narrowest bit of the path. At first it was the flowers that dazzled their eyes. They were everywhere, even beneath the feet of the six solemn men. It was like something in a painting, people said afterwards. It was like the horticultural show. It was like Heaven. Mr Fenner recognised his dahlias. The words formed in his throat, and then melted away, silenced. His huge White Alvas and his Purple Gems, woven across a bower of fir: they had never looked so beautiful. There were wildflowers too: buttercups, herb-Robert, toadflax, flowers from the hedgerows, cast wantonly over the piles of earth.

The children stared, astonished, enchanted. The adults looked from face to face, trying to make sense. Beautiful, unworldly, flowers. Sinister, terrible, stolen flowers.

And across the grave, the six solemn men stared back. Four in black suits and two in clerical robes, all of them serious and somehow familiar.

Somehow familiar.

Then suddenly Davie realised. He recoiled for a moment, because the man beside the Vicar was not, in any obvious way, the lad he had known before. His hair was mousy now, not blond, and the Sneddon curls were looser. The peach-bloom face was leathery. But once Davie saw it, he couldn't un-see it. It was inescapable, even through the fog of the cider.

"Bloody hell! That's *him!* It's bloody *him!*" And he pointed, straight at Ralph, and then, once it was spoken, everyone saw.

There was a cruel joy in the moment, like the baying of the hounds when the fox backs into a corner. Davie moved forward, with his friends either side, a kind of triumph in his face.

"You bastard! Bloody murderer! Get out of here! Get out! Get out now!"

"Yeah, get out. Out! OUT!"

"Out out out out!" The crowd took up the word. A few of them shouted "Murderer! Murderer!" and others echoed back "Get out! Get out! Get out!"

There were other voices further back, berating, reproaching, and women looking suddenly for their children.

Somebody picked up a stone and hurled it towards Ralph, but it clattered into the grave. Ralph took a step backwards but there was nowhere to run. Davie Vardon, rocking a little, made a step towards the coffin.

"You sick git. You bloody pervert. What the hell do you think..."

"No... No Davie, don't..."

But it was too late. Davie made a rush towards Ralph and punched him in the face, knocking over the Vicar in the rebound.

"Stop it! Davie no!" There were voices in the crowd calling him back – women's voices mostly – and Mr Vardon from the pub who grabbed him by the shoulders. "No, mate – give it a rest... not now son..." But Davie's friends rounded on the older man, and Ralph turned to help the Vicar, though his own nose was bleeding. As he bent down, Davie kicked him in the back of the knees and he stumbled as well, face down into the flowers.

The crowd surged forward then. The men were shouting and some of the children were screaming. Michael Crouch and a couple of younger boys jumped onto the coffin, to get a better look. Some others tried to follow and pushed the first ones off, and two little Sneddons fell into the grave. Another couple of stones flew from the back towards Ralph, but one of them hit Mrs Vardon, and there was much more shouting from the women then, and Max Pavis was standing by the coffin, shouting

"Stop! Stop!" But nobody took any notice.

Then the whistle went.

It was a good whistle. Under normal circumstances it was audible from the front door of the school to the back of the cricket pitch. It was the whistle they had all jumped to, at some time or another. But it wasn't particularly loud this time, because the Head was right there, looking over the fence from the playground.

The silence was abrupt, automatic, and for a second everyone froze, except for the boys on the coffin, who jumped off briskly, and pushed themselves back into the crowd.

"Stand up! All of you! Turn round!" Everyone under forty had the voice ingrained in their consciousness, and they stood up and turned like automata, just as they had done when they were children, caught in some transgression in the playground. All the village parents knew the voice as well, from encounters at Open Days, and occasional humiliations when their children misbehaved. The voice was a crisp staccato, but not loud. "David Vardon! I don't know what you're doing but you'd better leave this churchyard straight away. I really wouldn't want to have to call the police to a funeral but if I need to, I won't hesitate. You too, Peter Sneddon. And you, James Vardon." The three thus named looked sideways and scowled, but still they turned. Halfway back to the church they paused, but the Head spoke again, without turning round. "No, I mean it. I don't believe any of you has any business here. I dare say you would benefit from a brisk walk and a glass of water." He returned his attention to the crowd, who were looking more sheepish by the moment. "Joan Fenner – Mrs Sneddon: get your children out of that grave. Mark Fenner, Mark Vardon – you are both standing on the flowers. Get back on the path. You too Marjorie Fenner. Mary Crouch – come out from the shrubbery – we're not playing hide-and-seek. Children – all of you, get back to the playground and wait for your mothers. Mr Pavis, perhaps you would be so kind as to help up the Reverend."

All his years of teaching had served the Head well. His eyes roved round the group and he sensed that the crisis was over.

"Now, I don't know what's just happened and I don't *want* to know. But I suggest that all of you – unless any of you are *mourners* – might be well advised to absent yourselves."

With that, he made a little gesture, pointing the way they should go. May Pavis took her sister by the arm and nodded to her husband. "Come on. I've had enough." And as she moved forward, avoiding the Head's gaze, the crowd moved with her.

The Head turned to the little gathering round the grave. "Reverend, I am extremely sorry that you have been so…. disturbed. I trust you are not hurt?" The Vicar shook his head, mutely.

"Ralph Sneddon. Yes." He said the name slowly, feeling the weight of it. "Ralph Sneddon." In those fragile syllables he tried to encompass the bright young boy he had known long ago, the haggard figure before him, and all the terrible years in between. He shook his head, unable to make the leap. "Ralph Sneddon. It has been a long time since we met. The pleasure is… unexpected. I am sorry that it should be on such a sad occasion. I remember your mother well. She was… she was a woman of great… *fortitude*. Please accept my condolences."

Ralph bowed his head. The teacher saw the tears flow down his cheeks, and wondered what the poor man's intentions were. Perhaps it would be sensible to contact the police, just to let them know he was around. Or perhaps the doctor. Someone should be keeping an eye on him.

"Ralph. You may find things rather … changed since you were here. If you have the time for a little catching up, I would be pleased for you to call on me. But… it would not be best to come in school hours. I am usually in the school until six. You would be most welcome to call any evening *after five*. Yes. Really. I would be pleased." He looked directly at Ralph, and tried to smile, though it did not come naturally. "Do be careful now. It's a small village. I am sure Mr Barraclough will give you a lift – if you are staying somewhere locally. People in the village are upset, as you saw. It might be best not to walk."

\*\*\*

Mary Crouch, who had known all along that her hero would be there, had shuffled back to her place in the shrubbery. She still had her present to give him, the Key to Happiness. But she had lost her chance. He was walking away with the other black figures, his back to her.

She wondered what to do.

He would obviously be going back to the house. She wondered if his mother's ghost would still be there. She shuddered a little, remembering, but then told herself firmly that with all the flowers the ghost would be on its way to Heaven now.

Everything she had witnessed confirmed what she suspected. What had passed that day did not belong to ordinary times. It was something else. Something unheard-of was happening, in her own village, something enormous – and she was in the midst of it, part of the story. The scene in the churchyard had a biblical stature, with biblical emotions.

She thought of the crowd. Their church in Croydon had done a passion play, and some of the older children had been in it as citizens. Michael and Mary were too young, but Colin was in the scene called *Jesus is Hailed by the People in Jerusalem* – he had to throw a palm leaf and cheer as Jesus came by on a cardboard donkey. And some of his friends were in the scenes called *The Crowd Turn Against Jesus* and *Pontius Pilate Washes his Hands*. Colin kept the programme in his treasure box, because it had his name in it and the names of old friends whom he wouldn't see again.

What had happened at the grave had been somehow like that. *Ralph Sneddon Weeps at the Grave of his Mother... The People Throw Stones at Him... The Head Turns the Crowd Away...* The Head had talked in a special way to Ralph. Perhaps the Head knew too. Perhaps they all knew.

But nobody knew the part that belonged to Mary Crouch. She wasn't just a citizen. Whatever it was, she had a special part. The thing with weeing in her bottom had been nasty, but it meant something else. She was someone special.

She squatted behind the shrubbery till the last of the footsteps passed. She heard the chatter of children, and Michael calling from the playground. For a little while it was her name, then a few threats, then some bad things, then nothing. Mary's feet got pins and needles and her elbow, wedged against a rough branch, picked up the pattern of the wood, like a map on her skin. At last, when she was sure it was safe, she pulled herself up and stretched.

It was only five minutes to War Memorial and the little lane. She walked solemnly, clutching the Key to Happiness in its little felt pouch. Ralph would be there already, delivered by the big black car. She would comfort him. She would give him the gift.

*Mary Crouch kisses the head of Ralph Sneddon. Mary Crouch hands over the Key to Happiness.*

The late summer sun shone on the leafy verge. Skylarks were singing, high in the sky, and a cuckoo attempted a hoarse belated call. Summer was over. It was time for them all to leave now, back to the warmer south. Already, thousands of miles north, the clouds were gathering that would descend across the land, and cold winds were rallying, ready to bring snow.

But on Thursday, the thirteenth of September nineteen sixty-two, the day was sunny. The air was full of mystery and the sky was full of angels.

## 25. Parting Gifts

"Might be best to take the long way round," Jack Barraclough suggested to his father. "Up round the main road, like."

"Yeah," his brother agreed. "You can double back under the bridge. It'll save... well, you know."

Their father knew exactly. It was three times the distance, but none of them wanted to drive through the village, with this passenger on board. Not today. They had the hearse to think about. Old Mr Barraclough was wishing he hadn't got involved. Business was business, but if only he'd known, he'd have turned the job away. After all, he'd done the funeral for the girl who was murdered. He remembered the parents. So if he'd realised in time – which meant rather sooner than half-way to the village, with the coffin and the murderer already in the car – he could have claimed *conflict of interest* and got the Co-op to do it. The Co-op had the contract with the council and did tramps and paupers even – whereas *Barraclough & Sons* was a byword for 'respectable'. He wondered what the knock-on would be, when people got to hear of it. It might be quite a penalty, he felt, for a momentary lapse of memory. But there were so many bloody Sneddons in that village! Someone ought to have told him whose mother it was.

Despite his misgivings, if they'd been alone, he'd have spoken to his passenger. A murderer would have tales to tell and it would be something to talk about later in the pub. But his sons were only youngsters and they might have taken it wrong.

In any case, the business didn't owe the man anything. He wasn't their *client*. The woman had paid for the funeral herself, years back, and when the chap came in, he was adamant that he didn't want extras – at least, not anything that he'd have to pay for. He'd even had the cheek to ask for some money back, because the contract specified *four* pall bearers, and with him on one corner, they'd only need three. Old Mr Barraclough had never met such a skinflint, not in all his years. Even the flowers were a disgrace – a mountain of weeds and some blooms dragged out of the garden – not one of them came from a florist or had a scrap of cellophane.

So he wasn't surprised that there wasn't a tip when he dropped the man off. Some people were just cheapskates. There was no doing anything about it.

***

The child was sitting by the back door, stroking the white cat. She was simply there, like a gift left on the doorstep.

As Ralph opened the gate from the lane, she smiled at him: a shy, anxious smile.

He did not speak at first, just looked at her. Her square, plain face, with its freckles and badly cut hair. Her grubby knees pulled up to her chin, with a flash of grey knickers behind them. And he saw the expression in her face: a tender, pleading little smile. Mary Crouch.

Mary Crouch.

Like a solid thing, he felt the time that had passed. Everything that had happened, everything he had planned. He felt at that moment neither shame nor desire. All of it was something from another world, another life. If she had come a week ago, when his plan was crisp and ruthless, it would have been different. But now she seemed almost irrelevant. She was out of place, out of time.

An indescribable weariness washed over him. She was there. He didn't have any choice.

"Mary. What are you doing here?"

The child drew a sudden breath, as if relieved that he had spoken. "I came to see if you were all right. I was worried. Because of what happened – at the church. And I wanted to see you." She looked at him, pleading. She appeared to be waiting for something. A smile perhaps, or a gesture. "Please... Please... I'm really sorry. I'm really sorry I was... Last week... I'm sorry I didn't... I was just frightened. But I am... I do want to be..."

Then she stopped. A long silence rested between them before he spoke.

"Mary, you shouldn't be here."

"No! No, no... no please. I'm really sorry Mr Ralph. I'm sorry about your mother. I'm sorry about what happened. What they did. The people at the church. But I... I came here... Last week. I was looking for you... I wanted... But I saw her... inside. But it was... it was a ghost. I'm really sorry. Please let me..."

She stood up, and the pleading look in her eyes became something else. Her face began to crumple. "Mr Ralph, I'm sorry. I wanted to see you. Please..." Then she started groping in her pocket, as if looking for a hanky. But it wasn't that. She had something small and red in her hand, some tangle of fluff and cotton. "I've got something for you. I made it. A present. Please... I'm really sorry..." She held it out, stepping towards him, her hand held flat with the little thing in it, as if trying to feed a pony. He kept his hands behind his back and shook his head. He needed to go in, but she was standing in the way, in front of the door.

"No! Not now. Please. I'm in a hurry. I'm leaving now. I've just got to... Please Mary, go home now. I need to go in."

He twisted the broken padlock – left only for show now – and pushed passed her to the door. From the other side of the threshold, in the sunshine, the child looked up at him.

He should have closed the door then. A better man would have closed the door.

It wasn't that he meant to let her in. It was just that there was something in her face that unnerved him, calling to all the days they had spent together – the happiest days. Whatever had happened since, it seemed a lot to lose, those happiest days, without even a goodbye. He still should have shut the door, but instead he spoke. "I'm leaving Mary. I'm not coming back. You won't see me again. Not ever. I'm going away."

And suddenly she was in his arms, her legs around his waist, clinging to him, pressing her head against face, weeping.

He bolted the door against the world and put her down on the kitchen table.

\*\*\*

He noted, wryly, how quickly she rallied.

"Oh! You've made it all *nice*." She was looking round admiringly. "You've done the windows. I like it." She glanced towards the stairs, as if there might be something up there. But there were only the cats, a black one and a tabby, peering from the landing, and she went on conversationally. "And the walls. But you didn't finish the bit just there."

She pointed to a patch above the sink.

"I ran out of paint."

"Oh." She put her head on one side. "You could buy some more. They sell it in Woolworths."

"I haven't any money." Ralph shrugged. It didn't matter now.

The child was looking round again. "There used to be a dresser over there. And there was a telly. Did you finish mending the telly?"

"No. Someone stole it."

"Oh!"

"And the dresser. People came in and stole it all." He said it flatly, but there was something comforting in telling her. Another person who was interested. Another person who might perceive the injustice.

Mary appeared to warm to this topic. "They're burglars then. A house got burgled up our street. Did you call the police? There's a phone by the green. You have to dial 999."

"No."

He saw her looking curiously, as if trying to read him. Something flashed through his mind: the horrible thing. The thing that belonged to another life. He turned his back on her so she couldn't see.

"Mary, I'm leaving in a minute. You'll have to go." There was something he had to say, but the knowledge in his head made it hard to form the words. He had never thought of himself as a hypocrite.

*Stop it or I'll tell of you. I'm telling my Mum. I'm telling my Gran.*

Perhaps she had not meant it. But he had to know.

"Mary, you didn't tell anyone, did you? About what we... Last Saturday... What happened."

"No," she said at once. Then she looked a little awkward. "But I think my mum... I don't know."

"What do you mean – your mum?"

"I think she knows."

Ralph's throat tightened.

"Did you say anything to her?"

"No." But he saw the child blush, just a little. She must have said something.

"Mary?"

"Well... I just think she might know. She didn't want to talk about it though. I didn't say anything. Do you really have to go?"

"Mary what did you tell her?"

The child was silent then. A cat had jumped on the table and she was trying to stroke it. He touched the back of her neck. "You've got to tell me. What did you say? I mean it Mary; *you've got to tell me.*"

The child shook her head. "I just told her we were friends... and about you being special. Like Jesus. She said she knew and that it was all alright, and I mustn't worry about it. And that I'd understand it when I had the baby."

"Is that all? Is this the truth Mary?"

"Yes. Yes. I promise."

Ralph relaxed a little then. It sounded like prattle. Nothing to take notice of. She had *wanted*, however, to tell. He would never be safe.

"I've got to go now. I'm getting my things and then I'm going. You should go home now."

The child didn't move. She stood, four-square, looking up at him, fixing him. As if looking through a microscope he saw, in terrible, disjointed detail, the tear grow round in the corner of her eye, then drip down her cheek. But there was nothing soft in her face. Her jaw was tight, accusing almost.

"Mr Ralph," she said slowly. "Were you going to kill me?"

*\*\*\**

It was the question she had needed to know, most of all. The question that would define what lay between them, her specialness.

She heard the momentary stop of his breath and saw the sudden grimace in his mouth. But he did not answer. Not answering was an answer of a sort.

After a second, he took two steps backwards and then spoke. "Mary, you've got to go home. Please. Get out. Please." He looked quite frightened.

She looked at him, more softly. She didn't suppose that he had ever *wanted* to kill her. It clearly upset him that she had even spoken of it. She did not doubt that he loved her. Abraham had loved Isaac, too. The sacrifice would have meant nothing if there hadn't been *love*. It must have been terrible. But still she had to know. She had waited a long time to ask him this.

At the end of that terrible day, he had walked back through the trees, covered in blood.

"But you killed the little dog instead. God sent the little dog." She said it like a statement of fact, to encourage him, to let him know that she knew. But she needed an answer, a confirmation.

Ralph was staring with an expression she had never seen before. His face, moving a little without speaking, had a look that no human face should have.

"Get out Mary Crouch. Get out!" He stepped abruptly towards her as if he were going to push her, but just as his hands reached out, they dropped again. "Get out Mary. Please. Just go away. I'm sorry. Please Mary. Go away."

"But I..." Mary had no intention of going, not now. He was never coming back. Even Aslan had promised to come back, some time, though he wouldn't name the day. And what would happen to her, if she never saw Ralph again? What about the baby? What was it all about? There were too many questions that needed an answer. She did not move.

"You've got to go Mary." He said it softly now, not exactly as if he were relenting, but there was no fierceness now. Then he turned and walked upstairs.

She followed him.

She had never been further than the second step before. But the stairs were different now, bright and white down the edges, with the clean fresh smell of paint. Upstairs there was a bedroom, also clean and white. There was a blanket spread nicely across it, but instead of sheets there was a tablecloth. Three cats jumped off as she entered. Ralph was bending down with his back to her, cramming things into his rucksack. He was going away. He might never come back.

She felt the turning of immutable forces.

She remembered the terrible shouting at the grave. She remembered how he had wept. She remembered the people who had wanted to drive him away. Perhaps that was why. Or perhaps it was his mother dying. Perhaps it was the little dog.

She took a deep breath and spoke quickly. There were so many things she had planned to say, and others that came to her, as she spoke. They tumbled from her mouth like a string of little beads. "I'm sorry about the people at the churchyard. They didn't mean it. Please don't go away. Not for ever. You're my best friend. We haven't finished. I'm sorry about your mother dying. I love you Mr Ralph. I really love you. And I'm going to have a baby. You can't just go away, not if you're not coming back. I'm sorry I upset you. I'm sorry I was naughty. I'm sorry about your mum. But you've made the house nice now. You could stay here. You could make another den. I'm really sorry about the little dog. But it's what God wanted. Really it was. Please. Please don't go away. Not forever."

Then abruptly she stopped.

Ralph had sat down on the bed, hugging the rucksack on his lap. And he was crying.

It wasn't a silent weeping like he had done at the grave. It was a proper, sobbing sort of cry, like Mary herself might do. It grew with every moment till he became quite noisy. His shoulders were rocking and his nose was running and he was wiping it on his sleeve. Each sob was messier and louder than the last.

Things were clearly taking a better turn.

She climbed onto the bed and put her arms around him, like one should when someone cries. She kissed his cheek, and told him, in the proper way, like her mother would have done, that it would all be alright and he didn't need to cry. Then she kissed him again, in a business-like way, and told him that really he should take his jacket off, because it was a good jacket and the tears might spoil it. He did not resist as she pulled it from his shoulders. Then she fished about in her pocket and pulled out her hanky. It was the second time that she had provided him a hanky, so she felt rather pleased. She shook it out from the corner, like her gran would have done, and tried to wipe his nose. She felt properly in charge now. She was really rather happy.

"Come on, lie down," she said firmly. "I'll give you a cuddle." His whole body was racked with sobbing and it clearly wouldn't stop for quite a while. "It's all right," she said. "It's all right." Obediently, he rolled towards the pillows, but then curled into a ball with his back to her, rocking. He wasn't, Mary felt, very good at this. Even Michael, who didn't cry much but was awful when he did, knew it helped to have a cuddle.

She folded herself round him and stroked his shoulders through the starchy shirt. It was crisp and white and didn't smell like his clothes usually did. Beneath it, she felt the muscles in his back, the familiar firmness of his flesh. She felt the warmness of him, but he was shaking all over. He had done that before. He was clearly a person who felt the cold, just like her Gran did. His lovely leather jacket was hooked over the bed-knob so she pulled it over both of them. That made it rather better. Leather and oil and the smell of a man. His scratchy shirt was untucked behind, so she stroked his back. She didn't want to repeat what they'd done before – though she had come prepared to, up to a point. But she felt pretty sure that he didn't want that today, which was a bit of a relief.

He didn't even hold her. His arms were tucked into his chest and his knees pulled up. She felt round his body and found one of his hands.

"That's better," she crooned. "There there. Don't cry. There there." Grownups always said that when people cried, so it must be right. The crying was naturally about his mother, despite her being old and not at all nice.

Ralph's body was convulsed now, and he was gripping her hand, rocking and weeping. She didn't mind him crying but she was beginning to feel that it was time for him to stop. After all, he had said he had to leave, and there were things she needed to talk about. If they only had minutes, it wouldn't do to waste them. She wondered what she could say, to turn the tide of his grief.

Mary's Dad had gone on about the goldfish's "innings" having been good, which probably referred, Mary thought, to its inside bits. But it didn't seem quite nice to say that about a *person*, especially as it might not be true. Mary hadn't seen the old lady, except as a ghost, but from what Ralph had said, she had always been sick. So perhaps her innings had been rather *bad*. Mary thought for a moment of the ghost, but there was nothing ghostly in the house anymore. It had probably gone to Heaven.

This led Mary to a better train of thought. When Rita's Auntie died, the resulting thoughts from Heaven, on which Rita was clearly an authority, had been a matter of pronouncement and clearly considerable comfort. It was certainly worth a go. Mary propped herself up on an elbow and stroked Ralph's curls.

"There there. You shouldn't cry. Your mum's happy now. She's gone to Heaven. She's looking down on us now. She's looking down right now and wondering why you're crying. She's thinking *Here I am all happy in Heaven and there is my darling Ralph all crying. What a silly billy. He knows I love him very much and one day I'll see him again when he comes here. But till then I've sent him a nice friend to look after him and her name is Mary. He should stop crying and be happy.*"

Mary was quite pleased with this, which was more or less exactly what Rita's Auntie had said – after necessary adjustments. And possibly it was working with Ralph as well, because for a moment he did stop crying. But he didn't seem pleased.

"Mary, stop it..." He sat himself up and did one huge gasping sob. "Stop it Mary. Please go away. I've got to get ready. I don't want to... I don't want..."

His face was all wet and his nose was running again. It didn't seem quite right in a grownup man. Mary handed him the hanky and this time he took it.

"I'm sorry Mary. I'm sorry... You don't understand... I'm sorry. You don't know anything. Please Mary... Please go away. Please. I'm sorry about what happened. I didn't mean it. I'm really sorry. I'm going away now. Please just don't tell anyone... Even your mother... Please."

He was sitting on the side of the bed now, fussing over his rucksack. She could see he was really going, though they hadn't finished their talk. He handed her back the handkerchief and as she put it back in her pocket, she felt the Key to Happiness, resting in the corner.

"Wait. I've got something for you. A present. I made it for you." She held out the little pouch again, with its precious silver cargo. "Well, not the key, I mean... I... I found the key. After you left... after the dog... "She checked herself. This wasn't the way she wanted to go. Ralph was staring at the little red package in her hand. He wasn't picking it up. "The little pocket. I made it for you. It's got an R on. Look. It's for the Key to Happiness." So saying she gave the key a little push, so it poked out of the top and he could see it.

And something extraordinary, something wonderful, happened to his face.

One last sob became something like laughter.

"Mary! My key! Oh Mary! You darling!" And without another word he picked her up and gave her a kiss, right in the middle of her forehead, and whirled her round in the air, as he used to do, before. Then he put her down again quickly. "That's wonderful Mary. Really *wonderful*. Mary... thank you. That's really... really... the best thing Mary. The really best thing. The best present anyone..."

Mary beamed. It clearly *was* the Key to Happiness. Really.

"But Mary, come on. I'm going now. You must go too. Look, we'll go out together, but we'll say goodbye now, and then when I open the door you must go down the lane without saying anything else, and I'll go the other way. It's getting late. I've got to go."

He took her hand and led her out of the bedroom and down the stairs.

And both of them saw the brick come through the back-door window.

# 26. As a Moth to the Candle Flame

It was the matter of the Will that had sparked them off, in the back room of the pub where the villagers had gathered, after the shock of the funeral. The outrage about Ralph had overwhelmed them at first, though a few of the women said it was only natural – she was his mother, after all. Mrs Vardon, pulling pints, thought it best to be conciliatory.

"Now in the normal way, of course he shouldn't have... We all know that. But a funeral – well you can't really say... I mean, I suppose the Vicar must have told him. He probably had to."

"Or *Verity's lawyer.*"

It was a voice from the back of the snug, and the words dripped into the air like poison. Several people turned to see who had spoken. It was Old Sneddon from the farm, the head of the Sneddon clan. Old Sneddon who had led the foray to the house. Old Sneddon who had pulled out every drawer and box of papers.

All conversation in the bar had stopped. "What do you mean?" Sid Vardon asked, voicing everyone's thoughts.

"Well, you don't suppose she left the house to the bloody *cats,* do you?"

There was a moment's silence while the possibilities sunk in. Then everyone started at once, some denying it was possible, others pressing for details. One of the Vardons came right out with it and demanded to know if they'd found a Will. Old Sneddon tapped his nose and his eldest son said quickly, "That's Sneddon business. He can't discuss that," and the family closed round him. Someone asked something about the flowers then, and one of the Fenners started on about his dahlias, and for a while it seemed the topic might move on. But after a few minutes Max Pavis went back to it. "So, did anyone actually *see* it, eh? The Will? Has she actually left him the house?"

"That's our business, mate, not yours."

"But the house...We've got a right to know, for Christ's sake. Think of May and Ted. I mean... if he's coming back. Think of young John..."

The old man downed the rest of his beer, taking his time. Then he looked up. "Like I said, that's our business. I can't talk about it."

There was an uproar then. Davie Vardon, who'd had several more ciders since he stormed the churchyard, suddenly stood up and declared "Well I don't care if it's Sneddon business or whose bloody business. I'm goin' to find out from the bugger 'imself. If he's hanging about up there, I'll sort 'im out." He peered round the pub, emboldened by the looks on people's faces. "Yeah. Just watch me. I'll sort 'im out proper. An' old four-eyes up the school needn't go blowing 'is little whistle round *there*, I can tell you."

Davie Vardon, though well-connected, was not the most promising of the sons of the village. He hadn't been successful in any field of endeavour and he wasn't a stranger to prison. He worked, when he worked at all, as a casual at the farm – though they only called him when there were pigs to kill, which was little recommendation. So he wasn't an obvious choice as moral leader.

But at that moment, he expressed in pure culture the outrage of the village. His loathing of Ralph was a primitive thing, far older than the matter of the girl. From the day they started school together, he had felt a desire to *stamp* on Ralph Sneddon – to crush his soft face and grind his pretty curls. There was something about him, there always had been, that made Davie sick.

As he stood up, his companions from the churchyard rose unsteadily beside him. There was a moment when nobody spoke, but then his two brothers got up as well, and Max Pavis's granddaughter and her boyfriend, and a lad who was Pavis somewhere back, and the Sneddon girl who taught in Sunday School and wasn't very bright, and a couple of Sneddon men, younger than Ralph, who had suffered as teenagers for having the same name.

As the last of them left the pub, a silence descended. The older customers, particularly the women, looked shiftily at each other, as if waiting for someone to take a stand. But no one did.

Then Old Sneddon called for another beer and his son said something loudly about the weather, and the pity of the rain they had last week, when the wheat was ready.

"Lost a whole field of it, we did. Ruined. You lost some too, eh Max?"

Max nodded, without looking up. That had been a bad weekend, certainly, and he'd lost his dog as well. But he wasn't in a mood to talk about the weather. He thought of the little group who had gone – and

Jeannie, his own granddaughter, in amongst them. Perhaps he should have intervened. But they might have taken no notice, and he'd have lost face then, with Old Sneddon looking on. In any case, they were only youngsters, all of them. Nobody wanted Ralph Sneddon in the village. If they gave him a bit of a going over, it wouldn't be undeserved.

\*\*\*

The green was full of children. There were little ones from the infant classes, who'd been left to play while their parents joined the gathering in the pub. There were the juniors who'd seen everything in the churchyard and wanted to talk about it. As the train came in, with the older ones from the Secondary, some of them ran to the station to pass on the story. Nothing so exciting had happened, ever.

Some of the teenagers, too grownup for the swings, ambled over to the tables by the pub, stuffing school-ties into pockets and trying to look adult. When Davie came out, they swarmed around him. It didn't really matter that he was rather too drunk to explain. It wasn't the details that they wanted, but the action.

As they set off from the green, the children followed. The twins took up position at the front, swaggering along beside Davie: they knew him from the farm, and their dad was his boss. Michael kept trying to get in beside them, but Colin pulled him back. It wasn't wise to push in with Sneddons, and anyway, he was worrying about Mary.

Michael gestured, vaguely, to the children behind them. There must have been twenty or thirty of them, dancing around and giggling. Some of the youngest ones were lagging now, because the station was something of a boundary, so it wasn't very clear if they were coming or not.

Davie Vardon broke a stick from the cherry at Mrs Fenner's gate and was swishing it in the air. Several of the teenagers got one as well, and the older boys joined in. From an upstairs window, Mrs Fenner was shouting at them to lay off the tree or she'd come out and thrash them with it.

"But Mary..." Colin said, staring back to the group of children.

"She's probably with Rita," Michael said. He shrugged. It wasn't his job to look after her anyway. She hadn't bothered to wait for him at the school. "Come on. Let's get a stick."

The front part of the crowd was getting ahead now. Michael and Colin were in a no man's land between the older ones and the kids. Michael tugged at Colin's sleeve.

"Come on Col. Let's catch up with the twins."

"What do you think they're going to do?" Colin asked nervously.

"Dunno. Have a fight, I think. If he's there. They're gonna scare him off. He's no good."

Colin looked at his brother, rather awkwardly. "Do you know about it? Do you know what he did?"

Michael looked shifty. "Maybe. Do you?"

"Yeah. But I'm not supposed to say."

"Oh, come on Col. That's not fair. Rita's brother said he *went to prison*. But he wouldn't say what for. Come on Col, you can't not tell me. What did he do?"

Colin looked round. He didn't know the details. John had started telling him once, but then the twins had heard and told John to shut it.

"You won't tell mum I told you?"

"Nope."

"Cross your heart?"

"*Hope to die. Stick a needle in my eye.*"

Colin was satisfied. He stepped closer to Michael and breathed the words quietly. "He killed a little kid. A little girl."

"Crikey. Why?"

"I dunno."

"Who was she?"

Colin hesitated. That was the horrible bit. But he'd started now. "She was... she was John's *sister*. Before he was even born." He saw Michael's jaw drop.

"*Killed* her?"

"Yeah. John told me."

"Crumbs." The enormity of the secret brought a flush to Michael's face. "Do you think they'll kill him back?"

"I don't know," Colin said anxiously, seeing the excitement rising in his brother. "I think we'd better go home. They won't want us there. It's village stuff." Dimly, Colin knew about village stuff. It wasn't something they should get involved with.

"Nah." Michael said. "Don't be a sissy. Anyway, we'll just watch. We won't do anything. And... you know... Sounds like he deserves it."

Already the house was in sight. Up ahead, the older ones were hurrying now, and suddenly they broke into a run. Michael and Colin sped after them. They were only going to watch, but they didn't want to miss it.

Davie Vardon was rattling the back door. He swayed a little, and yanked at the handle, but the door didn't open.

"Give it kick, Davie," one of the teenagers said. "Go on. Kick it down."

"Nah. Let's break the window."

"Yeah, OK then. Stand back you lot."

Davie pulled up a brick from the path, and looked around, to make sure he was being appreciated. "There you go, matey!" he said as he threw it at the window. It wasn't a bad shot. The brick went straight through and the glass tinkled after. Another of the young men picked another brick, and threw it higher, to one of the windows upstairs. It missed and clattered down again. Everyone laughed.

After that there was a bit of a scrum, and a lot more bricks got thrown. The leaders of the gang were too drunk to be accurate and the upstairs windows were difficult. One of the twins got the skylight with a pebble, but it just bounced off. So Colin, who was good at things like that, got a bigger stone and skimmed it into the air. The skylight shattered with a satisfying sound, and everyone but the twins did a little cheer.

There was a bit of hiatus then. Both the doors were locked, and there was broken glass in the back one, so no one was keen on barging it.

"You gotta go in Davie," one of the teenagers called. "Go on Davie – do the front. He might be in there."

So Davie swaggered to the front of the house and kicked the front door. The old oak didn't even shake. "Bloody solid," he remarked, and barged it with his shoulder. Still solid.

"You won't get *that* down. Built like a bloody bunker."

"I bloody will! Come on you two, give me a hand. Let's kick it together. You too. Come on, let's ram the bugger down."

So the lads lined up and started kicking and barging, and were none too pleased when there was a call from the back. Jeannie Pavis, approaching the matter with more delicacy and less alcohol, had reached through the broken window and unbolted the back door. By the time the men were there, the children were swarming through the house.

Jeannie ran upstairs, and shouted down that there was nobody there. But just after that, the Sneddon girl, from Sunday School, said there was someone under the bed, and started screaming. So everyone rushed up, and a couple of cats ran hissing from the bedroom, and everyone laughed.

There was a great deal of shouting, and a couple of the little ones fell over in the glass which led to some blood and a lot of hysterics. There were boxes piled up in the kitchen and some of the children started throwing them about, in a little fight of their own. Then the twins found a bowl of cat food and smeared it on the wall.

There wasn't much in the house, not really. Nothing interesting, certainly. Some boys turned out the chest in the old woman's bedroom and held out her ancient underwear with hoots of mirth. Then someone else tried to open the wardrobe but it was locked, so they kicked it and heard glass break inside where there must have been a mirror. Three cats ran out from under the dresser, so they chased them down the landing, but they were quickly out of reach. Someone pulled the rest of the stuff from the chest, but it wasn't particularly funny the second time. There didn't seem much else to do after that.

The steam seemed to have left them. It had been, after all, just a bit of fun.

"Yeah. Well he'll think twice if he comes back now," one of the Fenner boys said, gesturing vaguely at the mess and the broken windows.

Davie Vardon nodded. "He won't be back. He's buggered off. Good riddance. He was always a bloody wimp anyway."

And so it might have stayed, if the Pavis girl hadn't commented, innocently enough, "And a fat waste of time it was, him painting the place up. Look at all that mess." She pointed to the wall, where the twins had smeared the cat food, and she laughed.

All that mess *on a newly painted wall.*

Davie Vardon had never done well at school, and he was currently very drunk. If he'd been brighter or less drunk, he would have noticed it sooner. The wall was definitely freshly painted. Now it was pointed out, it was obvious. There was also the smell, that he'd almost noticed before, without taking it in.

Everywhere. The whole house had just been painted.

"Bloody hell!" he said, as the meaning dawned on his muddied brain.

And he waved his arms about, trying to get the rest of his party to take notice. "Look at it. All of you. Look at it. He's bloody doing the place up! He's painted it up! He thinks he can bloody live here!"

There was a silence.

"Nah! He wouldn't."

"He bloody *would*. Why the fuck else would he have painted it all? The bloody witch not dead five minutes and he's painted the place up!"

***

Nobody, afterwards, admitted to starting the fire, though at the time it seemed rightful to everyone. Smashing the place up was one thing, and might have been enough if he only needed discouragement, but the incontrovertible evidence of the painted walls was really something else.

It was generally thought that it was one of Fenners, because everyone knew they had a point to prove – what with their mother, who had treated the witch like family. But after the curtains in the kitchen went up, it was certainly Davie Vardon who carried the fire to the staircase.

Davie didn't want to leave. He wanted to see the whole place go, but the curtains were all that was burning. From the floor he grabbed the boxes that the kids had knocked down, and hurled them onto the draining board, so the curtains would catch them, but they only smouldered a little, and there was nothing dramatic – just a lot of smoke.

Coughing, he ran out of the kitchen to the path at the back where the children were scurrying.

"Come on," he called to a friend. "Let's put some welly in it. There must be something somewhere. Come on!" He staggered to the shed. He wanted paraffin, petrol, anything that would go with a bit of a bang. At the back, thick with cobwebs, he saw a bottle of meths, and grabbed it with a yell.

"Come on then, let's do it," he shouted, waving the purple bottle like a trophy.

He ran into the smoking kitchen and smashed the bottle on the stairs. "Light it now, light it!" he called to the Fenner boy, who was wielding a box of matches. "Go on! light it up!"

But the boy didn't want to, in case it blew up, so Davie pulled the matches off him and lit five all at once and threw them down. It went up straight away and Davie was ready to go back for something else. But

Jeannie Pavis was tugging at his shirt, and pleading with him to come, and she was, after all, a girl he'd always fancied, so he thought he might as well leave it at that.

Perhaps it was just as well. The stairs were full of cracks and there were boxes beneath them, where the meths had dripped. In moments the wood was ablaze. Out in the garden the Sneddon girl was marshalling the little ones. "Everyone out of the garden. Go out... it's not safe here," she was shouting in her Sunday school voice. And it was true that the flames were coming higher now.

Reluctantly, with the last of their excitement as an armour, the children made their way into the lane. At the front of the house there was only smoke, billowing through broken windows.

Some of them were exchanging awkward glances. Others were pointing and whispering. It was Davie Vardon's fault and the Fenners'. And they were grownups, or almost so. The older girls – though they had been in the house all along – were pulling back, getting ready to disapprove. A few of the children, one of them with blood on his shirt, were still hysterical. The twins were dancing round and Michael was with them. "Whooooshhh!" one twin shouted, waving his arms towards the little ones and hooting with laughter. "Did you see it when he lit the mauve stuff up? Did you see the curtains? Whhooosh!"

Colin was looking around, aghast. There was a horrible question forming in his head. He peered round the little groups of girls. It wasn't a question he wanted to ask. And it was probably unnecessary, because he couldn't, now he thought about it, remember seeing her at all. She might have stayed at the village, because she would only have come if Rita did, and he couldn't see Rita either. But the question remained in his mind.

"Whooosh! Kapoing!" The twins were still lost in their fantasy of glory. "Look! It's coming out of the side now!" And it was true, there were flames coming out of the side, high up.

"Shut up you two. You're cretins. Go away." Colin pushed them rudely away and dragged Michael's arm. He had been staring at the house, his features rapt.

"Michael... Michael. Please. It's important." Michael looked at him, waiting for him to start on about getting into trouble. But it wasn't that.

"Michael. Do you know where Mary is?"

\*\*\*

When the brick came through the window, Mary and Ralph had both, without needing any discussion, run back to the bedroom and closed the door. There was a momentary squawking of cats, and then silence.

"Get down," Ralph hissed, and pushed her onto the floor beside the bed. He crawled across to the window. Peeking out, he saw half a dozen men, and further down there were more, a crowd almost.

He thought quickly. The bedroom looked out to the front, but the brick had come through the back, so they must be surrounded. He thought of the skylight and the passage at the back, but he'd still have to go through the garden to get out. He'd still be seen. And there was Mary.

He was in a locked house, on his own, with a little girl.

He remembered the ugly scene at the church.

At that moment, a stone came through the window of the bedroom, leaving a neat round hole like a bullet. A tiny shard of glass dashed Mary's face, and her nose was splattered with blood. A little spider-web of blood, sharp against the freckles. She didn't cry or scream, but she threw herself against him, clutching his legs.

Another brick clattered against the wall outside. He pushed Mary down, into the space between bed and wall.

"Get under the bed Mary. The glass – get underneath, it won't get you there."

It suddenly seemed that the whole house was under attack. All around was the sound of windows breaking and of stones hitting walls. And shouting. A horrible, high-pitched shouting. Children and women as well as men. They must all be there. All of them. He wondered how many there were.

On his own in a locked house, with a little girl. He did not doubt that if they found him they would kill him.

He thought of places to hide. He could get into the loft, but the hatch was on the landing, at the top of the stairs. From the back door, he'd be clearly visible through the window. And he'd need a ladder to get up, or at least a chair. The room next door was completely empty. Under his mother's bed was useless – they'd look there straight away. And whatever he did, there'd still be the girl.

Someone was kicking the front door. He heard the heavy thud of the oak, and the voices just outside. A man's voice shouting. And more shouting and more banging. Mary was shaking and moaning a little.

There was glass on the floor and she had cut her hand. He looked round. The chest was too small. There was either the bed or the wardrobe. A plan was forming in his mind.

"They're coming, Mary. You've got to hide. Now. In the wardrobe. I'm going to shut you in so they don't find you. I'll guard the door. Trust me Mary. When it's quiet, I'll let you out. You'll be safe there Mary."

"No, no please... Please..."

"Yes, you've got to. Just keep very quiet. Not a sound." He saw the blood on her hands but there was nothing he could do. He opened the wardrobe and pushed her into it. Then he turned the key in the lock. If he made a dash for it, he might get to the bike before they got him. Then he could get away. Like a palpable thing, he felt the possibility of escape, the leap of the engine, the air on his face, rushing into the future.

They wouldn't find her till he was gone. He'd have a chance then. Better a dash across the garden and a bolt down the road with the pack behind him, than pinned in the house, like a rat in a cage, in room with a little girl. He had the key. The bike was full of petrol.

Mary was whimpering in the cupboard, protesting. "Shut up," he snapped. "Be quiet." Her hands were scrabbling round the door, tapping on the wood and on the mirror. He wondered if there was air enough, but that wasn't his problem, not now.

He hesitated for a moment, thinking of the rucksack. It would slow him down. But everything was in there. Everything he needed. If he had his rucksack, he could go to ground for a bit. He wouldn't last long without it.

As he struggled with the straps, he heard the footsteps in house. Then the voices. Dozens of voices, men and women, flooding through the back, baying for blood. Hope evaporated. An image flashed through his mind of a fox torn apart by dogs. From the wardrobe, Mary was beginning to shout. He was about to be caught, on his own in a house, with a little girl locked in a wardrobe. There was nowhere to hide, no escape.

He unlocked the wardrobe, pushed Mary rudely into the depths at the back, and pushed himself after her. Then he pulled the door shut and locked it from inside.

Mary's shouting stopped at once.

"Ralph! I love you Ralph!" she whimpered, and in the vile darkness, rank with mothballs and cat-piss, she pushed herself onto his lap, and curled into a ball.

***

The wardrobe was airless. In the space that was left between clothes and unnameable packages there was barely room for a child – let alone a man as well, even a thin man, bent double. He pulled the key from the lock in case the child got ideas, and he kept his hand near her face, ready to silence her.

The next half hour was torment. Sounds like warfare rang all around the house, and at intervals people ran in and out of the room. Once someone tried to kick open the wardrobe, and the glass of the mirror shattered inside. He felt the glass fall, and then the warm wetness of blood running down his face. He put his hand over Mary's mouth. She didn't even struggle. There was a kind of submission in her limp little frame, though each time he shifted, she clung to him tightly as if afraid he might leave her.

They were smashing everything. It would not be long till they came – with axes perhaps – to smash up the wardrobe. Perhaps it was only the lack of air, but he found himself gasping. Time froze.

But at last he noticed that the voices were receding. Some of them were coming from outside again, and it was quieter in the house. They must be leaving. They had had enough. Relief flooded through him, and something colder, stronger. Whatever softness he felt earlier had gone. He knew what he wanted now. In the grief of his mother's death, he had lost his way. He had thought he did not care if he lived or died. But he knew now. He must live. Whatever else he must live.

After he was gone, they would find the child. Without thinking, he tightened his grip round her face, and she struggled a little to free her mouth. Alive or dead. Silent or speaking. Both were damning. There was little difference, really: they would want to hang him anyway.

Most of the voices were going now. There were other noises, that he couldn't pin down, but the people were leaving.

Alive was better. Doubtless they'd come back. Someone would find her, but not till he was gone. He could make the coast before nightfall. Or London. Anyone could get lost in London.

Or dead was better. If she was alive they'd find her sooner. They'd come and she'd be shouting. If she were dead, it might take longer to find her. It would buy him time. Again, his hand tightened round her face. He had to live. *He had to live.* He had not escaped all this, to fall at the final hurdle. It must not matter to him.

The last of the voices in the house had gone. Ralph felt their absence like an embracing friend. But Mary was wriggling in his arms, and squeaking, trying to free her mouth. As his hands relaxed, she jolted her face away.

"Ralph," she whispered at once. "I can smell smoke."

\*\*\*

She was right of course. He had been feeling, for some time, that the wardrobe was painfully stuffy, that the mothballs were ever more oppressive. But he had not registered, until she spoke, the thing that was suddenly obvious. Smoke. And the sound that he had not named. A quiet, rattling, rushing sound. The sound of fire.

He groped in the dark for the keyhole and tried to push in the key. But his hands were cramped and he dropped it in the dark. It took minutes to find it, groping inch by inch through the glass and packages at the bottom of the cupboard. As he did so, he glanced at the patch of light where the key should go. Fine smoke was whispering through the keyhole. His mother's room. The dampest room in all the house. It wasn't burning yet, but it would burn in the end. Airless as it was, the cupboard was probably the cleanest air in the house.

At last he found the key, and placed it, more carefully now, in the lock. The smoke drifted in as he swung his legs out. Mary tried to climb over him, but he pushed her back. "Stay there a minute. It's too smoky out here. I'll come and get you when its's safe." And he pushed the wardrobe shut again and locked it.

This time she was angry. "Ralph, let me out! I can't breathe! Let me out! I want to come out." She was screaming now and banging on the wood, but it didn't matter. Smoke was curling under the bedroom door.

As he pushed it open, he saw it was worse, far worse, than he had let himself imagine. Down the stairs, the kitchen was a furnace and the staircase was ablaze. There was no way down. The shattered skylight at the end of the corridor was drawing the heat, like a chimney.

Everything at the back of the house was burning. It wouldn't be long till the front went too. The whole house was going up.

And at that moment, he realised.

People who have survived a terrible danger sometimes speak of a moment when a presence appeared in the darkness and they saw the way to safety, lit as by an angel, and felt the touch of an angel, taking their hand. Such it was, in a way, for Ralph, as he stood in the choking smoke and looked along the corridor to the skylight. It was not simply the fire he might escape. It was everything.

To be properly understood as accidental and to arouse no suspicions, a tragic event must evoke an obvious story.

The house, that moments before had been full of adults and children, baying like dogs, was burning to the ground. When the floorboards went up, when the great beams fell from the ceiling, when the house caved in upon itself, there would be nothing left, but ash and blackness and metal and burnt brick. And the bones of a single unfortunate child, a child forgotten, who had not escaped.

Ralph Sneddon had served his time.

He had never met Mary Crouch. He had missed a week's work because his mother had died. He was there in the village for the funeral, that was all. Terrible things were done that day, but they were not of his making. He was a victim in a larger tragedy. He was not to blame.

There was no one to contradict. He was entitled to a life. Time could, after all, be bent to his will.

An angel, holding this burning light, helped him through the acrid smoke of the corridor, onto the tallboy and up through the shattered glass of the skylight. It cut his hands, but he didn't stop. The shards fell away round his shoulders, and he hurled himself out into the air. Then he let himself slither, gasping, onto the bathroom roof and into the passage. He fell awkwardly onto the dustbin and his head hit the ground.

\*\*\*

The face looking down at him was curiously familiar. It was a girl's face, blue eyes, framed with curly hair. He did not know her but could see she was a Sneddon. In fact she was his cousin Shirley, whom he'd last seen fourteen years ago, in a pram.

"Hey look!" she was shouting. "Come here! A bloke was in there. He just fell down. Come here – look."

Ralph jumped up, pushed past her, and bolted to the road. It was packed with youngsters.

"Hey! Get him!" a man's voice shouted from the back. "Don't let him get away! Hey, Davie, it's *him*!"

For a second, Ralph saw Davie Vardon, clinging to a tree on the other side of the road. He was bending over and retching. The drink and the smoke had got to him. "Fuck him!" Davie shouted, then he wretched again. "Tell 'im to fucking go away." His voice was slurred, but had, all the same, a kind of authority. "Tell him to go away and not come back. Get the fuck out..." And this time he threw up properly, and people looked away.

It was, after all, Davie's project. And Davie, it seemed, had run out of steam. As his friends looked uncertainly from one to the other, Ralph fixed his eyes on the little bend in the road, a few hundred yards ahead. He felt in his pocket and got out the key. Small and tight and ready. He had a tank full of petrol. He could do it. Ralph took his moment and darted forward through a group of girls.

But as he ran, two girlish hands – hands that he had discounted – grabbed him by the hair. And a knee that had seemed to hold no threat rose sharply and caught him in the groin. He fell to the road, rolling in the dust, groaning.

"Bastard!" the girl's voice said. She was young, perhaps only a teenager, and she was, he did not doubt, a Pavis. She had the fine, white skin and the greenish eyes, like Sonia.

Then her foot came again – too quick for him to dodge. Her shoe was pointed and it hit him in the eye. As the pain flooded through him, he saw red and black and flashes of light. They were not from any angel. And he felt the blood. He tried to push himself up, but the shoe came again, in his throat this time, and again, in his face. Then, as the redness flooded over the world, he heard her voice. "That's for Sonia, bastard. You can bugger off now. Go on. Bugger off."

He waited for the next blow, unable to move. But it did not come.

He pushed himself up and forced open an eye. His field of vision was full of her hard leather heel and the back of her fine leg. Everything else seemed patterned with blackness. She had turned her back to him and was pointing up at the house. He knew that something terrible had happened to his other eye. He pulled himself to a squat, expecting another blow, but she no longer seemed interested.

The girl was pointing at his mother's room and shouting something. Ralph forced himself to sit, though his head span round and patches of black spattered through his vision. There wasn't, it seemed, very much to see, but still she was shouting and pointing at the window. Other people were drawing round her and at last he could make out her words.

"You've got to get them out! There are cats up there. Look! They're trapped!" And sure enough, in the swirling smoke of his mother's bedroom, stretching up towards the broken pane at the top, there were cats. A white cat and a tabby, trapped in the room.

A man, little older than the girl, looked up and shrugged. "They'll get out," he said. "They're cats. They'll get through the top one when their bums get hot." And he laughed rather nastily.

Ralph saw the girl kick him, sharp in the shins, and the pain from Ralph's groin shot through him again, as if in sympathy.

"You're a bastard too," she said. "Go and get the ladder. Do it now. You've got to do it for me. Otherwise no more you-know-what." She laughed then, a short staccato laugh, bereft of amusement. "There's a ladder round the back. Poor pussycats. You can go up and get them down for me. I might keep one. I'd *like* a cat." Her voice was imperious. Knowing what she wanted, commanding what she wanted.

The young man bent to pick up a stone. "This'll let them out," he said, taking aim.

But the girl grabbed his hand and twisted it back. "No! The glass'll kill them! Get the ladder!" This time the lad avoided the kick, though his friends were smirking.

As the back of the house burned out, the children were shuffling away. Some of the teenagers were shepherding the little ones down the lane, but others – full, at last, of a sense of civic duty – were standing with the women and fretting about the ladder and the cats. Ralph pulled himself to his knees. He wasn't after all, such an interesting prey. The crowd had other sport now. He pulled himself to standing, feeling his head. A wrenching heaviness tore on one side.

Once he could stand, he started towards the bike. His field of vision was broken, but he still could walk. Nobody followed him. Then he felt his hand where the key had been. It was empty. He turned around, searching the spinning ground. The key was nowhere.

He heard the shouting behind him and looked back. A group of lads were triumphantly heaving a ladder that was well past rotten, dragged from the weeds in the garden where it had lain for years.

And it dawned on Ralph that they were going up. They were going to the room where the cats were, where Mary was. They would hear her shouting. They would find her, locked in a cupboard. And his key had gone.

There wasn't, after all, any hope. There was only redemption.

Ralph lunged, unsteadily, towards the people with the ladder. "No..." he said. "No... It's rotten. It won't hold you. Leave it. I know a way up."

# 27. On the Innocence of Adulthood

With his remaining eye, Ralph saw how they recoiled from his face. No doubt it was hideous. But his head was clearing, just a little, and the searing pain where his eye had been was reduced to a blackness that meant nothing to him now.

They stared but they did not follow as he staggered to the back of the house. The heat was intense, but the flames were lower now. There wasn't much left at the back to burn.

As he stumbled towards the passage, the world slipped in and out of vision. The back of the house had never seemed so broad. The dustbins had never seemed so high, the step to the roof so inhumanly far. But still he forced himself up, though his hands were seared on the tiles and the paint on the skylight was bubbling.

The fire was eating out the landing now. The floorboards were largely gone, and through the gaps he could glimpse the room below. Flames were nibbling along the beams, approaching the base of the ancient tallboy. He could not leap now, his body was broken, but he lowered himself into the heat, down to the tallboy and onto the largest beam. He felt the heat through his shoes, but it was only two steps to the bedroom and the door had held. He pushed it open and closed it at once behind him. The room was full of smoke. With his elbow, he smashed the glass from the lower window, and even before the smoke had cleared, the cats leapt down to safety. Ralph gasped at the air from outside, cooling his burnt lungs.

There was no sound from the cupboard. Ralph guessed it was too late. The smoke had been too thick. Or perhaps there'd been no air. He glanced out of the window and saw the people fussing round the cats. Shirley Sneddon was pointing upwards, saying something, but the others didn't seem interested. He had played his part. For a second, the Pavis girl looked up at him, and called, without any obvious urgency. "You all right then? Hot up there, is it?"

And a man shouted something else, less charitable.

He tried to call back, but his throat was burnt. He could make no sound. People were moving away. They were leaving him. Only Shirley was rushing from one to the other, tugging at their jackets, pointing back. But they did not turn.

So, it was over. He bent his head to the cupboard, but there was no tapping on the wood. There was nothing. He pulled the door open and the shape of a girl slid out. It landed on the floor with a sound like a bag of rotten apples. It did not move.

Then, abruptly, a horrible grunt came from Mary's throat, and she heaved a great breath. She opened her eyes and looked up at him. Perhaps it was adoration in her eyes, but Ralph could hardly see now. "I knew you'd come," she said. "I knew you'd come." Then she peered up at him, and he saw that she grimaced. "You've hurt your face. You look horrid."

Through mists and flashes he looked back at her. She had hurt her face too. There was a little spider of blood where glass had hit her, just beneath her eye, stretching over to the side of her nose. For a moment he saw the other child, with the purple mark. He tried to say something but no sound came.

***

The escape had a curious, dreamlike quality, and afterwards Mary found it quite hard to remember. Ralph seemed to go so slowly. Even wrapped tightly in his jacket, she could feel the fire and hear things breaking as they went. Looking down through a gap in the leather she could see the flames on the beams where he was walking. He was stepping from one to the next, walking through light, and everything was breaking as he walked. His shoes were on fire. The air was burning.

She was too frightened to speak, almost too frightened to breathe. Just once, she twisted her head to look upwards, and it seemed through the flames that Ralph's hair was full of light, breaking over his head. It wasn't just a halo. It was great beams of light, like a lion's mane, like a sun, burning around his neck.

Then he was climbing, and suddenly she felt herself pushed into the air, and then there was shouting below her, and she was going down, headfirst. A woman's voice was shouting, and there were strong hands taking her. There was a gasping behind her, and more shouting, and other people, talking much too loudly.

After a little while, Colin was there, and Michael, both terribly pleased to see her. And other people whom she didn't know. Then there were sirens, and lots of people, and blankets around her. She heard someone saying "She's fine, she'll be fine. Just give her some air. Not a scratch. Best see to the bloke." And she was a little indignant because she had felt the scratch on her face, but she was glad they were seeing to Ralph as well.

*\*\*\**

The rescuing of a child from a burning building is incontrovertibly evidence of heroism. At least, it was reported as such in the local press, which was not wholly sensitive to the feelings of the village. The Pavises were particularly put out by the headline, which implied that the saving of some random child, not even of the village, could offset the murder of their daughter.

Certainly, the village was more sober, afterwards. The burning down of the witch's house was not something people spoke of, though some of them kept the cutting, in the interests of history.

### *Local Bad Boy Makes Good*

*A house fire in Heckleford could easily have ended in disaster. This was averted by the prompt actions of a local girl, Miss Jean Pavis, (17). She was walking with her boyfriend, (Peter Fenner, 22) and went to investigate some smoke from a building on the outskirts the village. "Children had got in," Miss Pavis said. "They had broken in and were messing about. They must have started a fire by accident. I got them out and my boyfriend went for help."*

*It appears that the house was unoccupied, having belonged to a lady recently deceased. Her son (Ralph Sneddon, 31, notorious for the murder of a local child in 1948) was visiting for his mother's funeral.*

*"We thought we'd got them all out," Miss Pavis said. "But when Ralph Sneddon turned up he wanted to go in because his mum's cats were trapped upstairs. I told him to wait for the firemen because it wasn't safe, but then while we were waiting we saw the girl at the window. She was up there with the cats, banging on the window. And the fireman weren't there yet, so Mr Sneddon went in, and I helped him get her out through the window. It was lucky we saw her, a miracle really, because the house was all on fire. She could have died."*

*Another eye-witness, Miss Shirley Sneddon (16, no relation) said "It was all thanks to the cats really. If he hadn't been worried about the cats, he wouldn't have found the little girl."*

*The blaze was finally extinguished by firemen. A spokesman from the Fire Brigade said it was never sensible to go back into a house for pets, but commended Mr Sneddon for his brave assistance to the child. The rescued child, Miss Mary Crouch, 7, was released from hospital that evening. Mr Sneddon, the unexpected hero of the hour, has been transferred to the Burns Unit in East Grinstead, where a spokesman reports that he is comfortable. There were no other casualties. Local policeman PC Edward Fenner warned parents of the dangers of children playing in empty buildings, and commented "They shouldn't have been there and they all had a lucky escape. It could so easily have ended in tragedy."*

\*\*\*

That was more than enough, all things considered. It doesn't do to say too much, it only leads to trouble. Even Mary did not say too much.

In any case, everything seemed a little distant after that, through the frozen days of the long, bitter winter that followed, when the roads were icy for months, and she got a series of colds, and drew into herself, and school was a bit of a burden and she wasn't doing well.

Janet told the boys that they mustn't speak of the fire in front of her. It wouldn't be nice to remind her about it. Especially they mustn't tell her about the man who had carried her out, or what it had cost him. People in the village said that even if he lived – and some were adamant he wouldn't – he would never recover from the burns and other injuries. Mary was a soft-hearted girl and it would only upset her. In any case, Janet knew the history now, and it was most unfortunate that it was *him*, of all people, who had got her out: he certainly wasn't anyone who Mary should be told about. So it was good, all in all, that they were moving to Manchester. Good houses were cheaper there, Rick said, and work was easier to find.

It would do Mary good, Janet felt, to make a fresh start. Her behaviour had been rather difficult recently, and her appearance rather *peaky*. She had taken to praying before bed, which wasn't, Janet felt, quite healthy. For a while she'd also been peculiar about her clothes, and a little while later she got a thing about *babies* and kept asking naughty questions which she must have picked up at school. A school with farmers' children wasn't really very nice: such children lost their innocence altogether too young.

But gazing on her daughter with all the innocence of adulthood, Janet knew that Mary was a good girl – so she kept her home from school, ignored the naughty questions and fed her treats to build her up when the boys weren't looking. After a while, Janet guessed that the fire was forgotten. Mary did not speak of it, and really, she had no reason to remember – what with the excitement of the snow and her birthday, and the nice white cat that they got for her, because a dinner-lady at school was giving them away and Mary said she really wanted it.

In all likelihood, Janet felt, it wasn't the fire that had bothered her, anyway. All of that drama had been over in minutes and Mary hadn't been hurt.

What had really upset her – to judge from the things she mumbled in her sleep – was all about Rick going off like that, and not even writing, and then coming back and favouring the boys. It was clear from her restless calling that Mary did still love him, even if she wouldn't express it to his face. All of that winter she wouldn't let Rick kiss her, and she turned away rudely when he held out his arms. It was naughty of her, certainly, and in a ritual way, to keep the peace, Janet told her off for it – though she felt, deep down, that actually it was Rick's fault, all of it, so he had no right to mind.

Men were quite impossible really, all of them, and they all had things too easy.

\*\*\*

Much later, white-coated figures would ask Ralph if he thought of the other child, the child he had killed all those years before, at the moment when Mary Crouch appeared at the window.

And he would think of how the story must be written in their file, and how everyone must have lied.

Then, because they prompted him and made him go back in his mind, he would remember the day and the warmth of the afternoon. He would think of the cats at the window and of Mary tapping and calling to him. He remembered how she trusted him: the terrible irony of that.

Of course he had thought of the other child. The other child was always with him.

The other child had a mark on her nose: a spider of thread-veins, stretching to her cheek. Yet she had been beautiful, which Mary wasn't.

He did not say that though. He knew it would not help to mention that.

So in the end he would shake his head and form the lie again. *No. It was nothing like that. When I saw Mary, I never thought of the other child. There was no connection.*

On other days they asked him why he did it, as if, because of what he was, it was necessary to ask.

He knew what the newspapers called him and the word disgusted him. He knew what he was. He never claimed to be a hero.

He would try to think of nothing.

But in the pressure of the silence, he would remember the final moments – when Mary was struggling in his coat, and he covered her face, when he felt her life in his hands and the imperative engulfed him, when all of his body was on fire and he knew what it would cost him but he did not care.

And even then, as they watched him and waited for his answer, he felt a kind of exultation. In all his pointless life: those few pure moments of glory. He had been, in those moments, a man.

*I didn't have a reason. I did it because she was there.*

They did not push him further. They were professional. They dealt with him, processed him, followed correct procedures. He would hear them writing on their boards, and then they would go.

There was only one, a woman, Irish, who would hang behind as the others left. Her words would hiss behind his head, and she would ask him, her voice contorted with loathing, *if he thought about burning in hell.*

"You had nothing to lose, did you?" she would say. "Did it make you feel big? Are you proud of yourself?" And she would tell him, as if it gave her the right to speak, that she had a little girl herself, and that nothing, nothing he ever did, would make up for what he had done.

Then he would hear her sucking on her tongue, and he would wait for the spit on his cheek.

He never spoke of it.

Only occasionally, waking in the night, he would sense without remembering that he had dreamt of them both together. Mary and the other child, point and counterpoint. A little stain on both their faces.

But really, the two events were separate and there was no connection. He was thirty-one that day with Mary, not a boy of seventeen. He knew what he was doing. Perhaps because of what he was, and what he had done before, he did not count the cost as he might have done. But it did not mean that he did not choose. He had free will.

And which of us sees the strings that tweak our legs and arms, making us dance?

## Message from Carly Rheilan

Thank you for reading "A Cats Cradle". If you enjoyed it, I would be *so pleased* if you would write a brief review on Amazon – even a few words – to tell other readers.

If you would like an advance e-copy of my next book, please just email me. I'm always happy to hear from readers and will usually answer emails.

carly.rheilan@freepeoples.space

# About the author

Carly Rheilan was born in Malta and lives in the UK. She was educated in Oxford University (which she hated and left) and then at Brunel (a small-town technological university where she stayed for a PhD). As an academic and a psychiatric nurse she has done research into criminal justice, taught in universities and worked for many years in the NHS. She has children of her own and has also fostered two children with mental health problems.

Like this book, all of her writing addresses issues at the edges of psychiatry, crime and personal trauma.

- Asylum tells the story of Cabdi, the survivor of an African massacre, and Mustaf, a trafficked child
- Birthrights is a story about a childless psychiatrist seeking a fraudulent motherhood

When not writing herself, Carly promotes the work of other indie authors through her book promotion company Coffee and Thorn, whose takings are used to educate destitute girls in Sierra Leone. She also boxes (joyfully but badly), rages against the politics of her unequal country (pointlessly), campaigns for the introduction of parole in Mississippi (without success), and fights a solitary battle against acres of nettles in a community garden (so far the nettles are winning). But most of all, she loves to spend time with her family, who forgive her failings and make her happy.

# Also by Carly Rheilan

**Asylum**

*The child's hand groping out of the earth is undoubtedly real. As real as Cabdi's own hand, when it lay on the earth after the machete fell, long ago.*

*But this hand is alive. And it isn't in a warzone, far away. It is in the playground of a school, just outside the grounds of the English psychiatric hospital where Cabdi is now held. And the man who is stamping on the moving hand is a pigeater. Pigeaters are in charge of everything.*

*As an accidental asylum seeker, Cabdi is friendless in a country he does not know. He cannot speak English. But he knows that he should not have gone into the playground. He should not have seen the hand in the earth. And whatever lies behind this, it is not his war.*

*He walks away.*

*Why should the crime have a witness, anyway?*

## *Readers' comments about Asylum:*

"Awesome book. Asylum by Carly Rheilan is a dark, twisty kind of book that will keep you guessing. This is not a feel-good book at all, but rather a tale that will stay with you in all of its dark glory… The author writes with confidence, and that dark mood that permeates this novel sets the tone for an intriguing and exciting story. Not only is this book dark and disturbing, but is so well written you may forget you are reading about horrible things. Highly recommend for a chilling thriller in the classic noir style."

"Dark, heavy, creepy yet beautiful. Asylum is one of those unique stories that leave a deep imprint on your mind and makes you think of all the darkness that is present in this world and yet, there is a specific beauty that makes you believe in life's goodness and gives you the will to live on….The book is grim and very engaging."

"Tense, very dark, but securely written by an author about whom we most assuredly will be hearing more. A fascinating, disturbing book."

## BirthRights

*Sometimes the perfect pregnancy is less than skin deep…*

*A young man watches as a heavily pregnant doctor is stabbed in the street. He sees the knife, swinging down into that rounded belly, again and again, deep to the hilt.*

*A few minutes later, the doctor has gone. Nobody believes what the man has seen.*

*For Ana, the doctor, the incident is problematic. Back home, she peels off the damaged pretence of her pregnancy, a beautifully crafted garment, padded and slung across her abdomen. And she begins to realise that a story she has crafted with even greater care, is about to unravel.*

## *Readers' comments about BirthRights:*

"I have just finished this book and am in awe. I don't say this lightly. It is one of the best books I have read in years. Carly Rheilan takes the reader onto a journey into the minds of several people, linked by the profound emotional scar tissue of the protagonist. Everything rings true. The dialogue, the many perspectives the author juggles with ease, the complex storylines seamlessly woven together, and the daring exploration of difficult subjects such as the pitfalls of the medical establishment, treatments for mental illness, surrogacy, loss, and infertility, among others. I couldn't put it down, and it will stay in my thoughts for a long time to come. I cannot recommend this book highly enough."

"BirthRights is a novel that *'celebrate(s) the troubled, troubling, remarkable life'* of Dr. Ana Griffin. She is a psychiatrist who suffers from her own mental health disorders yet dedicates herself to helping others with similar challenges. It's a dark and thrilling look at the complexities of mental health disorders and the inadequacies of the systems set in place to help sufferers. It is a story that will leave you on the edge of your seat, both rooting for and against the events as they unfold.

*'We are all fractured, there are no unbroken planes in the human spirit.'* A truth that would hold us all to good stead if we accepted it, but we

mere mortals instead always put perfection on a pedestal instead. Carly Rheilan's new psychological thriller 'Birthrights' is more than just plots and twists you don't see coming. It is a very intrinsic and instinctive look deep down into our souls. It reaches out and grabs at your very fabric and that of the people that surround you."

## The Angel – to be published in 2025

*"Jackie slept little in the nights before a killing night. She would sit in the dark, emptying her head of all the voices that rattled through her thoughts, with their opinions, one way or the other. She would wait until her head was silent and empty, like a church after all the singing and praying were finished, and she would think of the one who was to die.*

*There was a secret pleasure in it. She would go through the stories in her head, the biographies half told in the medical files, the snippets let drop by relatives when they visited. And from whatever threads she found, she would compose the poem in memoriam. She always wrote a poem. She kept them all in a carved wooden box she had bought from Oxfam, years back. She meant to publish them all one day, when her work here was finished: a slim volume in a dark cloth binding. Poems from the Edge of Darkness she planned to call them. It was not a great vanity, but there was a vanity in it.*

*So it was on this night. The poem was written."*

Written in the wake of the Shipman case – an English doctor who was eventually convicted of the murder of 15 patients and was believed to have murdered many more – The Angel explores the complex issue of medical homicide. Is Jackie the angel of the title? Or does that name belong somewhere else?

Printed in Great Britain
by Amazon